# OF GODS AND ELVES

# THE GODLING CHRONICLES

# OF GODS AND ELVES

## BRIAN D. ANDERSON

4 Horsemen
Publications, Inc.

Published By: 4 Horsemen Publications, Inc.

4 Horsemen Publications, Inc.
PO Box 417
Sylva, NC 28779
4horsemenpublications.com
info@4horsemenpublications.com

Cover & Typesetting by Autumn Skye
Edited by Joseph Mistretta



*Paperback ISBN-13: 979-8-8232-0533-7*
*Hardcover ISBN-13: 979-8-8232-0534-4*

# DEDICATION

In loving memory of Magdaline Panagos
(1923-2006)

# CONTENTS

# PROLOGUE

Gewey felt cold, smooth stone pressed against his face, and a terrible wind roared in his ears. He opened his eyes. Nothing but pitch-blackness surrounded him. He remembered his fight with Harlondo. He felt his body, searching for the wounds that the half-man had inflicted. No injuries!

"We have healed you," said a voice from the darkness. It was soft and musical, but neither male nor female.

Gewey tried to tell where the voice originated from, but it was as if it came from everywhere. "Where am I?" He got to his feet as his voice echoed. "Who are you?"

"You are home," said the voice. "You are with us. We have been waiting so very long."

"You haven't answered my question."

"There is plenty of time for questions. For now, you must take your ease."

A light appeared several yards away, piercing the darkness. He was stood on a raised stone walkway surrounded by pure nothingness that went on forever. The only other thing he could see was a silver door at the end of the path. Gewey crept forward, careful not to step too close to the edge.

When he was only a few feet away, the door opened, and the light dimmed.

"What's in there?" he asked, but received no reply.

He stepped inside the door and found himself in his own house. A fire burned cheerfully, and a hot plate of roast lamb and honey-split bread was on the table. Harman Stedding, his father, sat at the far end of the table, smiling at him.

"Finally," said Harman. "Did you have a good day?"

Gewey turned pale and tried to back out of the door, but it was no longer there.

"What's wrong, son?" Harman asked.

His father was just as he remembered him, tall and lean with salt and pepper hair. Gewey had always thought he looked more like a teacher than a farmer. He wore the same green linen shirt and trousers that he'd always worn in the evenings after the day's work.

"Who are you?" Gewey demanded. He reached for his sword, but it was no longer at his side.

Harman looked concerned and tried to walk over to him, but Gewey ran to the other end of the table, looking for something to use as a weapon.

Harman sighed, shaking his head. "He told me this might happen. Gewey, let me explain."

"Explain what? You're not my father. My father is dead."

Harman backed away. "Son, please. You've been through a terrible ordeal. Let me help you."

"Liar! Get away from me." He found a knife on the table and snatched it up.

Fear struck Harman's face. "If you'll just let me speak to you for one second."

Gewey tried to calm himself and focus. "Speak," he growled. "But if you come near me, I swear I'll kill you."

Harman slowly pulled up a chair and motioned for Gewey to sit as well, but Gewey backed away and put himself near the front door.

"You've been ill," said Harman. "Very ill. Lord Starfinder took you to Gath for treatment. You've been back for three days now."

"Gath, eh," said Gewey. "I was in Gath with Lee, and so far that's the only true thing you've said."

"I'm not lying, son. This is the third time you've lost your memory since you've been back. It's the medicine they gave you. Lee told me that the healer said this might happen."

"You expect me to believe that?" Gewey snorted. "You've been dead for two years. I buried you myself."

"Your fever is causing you to hallucinate," said Harman. "Last time you lost your memory, you thought you were a god. You even told me I wasn't really your father."

Gewey glared. "This won't work. Tell me the truth, or I'll gut you right now."

Harman bowed his head. "You're not going to make this easy, are you? We really hoped that being here, and seeing your father alive and happy, would be enough for you just to accept this."

Gewey raised his knife and readied himself to attack. "What are you?"

"I'm here to care for you," he answered. "You are with us now. Your body has been left behind."

"My body? What have you done to my body?"

"Your body was destroyed. Only your spirit remains. However, you shouldn't fear. We love you, and we will care for you. Anything you want is yours."

"You still haven't told me who you are."

"We are the first," he replied. "We are the lovers of the gods. We have been waiting for you. We love you."

"Return me to my body now," Gewey demanded. "You can't keep me here. You don't have the right."

"I cannot return you," said Harman. "Please don't worry. Soon you will forget about the troubles of that other world.

Here, you can be anything you wish. All we ask is that you love us as your kin had once done."

"My kin? You mean the gods? What do you know about them?"

"We were favored by them, above all others. When the Dark One trapped them, we were left all alone. We had you once and should not have let you go. But we were betrayed."

"You're not making sense," said Gewey. "Who betrayed you?"

"Felsafell," he said bitterly. "He convinced us to let you go. Then he left us too."

"You're spirits. That's what you are. What do you want from me? I have nothing to give you."

"We only desire your love," he said. "It is everything to us. We need it. We are so lonely."

"I cannot stay with you," said Gewey as he moved to the door. "I don't belong here."

"You cannot leave," cried Harman. "There is nowhere to run. Soon you will forget. Soon you will love us as we love you."

Gewey couldn't help but feel pity for the creature, but he knew he had to get away. He opened the door and ran from the house. The figure of his father appeared in front of him.

"Get away from me," screamed Gewey. "Let me go." He pushed his way past the spirit and ran in the direction of town.

"You are with us." The voice of the spirit carried on the wind, following him as he ran.

Gewey ran until his legs burned. When he reached the village, all the familiar faces he knew as a child were there to greet him, but he ignored them and made his way toward Lee's house.

The trees and brush whizzed by as he ran at full speed down one of the many roads Lee had built. Gewey stumbled to a halt. He couldn't remember why he was running or where he was going.

"Wait up." His father ran up from behind. "I'm too old to keep up with you anymore."

Gewey stood there, scratching his head. "What happened?" he asked. "Why was I running?"

"We're going fishing," Harman replied. "Don't you remember?"

It was then that Gewey realized he was holding a fishing pole in his right hand. Harman carried one as well, along with a bucket of bait in the other.

"Yes," said Gewey after a long pause. "Of course I do. I'm sorry, I was just confused."

Harman smiled warmly and threw his arm around Gewey's shoulder. "That's all right, son." He laughed. "It happens to everybody."

Gewey and his father walked for about three miles to a spot along the Goodbranch River where they had fished since he was a small boy. The sun shone brightly, and the birds chirped merrily as father and son sat on the bank near a large oak and fished throughout the day.

Gewey landed three nice-sized trout, and Harman four others. His father always had better luck at fishing. As the sun began to sink closer to the horizon, Gewey lay back on the grass and took a deep breath of the fresh spring air.

"Are you happy, son?" his father asked.

Gewey looked at Harman, mildly surprised. "Of course, I am. Why wouldn't I be?"

"I'm glad." He stretched his arms with a satisfied moan. "I think it's time for us to go home and eat some fish."

It was nearly dark when they arrived back at the farm. Gewey cleaned the fish on a wooden table next to the house, while his father prepared the stove and wash water inside. After they had both cleaned up and cooked dinner, they sat down to eat. The fish tasted better than any Gewey could remember.

"I have a surprise," said Harman, getting up and bringing a pitcher down from the cabinet. Gewey could smell orange juice as his father placed it on the table.

"Where did you get that?" asked Gewey.

Harman just smiled and poured Gewey a cup. "My little secret." He winked and returned to the chair.

There was a knock at the door. Harman sprung up and looked out of the window.

"Who is it?" asked Gewey.

"It's no one. No one at all."

"No one? Someone knocked." He got up and started to the door. Harman rushed in front of him, barring Gewey's way.

"I told you, it was no one," said Harman, this time with more force. Again, there was a knock.

"What's wrong with you?" said Gewey. "Why won't you open the door?" Gewey tried to push his way around his father, but Harman shoved him hard, sending him flying across the room and crashing into the wall.

"I said leave it!"

Gewey stared in horror as his father changed and distorted until he became a creature of quivering mass and swirling colors. "What are you?"

"She doesn't belong here," cried the creature. Its voice echoed loudly. "She must leave."

Gewey felt panic grip him as the creature closed in. He bolted around the table and tried to get to the door, but the creature got there first. "You must stay. We love you."

Gewey slowly backed away until he was stood next to the window. Without thinking any further, he propelled his body through the glass and onto the porch.

"Gewey," a familiar voice called out.

Gewey tried to focus, but the world around him blurred. "Who's there?" he cried, as he tried to regain his feet amongst the shattered pieces of glass. A figure stood in front of him, but he couldn't tell who or what it was.

"It's me, Kaylia."

As soon as he heard her name, it all came rushing back to him. The figure cleared, revealing Kaylia dressed in the same shirt and trousers she'd been wearing when he'd first met her in the forest. "Kaylia," he cried, his voice filled with relief and joy.

She took his hand and pulled him from the porch. "Hurry," she ordered. "We must get out of here."

The door to the house shattered, sending splinters flying. Gewey and Kaylia ran as fast as they could, paying no attention to where they were going.

"You must not leave!" the creature screamed as it pursued them. It appeared to float just above the ground.

"Where are we going?" asked Gewey while they ran.

"How should I know? Anywhere but here."

Gewey nodded in agreement as they continued heading down the road east, away from town. After a few minutes, he glanced over his shoulder, but he couldn't see any sign of pursuit. "Hold on," he said, grabbing Kaylia's arm and bringing them to a halt.

"We need to keep going."

"But where to? I don't even know where we are, let alone where we should go."

"We're in the spirit realm." Kaylia looked around for signs of the creature. "You became trapped here after your battle with Harlondo."

"The spirit realm?" said Gewey, frowning. "Then how are you here?"

"We took you to Valshara to be healed. But your spirit was lost. I used our bond to find you."

"Valshara," whispered Gewey. "How long have I been here?"

"Not long," she said. "Two days. But time may not flow the same here. For all I know, we've both been here for weeks, maybe even months."

"How do we get out?"

"You don't," called a voice from behind them. They turned and saw the form of Gewey's father smiling at them.

"Who are you?" Gewey demanded. "And why are you keeping us here?"

"We did not bring her," said Harman, looking at Kaylia. "We only want you. She does not belong here. She must leave."

"We will both be leaving," said Gewey. "Release us."

"I cannot," he replied. "We need you here. We have been so alone."

"What are you?" asked Kaylia.

"We will not speak with you," said Harman. His hand flashed from his side, and a dagger flew through the air straight at Kaylia's heart.

Gewey shoved her out of the way just in time. Instead of finding its target, the dagger buried itself deep into his arm. Pain shot through him as he fell to his knees. Kaylia rushed over and pulled out the blade. Blood soaked his sleeve and dripped from the ends of his fingers.

"That was foolish," scolded Harman. "But no matter." He waved his hand, and the wound was gone. "You will come to no harm, but she must be destroyed. You cannot stop this."

Gewey stared in amazement at where the dagger had struck. "If you hurt her, I'll kill you all." He got to his feet and squared his shoulders.

Harman looked amused. "You cannot kill us. The dead cannot die." He stepped toward Kaylia menacingly.

Without warning, there was a blinding flash of light. When Gewey's eyes adjusted, he gasped. Felsafell stood between Harman and Kaylia. He was dressed in his animal skins and carried his walking stick.

"Leave her be," Felsafell commanded.

Harman's face twisted in anger. "Traitor!" he shouted. "Leave this place!"

Gewey looked into Kaylia's eyes and smiled. "Are you okay?"

Kaylia nodded, still staring at the scene.

"Your heart is rotten," said Felsafell. "It's rotten and cold. You take what is not yours. You seal your own doom. Yes, you do."

"You left us," said Harman. "You broke your promise."

"There was no promise," Felsafell replied. "Oh, no. You are doomed and foul. I no longer care for your words. Our people are gone, and I will join you soon enough."

"We will not let him go." Harman clenched his jaw. "You can't make us."

Felsafell shook his head slowly. "I can't make you. But I'll tell him not to love you. Yes, I will. You'll still be alone. Alone forever. Unloved and alone."

"I will never love you," cried Gewey. "Not if you hurt Kaylia."

Harman shifted his eyes to Gewey. "You will love us," he said. "Your father and mother loved us. So will you."

"You're wrong," said Gewey. "But I will release my mother and father. Then you can be with them again."

"You see," said Felsafell. "You are a fool. The fool of fools. You keep the one who can give you love, but if you do, he will never love you."

Harman turned his back and lowered his head. "Will you return to us, brother?" he asked.

Felsafell walked up and placed his withered hand on Harman's shoulder. "I cannot. I must help free the fathers and mothers. And more there is to do for me. But I will join you soon enough."

Gewey watched as Harman faded and disappeared. "What happened?" he asked. "Is he gone?"

"Gone?" Felsafell replied. "No, not gone. Just far away."

"Thank you," said Kaylia. "I owe you a debt."

Felsafell smiled. "You will repay," he said. "Oh, yes. Then I can rest my old bones and tired head."

# CHAPTER 1

Millet, Maybell, and Malstisos made their way toward Hazrah. The first snow began to fall just as they had rounded the western end of the Razor Edge Mountains. Luckily, the snow was light and didn't bar their way, but Millet feared for Maybell's health, nonetheless. As strong as she was, he knew the long days of travel and the cold weather took a toll on her aging body. He and Malstisos kept a close eye on her and did their best to lighten her burden, though she didn't make it easy for them. Maybell had an annoying habit of taking on extra work, especially if they tried to do anything she saw as her duties.

Aside from the dropping temperatures and light snow, travel was pleasant. Malstisos was open, friendly, and free with his humor. Millet couldn't help but be pleased to have him along, and his skill as a hunter came in handy, as did his ability to know when harsh weather was coming.

They had done well avoiding other travelers, and only once had they been forced to seek shelter at a village inn. Malstisos insisted on accompanying them, stating his desire to see humans from other parts of the world. At first, Millet and Maybell objected but soon realized that he could remain unnoticed, even in a crowded tavern.

They were three days outside of Hazrah when they encountered the first indication that things had changed in the north since Millet had last been there. Malstisos stopped abruptly and led Millet and Maybell into the nearby brush.

"Wait here and keep silent," he whispered, then disappeared into the woods parallel to the road.

Maybell and Millet did their best to stay hidden and keep the horses calm, but as the minutes passed, the cold set in. Maybell began to shiver uncontrollably. Millet held her close in an attempt to keep her warm. At first, she tried to shake him off but eventually relented. Thirty minutes later, Malstisos returned, his expression grave.

"Five soldiers are camped three hundred yards down the road," he said. "They bear a standard I'm unfamiliar with, though admittedly I know little of human nations in the north."

"What did it look like?" asked Millet.

"Red with a gray background, and it bore the image of broken scales."

Millet and Maybell looked at each other. "That's the standard of Angrääl," grumbled Millet. "We must not let them see us."

"We should go around then," said Malstisos. He turned to Maybell. "I'm sorry, but we cannot rest yet."

"I'll be fine," said Maybell. "It's not riding that bothers me, it's standing still that chills old bones. Lead on."

Malstisos led them northeast, away from the road and through some forest. Millet could feel the wind picking up as it howled through the bare limbs of the trees. They rode for two hours before Malstisos finally called for a halt and built a small fire.

"Rest here," said Malstisos. "I'll scout ahead." He pulled a small flask from his pack and handed it to Maybell. "Drink this. It will help you stay warm."

"What is it?" she asked. "Not jawas tea, I hope."

Malstisos smiled warmly. "It's elf brandy," he said. "A small sip should take the chill away. I'll return before dawn." He strode off into the woods.

Millet watched Maybell's hands trembling with the cold as she lifted the flask to her lips. The concern showed on his face.

"I'm fine," said Maybell. "Quit looking at me like that."

"I'm sorry," he said. "But please understand, I'm only thinking of your well-being. Even a young man couldn't stand this cold for very long."

"Then worry about yourself," she said. The warm rush of brandy filled her, putting color back into her cheeks. "I may be an old woman. But you're no spring chicken either."

Millet laughed as Maybell passed him the flask. "Point taken."

Neither of them was able to sleep. The fire and the brandy kept them warm, but soon the howl of wolves mixed with the howl of the wind.

"How close do you think they are?" asked Maybell, trying her best to hide her fear.

"Not far from the sound of it," he answered. "But don't worry. Wolves rarely trouble travelers, and they won't come near the fire."

Malstisos returned just as the sun was breaking the horizon. "There is a garrison due east of here bearing the same standard as the other soldiers," he said. "But I have found a way around that should keep us out of sight."

"If they have built a garrison this close to Hazrah, then it's likely they've already taken the city itself," said Millet.

"The king would never allow a foreign army to go unchallenged so near to the capital." He turned to Maybell. "There is a mining village a day's ride from here. I have a friend there who can shelter us while we gather information and form a plan. I don't want to march headlong into the sights of Angrääl unless there is no other choice."

"If Hazrah has fallen, this trip may have been for naught," said Malstisos. "The garrison is organized, and they are well prepared. Whoever leads them is no fool. Entering the city unnoticed may be impossible."

"If getting into the city unnoticed isn't an option, then we'll hide in plain sight," Millet replied. "This is not my first dangerous mission."

"I may be able to help," said Maybell. "If your friend can get word to the Hazrah temple, then perhaps they can find us a way in."

"There may not be a temple to contact," said Millet. "Remember what Salmitaya did to the temples in Kaltinor?"

Maybell's heart ached at the thought. "I should have killed her when I had the chance."

"Don't second guess yourself," replied Millet. "Your actions were correct and merciful. I, for one, am glad you spared her. Once her masters discover her failure, I'm sure they will be less than pleased. I doubt that her comfortable life in Kaltinor will last for much longer."

"I hope you're right." Maybell wiped a tear from her cheek.

Millet explained to Malstisos their position relative to the mining village so that he could scout ahead for patrols. As it turned out, they were forced to change direction three times to avoid detection. When they eventually reached the edge of the village, they hid behind some bushes and watched for a time. No soldiers came into sight, so Millet told Maybell and Malstisos to wait while he entered and made contact with his friend.

"I don't like you going alone," said Maybell.

"Until we know what's going on, we can't risk being taken together," he replied. "I'll need to talk to Markus and make sure it's safe."

"Don't worry, Maybell," said Malstisos. "If he is taken, I will free him."

"Fine," said Maybell, scowling. "Who is this Markus person, anyway?"

"He's the foreman of the Kessel copper mine," said Millet. "He and I were good friends when we were young."

"How do you know you can still trust him?" she asked.

"I don't. But when we were young, he was the most honest and dependable man I knew. Besides, it's either this, or we ride blindly into danger. I'd rather try to escape from here than from the city gates."

"If you are captured, be certain to make enough noise so that I know to come get you," said Malstisos.

"Absolutely," Millet agreed.

Millet scanned the area one final time to make certain he wasn't being watched and then hurried to the nearby street. Malstisos handed Maybell the flask of elf brandy, which she gratefully accepted. An hour later, Millet returned.

"I spoke to Markus," he said. "He offers us food and shelter."

"What news of Hazrah?" asked Malstisos.

"It's not good," he replied. "We can discuss it at Markus's house. Keep your hood on until we're inside. Markus knows you're with me, so there will be no reason to hide your identity once we get there."

Millet led them into the village. It was typical of a mining town, mostly single-story wooden buildings built for utility rather than aesthetics. The streets were empty aside from a few workers on their way home from the mines.

Being the mine foreman, Markus lived in one of the larger houses. Even so, it was still not much bigger than the average farmhouse. Millet tied the horses to a nearby hitching post, then walked straight up to the door and opened it. The interior was modest, yet comfortable. A sturdy dining table was already set for the evening meal at the far end of the great room, and a fire crackled in the fireplace just inside the door. A balding, stocky man with deep-set eyes and a weathered face stood next to the table, slicing a loaf of fresh bread. He looked up and smiled as the party entered.

"Welcome," said Markus. "Please have a seat. Supper will be ready shortly."

"Thank you, old friend," said Millet. "This is Maybell and Malstisos."

Markus walked over and took Maybell's hand. "My lady, you are most welcome. A Priestess of Ayliazarah is sorely needed here."

Maybell curtsied. "I cannot tell you how grateful we are for your hospitality."

"It's my pleasure," he replied and turned to Malstisos. "And you must be the elf Millet told me of. Truly, the world is changing."

Malstisos smiled and bowed low. "I am at your service and in your debt."

Markus smiled broadly. "Not at all. Millet is an old friend, and his friends are mine."

They sat at the table while Markus passed around the bread and retrieved a small pot of beef stew from the stove. "I'm sorry that there's not more, but this is considered a feast in these dark times."

Millet reached into his purse and brought out a gold coin. "Take this." He pushed the coin to Markus.

Markus pushed the coin back, shaking his head. "I don't need the money, my friend. It's food we lack here. Most of what we have is sent north to feed the armies of Angrääl. I'm one of the lucky ones. As foreman, I'm given extra provisions."

"So the Dark Knight has taken Hazrah," said Malstisos.

Markus stared down at the table. "He has. And he's brought misery with him. Of course, they call him the Reborn King, and not the Dark Knight."

"How long ago did his armies arrive?" asked Malstisos.

"Three months ago. But his agents were here long before that. They negotiated our surrender. We didn't even put up a fight."

"Why not?" asked Millet. "The King's army could have held out for years. The city walls have never been breached."

"I don't know," said Markus. "Those kinds of questions land you in prison these days. As far as the King's army is concerned, most have been sent north to Angrääl. Some have returned carrying the banner of our conquerors. It's like The Dark One is trying to eat the world and we're the appetizer."

"What of Lady Nal'Thain?" asked Millet. "Is she well?"

"If that's why you've come, you've wasted your time," replied Markus. "No one has seen or heard from the house of Nal'Thain for weeks. The rumor is that the Lady has been sent north, but I don't know how much truth there is in that."

Millet lowered his head. "What of her son?"

"I'm afraid that I have no news of Jacob's whereabouts. There are whispers that he was the one who convinced the King to surrender. After that, he seems to have vanished."

"I don't believe it," cried Millet. "The son of Lee Nal'Thain would not betray his people."

"I only know what I hear," said Markus. "Whether there is truth in this—who knows?"

"We must find them," said Millet. "Can you get us inside the city?"

"I doubt it. They check everyone coming in or going out. But I may be able to help. I make monthly production reports to the city clerk, and the next one is due in two days' time. I could try and contact them for you."

"What about the temples?" asked Maybell. "I could claim to be sent from Baltria. Certainly they wouldn't stop a priestess?"

"I hate to be the one to tell you this," said Markus, unable to meet Maybell's eyes. "But the temples have been shut down. They house Angrääl's soldiers now."

"What?" she cried. "Foul beasts!"

"I'm sorry," said Markus. "Worship of the gods is forbidden now. Most of the priestesses and monks were sent north for re-education a week after the soldiers arrived."

"I still can't believe that the King has done nothing to stop this!" said Millet.

"The time is long past for the King to take action," said Markus.

"Is there no resistance?" asked Malstisos.

"There was at first. But Angrääl crushed it. I know you won't want to hear this, Millet, but it was Jacob Nal'Thain who helped them rout out the resistance. This I saw with my own eyes."

Millet shook his head, rubbing his temples. "It doesn't matter," he finally said. "I was sent to retrieve My Lord's family, and I will do as he has commanded me."

Markus sighed. "Very well. Tonight, you and your friends will sleep in the basement. I will leave in the morning. But I cannot promise that I will succeed."

"I thank you for your help, old friend," said Millet. "I know how much you're risking by aiding us. You can come with us if you wish. We can offer you sanctuary."

"My place is here with my men. I cannot abandon them."

"I understand," said Millet.

After their meal, Millet retrieved their packs from the horses, which were then put in a small stable behind the house. Markus gave each of them extra bedding and led them into the basement. "Please keep as quiet as possible," he said. "The soldiers rarely check my house, but a little extra caution won't hurt." He walked up the stairs and closed the door. The clank of the latch echoed throughout the basement.

"I don't like being trapped," said Malstisos. "If we are discovered, there is only one way out."

"I don't like it either," agreed Maybell.

"What choice is there?" said Millet. "We are asking Markus to take a huge risk. If he says we should stay here, I must trust him."

"I hope your trust is justified," remarked Malstisos. "Hardship can do strange things to a person's loyalty."

"I don't like what you're implying," said Millet. "I've known Markus for more than forty years. He is as solid and honest a man as I've ever known."

"We shall see," said Malstisos.

They set up their bedding and went to sleep. Bad dreams troubled Millet, causing him to wake up several times. Eventually, he decided to forgo sleep completely and spent the rest of the night huddled in a corner. After a few hours, he heard the door slowly creak open. Malstisos woke immediately and drew his knife. Maybell stood up and moved behind him.

"What?" Millet asked in dismay.

"There are a dozen soldiers upstairs," Markus announced as he descended the steps. "If you don't disarm, they'll burn you alive down here."

"Traitor," shouted Millet. His fist shot out, landing solidly on Markus's jaw. Markus stumbled back and fell to the ground.

"It's not my fault," said Markus, still sitting on the ground and rubbing his jaw. "You were seen coming in here by one of their spies. Please understand, if I didn't do this, they would have killed me, and half of my men as well."

Malstisos glared furiously at the door. "I say we fight our way out."

"No," said Millet. "Let me speak to them first." He looked down at Markus. "Lead me upstairs."

Without a word, Markus got to his feet and led Millet up the stairs and through the door. He entered the main part of the house and immediately saw twelve soldiers in full armor, swords drawn.

With them was a man in a dark blue velvet suit, carrying a white ash walking stick. He had long, dark blond hair and fair skin. He smiled as Millet entered.

"You must be Millet," he said. "My name is Brandis. I am here to escort you and your companions to Hazrah if you wish."

"We will not be used as hostages," said Millet. "If that is your intent, you might as well kill us now."

Brandis laughed. "No, no, no, you are not my captives, you're my guests."

"And if I decide not to accept your hospitality," said Millet. "What then?"

"Leave if you wish," he said. "But I believe you are here at the direction of the former Lord Nal'Thain. Is this not so?"

Millet remained expressionless and silent.

"No need to answer," said Brandis. "I already know. Markus was kind enough to fill me in. It's a good thing he did. Otherwise, you may have been foolish enough to attempt sneaking into the city. Naturally, you would have been caught. Heaven knows what may have happened before I could get to you."

"What do you want with us?" Millet demanded.

"To help. You're here to retrieve the Nal'Thain family, and I'm here to see that you accomplish your task."

Millet looked warily at Brandis. "So we can simply take them and leave?"

"Certainly," he said. "Jacob Nal'Thain is a troublemaker we would be happy to be rid of. As for Lady Penelope, you have a choice."

"What might that be?" asked Millet.

"She has traveled north to the court of the Reborn King," said Brandis. "It will take several weeks for her to return. You may wait, or you may take young Jacob and leave immediately."

"If you are being truthful, then have Jacob brought here," said Millet. "Now."

"I see your suspicions abound." Brandis chuckled. "As you wish. But I must ask that you remain here until he can be brought." He turned to leave. "Oh, I nearly forgot. You must surrender your weapons first, of course."

Millet made no move to comply.

"Come now," said Brandis. "They will be returned when you leave. A small thing to ask, all things considered."

Millet nodded and went back down to the basement. Malstisos was still standing in front of Maybell with his knife drawn.

"I could hear your conversation," said Malstisos. He handed Millet his knife. "We have little choice."

"I'm sorry for this," said Millet. "Clearly, Markus is no longer the man I knew."

"You are not at fault," he replied. "There was no way for you to know."

"If you would all join me," called Brandis from upstairs.

Millet led Maybell and Malstisos up and handed their weapons to him.

"Thank you," said Brandis. "Very wise choice."

"What happens now?" asked Millet.

"Now we wait," he answered. "One of my men is on his way to bring young Jacob. Then you may leave. That is ... unless you choose to wait for the Lady Nal'Thain."

"If she still lives?" said Millet.

"As I told you," said Brandis. "She is at the court of Angrääl. I have no reason to lie." He looked at Malstisos. "I am honored to have an elf among us."

Malstisos said nothing.

"No reason for apprehension," continued Brandis. "My Lord holds your kind in high regard. Certainly, you know of our offer of friendship."

"I know of the lies your master has told," said Malstisos. "Empty promises of glory made to a generation that still clings to the past. You will find that I am not so easily swayed as some."

"Not empty promises," replied Brandis. "Soon we will spread our message of hope throughout the land. And when that happens, those who have seen the wisdom of our cause will benefit the most."

"Your cause?" snapped Maybell. "You've destroyed temples and murdered their followers."

"Ah, the priestess." Brandis sneered. "I had almost forgotten about you."

Malstisos moved his body between Maybell and Brandis.

"There's no reason to be alarmed. I have no intention of harming any of you."

Maybell seethed with rage. "You've killed innocent priestesses and monks. You are an abomination."

Brandis laughed and shook his head. "I haven't murdered anyone. Your own people betrayed you. Not me, and not my master. All we have done is told people the truth."

"And what truth is that?" asked Millet.

"That the gods are as corrupt as the people who serve them. Your elf friend will certainly agree with this. They have caused nothing but harm to man and elf. They are greedy and petty, and now, thanks to the Reborn King, they are gone."

"You assume that all elves believe the old tales," said Malstisos. "Not all of us blame the gods for the split."

"You are wise," said Brandis. "You do not take what you are told at face value. Sadly, in this case, you are wrong. It was the gods that cursed the elves. But what you do not understand is that they cursed man as well. They turned us into slaves. We were sent on a path of endless destruction without guidance. However, that horrible chapter of history is coming to an end. Soon the world will be at peace, and both elf and human will be able to live as they were meant to—in peace."

Maybell sneered. "You speak of peace and freedom, and yet here you stand, conquerors and invaders."

Brandis laughed. "We have taken Hazrah without spilling blood. When before in history has that happened? We allow you and your friends to leave in peace, even though you have sworn to destroy us. We give you Lee Nal'Thain's family as a token of goodwill, and still you accuse."

"You tried to have us killed," replied Millet. "You've destroyed temples, and only the gods know what you've done to the clergy. Whatever your motivations are for letting us go, I suspect they are part of some grander design. You allow us to leave because it serves your needs to do so, though I don't yet know what those needs are."

"The attempts on the lives of you and your friends were unfortunate," he said. "The people responsible have been dealt with. Of course, I don't expect you to believe that. And frankly, it doesn't matter. You will think my master is your enemy until the very end. But when that end comes, you will see the truth."

"I see the truth now," Millet shot back. "And unless you force me to do so, I will hear no more of your lies."

"As you wish," said Brandis. "My soldiers and I will wait outside." He spun on his heels and left the house. Markus and the soldiers followed close behind.

"Do you think they actually intend to let us just walk out of here?" asked Maybell.

"Millet was correct," said Malstisos. "If it serves their objectives, they will. This may well be a deception, but I cannot divine the purpose. If they want us, they have us."

"We'll know soon enough," said Millet.

Two hours later, the door opened and Brandis entered. Behind him was a tall, thin youth, aged no more than twenty, with light brown hair that fell in loose curls to his shoulders. He was dressed in tan leathers and boots and carried a pack over his shoulders. Apart from being a bit more rounded at the chin and having eyes that were deep green and wider set, his face was strikingly like Lee's.

"I give you Jacob Nal'Thain," said Brandis.

Millet looked Jacob over for several moments. "How do we know this is Jacob?"

"Who else would I be?" Jacob sneered. "And who are you?"

"I am Millet Gristall, the personal assistant to Lee Nal'Thain."

"My father?" said Jacob. "So this is what you brought me here for? You drag me from my cell for this?"

Millet cocked his head. "Your cell?"

"Young Jacob has been somewhat of a troublemaker," Brandis explained. "We have had to lock him away for the good of the city."

"I see," said Millet. He turned to Jacob. "Where is your mother?"

Jacob glared. "This dog knows where she is. In Angrääl, where they took her."

"How many times must you be told?" said Brandis. "She went there of her own free will."

"I'll never believe that. And if you expect me to go willingly with these people just so they can kill me when we're out of sight, then you're mistaken. Kill me now, for all to see."

Brandis sighed. "For the last time, if we wanted to kill you, we would have done so long before now. You will either go with these people or leave on your own. Either way, I tire of you and will no longer tolerate your presence."

"You will come with us," said Millet. "I was sent to retrieve you and your mother. Being that your mother is not here, I will at least retrieve you."

"Why should I believe you?" asked Jacob. "What's to prevent you from killing me the moment we're out of sight?"

"As much as I hate to admit it," replied Millet, "Brandis is correct. If they wanted you dead, they wouldn't need such an elaborate deception. In fact, we are in more danger from you than you are from us."

Jacob thought for a moment. "Very well, I will go with you. For now."

"Good decision," said Brandis. "I'll leave you to it then." He started to the door. "Please tell Lord Nal'Thain that we will allow him to see his wife any time he wishes. And as for Gewey Stedding, the Reborn King still wants his friendship. Please convey the message to both of them, if you would."

"I'll tell them," replied Millet.

"Good," he said. "You will not be hindered when you leave. I'll wait outside until you're ready." He turned and left.

"I'm not sure what your game is," said Jacob. "But if you wish me harm, even your friend the elf may find that difficult."

Malstisos stepped forward. "If I wanted you dead, I would have killed you the second that door closed. It is not we who need prove our intentions."

"I agree," said Millet. "You look like my lord, but I have no way of knowing for sure."

"What do we do?" said Maybell. "Certainly we cannot trust that this is not a deception."

"We won't," said Millet. "There is one way of finding the truth. But in order to do so, I must contact Lord Starfinder."

"I've heard that name before," said Jacob.

"Of course you have," he replied. "That was the name of your father before you were born, and it is the name he goes by now. I'm sure your mother has mentioned it."

"No," he said. "I heard it when I was in prison. The Dark One wants him. They mean to kill him."

"They've already tried," said Millet with a wicked smile. "So far, they've failed miserably."

"Enough talk," said Malstisos. "We need to leave while we still can."

"Agreed," said Millet. "We'll head west for now."

"Then what?" asked Maybell. "We can't bring him back with us. At least, not until we know with certainty that he is who he claims to be."

"I have no intention of being taken anywhere," said Jacob. "As soon as I'm able, I'll be going my own way."

Millet looked irritably at the boy. "I suggest you accept our company for the time being. At least until we're away from here."

Jacob looked disgusted and walked to the door. "I'll be outside when you're ready." He slammed the door behind him.

# CHAPTER 2

Millet, Maybell, and Malstisos gathered their gear and left the house. Jacob was sat on the front steps fiddling with a small knife. Their horses were ready and waiting. Brandis stood a few feet away, along with two guards.

"Here are your weapons," said Brandis. He motioned to one of the guards who handed them over. "I trust you will not need them anytime soon. And we have provided young Jacob with a sword as well as a mount. If you wish an escort, one can be provided. But I suspect you do not."

"No escort is necessary," replied Millet. "We know the way."

"In that case, I wish you a safe journey," said Brandis. He nodded to the guards, who followed him as he headed off down the street.

Millet led them through the village to the west road. The street was conspicuously empty.

"Do you think they plan to ambush us?" asked Maybell, as they mounted their horses.

"I doubt it," answered Millet. "They could have killed us already if they wanted to. Malstisos is the only one who might have escaped. No, whatever their plan is, it involves us removing Jacob from Hazrah." He looked suspiciously at the boy.

They continued until dusk and made camp along the road. While on their way earlier, they had passed a patrol, but the soldiers simply ignored them.

"It would seem that Brandis intends to let us leave without incident," said Malstisos.

Millet stared at the fire and rubbed his hands together. "So it would seem." He watched as Jacob checked his horse and unpacked his gear. "We must find a way to contact Lee without giving away his location. Until then, I'm afraid we have no way to trust the lad."

"I have exceptional hearing," said Jacob. "From my father's side of the family, I assume. Contact him if you must. As for me, I'm headed for Baltria once we're safely away from here."

"You intend to abandon your mother?" asked Millet.

Jacob glowered. "There's nothing I can do for her." He placed his blanket near the fire. "They won't send for her. I don't care what they told you. I doubt she's even alive."

"They let you live, didn't they?" said Malstisos.

"That may be. But I'm in Hazrah, and my mother is not. The house Nal'Thain still has a good name among the people. To kill me without scandal or reprisal, they would need to do it away from the city."

"We were told that you helped Angrääl take control," said Maybell, huddled close to the fire and sipping elf brandy.

"That's a lie," spat Jacob. "I did everything I could to stop them."

"That may be," said Maybell. "But if the people believe it, I doubt your death would cause much of a scandal."

Jacob pulled his blanket close and stared into the fire.

"What did happen?" asked Malstisos. "From what we have seen, it didn't take much of an effort for Angrääl to seize control."

Jacob scowled. "It was the King," he muttered in disgust. "He sold us out."

"You're not making sense," said Millet. "Even the King couldn't simply hand over control of the land to a foreign power without resistance from the nobles."

"That's not what happened," replied Jacob. "They were far more subtle than that. A year ago an ambassador arrived at court with a message of friendship. He said he was from a kingdom in the north and desired to establish relations and trade. Naturally, the lords were skeptical. All the old tales of the northern kingdoms are of terror and war, but the ambassador assured us of his good intentions and suggested that we send an envoy to meet with his lord. After much deliberation, the King agreed. I wanted to be the one to go, but Mother wouldn't allow it."

"Wise woman," said Millet.

"In this case, she was." Jacob nodded in agreement. "The King sent his second cousin to gauge the truth of matters. Sadly, though loved dearly by the King, he has no skill with diplomacy. He returned two months later, accompanied by a full entourage of representatives from Angrääl, enough to occupy a proper diplomatic embassy. At first, the King protested, but his cousin convinced him that relations and trade would be in the best interest for the kingdom. Before long, they had bought a building close to the palace and had established themselves as the embassy of the 'Reborn King of Angrääl.'"

"Didn't that send up warning flags?" asked Millet. "The 'Reborn King' can only be referring to the Demon King, Rätsterfel. Surely the temples intervened when they heard this?" He retrieved a loaf of bread and dried meat from his pack and passed it around.

"I believe the temples had been infiltrated long before the arrival of the ambassador," replied Jacob.

"Why would you think that?" asked Maybell, trying to contain her irritation.

"From the moment they arrived, they showed their contempt for the gods. They refused to have their embassy blessed and turned away any offer of friendship the temples made. On the streets, they openly mocked the gods and said that anyone who trusted in them was a fool. A few of the temples were even vandalized. Everyone knew who did it, but there was no proof. More than that, the temples did little to stop it."

"All this, and the King still did nothing?" said Millet.

"There was nothing to do," said Jacob. "The temples made no complaint. Not to the King, nor anyone else. In fact, it was widely known that many of the high priestesses and senior monks had dealings with them on a regular basis. I, myself, saw the chief librarian of the Temple of Gerath riding with the ambassador, talking and laughing as friends."

"That means nothing," said Maybell. "You can't know why they were speaking."

"True," he answered. "But the next day the library was robbed and nearly every important text stolen. The culprits were never found, despite the fact that I told the magistrate what I had seen. Naturally, after that, life became more difficult for my mother and me. Several of our trade caravans were attacked, and our interests in the copper mine were suddenly audited. I went to the magistrate to complain, but I fear he had already been bought. The chief finance minister manufactured reasons for our mining assets to be stripped away. Of course, they were sold to an unknown party—and by unknown, I mean Angrääl."

"Was anyone else attacked like this?" asked Millet.

"Oh, yes, I was not the only Lord of Hazrah with the courage to stand up to these interlopers. But our resistance was short-lived. With the King and the temples against us, we were reduced to simple acts of defiance and petty acts of vandalism. Unfortunately, in my case, they found my weakness."

"And what might that have been?" asked Malstisos.

"My mother. As I became more brazen in my resistance, they threatened to kill her if I didn't fall in line. My first reaction was to send her away. We have friends in Baltria, and I thought she'd be safe there. But they got to her before I could make the arrangements. I was told that she had volunteered to attend court in Angrääl as the personal representative of the King, but the truth is they were using her as leverage against me. It was a week after she left when the first Angrääl troops arrived. The King announced that there was a growing threat from the southern kingdoms and that they were only there to assist in our defense. But it was soon clear that it was an occupation."

"It's difficult to imagine all this," said Millet. "The people of Hazrah would have risen up and fought in my day."

"Some tried," he said. "But any who actually took up arms were slaughtered and called a traitor to the throne. Most were arrested and sent north before they could organize properly."

"Is that how you ended up in prison?" asked Maybell.

Jacob nodded slowly. "At first they said I was being held for questioning about a raid on a grain shipment. There was, of course, no such raid. It was clear I was framed to get me out of the way. They made it seem as if I was cooperating in order to coerce me into furthering their goals, but I refused. I think the only reason I've kept my head is that my mother has agreed to work with them."

"I can't believe Lady Nal'Thain would side with the Dark Knight over her own people," said Millet. "She would rather die."

"You're right," said Jacob. "But it was my life, and not her own, that she was protecting. That's what they do. They use the people you care for against you."

"How long have you been in prison?" asked Maybell.

"Six months," he replied. "I was released once, but immediately rearrested. When I was jailed for the first time, their troops were just arriving. Now they are at least two thousand strong."

"What do you intend to do?" asked Millet. "If you go back, you'll be imprisoned—or worse."

"What I told you earlier," said Jacob, "was not entirely truthful. I will most certainly not abandon my mother. I do believe she still lives. But I am indeed going to Baltria. I have friends there who can help me. Then I'm going to get her out of Angrääl."

Millet thought for a moment. "In that case, I'll go with you." He turned to Malstisos. "You and Maybell, go back and tell Lord Starfinder what has happened."

"I don't need you slowing me down," said Jacob.

Millet laughed. "If you are who you say you are, then you will need my help. I traveled with your father for many years and am far more capable than you might think."

Malstisos smiled. "You should listen to your elders, young one. Millet is far more traveled than you. Besides, I doubt they left you with any coin. How do you intend to eat and lodge?"

"I can hunt," said Jacob stubbornly. "I've learned to survive on my own."

"That may be," said Millet. "But I serve the house Nal'Thain and have an obligation to see to your well-being."

Jacob met Millet's eyes. "You serve my father, not the house Nal'Thain. He gave up his right to use that name when he abandoned us."

"You speak from ignorance," said Millet. "But now is not the time for me to enlighten you." Millet straightened out his bedroll. "I am going with you." He then turned to the others. "We'll take the road east to Manisalia. There is a crossroads a few days from the city. We'll split up there."

Maybell's eyes lit up. "Perhaps we should see the Oracle?"

"You can try," said Millet. "But I would not tarry long. If she will not see you right away, you should move on."

"I too would relish the chance to see the Oracle," said Malstisos. "She is well known to my people."

"I think you will be disappointed," said Jacob. "The rumor is she has left Manisalia to escape the armies of Angrääl. I even heard that she is dead."

"I hope you're wrong," said Maybell, settling into her blanket. "It would be a great loss to the world. Her wisdom has helped guide the world away from destruction for many decades."

"Decades?" said Malstisos. "My people have tales of her that go back to before the Great War. I have always assumed her to be more than one person, the title passed down, but perhaps not."

"You think she is that old?" asked Maybell. "She is human, after all."

"Are you so certain of that? Our stories always describe the same person, always looking the same way. That in itself means nothing, but I've also heard human tales of her. Recent ones. They are too similar in her description to think it a coincidence. At least, it seems that way to me."

"Maybe you can ask her if she is still there." Millet pulled his blanket over his chest and yawned. "We still have a long journey ahead. We can continue this discussion tomorrow."

# CHAPTER 3

The next day, they rode in silence. At midday, they stopped to eat and to rest the horses. Several groups of soldiers and a few local farmers passed, but all of them ignored their presence. The temperature had dropped substantially, and a strong north wind cut straight through the group's clothing. Soon they were underway once again, but it quickly became clear that they would need to risk a town and an inn.

"No need for us to hide at this point." Millet's voice trembled from the cold. "Whatever their plan, it's obvious they do not intend to hinder our departure."

"I agree," said Malstisos. He glanced over at Maybell, who was riding in silence, her eyes down. He couldn't help but worry. Despite remarkable resilience for a woman of her advanced years, he knew the elements must be taking their toll. "In fact, I intend to remain in plain sight for as long as possible," he added.

Jacob chuckled and slowly shook his head. "It would do no good to run. They have trackers from Angrääl following us even now. Of that, I have no doubt. Where we go, they will follow."

Millet grunted with displeasure. "When we split up, they may have a harder time of it. I have a feeling it is you and I who they will be following, and my skills in evasion should not be underestimated."

Jacob sniggered.

"You should not let your eyes always be your judge, child," scolded Malstisos. "Your father has great confidence in Millet. And thus far, he has shown his worth more than once since I've traveled with him. I daresay his skills and usefulness outweigh yours."

Jacob suddenly halted his horse, his face twisted in anger. "Mind your tongue, elf." His hand slid to his sword.

"Don't be foolish." Malstisos's voice became low and dangerous. "I will not be threatened, no matter who your father might be."

The two stared at each other intensely for what seemed like an eternity.

"Enough of this!" Maybell's voice echoed over the trees. The ferocity of the woman's tone startled the others.

Malstisos bowed his head. "I am deeply sorry, sister. I know you must be cold and tired." He turned to Jacob. "I'm certain we can conduct ourselves with better manners."

Jacob continued to fume but nodded sharply. "For now," he grumbled.

Maybell snorted in disgust at the scene. "How much farther to the next village?" she asked Millet.

"Two days," he replied. "But there's a hostel we could reach before sundown if we keep our next rest short."

"Good," said Maybell, trying to hide her relief.

Abruptly, Malstisos's back stiffened. He drew his long knife.

"What is it?" whispered Millet.

"Something follows." The elf dismounted.

"I told you," scoffed Jacob. "They have sent trackers. Weren't you paying attention?"

Malstisos shook his head. "This is no tracker. Whatever it is, it smells wrong." He closed his eyes for a moment and sniffed the air. "Stay here." He placed his hand on Millet's shoulder. "If I do not return in one hour, flee as fast as you can."

"Where should we go?" asked Millet, alarmed.

"Stick with your plan," the elf replied, then turned to Maybell and smiled. "Don't worry. I may only be chasing shadows." He disappeared into the nearby trees, leaving the group behind.

Many minutes passed before anyone dared to move. Finally, Millet reached into his pack to retrieve a loaf of bread and passed it out to the others. Maybell reluctantly took a piece, then found a spot a few yards from Millet and Jacob to sit alone and nibble.

"What do we do if he doesn't return?" asked Jacob through a mouthful of bread.

Millet met Jacob's eyes. "We'll do as Malstisos said and continue to Baltria. There, I will contact your father. Now, if you don't mind, I would rather not speak until Malstisos returns."

"If he returns," muttered Jacob.

Millet shot a furious glance and stormed away.

Minutes seemed like hours as the group stared into the surrounding forest, hoping to see Malstisos return. Finally, just as Millet was about to tell the others it was time to leave, he caught sight of the elf, head bowed low, holding what appeared to be a severed head in one hand and his long knife in the other. Maybell gasped. Millet and Jacob stared in horror as the elf tossed the head to the ground beside the horses. The elf's knife and hands were covered with thick, black ooze, and the stench of rotting flesh filled the air. The head resembled a human man, but its features were distorted and grotesque as if burned by fire, its hair tangled, stringy, and covered in filth.

"What is that thing?" whispered Maybell with a shudder.

Malstisos looked at Jacob. "I was hoping our young friend here might be able to enlighten us."

Jacob's eyes went wide. "Me? How should I know? I've never seen such a creature."

Malstisos studied Jacob, then looked down at the remains. "I found it about half a mile behind us. It was clearly following our trail. I tried to approach unseen, but it must have had a keen sense of smell because it knew I was there the moment I saw it. I am no seeker, but no human I have ever encountered, save perhaps Lord Starfinder, could have heard my approach. When I knew I was discovered, I decided to withdraw, but the thing was on me in an instant. It moved as quickly as any elf, though not as graceful. It struck at me with bare hands but with power beyond human strength. As it was unarmed, I had the advantage and buried my knife in its heart."

"Then why cut off its head?" interrupted Jacob. "And why bring this disgusting thing here?"

"Like I said," Malstisos replied in a low tone, "I was hoping you could help to identify it. You have been here throughout the entire occupation. Have you never heard of such a creature?"

He reached into his saddlebag to retrieve a flask and a small cloth and began cleaning his hands and knife. "But that's not the only reason I bring it with me. I have the creature's head because it was the only way I could kill it. My blow through its heart served only to enrage the beast. As I pulled my blade loose, it charged in yet again with a ferocity I have never before encountered. Again and again, it charged. I was barely able to avoid its blows. I slashed away at every part of it and watched in horror as my strikes had no effect. It wasn't long before I knew I had to either kill this beast or flee, so I waited for it to charge one last time. Then I brought my blade across its neck. To my great relief, my stroke fell true, and the creature died."

"What should we do now?" asked Millet. "If there are more of these things around, we don't stand a chance."

Malstisos dried his hands and wiped his knife with oil. "If there are more, then we are in mortal danger." He checked his pack and sheathed his knife. "I cannot protect everyone at once. Still, I don't see that we have any other choice but to continue with our plan. If we are lucky, there will be no more of these things about. If there are, then I'll do my best to kill them before they are upon us. Now that I know how to kill it, one will pose me little danger. And with only Maybell at my side, I should be able to keep her safe."

"It's settled." Millet mounted his horse. "The crossroads. Then we will part ways. By then, we should know if there are more of these ... creatures."

The party rode on through the rest of the day in silence, and it was nearly sunset when they arrived at the hospice. This was little more than a small cabin with a small adjoining stable, but the smoke from the chimney and the aroma of roast pork filled their hearts with joy. Millet dismounted and motioned for the others to wait. "I'll see to our accommodations," he said. "I won't be but a moment."

The interior was as he expected. The single room was large enough to hold a dozen beds and a roughly made dining table. A fire crackling in the hearth was the sole source of light, giving it a comfortable, albeit dim, atmosphere. A thin young man sat at the table carving a piece of roast pork. His blond hair and fine features indicated that he had not seen many winters. He looked up as Millet opened the door and frowned.

"If you're here to rob me, I have nothing to take but some roast pork and a half bottle of wine."

Millet stopped and bowed low. "I am not here to rob you, young man. My companions and I seek a bed for the night."

He scanned the room for signs of other people but saw none. "Are you master here?"

"I am," the boy replied. "At least, until my uncle returns." The boy stood, wiping his hands on his trousers. "I'm Gerald. And you are welcome here, though I have little to offer." He walked to the hearth and stirred the fire. "How many are you?"

"Four," Millet replied. "And we ask only for a bed and perhaps a bite to eat." He fished three coppers from his pocket and placed them on the table. "This should cover our expense."

Gerald's eyes widened as he retrieved the coins, clutching them tightly. "In that case, you are very welcome."

Millet smiled warmly. "If you would allow me to stable my horses."

"Of course," said Gerald. "I'll do it for you if you'd like." He headed toward the door, still clutching the coins.

Millet grabbed the boy gently by the arm. "That won't be necessary. But I would be grateful if you could prepare us a meal."

"Yes, yes," said Gerald. "It will be waiting."

Millet thanked the boy and returned to the party. After they'd unpacked and stabled the horses, they entered. Four plates and cups had been placed around the table. Malstisos was careful to hide his features beneath his hood.

Gerald whistled merrily as he placed blankets on the beds. The roast pork, though a bit plain, was well received, and soon they were laughing and talking as if they hadn't a care in the world.

"Hostels in this area are usually filled to bursting this time of year," said Millet once his belly was full. "Why are you so empty?"

Gerald's face twisted in anger. "Angrääl," he spat. "It's because of those damn soldiers. Most people are too afraid to travel, and the few that do are agents and officials of the invaders. They take what they want and leave us to starve."

His hands trembled as he drank from his cup. "This hostel has been in my family for three generations. We've never had much, but donations from the temples and travelers kept us fed and clothed. We were able to help hundreds of people who might have otherwise perished on the road. I always took great pride in the work my family has done here. Now I can barely survive."

"You mentioned your uncle," said Millet, his voice filled with compassion. "Where is he?"

"Hunting," replied Gerald, regaining his composure. "We can't afford to buy food most times, so my uncle hunts for what we need." He nodded to the leftover pork. "Without it, we'd starve."

Maybell reached over, took Gerald's hand, and said softly: "You're very brave to stay here alone."

Gerald managed a weak smile. "It's my uncle that's brave. The forests are riddled with bandits and thieves. So far he's avoided them, but it's only a matter of time before I fear his luck runs out."

"I'll pray for you," said Maybell, tears welling in her eyes.

Gerald jerked his hand away. "Save your prayers," he uttered sharply. "The gods care nothing for me." He stood up and faced the wall. "I'm sorry." His voice cracked as he forced back his tears. "I know you mean well. It's just that it has been so long since hope has been in this land. I've prayed and prayed, but I think the gods have abandoned us."

"Perhaps not," said Millet. "Perhaps help is on the way."

Gerald turned and sighed. "I hope you're right."

They soon retired for the night. The earlier cheer was overcome by sadness, and none slept peacefully.

# CHAPTER 4

Lee sat by the fireplace in the main library of Valshara, reading quietly. Over the past eight days it had become his favorite way to pass the time, and the only thing that took his mind off his wife and son, not to mention Gewey and Kaylia. He had always been proud of his own collection of rare books, but Valshara held treasures beyond his imagination.

When he wasn't in the library, he spent time with his mother. She told him of her life in the temple and recalled memories of his father. It soon became clear to him the love she held for the man and the pain she felt after his death. He found it difficult at times to fight off feelings of guilt for the anger he had felt toward her for so long.

Gewey and Kaylia had shown no signs of reviving. Lee visited them at least twice a day but was only allowed to be in the room for a few minutes at a time. The healers clearly thought any intrusion an imposition, and Lee was not inclined to argue. Besides, there was nothing he could do, and he did not enjoy feeling helpless.

Dina spent her time recounting her experiences in her journal. Selena had held a small ceremony signifying her elevation to full cleric and then set her to task. Lee had scarcely seen her except for when they happened to run into each other on their way to check on Gewey and Kaylia.

Word had come that Linis was seeking out Theopolou and that he hoped to have the sage there soon. He'd arrived in Althetas two days after the battle between Gewey and Harlando and had been contacted by Valsharan agents. Lee took comfort in this. He knew if anyone could hasten the arrival of Theopolou, it was Linis.

The door to the library opened. Lee looked up and saw Ertik. His face was grave, and he was dressed in white ceremonial robes, something Lee had only seen at Dina's elevation to cleric. Lee placed his book on the table beside his chair and rose to his feet as Ertik strode over.

Ertik bowed. "Lee," he said in a respectful tone.

Lee smiled warmly. "Why so formal today?" He reached out and shook Ertik's hand.

"Theopolou has arrived," he replied. "The High Lady asked me to tell you that we will be meeting with him this evening in the main receiving hall. Appropriate clothing has already been brought to your room."

"I see," said Lee, noting Ertik's demeanor. "How many are with him?"

"He has brought an escort of ten elves. Linis is also with them."

Lee nodded. "I'll be there."

"Mind what you say. These elves are not like others you have encountered. They do not enjoy the company of humans. That we possess the Book of Souls is the only reason they've agreed to come." Ertik lowered his voice to a whisper. "This may not go well. Be prepared." With that, he bowed and left.

Lee stood for a long moment, his brow furled with worry. He knew the elves thought the Book of Souls was rightfully theirs, but his experience with more enlightened elves left out the possibility that they may try to take it by force. Since he had arrived, he had counted maybe a dozen men that belonged to the Knights of Amon Dähl. Though he knew their reputation, he alone had actually fought an elf. Lee doubted very much that he and twelve men would fare well against ten trained elf fighters. If Theopolou was as great among his people as he was told, he was likely to have brought elves of great skill.

It was midday. With several hours until the meeting, Lee decided to check on Gewey and Kaylia again. He wound his way through the stone hallways, nodding and smiling at the passers-by. Word had spread quickly that he was the son of the High Lady; at first, he had become a bit of a celebrity. People practically tripped over themselves to shake his hand or help him find his way around. After a few days, however, the excitement died down and most of the temple simply became a bit more cheerful when they saw him.

The door to the healing chamber was usually unattended, but to his surprise, he now saw a tall elf standing guard on either side of the entrance. Both had light bronze skin and shoulder-length black hair tied neatly into a small ponytail. They wore well-oiled, studded leather mail over emerald green shirts and trousers. Their feet were clad in soft buckskin boots adorned with tiny beads that formed multiple interlacing patterns. Vicious-looking curved swords hung from their belts. Lee found this curious. From what he had learned, elves preferred to use a long knife or dagger, though Kaylia had mentioned that they did use swords when in pitched battles. This thought put his nerves on edge.

Lee stopped a few feet away. The elf guards did not look at him, though clearly they knew he was there.

"Excuse me," said Lee. "I would like to pass."

Both elves now turned their gaze on him. The one nearest to Lee took a single step forward and bowed his head slightly.

"You cannot enter at this time," he said. His voice was deep and masculine. "I would ask that you return later."

"I will not return later," Lee insisted. "Two of my friends are inside, and I will see that they are all right."

"I cannot allow you to enter," the elf insisted.

Lee could see the elf's muscles tense. He didn't want a confrontation, but neither could he leave until he knew that Gewey and Kaylia were unharmed.

"Who is in there?" Lee demanded.

"That is none of your affair," the elf replied. The other guard stepped forward, and both of their hands crept to their swords.

"It is my affair," Lee countered. "And I will see to my friends." He also stepped forward, positioning himself less than a foot away from the first elf. He knew that should things turn violent, he needed to be close. He was unarmed, and swords were awkward in tight quarters.

The door to the chamber flew open and Lee's mother stepped quickly into the hall. "It's all right, Lee." She pushed him back and placed herself between her son and the elves. "Gewey and Kaylia are fine."

"Why am I being kept out?" growled Lee.

"Theopolou is in there with them," she replied. "He has asked not to be disturbed, and I have agreed." Selena placed her hands on Lee's chest. "Please, son. I give you my word they are safe."

Reluctantly, Lee yielded. "Very well." He slowly backed away and headed for the parlor.

When he arrived, he found Dina sitting on the couch next to Linis. Linis beamed as Lee entered the room. He sprang to his feet and grasped Lee's shoulders tightly. Lee returned the gesture.

"It's good to see you, my friend." Linis laughed. "Though I wish it were under better circumstances."

"It's good to see you too," said Lee, giving Linis's shoulders one final fond squeeze before releasing him.

They took a seat on the couch across from Dina. She was in her formal robes, just as Ertik had been, and her hair was wrapped in a tight bun.

"Dina was telling me details of your travels since we last parted," Linis said. "It would seem I have missed much."

"Indeed," Lee replied. "Much that I wish I had avoided."

"I understand," said Linis. "But often we are beset with hardship in order to prepare for greater challenges ahead."

Dina laughed. "I don't think I want to know what those challenges are ... if this is what it takes to prepare."

"No doubt," Lee agreed. "But I fear this is but a taste of what's to come. Angrääl is on the move, and if Gewey doesn't recover..."

"Do not despair, my friend," said Linis. "If the boy fought a half-man and was victorious, as I have heard, then I am certain that he has the strength to overcome this. His true nature is still a mystery to me, but I do believe that his part in what is to come has not yet been played out."

Lee realized that Linis was still unaware of just what Gewey was and made the decision to tell him.

"I know how the elves feel about the gods," said Lee, once he had recounted the tale. "And I hope you can see beyond old hatreds, as you have in the past."

Linis was stunned. He rose and moved slowly to the fireplace. He stood in silence for several minutes.

"It is good that you have kept this secret from me until now," said Linis finally. "And I am honored that you have chosen to share it. Had I found out about this before I had come to know the boy, I am unsure how I would have reacted."

"I think you would have been fine," said Dina. "When you found out about me..."

"You are different," said Linis. "You are the natural result of two people sharing the same world. Gewey's nature, on the other hand, stirs feelings even in me of the old hatreds. It is a thing no elf would ever expect to be faced with." He turned to Lee. "You must keep this from Theopolou and the others."

"I only tell you because of our friendship," said Lee. "The presence of your brethren is causing me great concern, and not only because of Gewey."

"The Book of Souls," whispered Linis. "To think I traveled with both The Book of Souls and a god at the same time." He burst into laughter. "A thing worthy of a tale, wouldn't you say?"

Lee joined his laughter. "No doubt it will be told for ages to come." Lee motioned for Linis to rejoin him on the couch. "Tell me about Theopolou."

Linis's eyes shifted back and forth from Lee to Dina for a moment. "He is great among my people," he began. "And his knowledge, vast. His family had been the keepers of the Book of Souls for generations until its disappearance."

"How does he feel about what you and the others are trying to do?" Dina asked.

"You are referring to our contact with humans." Linis breathed deeply. "He is of the old way of thinking, but so far has done nothing to hinder our efforts. Some elders distrust him for that very reason. They imagine that he secretly aids our cause. That is untrue, of course, though his presence here will not help to quell the rumors."

"Surely they understand that he comes because of the Book?" said Dina.

"None of the others know," Linis replied. "Aside from his personal guard, I am the only elf that knows of his reasons."

"Why?" asked Lee. "Wouldn't it be to his benefit to allow the other elders to understand why he is here?"

"Yes," said Linis. "But there is another complication. As you know, Kaylia is to be killed should she be found."

"I know," growled Lee. "I went to see her and Gewey just before I came here. I was stopped at the door by two elf guards. Theopolou was inside, though I didn't see him."

"You needn't worry about Kaylia," said Linis. "She is the reason he is here, not the Book. He is her uncle."

Dina straightened in her seat and gasped. "Her uncle? I thought her uncle was one of the elders who want her dead?"

"No," replied Linis. "He cannot support her publicly, but he was strongly opposed to having her killed before judgment could be passed. Understand that, after the death of her father, he took her for his own daughter. Theopolou may be set in his ways, but he loves Kaylia. He could not abide her assassination. Especially when such an act breaks our traditions."

"I see," said Lee thoughtfully. "Then he is here to do what? Heal her? Take her to be judged? What exactly?"

"To be honest, I'm not sure." Linis shrugged. "He knows I will not allow her to be taken. I've told him as much."

"I hate to point this out," said Lee. "But he has ten guards with him. There are maybe a dozen knights in Valshara, and most of them are either too young to have seen battle, or too old to be effective against a trained elf warrior."

"I don't think it will come to that," said Linis. "But still, I have sent word to the other seekers. They'll be here soon. I've instructed them to guard the way from Valshara. If Theopolou or any of his guards try to take Kaylia, they will be stopped."

"That is good," said Lee. "Still, I am concerned. If this meeting goes badly..."

"If that happens," Linis interrupted, "I will give you time to get Dina and your mother out of danger. My brethren will be reluctant to fight me, and that should give you enough time to escape."

Lee nodded. "Though I hate the idea of leaving you to fight alone, it seems the best option."

"I don't like this discussion," said Dina. "Nothing is going to happen, and talk of killing and escaping upsets my stomach. If it goes wrong, we'll deal with it then."

"Quite right." A smile returned to Linus's face. "We have so little time for good company and pleasant talk. It would be a pity to waste what we have been given."

The conversation was light for the next few hours. Linis told them that he had sent his band of seekers along the coast of the Western Abyss to open relations with the coastal villages, while he had made contact with several small groups of elves in an attempt to sway them to his cause. But this had so far met with only marginal success.

After a time, they decided to take their afternoon meal and then retire to their quarters in order to prepare for the meeting with Theopolou.

"I would caution you," Linis warned Lee as they parted. "Theopolou is soft-spoken but dangerous. He may not want to see his niece come to harm, but I doubt that sentiment extends to you or the rest of the people here. If you notice his escort becoming agitated, get ready to make your escape."

Lee nodded grimly and went to his room.

A fine white linen shirt and trousers embroidered with gold runes, along with a pair of black leather boots and matching belt, lay neatly on his bed. Steam rose from the hot water, filling a large washtub in the corner. Lee smiled. He enjoyed a long soak, allowing the tension to flow from his body as he meditated on the situation.

Once clean and dry, he got dressed, careful not to wrinkle the linen, and attached his sword to the belt. It wasn't long before a light tap sounded on his door. Lee opened it. Dina was stood there dressed in her best ceremonial robes, smiling sweetly.

"I take it you're my escort," said Lee.

"Indeed, I am. Your mother and the elves have just entered the main receiving hall. They will begin as soon as we arrive."

Dina led Lee through the passages of the temple to the western wing and down a long arched hallway. A large oak door stood at the end. Dina entered first.

The main receiving hall was one hundred feet long and nearly twice as wide. The walls were lined with paintings and tapestries depicting monks, priests, and priestesses involved in various acts of charity and bravery. Four immense brass chandeliers hung from the ceiling, illuminating the hall. At the rear of the room, a cushioned mahogany chair stood on a small crimson rug. There sat Lee's mother, dressed in the same white robes that Dina wore, but with a deep blue sash tied loosely about her waist.

A long wooden table was positioned in front of the high priestess. The elves were standing, backs to the door, next to their chairs. They had discarded their armor in favor of multicolored shirts and trousers made from a material that caught the light and made them shimmer. Each had a long knife attached to their belt. The fact that they wore no swords somehow made Lee feel better. The elf in the middle, though dressed similarly to the others, had a long silver ponytail tied tightly by a black cloth and wore no weapon.

A chair had been placed on either side of Selena. Dina motioned for Lee to occupy the one to her right. As he passed in front of the table, he glanced over to the elves. Their faces were grim as they watched Lee stand next to his seat. Theopolou was clearly the eldest.

His skin was pale compared with the others, and the tiny lines around his eyes and the corners of his mouth spoke of many winters and many worries, though only Lee's keen eyesight would have noticed this. Dina stood next to the opposite chair. Lee scanned the room for Linis but could not see him anywhere. In fact, there were no temple guards of any kind present. This made Lee nervous. The only way out was the way he'd come in. Should the meeting go poorly, it would not be easy for him to get his mother and Dina to safety.

Selena stood and addressed the room. "I bid you welcome. I am Selena Starfinder, High Lady of Valshara and leader of the Order of Amon Dähl. This is Sister Celandine, a historian of our order, and this is my son..."

"We know of the half-man," said Theopolou. His voice was deep and stern but tempered. "And as you and I are acquainted, we should forgo introductions. My companions prefer not to be named at this moment. Time is short, and we have much to discuss."

Selena nodded and took her seat. The rest followed suit.

"I would have Linis here," said Lee. "It is because of his efforts that we are together today."

Theopolou furrowed his brow. "You speak out of turn, half-man. Your presence here is only allowed out of courtesy."

Lee leveled his gaze. "My presence is not an option," he corrected. "You would do well to remember that."

The other elves shifted in their seats, but Theopolou shot them a glance and they settled down.

"Son, please," whispered Selena. "Mind your temper." Lee ignored her. His eyes never left Theopolou's.

"You are bold," said Theopolou. "I was told as much. I was also told you ended the life of Berathis."

Lee's expression did not change. "I did. He died with honor, facing me in single combat. His passing weighs heavy on my heart."

The elves whispered to each other, but Theopolou only nodded somberly. "If you are concerned for the safety of your mother, you needn't fear. I gave my word to Linis just before we entered this hall that we will commit no violence within these walls. It was the only way to keep him out."

"Why would you want to keep him out?" asked Lee.

"That is between Linis and me," the old elf replied. "But rest assured he is not far. I can have him summoned if he is needed." His eyes fixed on Selena. "I assume you have brought it with you."

Selena reached beneath her chair and pulled forth the box containing the Book of Souls. An audible gasp came from the elves as the High Lady held it aloft.

"As I promised, it is here," she said.

"That belongs to the elves," blurted out a young elf sitting at the end of the table.

"Silence," commanded Theopolou.

The young elf lowered his eyes in obedience. "May I approach, High Lady?" Theopolou asked.

Selena nodded, and he rose to his feet and walked over to her chair. She handed him the box. Theopolou gently ran his fingers across the ancient letters.

"It is the Book of Souls." He handed the box back to Selena. "How did you come by this?"

"It was in my possession," said Lee. "I inherited it from my former lord and master, Dauvis Nal'Thain."

"I see," Theopolou muttered. He returned to his seat. "The Nal'Thain family is known to me. They were fierce adversaries during the Great War. It is likely that it was they who stole the book in the first place."

"Some may say it was stolen," said Lee. "Some might call it the spoils of war."

"Some might," said Theopolou. "It matters little. What concerns my people is what is to become of it now. We were the keepers of the Book of Souls for generations and believe it best left in our care."

"I don't understand," said Lee. "From what I've learned, the Book of Souls was written by the gods. Unless I'm mistaken, you and your people don't exactly hold the gods in high regard."

"You are not mistaken. But we do not believe it was written by the gods alone. We believe it was written by the hand of the Creator, then passed into our care. We were charged with its keeping until the time of the 'Coming of the Emancipator'. The Emancipator will free us from the curse that took away our understanding of The All Father. Without the Book of Souls, we will be forever lost."

"I understand why you would want it so badly," said Selena. "But we believe it may hold the key to our own salvation as well."

"You refer to the power that grows in the north," said Theopolou. "We are aware of the one you call the Dark Knight, and know that he seeks your destruction, as well as the destruction of the gods."

"And we are aware that he has contacted your people," said Selena. "And that many believe him to be the reincarnation of the Demon King Rätsterfel."

"You know much," said Theopolou. "Then you must also know that we have not agreed to join his cause." His tone darkened. "At least—not yet."

"A threat?" asked Selena.

"No, High Lady. A fact. There are many who feel that should Angrääl march, we should join them. But we have not decided to do so. We are still uncertain of his true intentions."

"I'll tell you what his intentions are," roared Lee. "He wants to destroy everything and reshape the world in his own image. If he is not stopped, blood will cover the land."

Selena placed her hand on Lee's forearm to calm him. "Do you truly believe that there will be a place for your people in his new world?"

"It is that question that has caused much debate." Theopolou kept his eyes on Selena, ignoring Lee's agitation. "And also why it is important that you return the Book to us."

"If the Book of Souls was in your possession," said Lee, "what's to stop you from giving it to the Dark One?"

"How dare you!" Theopolou's age melted away, and suddenly he looked very much an elf warrior. The other elves jumped to their feet, shouting curses, but none reached for their weapons.

"It's a fair question," said Selena calmly. "Should we hand over the Book, what is to say that it will not be used against us later? It is said that it only can be opened by one who possesses the power of heaven. The Dark Knight has the Sword of Truth. He may be able to use it to open the Book."

"We would never give it to him." Theopolou settled back down. "This I swear."

"Yet it may be taken from you if he knows you have it," said Lee. "It was taken once before."

"It may be taken from you as well," Theopolou shot back. "From what I have seen of your defenses, that could easily happen."

"Aside from you, your escort, and a few others," replied Selena, "none know the location of this temple. And though you may not think so, we have the means to defend ourselves."

"This location is not as secret as you think. My people have known of it since it was first built. It would not be difficult for the spies of Angräal to find it ... if they have not already done so."

"You assume the Book would be kept here," said Selena with a wry smile.

"I assume you have summoned me to return it."

"Let's not play games. You know why I summoned you here."

"I saw Kaylia and her young friend," said Theopolou. "I told you there is nothing I can do for them. They are beyond my reach."

"We had hoped that you would know a way to open the Book," said Selena. "Perhaps within its pages, we could find a way to help them?"

Theopolou shook his head. "I cannot. My family has been the Book's keeper and guardian, but we have no knowledge of how to open it, or what is truly inside. Even if I knew, I wouldn't. It is not meant for me, or any but the Emancipator."

"Perhaps not," said Lee. "But the thought of handing over a potential weapon to a people who have such deep hatred of humans does not sit well with me."

"I understand," Theopolou replied thoughtfully. "As I have given my word, we will not take it by force. But you must know that once word of this reaches my people, they will not suffer you or anyone else to possess it. They will come for it."

"Any attempt to attack this temple will fail," warned Lee. "And many will die in the attempt."

"All the more reason for you to return it," he replied. "I have no desire for bloodshed, but I cannot prevent it from happening. My kin will take back the Book of Souls. Of this I am certain."

"As the High Lady of Valshara, I will tell you this." Selena's voice was commanding and firm. "Any attempt to take the Book of Souls by force will fail. You may know of the location of this temple, but you do not know its secrets. Even should you succeed in breaching our walls, you will never find the Book. It will be lost forever." She slowly rose to her feet. "I promise you that the moment a single elf steps inside without invitation, this will be the last moment the Book of Souls will see the light of the sun. I will cast it where no one will ever find it again."

"This is getting us nowhere." Theopolou's frustration bled through in his voice. "What will make you see reason?"

The door to the hall flew open and Sister Wileminia ran straight to the High Lady. As she whispered in her ear, Selena's eyes widened.

"We must resume this later," Selena announced. "Lee, Dina, and Lord Theopolou, I need you to come with me at once."

"What's happened?" asked Dina.

"Gewey and Kaylia are awake. Sister Wileminia, will you see that Theopolou's companions are fed?"

Wileminia gave a quick nod and Selena rushed out of the room. Lee, Theopolou, and Dina followed closely behind.

# CHAPTER 5

When they arrived at the healing chamber, they found it nearly empty. A single healer was mixing herbs with a stone pestle in the corner, and Gewey and Kaylia were sitting up in their beds talking quietly to each other. Their faces lit up when they saw Lee and Dina, but Kaylia's expression quickly changed to concern when Theopolou entered.

"It's about time you two woke up," Lee said, laughing.

"It's good to see you, too," said Gewey. His voice was weak and cracked.

"They mustn't speak too much," said Selena. "At least, not until they've had a few days to regain their strength. We've kept them alive with herbal mixtures, but that's not a replacement for a good hot meal."

"We're both fine," said Gewey. "Although I wouldn't turn down a bit of food."

"I've already sent word to the kitchen, High Lady," said the healer in the corner. "It should be here shortly."

Theopolou moved next to Kaylia's bed, ignoring the others. "It is good to see you well."

Kaylia nodded. "I am pleased to see you, uncle. I am confused, though. How did you come to be here?"

"Your ... friends sent for me. They hoped I could heal you." He motioned, indicating Gewey. "And this one too. But it seems this was unnecessary."

"Healing me cannot be the only reason you have come," said Kaylia. "I am to be killed on sight. Am I not?"

"That is not of my doing," replied Theopolou. "I have opposed it from the beginning. I despise what you are doing, but I would never see you put to death without judgment."

"But you would see me put to death," she shot back.

"Have you not broken the law? Are you not in the company of humans? Have you not chosen to travel with them openly?"

"And why should that be a crime?"

"You should know better than most."

Kaylia fumed, but Gewey reached out and took her hand.

"I thank you for coming," said Gewey. "But as you can see, neither of us is in need of help."

Theopolou stared for a long moment at Gewey, holding the hand of his niece. "I see," he said finally. "Then you have committed yourself to treason, and there is nothing more I can do for you."

"Treason?" Kaylia scoffed. "Then what have the elders who sent assassins to hunt me down committed?"

"I agree," said Theopolou. "But that changes nothing. If you come home now, then I might just be able to persuade the elders to let you live. However, the look in your eyes tells me that this will not happen."

"You're wrong, uncle. I have given my word that I will face judgment, and I will do so. But not until my task is finished."

"And what task is that? What business could you have with these people?"

"That is not for me to say. At least, not yet."

Theopolou sighed heavily. "Then if you no longer are in need of aid, that only leaves one final matter." He looked over to Selena. "The Book of Souls."

"That can wait," said Lee. "I would speak to Gewey and Kaylia first. There is much I have to tell them and much I would like to know."

"Very well," said Theopolou. "I too, would hear their account. They have journeyed where no elf has gone. How this could have happened has weighed on my mind."

"Forgive me," said Gewey to Theopolou. "But there are things you cannot know."

"Then please omit any details you feel necessary," he replied. "I already know that you are not what you appear to be. That your spirit traveled beyond my reach or understanding tells me as much. And that Kaylia was able to join you tells me even more."

Gewey looked at Lee, who just shook his head and shrugged. "Fine," said Gewey. "But only if Kaylia allows it."

Kaylia stared hard at her uncle. "He is wise and will learn the truth if he stays, no matter what you leave out."

"You know me well," stated Theopolou with a hint of pride. "But I already know that you have bonded your soul to the boy. That is clear. And the places his spirit has traveled say that he is either one of Felsafell's race or something ... else."

Silence fell over the room for a moment. Hearing Felsafell's name caused Gewey's chest to tighten.

"What do you know about him?" asked Gewey.

"I know that he is neither human nor elf. And that he is ancient. His people were here before humans walked the earth. Some believe that they were here even before the elves, but there is no way to know. Perhaps you could ask Felsafell if he allows you to find him. I know that his race was able to project themselves into places unreachable by any, save the gods."

"I have met him," admitted Gewey. "I spent the night in his home, and I saw him again just before I woke."

Theopolou looked at Gewey in wonder. "Then I think I would hear your tale now."

Gewey nodded and recounted the experience he and Kaylia had had in the spirit world.

When he had finished, Lee doubled over in laughter. "You are a wonder. Just when I think I've heard everything, you tell us this."

"You are a wonder indeed," agreed Theopolou. "And the only one of your kind, unless I am mistaken."

Lee tensed. "Whatever you may think, I'm sure you are mistaken."

Theopolou raised his eyebrow and smirked. "I see that you believe I shall reveal his secret. Perhaps I would if circumstances were different. But, as my niece has bonded with him, I will not. Besides, if I did, I would be put to judgment for not killing a god when given the chance. Even my own guards would turn on me."

Hearing Gewey's true nature said aloud brought a wave of anxiety throughout the room.

"How long have you known?" asked Selena.

"I suspected from the moment I discovered where his spirit had traveled," he replied. "But when I heard about your experience with Felsafell, there was no question in my mind. And it does explain Angrääl's sudden mobilization in the north and their pursuit of a young boy."

"What do you mean?" asked Lee. His thoughts turned to his wife and son.

"Our seekers tell us that his armies gather. He will be ready to march by spring at the latest."

"When did you learn this?" asked Lee.

"Just before I came here. The information can be no more than a week old."

"How is it we have heard nothing of this?" Selena's eyes flashed with anger.

"If you have sent spies north, they would not likely have made it far enough to have seen anything," replied Theopolou. "The way is well guarded. Even my people have difficulty moving undetected."

"We need to start building alliances here," said Lee. "As the elves will not join us, we should finish our business and move on."

"Quite right," Theopolou agreed. "But as we are at an impasse, I do not see what there is left to say."

"What business?" asked Gewey.

Lee told Gewey about the meeting. Gewey sat up straight in bed and rubbed his chin. "I would like to speak to Kaylia and Theopolou alone."

Lee and the others paused for a moment before obeying.

"What do you suppose they're talking about?" wondered Dina as they waited outside the chamber.

Lee shook his head. "If I know Gewey, he's doing something foolish."

"Give him some credit," said Dina. "He's managed to do pretty well so far."

Lee grunted and crossed his arms.

Selena placed her hand lightly on Lee's shoulder. "It will be fine," she said softly. "If what you've told me about the boy is true, his heart will guide him well."

For over an hour, they waited, the only interruption being a healer who brought Gewey and Kaylia a bowl of stew and some apple juice. Lee was just about to lose his patience when Theopolou came to the door and invited them inside.

"We have come to an agreement," said Gewey. "But I don't think you're going to like it."

"No doubt," remarked Lee.

"Don't worry," interjected Theopolou. "It's conditional on the approval of the High Lady. And you, of course."

"What is it?" asked Selena.

"I have agreed to allow Theopolou to possess the Book of Souls," said Gewey. "In return, he will help me persuade the elves to join us."

"Assuming I agree," said Selena. "How do you propose to do that?"

"I will open the Book of Souls."

"You'll what?" exclaimed Lee. "How?"

"If the boy truly is a god, then he possesses the power of heaven," Theopolou explained. "With that power, there is a possibility that he may be able to open the Book. If he can, that will go a long way toward swaying my people—if not into joining you, at least into not opposing you."

"And when they find out what he is?" argued Lee. "What then? Even elves that befriend humans hold no love for the gods."

"Nor do I," said Theopolou. "But I do not subscribe to the notion that it was the gods that caused the Split. I was there." He turned to Kaylia. "As was your father. I saw no evidence of divine intervention."

"Then what do you think really happened?" asked Lee.

"That is not a thing I would discuss here. It is the business of the elves. I only say this much to set your mind at ease regarding my intentions toward Gewey. I may not wish to befriend humans, but as Gewey is not human, I bear him no ill will."

"I wish you could let go of the old hatred, uncle," said Kaylia. "They're not as we have been told. At least, not the ones I call friends."

"You did not suffer through the Great War or the Split. I watched the humans take advantage of our weakness and decimate our people. I could never trust them, and without trust, there can be no friendship. If I can help Gewey convince my people to help your cause, it is only to fight a greater threat. I do not believe the promises made by the Dark One. Once he has defeated his human enemies, he will turn on us and destroy us, too."

"I'm still concerned about the Book falling into the hands of our enemies," said Selena. "How does this agreement prevent that?" She walked to the bed and sat beside Gewey.

"If I fail to help sway my kin, I will take the Book and hide it away where it will never be found," Theopolou replied. "You have my solemn vow on this."

"And just how do you propose to sway them?" asked Lee.

"Gewey and Kaylia will accompany me to my home. There, the elders will meet and decide."

"Hold on a minute," said Lee. "Do you really think we would allow Gewey and Kaylia to simply leave with you and deliver themselves into the hands of people who want nothing more than their deaths?"

"They will be under my protection," replied Theopolou. "No elf will harm them while I give them sanctuary. That I return with the Book of Souls will also go far in aiding our cause."

"If you do this, I will go with you." Lee planted his fists on his hips.

"No, Lee," said Gewey. "It can only be Kaylia and me. If we have any hope of bringing the elves to our side, we must show them we can be trusted."

"You will not be welcome among us, half-man," said Theopolou. "If you come, our efforts will surely fail."

"Find a way to make them bear my presence if you are so bloody wise." Lee could barely contain his frustration.

"Insults are not called for. I have given my word that the boy and Kaylia will not be harmed."

"And what of Kaylia?" Dina was careful not to come too close to Theopolou, afraid he might discover her heritage. "What if they decide to judge her?"

"Kaylia will face judgment," he replied. "But not at this time. I have granted her my protection, and my people will honor it."

"Let us think on this," said Selena. "I will give you my answer tomorrow. In any event, they cannot travel until they are stronger."

"I would like Dina and Lee to stay awhile," said Gewey. "They've heard my story, and now I'd like to hear theirs."

Selena smiled. "Only for a short while. You must regain your strength." She turned to Theopolou. "I'll have rooms made ready for you and your escort."

Theopolou nodded. "Thank you, High Lady. If you can provide us with rooms that are, how shall I put this—secluded? That would make our stay more pleasant for everyone."

"That can be arranged." She showed no sign of being insulted. "I can have your meals brought to you as well, if you wish."

"That would be fine."

"Then, if you will follow me," she said, leading Theopolou from the room.

"You certainly wasted no time in causing me trouble," said Lee once the door had closed.

"I'm sorry," said Gewey. "But there is no other way."

"I didn't say you were wrong. I just don't like it."

"Enough," said Kaylia. "I want to know what has happened while I was asleep."

"Yes," agreed Gewey. "So would I."

"Fine." Lee sighed.

Lee recounted the events up until that day. Gewey smiled when he heard about the meeting between Lee and his mother.

"It's hard to believe," said Gewey once Lee had finished. "All this time, and she was living right here."

"Yes." Lee chuckled. "The world is full of surprises." His eyes grew sad. "Now, if only I had word from Millet."

Gewey thought for a moment. "I think I may be able to find them—with Kaylia's help."

"How would you do that?" asked Lee, unable to contain his excitement.

"I believe I can touch the mind of Malstisos. With a healthy dose of jawas tea and Kaylia lending me her strength, it may just be possible."

Lee looked at Gewey doubtfully. "They're hundreds of miles away. How could you do such a thing?"

Gewey smiled widely. "One thing I realized when I was with the spirits is that time and distance don't amount to much there. Now that I know the way, I can return."

Dina became alarmed. "But won't you risk being trapped again?"

"Not likely. The spirits will leave me alone now, and they are the ones who trapped me in the first place. Without them in my way, I should be able to come and go as I please. With Kaylia there to help me find him, I think I can reach Malstisos no matter how far away he is."

"I still can't ask you to risk it." Lee shook his head. "If you're wrong..."

"He is not wrong," said Kaylia. "Reaching out and returning is not the challenge. Finding one particular mind is. We have an advantage in that Malstisos will probably be the only elf in the area, so it will be easier to single him out. That's where I come in. Our bond allows me to travel with Gewey, and my familiarity with an elf's mind should increase our chances."

"When you say travel..." said Dina.

"I mean it literally," replied Kaylia. "It's different to when one touches the mind of another, the way you or I would do. The world where we go is as real as this one, in a way."

"I am familiar with this sort of contact, as you know," said Lee. "But it's still difficult to understand."

"As much as I'd like to show you, I'm not sure what the risks would be," explained Gewey. "Just imagine yourself in a dream where anything is possible, only you're wide awake."

"Sounds wonderful," said Dina.

"It is." Gewey nodded. "But it can be terrible, too. If it wasn't for Felsafell saving us, we'd probably still be trapped."

"That's probably the most confusing thing about your tale," remarked Lee. "Little is known about him, and if Theopolou is right about his being a part of some ancient race, then his motives are a mystery. I don't like mysteries."

"Whatever he's after, it doesn't seem he means to harm me," said Gewey. "Until I can see him again, that will have to be enough."

"But he was the one who freed you," said Lee. "What if the spirits decide to keep you there again?"

"They won't," said Gewey. "Even if they did, I think I could escape them if I needed to."

"And you really think you can contact Malstisos?" asked Dina.

"I do," Gewey nodded. "Tonight, I will try."

Lee nodded reluctantly.

With that settled, Kaylia turned to Dina. "I see you are in full dress."

"Indeed, I am. While you and Gewey slept, I was elevated to full cleric. I'm a temple historian now."

"That is wonderful," said Kaylia. "I know you'll do well."

"I'm going to try. The High Lady has put a great deal of trust in me."

"You won't disappoint her," said Gewey. "I know it."

Dina smiled and her cheeks flushed. "I hope you're right. It's everything I've hoped for. I just didn't think it would happen so quickly." She choked back tears of happiness. "But enough of that. Do you really think you can open the Book of Souls?"

"I'm not sure," Gewey admitted. "I do believe it's the only way to bring the elves over to our side."

"I agree that we need them," said Lee. "But I'm not sure this is the best way to go about it. Why not leave it to Linis and the others to sway them?"

"Do we have that kind of time?" asked Gewey. "If the Dark Knight moved on us today, what would happen? Could we fight him?"

"Then perhaps if I can't go with you, Linis can," suggested Lee. "We could insist upon it."

"We could request," corrected Kaylia. "But Linis is an outlaw as well. It may prove difficult. But, I agree that it's worth a try. Outlaw or no, he is among the greatest of all the seekers, and his presence carries weight."

The door opened and Selena returned. Lee told her about their idea of Linis accompanying them.

"I like it," said Selena thoughtfully. "I think if I agree to allow the Book of Souls to return to the elves, Theopolou will agree also. I'll approach the subject in the morning." She took a long look at Gewey and Kaylia. "I think it's time you two rested. We can talk more in the morning."

Gewey protested, but Selena stopped him with one stern look. Lee and Dina embraced them tightly and bid them goodnight.

"I'll wake you if I'm successful," Gewey called to Lee as he was leaving. Lee nodded and shut the door.

# CHAPTER 6

Malstisos felt a cool breeze caress his cheeks as he walked between the massive redwoods. The noon sun shone through the leaves, making the grass sparkle like a million tiny emeralds. The forest was familiar but like a distant memory from childhood. He reached over and touched the almost black bark of a nearby tree. It should have been hard and coarse, but it wasn't. It was soft and smooth and yielded to his touch. He withdrew his hand in amazement. He reached out again and gently moved his hand over the bark. Light rippled up the length of the tree and back down again. Malstisos stood transfixed by the sight.

"This can't be real," he whispered.

"It's real," a voice called from behind.

Malstisos spun around, but there was no one there. "Who are you?" There was no answer. He reached for his knife and found that it was no longer at his side. "Show yourself."

"I am here." This time, the voice was softer and clearly feminine.

"Why can't I see you?" he asked, straining his eyes. The forest began to blur and shift. "What's happening?"

"Don't be afraid. We are friends."

"We?" he said. "Who are you, and what do you want?"

"It's Kaylia. I'm here with Gewey."

"Kaylia? Why can't I see you? What is this place?"

"You are at the edge of the spirit realm. Why you can't see me, I do not know. I suspect that you would in time. But time is not a luxury we have. We have guided you here, though I do not know how long you can remain."

"How do I know you are who you say you are?" he challenged. "How do I know this isn't just a vivid dream?"

"Does it feel like a dream?"

"Yes—and no," he said. "I feel awake, but all this…"

He looked around as the forest ebbed and flowed like a green tide. "It can't be real."

"It is real," said Kaylia. "At least, in the sense that this is a real place. This is only our second time here, but I think that it changes with your thoughts and emotions. I do know that the dangers here are very real."

"Dangers," said Malstisos. "What dangers?"

"There is no time to explain. Gewey is struggling to keep you in this world. Did you succeed in saving Lee's wife and son?"

"His son is with us," he replied. "But I'm sad to say that his wife has been taken north to Angrääl. Millet is taking the boy to Baltria, while I escort Maybell to Althetas."

"I see." She paused. "Stick to your plan. Lee will find Millet in Baltria. Gewey and I have our own task, but you will be met in Althetas. Go to the Frog's Wishbone when you arrive. An agent from Valshara will contact you there."

"How am I to know…?" Malstisos began, but he was already losing contact. The forest turned into a swirl of light and color. He felt as if he were falling. Then blackness.

Malstisos awoke drenched in sweat, his heart pounding. For a moment, he didn't know where he was. As his mind cleared, he heard the sound of Millet, Jacob, and Maybell's deep, regular breathing. He reached over and shook Millet.

"What's wrong?" asked Millet groggily. Malstisos recounted his experience.

"Do you believe it was them?" Millet asked.

"I do. How they accomplished it I can't imagine, but I sensed no deception."

"Then we should keep to our plan," said Millet. "It's several hours until dawn, so we should try and sleep. Maybell can be told of this in the morning."

Malstisos nodded in agreement and drew his blanket tightly around him. Sleep came slowly, and his dreams were troubled.

The morning brought the smell of crisp bacon and fresh bread. Gerald was busy setting the table and humming.

Millet was first to rise and helped with breakfast. At first, Gerald protested, but soon realized Millet wasn't one to be deterred. The duo had the table prepared a full ten minutes before Malstisos and Maybell stirred. Jacob was last to awaken.

"Things are in order from the smell of it." Maybell yawned and stretched. She looked over to Malstisos, who was just waking up. "I always imagined elves to be early risers."

"My sleep was troubled—and eventful," he replied. "But we'll discuss that after breakfast."

About halfway through their meal, Gerald excused himself and left them alone at the table. Malstisos informed Maybell and Jacob of his dream experience.

"Amazing," remarked Maybell. "Well, I'm happy that you'll be met in Baltria."

"I'm not," Jacob growled. "I have no need of my father and have no intention of seeing him."

"If you intend to go to Baltria, you won't have much of a choice," stated Millet. "According to Malstisos, he will certainly be there, so you had better get used to the idea."

Jacob folded his arms. "He had better stay out of my way."

"Calm yourself," said Malstisos. "First, you must arrive at your destination, and that may not be easy."

"We'll get there," said Jacob. "If I have to kill every soldier I see on the way."

"Young man, you would do well to take Millet's lead," said Maybell. "He has seen much more of the world than you. If getting to Baltria means saving your mother, then you'd do well to keep your mouth shut and your eyes and ears open."

Jacob glared at Maybell but could find no words to reply.

"I do not think you should take time to speak to the Oracle when we arrive in Manisalia," said Malstisos.

Millet nodded. "I agree. In fact, I would have you avoid the city entirely if it's possible."

"I'm sure I can find a way around if need be," said Malstisos. "But, seeing as how I intend to leave you with the remainder of the provisions, Sister Maybell and I will need to resupply once you're departed. There is no way we can avoid the city, at least for a few hours."

"Good," said Maybell. "And I most surely would like to consult the Oracle—if she's still there."

The front door opened and Gerald entered, smiling. "I see you've nearly finished breakfast. I hope you enjoyed it."

"Very much." Maybell returned the smile. The rest nodded in agreement.

"I've readied your horses," said the boy. "I'll bring them 'round front whenever you'd like."

"We'll be leaving shortly," said Millet. "You can bring them now." Gerald nodded and dashed off.

They gathered their belongings and filed out of the front door. As promised, Gerald had saddled their horses and had them lined up a few feet away. He bowed to each in turn, handing them a cloth wrapped around a piece of roast lamb and a loaf of bread, thanking them for their kind donation.

Maybell embraced the lad tightly and whispered into his ear. Gerald smiled sadly, turned, and entered the hospice.

Travel that day was slow and miserable. By noon, the wind howled through the trees and the sky filled with clouds that promised snow.

Malstisos stopped periodically to check for signs of pursuit but found none.

"I think perhaps whatever that creature was, he must have been alone," said Malstisos during one of their stops. "That is not to say that more are not waiting for us ahead."

Millet shivered at the thought. The monster's distorted features still burned in his mind.

"Let them come," boasted Jacob. "I don't fear them."

Malstisos snorted loudly. "Then you're a fool. Fear may keep you alive. You are no warrior. That I can clearly see. If you encounter one of them, you should run if you can."

Jacob leaped from his horse and drew his sword. "I have had enough of your insults, elf."

Malstisos stared down at the boy for a moment, then casually slipped out of the saddle. "Come then," he said. "Let us see what you're made of." He didn't bother to draw his blade.

Jacob's mouth twisted into a malevolent grin. He lashed out at the elf, his blade seeking flesh, but it found only cold, winter air. Though Jacob moved with uncanny speed, he was no match for Malstisos.

"Come now, boy," Malstisos taunted. "Certainly you can do better than that."

Now thoroughly infuriated, Jacob ran headlong at the elf, slashing maniacally. Malstisos ducked quickly, spun around, and brought his heel into the back of the boy's knee. Jacob's leg collapsed, and he fell hard onto his back. Malstisos stepped on Jacob's blade, trapping it. Jacob struggled to pull the blade free, but Malstisos bent down, pressing his knee on Jacob's throat.

"You have passion," said Malstisos. "But no discipline."

Jacob bucked and twisted, but Malstisos only pressed harder. Slowly, Jacob stopped struggling and relaxed. After a moment, Malstisos released him and held out his hand, but Jacob only glared, his eyes filled with hate and anger.

"Take my hand, young one," said the elf. "The fight is done. You have lost, but there is no shame. You did well, considering your lack of training."

Jacob reached up, took Malstisos's hand, and allowed the elf to pull him to his feet. He brushed himself off and retrieved his sword.

"Now, if we are done with all this foolishness," said Maybell. "We have distance to cover."

"That we do," agreed Millet. "If we quicken our pace, you and Malstisos should be able to reach Manisalia in three days."

"As we are no longer followed, that should be easy," added Malstisos. He took another look at Jacob, who was mounting his horse. "It appears you are uninjured."

"I'm fine," Jacob grumbled. "It takes more than that to hurt me."

"I do not doubt your toughness," said Malstisos. "But mind your pride and your anger. It will be your undoing if you are not careful."

"That comes from his father," said Millet. "He was the same way."

"I'm nothing like him," said Jacob.

Millet shook his head sadly. "I know you must think he abandoned you and your mother. But he only left to protect you. One day you'll understand."

"Then explain it to me," said Jacob in disgust.

"It is not my place," said Millet. "Your father is the only one who can reveal his motives. For me to do so would be a betrayal."

Jacob sniffed and turned his horse. The others followed close behind.

The rest of the day, the group traveled without speaking, and when they made camp, Jacob chose to sleep far away from the others. Millet tried to convince him to come closer to the fire, but he was met with cold silence.

The next morning, snow began to fall. Gently at first, but by midday, it was well on its way to becoming a full-blown blizzard.

Millet shivered. "If this gets much worse, I'm afraid we will freeze to death long before we reach Manisalia."

Malstisos nodded in agreement and glanced back at Maybell. She was slumped in her saddle with her coat and a blanket wrapped tightly around her.

They trudged on for several hours until they were virtually frozen. About an hour before dark, Malstisos motioned for everyone to stop.

"There is a large group of humans ahead," he said. "They have many horses and wagons."

"Could be a merchant caravan," suggested Millet.

"Or soldiers," said Jacob.

Malstisos slid out of his saddle. "Wait here." With that, he disappeared into the brush.

"I'm hoping for merchants," said Maybell, rubbing her arms. "We can barter for a place by a fire."

Millet nodded in agreement.

By the time Malstisos returned, the snow was coming down in earnest. "Merchants," he announced. "Ten wagons strong. And something else..." His face wore a strange expression.

"What is it?" asked Millet.

"There are elves among them. I didn't notice their presence until I was nearly upon them, but there is no mistake."

"What difference does that make?" asked Jacob. "At least you don't have to hide."

"You don't understand," said Malstisos. "In the west, there are places where we have dealings with humans. But as far as I know, no such alliances exist here."

"Did they know you were there?" asked Millet.

"I don't think so. But I cannot be certain."

"What should we do?" asked Maybell.

Malstisos shrugged. "What choice do we have? Winter has come early, and we are not prepared for this type of weather. If we don't seek shelter, we will freeze to death."

Millet sighed heavily and urged his horse forward. The caravan was camped a quarter of a mile away in a large clearing on the north side of the road. Several large canvas tents stood in a semi-circle, and a half dozen cooking fires flickered in the center. At least three dozen men and women, all wrapped in thick coats, were busy preparing the evening meal. As they came closer, two cloaked figures walked toward them. They were tall, lean, and wrapped in heavy wool blankets.

"Elves," said Malstisos under his breath, and looked to Jacob. "Do not speak until we know why they are here."

Jacob scowled. "I'm not stupid."

"I did not say you were."

The elf turned his attention to his approaching kin. He jumped down from his horse and raised his right hand in greeting. The other two elves returned the gesture.

"Greetings, brother," said the elf on the left. His voice was deep and rough, unlike the elf voices Millet and Maybell had heard before. "I am Grentos, and this is Vadnaltis."

Malstisos took a step forward. "Greetings."

The two pushed back the blankets from her heads, revealing their features. Both had honey-blond hair, pulled tight in a long braid that disappeared into the folds of the wool. Their skin was ivory pale and flawless.

"I see you are from the Northwestern Steppes," remarked Malstisos. "I have not seen those of your tribe in many years. I am Malstisos of the Finsoulos clan. What brings you here?"

"It has been long since we have had dealings with our southern kin," said Grentos. "And what brings us to this frozen land is a discussion to be had over a hot meal and good wine. You must be near death in this frigid cold."

"We were hoping to take shelter with the caravan," admitted Malstisos. "But I did not expect to find elves among humans."

"Nor did we expect to see the same." Grentos smiled broadly. "But you need not fear. The humans here are from the shores of the Abyss. Elves are not unknown to them, nor do they fear us. A tent has been erected to shelter the horses near the tree line. Vadnaltis will show you the way. I'll prepare a meal and a place for you and your friends to rest."

Malstisos bowed low. "I thank you." He motioned for the others to dismount. They followed Vadnaltis around the outskirts of the camp to the horse tent. Two boys sat next to a fire near the entrance. They sprang to their feet and took the visitors' mounts. Millet gave both boys a copper and their eyes lit up.

"I promise they'll be well-tended, sir," said the older boy, a dark-haired, scraggly youth, barely eleven years old.

Once they'd removed their packs, Vadnaltis led them through the heart of the camp. A few people turned to glance at the newcomers, but most ignored them. They stopped at the far end of a large, red tent with smoke rising from a small opening in the top. Vadnaltis held open the tent flap, allowing Malstisos and the others to enter.

The interior of the tent was simple. Six bedrolls surrounded a small fire in the center. A lantern in each corner combined with the firelight to give the tent a cheery glow. Grentos was at the far end, pouring hot stew from a large pot into six bowls.

"Please, choose a place to sleep," said Vadnaltis. His voice was even rougher than his comrade's and just as deep. "It matters not where."

Grentos passed out the bowls and retrieved a large jug of wine and some cups from his pack. "First we eat," he announced. "Then we talk."

Malstisos and the others gratefully accepted the food and wine, but as Grentos and Vadnaltis did not speak while they ate, the others remained silent as well. The stew was unlike anything Millet, Maybell, or Jacob had ever tasted. Each smiled with delight after their first bite. Malstisos seemed to be more accustomed to the taste and gave no reaction other than a slight nod of approval. Once their meal was complete, Vadnaltis collected the dishes and left the tent. The cold air chilled them when the flap opened, and a wisp of snow blew inside to remind them of how close to death they had come.

"I hope you are satisfied with our poor fare," said Grentos.

"It was the best stew I've ever tasted," said Millet.

Maybell and Jacob agreed enthusiastically.

Grentos smiled and bowed his head. "You are too kind. But now that we have eaten, I believe you have questions— as do we."

"Should we wait for Vadnaltis?" asked Maybell.

"That will not be necessary," Grentos replied. "As your host, I will have you ask of me what you will. I expect he shall return before you are finished."

"In that case, I'll be direct," Malstisos began. "How is it you are here, and in the company of humans? I was not aware your tribe had started relations with them."

"Only a few of us have," said Grentos. "We have heard of the progress made in the coastal cities with elf/human relations, and it has inspired some of us to do the same. We realize the world is getting smaller. We need to learn to live in this world alongside mankind or face destruction. The old hatreds must be left in the past."

"I agree," said Malstisos thoughtfully. "But that does not explain your presence here."

"We came to gain intelligence on the gathering power in Angrääl," said Grentos. "Unfortunately, we were only able to get as far as Hazrah. We were unable to find a clear way further north, at least not one where we could pass unnoticed. They have every inch of ground well-guarded. We gained passage with this caravan in Althetas so that we might travel without drawing attention."

"So you are returning home?" asked Malstisos.

"Yes," he replied. "We will stay with the humans until we reach the Western Abyss. Then we head north, back to our people."

"Have you learned anything?" asked Millet.

"Sadly, no." Grentos sighed. "At least, nothing we didn't already know. The armies of the north are gathering. For what purpose, we can only guess."

"Don't be a fool," said Jacob. "You know why they gather."

"Young one," said Grentos. "I can see you are of this land, and dismayed that it has been conquered, so I will overlook your insult. But you know nothing." He reached over and took the jug of wine. "Armies gather. Still, motives may not be known. We have no way to be certain that they intend to march further. They may not have the strength for such a campaign."

"I think they have the strength," said Millet. "And I think they intend to keep marching. It's when that troubles me."

"You may be right, Millet," said Malstisos. "But I know my brethren. They will not come to arms easily. Without proof of a threat, they will be content to do nothing."

Grentos nodded. "Without proof, I can do nothing to persuade them."

Jacob jumped to his feet. "Proof?" he shouted. "They've invaded the north and practically enslaved my people. What more do you need?"

"Calm yourself," said Grentos. "I did not say that I disagreed with you, only that I cannot convince my people without more evidence."

Jacob glared at the elf for several moments, then marched out of the tent into the bitter cold.

"That one needs to govern his passions." Grentos took a long drink from the jug.

"He's young," said Millet. "And his land is invaded. I share his frustration. I too am from here, and it pains me to see what has become of my home."

"I am sorry," said Grentos. "I will try to be a bit more—delicate."

"Perhaps we should address more practical issues," suggested Malstisos. "The road splits about twenty miles west. If you are headed for the Western Abyss, I assume you will be taking the northwestern road through Manisalia."

"Indeed," Grentos affirmed. "It's the best way."

"Millet and Jacob will be taking the southwestern road," said Malstisos. "But Sister Maybell and I would like to accompany you, at least through Manisalia, once they leave us."

Grentos smiled broadly. "We would be pleased to have your company. You may stay with us as long as you wish."

Malstisos nodded. "Thank you, brother. I am grateful."

"As am I," Maybell added.

"It is I who am grateful," said Grentos. "This journey will allow us to strengthen bonds long neglected."

They spent the rest of the evening in cheerful conversation. The wine flowed freely, and soon the tent was filled with laughter. Jacob returned after a time and proceeded to sulk on his bedroll, despite Grentos's efforts to make amends. By the time the wine was gone, they had all but forgotten their troubles and fell into a deep, peaceful sleep.

# CHAPTER 7

Lee was woken by the gentle, feminine voice of one of the young healers who had attended Gewey. It had taken him quite some time to fall asleep. Despite his cool demeanor, he was excited by the prospect of Gewey finding out what had become of his wife and son, not to mention Millet, Maybell, and Malstisos.

"What is it?" Lee groggily asked.

"I'm sorry, but Master Gewey wishes to speak with you. I told him to wait until morning, but he insisted."

"Don't be sorry," he said, trying not to knock the girl down as he sprang from his bed and headed swiftly to the healing chamber.

When he arrived, Gewey was sitting up and sipping a cup of hot tea. Kaylia was still fast asleep in the bed next to his. He looked tired and worn but managed a thin smile.

"We did it," said Gewey.

Lee was stunned. He had prepared himself for bad news. "Are they safe?"

"From what I was able to tell, they're all just fine," he answered weakly. "They're a few days from Hazrah. Your son is with Millet, and he is escorting him to Baltria."

Lee sighed with relief. "And my wife?"

Gewey's eyes fell and his face clouded over. "She isn't with them. She's been taken north to Angrääl. There was no time for Malstisos to tell us anything more than that."

Lee's heart froze. "To Angrääl," he repeated. "Why would they take her there? Unless..."

While Gewey remained silent, Lee began pacing, rubbing his temple. They must have taken her there as some kind of hostage, he told himself. It was the only logical explanation. If the Dark Knight had wanted his mother killed, that could have been done easily enough without dragging her all the way to Angrääl. For a moment, blind rage clouded his judgment, and he had to battle against a wild impulse to set off on a one-man rescue mission immediately. Gradually, though, the red mist of anger began to dissolve and common sense took over.

If she were a hostage, then she was obviously being kept alive for a purpose, and unlikely to be in any immediate danger. On the other hand, for him to go rushing off to Angrääl with no knowledge of his wife's situation or exact whereabouts could change everything and place her in great peril.

Lee thought some more. Maybe his son was planning a rescue mission of his own! From what he had heard, Jacob was hot-headed enough to do just that. Yes, of course, that was why he was heading to Baltria. Jacob and his mother had friends there who would most likely be willing enough to help him in such a mission. But his son was still a mere child, with no experience whatsoever of such things. For him to make such a rescue attempt would be suicide. With a rush, Lee could see the truth and knew what he had to do.

"I must go to Baltria." He looked up at Gewey. "I'm sorry, but I must."

"I know you must. Besides, there is nothing you can do here. The elves won't allow you to go with me, anyway."

"I'll leave after you've gone," Lee said. "I should still be able to beat them there easily enough." Gewey nodded, clearly exhausted. Lee frowned. "Are you all right?"

"I'm fine," Gewey replied. "It took a lot of effort to reach Malstisos. I wasn't ready for it, that's all."

"And Kaylia?"

"She'll be okay after a good night's rest."

"I'll let you both sleep then. I can't thank you enough for this." Gewey nodded slowly and sunk back into his bed.

Lee returned to his room, but sleep took a long time coming. Thoughts of his wife trapped in Angräal were bad enough. But even more important at this stage was for him to reach Baltria. If Jacob were to set out on such a foolhardy rescue mission before he got there, his son's chances of survival would be almost nil. Even worse, a bungled attempt may well bring about the death of the boy's mother as well.

Much as these thoughts troubled him, Lee finally accepted that it was pointless dwelling on them. There was nothing he could do until he reached Baltria, and he had others to think of as well. Having accepted this, sleep at last came.

The next morning, Lee joined Gewey and Kaylia for breakfast in the healing chamber. The healers insisted that they rest for at least one more day. A small table had been set up, and Dina and Selena soon joined them. Conversation was light, much to Lee's relief. He never enjoyed serious talk over a meal.

"Theopolou has agreed to allow Linis to accompany you," said Selena after the table was cleared. "But I fear you may be forced to leave before you are fully recovered."

"We could leave now if necessary," stated Kaylia. "I am rested and not accustomed to being idle."

Selena's eyes wandered to Gewey.

"I'm fine, too," said Gewey. "Besides, it's no good for a farmer to be lazy."

Selena smiled warmly. "Don't worry. Neither of you will be idle for long." She turned to her son. "I did try to convince Theopolou to let you go..."

Lee stopped her short and told her about Gewey's contact with Malstisos.

"I'll do my best to find out what has become of your wife," she said. "In the meantime, I'll have preparations made for your journey. We have friends in Baltria. You will have whatever help you require." She reached over and took Lee's hand. "Don't worry, son. I will do what I must to ensure their safety."

Lee gave her hand a tight squeeze. "Thank you, Mother."

"I'll go with you," said Dina.

Lee smiled. "I appreciate it. But I won't put you in unnecessary danger."

"Don't be a fool, Lee. You can't go alone, and I grew up in Baltria. You may need me."

"I think it's a great idea," said Selena. "I'd feel better knowing you had someone I trusted along with you, and as a temple historian, it's her duty."

Lee sighed heavily. "Very well. Meet me in my chambers after the noon meal to discuss our plans."

Dina grinned with satisfaction.

"When does Theopolou want to leave?" asked Kaylia.

"In two days," said Selena. "He has already sent word to the other elders. They should be there upon your arrival."

"I don't like it," said Lee. "I'd rather Gewey and Kaylia arrived first. Less chance for a trap to be set."

"Linis agrees," said Selena. "That's why he's sending his people ahead, just in case."

Linis opened the door, his face grave. His hand gripped the handle of his long knife so hard his knuckles had turned white.

"What is it?" asked Lee.

"I just received a report that the roads are being watched."

"That's not surprising," said Selena. "We know that the elves are aware of this place."

"It is not elves," said Linis.

"Men?" asked Kaylia.

"No. We do not know what they are. But they're fast and cunning. My seekers have only been able to catch a glimpse of them before they disappear. But there is little doubt that they are stalking the routes away from here."

"If the Dark One has discovered the location of this temple, then you must evacuate," said Lee.

Selena lowered her head. "We will hold if attacked. Our walls are strong, and the Dark One has no army here."

"Don't be foolish," said Lee. "You have few men here that can fight or mount a defense. To cover the walls, you would need a hundred soldiers, at least."

"A hundred we shall have," said Selena. "What you see here is not the entire strength of the Order. I shall send word for all of the knights to gather here. That will be enough to hold this temple indefinitely."

"How long will this take?" asked Linis.

"I can double my strength in a week," answered Selena, her hands firmly on her hips. "In three, I can defend this place against any attacker."

"Then I shall stay until your men arrive," said Lee.

"No! You will protect my grandson."

Lee sat back in his chair, stunned by his mother's sudden anger.

Selena's face softened. "You must protect your family, as I could not. Don't worry about me. If these walls are breached,

I can escape. There are secrets here that only I know. I will not be captured."

Lee took his mother's hands and pulled her close. "Swear it!"

Selena smiled. "I swear," she said tenderly. "We will not lose each other again."

Lee lowered his head and sighed heavily.

"We should leave right away, Gewey," said Linis. "Tonight, if you are able." He turned to Selena. "You said there are ways out of here that wouldn't be noticed?"

"Yes." She wiped her eyes. "I can get you and the others out of the temple unseen."

"Good. I'll inform Theopolou." Linus nodded curtly and left.

Lee rose from his chair and looked at Dina. "Prepare to leave," he commanded. "I want to be gone ahead of Gewey. Perhaps we may draw off any pursuit."

"Of course." Dina rushed off to pack.

For the rest of the morning, the temple was a beehive of activity. Lee and Dina were ready to leave by midday. Selena provided them with gear and enough provisions to last more than a week, along with three strong horses. Lee had decided to leave Lord Ganflin's steeds behind and made his mother promise to ride one to safety if the need came.

Gewey and Kaylia had been informed by Theopolou that they would be traveling on foot, which pleased Gewey. He had not been looking forward to saddle sores and preferred to travel light. Linis spent the morning going over the plans with Theopolou and his guards. Theopolou was troubled when he heard the roads were being watched, but agreed that there was little to do but move forward with their plan. The healers made the loudest protests, insisting that Gewey and Kaylia were not ready to be out of bed, let alone travel. However, neither one of them was showing any ill effects from their ordeal, and the insistence of Selena was eventually sufficient to quieten the healer's opposition.

Just before one o'clock, Lee and Dina made their way to the front gate. The entire temple had gathered in the courtyard to see them off. Selena, Gewey, Kaylia, and Linis stood by the large oak doors, each one trying to hide the concern in their heart.

"Be careful, son," said Selena as she embraced him. "And you," she said to Dina with a smile, "keep yourself safe at all times. I won't have my most valued historian getting herself killed." She embraced Dina tightly.

Linis handed Lee and Dina a small flask each. "Keep this with you," he told them. "Should you find yourself lacking food and drink, it will keep you strong for several days. Only a mouthful is needed."

They received their gifts gratefully and bowed in turn.

"Thank you, my friend," said Lee.

Linis took Dina's hand. "I look forward to our next meeting."

Dina blushed and smiled. "As do I."

Kaylia embraced Lee and then turned to Dina. Dina laughed as Kaylia whispered something into her ear.

Gewey hugged Dina before looking at Lee. "Be safe, and bring your son home."

Lee placed his hands on Gewey's shoulders and studied him for a moment. "You have grown up so much in such a short time. Still, listen to what Linis says, and be careful whom you trust. I don't like the idea of delivering you into the hands of the elves, but I think you're right. It is the only way."

"I'll be careful," said Gewey.

Lee smiled, and then he and Dina mounted their horses.

As they rode through the doors, they could hear the farewells of the temple calling after them. Nonetheless, Lee's mind was immediately focused on their journey the moment he heard the boom of the doors closing behind them. They hadn't ridden a hundred yards when the hairs on the back of his neck stood up. They were being watched. He knew it. But from where exactly, he couldn't tell. The rocky terrain made it impossible for him to spot anyone, and if whoever it was could evade the elf seekers, then he had very little chance of catching him.

Lee turned to Dina, who was looking around nervously. "I feel it too," she whispered.

"Be ready," warned Lee.

Dina's hand slid to the knife in her belt. By the time they reached the end of the path, her nerves were frazzled. Lee, however, seemed calm and alert.

"We should head in the direction of Althetas," he said. "If we are still being followed by nightfall, we'll continue on to the city and try to throw them off. If not, we'll start west. There's a road about a day's ride that will take us to Idelia. From there, we can make our way to the southern coast."

By the time the sun began to set, Lee no longer thought they were being followed. He and Dina found a small clearing and made camp.

"It seems we are not worthy of further attention," Lee said as he laid out his bedroll. "Which means Gewey and the elves are the likely targets." His eyes scanned the nearby brush. "Still, I should scout the area. Wait here."

He disappeared into the fading light, leaving Dina to munch on a piece of bread and some dried fruit. About an hour later, he reappeared.

"Whoever or whatever it was is gone," Lee said. "For now, we aren't the objects of their interest."

"I hope they feel the same way about Gewey and Kaylia," said Dina.

Lee nodded slowly, lay down on his bedroll, and stared at the night sky.

# CHAPTER 8

Gewey, Kaylia, Selena, and Linis joined Theopolou and his companions in the receiving chamber shortly after Lee and Dina's departure. Their gear lay next to Selena's chair at the far end of the hall.

"Follow me," said Selena. She walked to the far left corner of the room where a tapestry depicting the symbols of the nine gods hung. She reached behind it and a loud clack echoed throughout the chamber. A hidden trapdoor in front of her fell open, revealing a ladder leading down into a dark hallway.

"Follow the passage below for about one thousand feet. There, you'll find a small iron door." She handed Gewey a key. "This will unlock it. The passage will let you out along the western wall of the temple. From there, follow the trail west until you reach the Sintil Sans Road."

Gewey nodded and put the key into his pocket. "Thank you, High Lady."

They gathered their gear and readied themselves to climb down the narrow ladder. Selena had packed the Book of Souls in Gewey's satchel.

Theopolou and the other elves thanked Selena for her hospitality. Linis bowed low and held out a small silver dagger sheathed in an ivory scabbard. The handle was wrapped in soft leather, and it was crowned with a large blood ruby. "Take this as a reminder of our friendship," he said.

Selena smiled and took the dagger. "Thank you, seeker. You and your kin are always welcome here."

Kaylia took Selena's hand in hers. "I can never repay you for your kindness, High Lady."

"Nonsense," she replied. "Your bravery has saved us all. Without you, the only hope we have for survival would still be lying helpless in the healing chamber."

Kaylia lowered her eyes and smiled.

"As for you," she said to Gewey. "I charge you with keeping yourself alive and well."

"I'll do my best," Gewey replied with a smile, then made his way to the ladder.

Gewey went first, followed closely by Kaylia, Linis, and the others. The narrow hallway was pitch black, and it took a few moments for Gewey's eyes to adjust. The air was stale, and the rough stone walls echoed their footsteps. Just as Selena had said, the passage sloped gently up for about one thousand feet. There, at the end, he could make out the outline of a small door. After retrieving the key he had been given, Gewey felt around until he found the keyhole. The lock was old and rusted, and for a moment he feared the key would break; but then, to his relief, he heard the sound of grating metal as the lock gave way. Gewey pushed hard with his shoulder and the door screeched open.

He breathed deeply, allowing the welcome fresh air to fill his lungs. The sun was still high in the sky, and for a moment he was blinded.

"I should take the lead for now," said Linis.

Theopolou nodded his approval.

They followed the trail west for a few miles before Linis ordered a halt. "I assume you have no intention of traveling the main roads?" he asked.

"Correct," said Theopolou. "Once this path ends, I will lead the way."

They continued for several hours. The terrain became less and less rocky, replaced by thinly spaced oaks and pines. The long grass bent and shifted as a constant breeze blew in from the west. What struck Gewey as odd was the utter silence. With the exception of their footfalls and the sound of the wind, nothing, not even birds, could be heard. The elves also appeared to notice this oddity, and Gewey could see that it was making them uneasy.

"Something foul is near," whispered Linis.

"What do you mean?" asked Gewey.

"I'm not sure. But I intend to find out."

Linis motioned for a halt and disappeared into the thin brush. A while later, he returned, muscles tensed and eyes wide.

"We are being followed," said Linis. "But by whom or what, I can't say."

"How?" said Gewey. "I thought this way was secret."

"So did I. It would seem the High Lady was mistaken. I tried to spot our pursuer, but it is as crafty as my seekers reported, assuming that what they saw is the same thing that hounds us now."

"We should try and capture it," said Theopolou. "I would know who this is, and why they risk following elves."

"Whatever it is, it's neither human nor elf," said Linis.

"How do you know that?" asked Gewey.

"No human alive could avoid me. Not even a half-man could manage it. As for it being an elf—no elf feels like this creature. Life flees from it. Not even the birds come near."

Theopolou looked troubled as his brow furled, and his eyes surveyed the area. "Take as many from my escort as you need."

"I should need no more than three," said Linis. He turned to the other elves. "Who among you have had seeker training?"

Stintos and Haldrontis, two tall blond elves, stepped forward. "And I make three," announced Gewey.

Linis looked at Gewey skeptically. "I know you have training, but I do not think Lee would approve of this."

"Lee is not here," said Gewey. "And if he were, I am still the best choice."

Linis's mouth tightened. Then he sighed. "Very well. But you must do exactly as you are told."

Kaylia grabbed Gewey's arm. "You should let me go instead."

Gewey squeezed her hand. This drew uneasy stares from the elves. "Don't worry. I won't do anything too stupid."

Linis motioned for the volunteers to follow him into the brush. They walked north for about one hundred yards, then he told them to halt.

"You two split up east and west. See to it that you make enough noise to announce your presence. I will move north while Gewey follows slowly behind." His eyes met with Gewey's. "Make sure you are at least three hundred paces behind me at all times. The thing that follows us fell back north as I approached. Ahead is a clearing. The creature will likely try to avoid being exposed, which means it will double back and try to sneak by me. When it does, we will close the trap." He looked hard at the entire group. "If you encounter whatever this is, do not take it on alone."

Everyone nodded in agreement. Gewey began to feel the pulse of the earth flowing through his limbs. The world around him opened up, and he could sense everything around him. He closed his eyes, listening for their prey.

"It's one hundred yards north," he quickly announced. "And you're right. It's neither human nor elf."

"How is it you know this?" asked Stintos.

"Never you mind," shot Linis. "If Gewey says the creature is there, then you can count on it." He turned to Gewey. "Do you know what it is?"

Gewey shook his head. "No. But I think it knows we're coming."

"All the more reason to be mindful," said Linis.

Stintos and Haldrontis drew their long knives and headed in opposite directions. Linis gave Gewey a final glance and set off north. Once he was out of sight, Gewey crept slowly forward. With his heightened senses, he could hear the movements of the creature ahead. Slowly, he slid his sword from its scabbard; it felt warm as it throbbed in his hand. Energy rushed through him like a torrent. He could feel the sinews of his arms and legs pulsing and growing stronger.

Gewey heard Linis as the elf neared the creature. Linis had not yet spotted it, but Gewey was certain he would very soon. How could he not? He was practically on top of it. Even so, it quickly became clear that he had missed it entirely. Linis continued past the creature without showing any sign whatsoever he had noticed it. With a rush, Gewey realized that the hunters had become the hunted.

From the east, Gewey heard two more of the creatures moving, closing in on Stintos's position. He knew he had to decide quickly what to do.

"Linis, it's a trap!" Gewey yelled at the top of his lungs. His legs burst to life as he sped toward Stintos.

The creatures revealed themselves just as Stintos came into Gewey's view. Their figures were that of a man, but this was the only thing they had in common. They wore tattered clothes, blackened with grime and decay. Their faces were burnt, misshapen, and covered with deep scars as if they had been assembled from the rotting corpses of a dozen dead men.

But despite their outward appearance, their movements were unearthly—their speed unmatched by any Gewey had seen, save for Lee.

They were on Stintos before he knew they were there. Each beast held a cruel dagger in hand, and with these, they slashed at the elf's throat. Stintos only just avoided death by falling back onto the ground. But this put him at a greater disadvantage. One of the creatures moved to plunge his dagger into the elf's chest, but Gewey got there just before the fatal blow could be struck. He removed the creature's head with one swift stroke. Thick, black blood poured from the beast's neck as the body fell.

Gewey turned his attention to the second creature, which was already in striking distance. The creature struck at Gewey's heart, but the power that flowed through him allowed him to easily avoid the attack. He brought his sword down across the creature's chest, splitting it open and sending it tumbling to the ground. But to Gewey's dismay, this did not end the battle.

No sooner had the creature landed than it sprung to its feet and charged again, this time at the elf. The creature slashed at the left arm of Stintos, who deftly moved aside and spun around, bringing his long knife across its back. But this did nothing to slow it down, either. The creature also spun, swinging its own knife wildly. This time, the blade struck home and slashed across the elf's ribs. Stintos groaned and staggered back.

Gewey knew this must end now. Linis was alone with one of these creatures, and he knew he must hurry to his aid. The head, he thought, aiming his sword at the creature's neck. The blade found its mark, and the beast fell.

"Go back to the others," Gewey commanded Stintos before tearing off in the direction of Linis.

He found the elf three hundred paces north, kneeling beside the dismembered body of the third creature—dismembered, except for the head.

"Are you injured?" cried Gewey, relieved to see his friend alive.

"I will live." Linis panted. "But as for this ... thing, it has seen better days."

Gewey moved closer. His eyes shot wide as he realized the beast still lived. The ground was covered with the creature's thick, black blood, and its limbs were hacked and scattered about the ground. Still, the thing snarled and growled, its eyes fixed on Linis. Linis stared in return.

Gewey touched Linis's shoulder. The elf looked up at Gewey and forced a smile. Blood soaked Linis's shirt—elf blood.

"We must tend to your wounds," said Gewey. "Stintos was hurt as well."

"Is he seriously injured?" asked Linis.

"I don't think so. He was on his feet when I left him."

"Good." Linis sighed. "As for me, I am fine. Thanks to your warning, it is only a scratch."

Gewey's eyes turned to the creature. "How does it still live?"

"I don't know," said Linis in a whisper. "How do you live, beast?!" His voice boomed, startling Gewey.

"I was never alive," hissed the creature. Its voice was like the wheezing of a dying man, sick and labored.

"It speaks," gasped Gewey.

"So it does," remarked Linis.

"You shall all fall by the hands of my brothers," spat the creature. "The master will see that it is so."

"You mean the Dark Knight, don't you?" said Gewey.

The creature let out a gurgling laugh. "I know you. The god who will die like a man. The master will see to you soon enough."

"What manner of beast are you?" demanded Linis.

"We are the Vrykol. We are the instruments of your demise."

Linis gripped his long knife so hard that his knuckles turned white. "We shall see." His blade flew down, cutting off the Vrykol's head.

"Are you all right?" called Kaylia's voice from behind.

Gewey turned to see Kaylia, Theopolou, Haldrontis, and three other elves running up with weapons in hand. They stopped short when they saw the mangled body of the Vrykol strewn about the ground.

"What is this ... thing?" gasped Kaylia in horror.

"It's a creature of Angrääl," said Linis. "It called itself a Vrykol." He turned to Theopolou. "Have you heard of them?"

"I have. But they are supposed to exist only in legend. They are said to be damned souls, forced from paradise to walk the earth. But I have never heard of them as physical beings, only spirits."

"They're physical beings for sure," said Gewey. "They almost killed us."

"So you spoke to it before it died," said Kaylia. "What did it say?"

Linis described his encounter and the short conversation with the Vrykol.

"You should have waited until I had a chance to interrogate it," said Theopolou.

"It wouldn't have told you anything," said Gewey.

Theopolou shot a glance at Gewey. "You know very little, young one. I may have been able to discover more than you could guess." He paused. "But there is no use belaboring the point. As it stands, we know they are intelligent and resilient. Whether or not they are in fact Vrykol, or just use the name, matters not. They are on our trail."

"How fares Stintos?" asked Linis.

"His wounds are being tended," Theopolou answered. "But he will slow us considerably. I'm sending him back to

Valshara with Haldrontis until he can travel." Theopolou noticed Linis's wound. "Are you able to travel?"

"I am," replied Linis, seeming to just notice the wound on his arm. "Thanks to Gewey's warning, the Vrykol's blade did not bite deeply."

"Still, it needs to be dressed," said Kaylia. "Come. I have salve and bandages in my pack."

The group started toward the trail, but Theopolou paused. "Bring the head," said the old elf.

Linis nodded and picked up the head by its grimy hair. A wave of nausea washed over Gewey as more of the black blood poured onto the ground.

When they got back to the trail, Linis immediately unpacked a spare cloak and wrapped the Vrykol's head inside. Stintos was there, leaning against a tree while two elves treated the wound on his ribs. He noticed Gewey's approach and motioned for him to come near. Gewey reluctantly obeyed.

"You saved my life, human," said Stintos. He winced as an elf rubbed salve into the deep cut. "I owe you a debt."

"Forget it," said Gewey. "I didn't do anything you wouldn't have done in my place, I'm sure."

Stintos smiled. "That you think an elf would come to your aid is remarkable, and speaks to your character. However, I don't understand how you knew to come. I was far out of sight and earshot. Only an elf seeker could have heard them coming, and even a seeker would have had difficulty."

Gewey was unsure what to say. "I ... I," he stammered at first, before adding: "Kaylia and Linis have been instructing me."

Stintos looked at Gewey skeptically. "I see. Then their training has heightened your senses. I was not aware that humans could gain such abilities." His eyes fixed on the boy, then his smile returned. "It matters not. You saved my life, and for that, you have gained my friendship."

"I value it," said Gewey, bowing his head.

"Gewey," called Linis.

Gewey turned to see Linis standing near the packs. Kaylia was dressing the cut on his left arm. He took his leave from Stintos.

"We leave at once," said Linis. "Theopolou says we should arrive at his home in six days if we press our pace, but I disagree with moving at too great a speed. With these so-called Vrykol about, I would not risk being taken by surprise. I would ask you to remain extra vigilant. You can hear what I cannot, it would seem."

"I'll do my best," said Gewey. "But I heard the Vrykol because I channeled the power of the earth. I've never done it for more than a few minutes at a time. To do it for six days..."

"You must try," said Linis. "Our lives may depend on it."

Gewey's stomach knotted at the thought of so many lives depending on him.

"I will not have him put his life at risk," said Kaylia, fiercely.

"I doubt it will harm him," said Linis. "Seekers use the same power at times. I have used the flow, as we call it, for two straight days and it did me no harm."

"He's not an elf," countered Kaylia. "Or have you forgotten?"

"I have not forgotten," Linis shot back. "But we also both know what he really is, don't we?"

"Mind your tongue," hissed Kaylia, looking around for prying ears. "Would you have Gewey exposed?" She jerked Linis's bandage tight, causing him to wince. "I thought Lee confiding in you might be a mistake."

"It was not a mistake, child," chided Linis. "Lord Starfinder thought I should know what is at stake. He confided in me out of friendship and trust. I will not expose Gewey, and I will not be scolded by you. I am a seeker."

Gewey had never heard anyone speak to Kaylia as if she were a mere child. He could see the fury in her eyes, but she managed to contain her rage.

"You are correct, of course," growled Kaylia. "My apologies—seeker."

Linis's face softened. "I know you love him. But remember, I have named him friend and care for him as kin. I only ask of him what I must."

"I know," replied Kaylia weakly. "I just want to keep him safe. The bond we share can be maddening at times."

"You are young to have done such a thing," said Linis. "But it seems to have been the right thing to do." He bent and flexed his arm as Kayla finished dressing the wound. "Gewey, if you feel any ill effects from the flow, release it at once and consult me."

"I will," said Gewey.

Theopolou approached, his pack already on his back. "We must depart. Gather your things."

Once everyone had donned their gear, they said farewell to Haldrontis and Stintos and continued down the trail. Gewey allowed the flow of the earth to saturate his body, taking great care to listen for anything out of the ordinary.

After an hour, they left the trail and headed south across country. The ground was level and the trees still sparse. Gewey was relieved to hear the return of the birds and small animals. The flow was difficult to maintain at first, but after an hour or so it felt more natural. By the time they halted to make camp, he couldn't imagine what it would feel like to be without it. Kaylia and Linis had been keeping a close eye on him, constantly asking how he was. Kaylia was clearly relieved that he had shown no sign that it was hurting him. Linis, on the other hand, maintained a look of deep concern.

Once they made camp, Theopolou sat next to Gewey and handed him a cup of honeyed wine and a small loaf of bread.

"How much rest do you need?" asked Theopolou.

"None," answered Gewey. "I am ready now ... if you'd like."

Theopolou raised an eyebrow. "Is that so? Well, you must at least appear to rest. The flow has made you strong, but it would raise suspicions among my guard if you didn't look a bit fatigued. I would have them in the dark for now." He looked more closely at Gewey. "Why do you still use the power? There is no danger near."

Gewey's features were hard and determined. "So I'll know if it approaches."

"Linis has asked you to do this, I take it." Theopolou shook his head. "You should not. Even a seeker such as Linis cannot hold on to it indefinitely. It can be dangerous."

"What do you mean?" Gewey's eye wandered to Kaylia, who was a few yards away changing Linis's bandages.

"Linis is a worthy seeker, likely the best that still lives, but he does not know all. Seekers learn to use the flow from a very young age, but they are too busy with other training to learn the nature of the power that fuels them."

"And you know these things?" asked Gewey.

Theopolou laughed softly. "More than most. I know that to hold the power of the earth for too long can break the mind. Seekers are taught to use it when they must, and rarely hold it for more than a day, so they are in no danger."

"In danger of what?" Gewey demanded. "Linis said he has held it for two days and he was fine."

"Linis is strong," Theopolou replied. "His mind and spirit are resilient. He is counting on your ... heritage to keep you safe. But I'm not as certain. I would not see you possessed."

"Possessed?" laughed Gewey. "Possessed by what? The earth?"

"Precisely. The power you use can become addictive. In time, you will not be able to release it without great pain."

Gewey shrugged. "So what? I'm stronger—faster. I can hear and see better, and more importantly, I'm better able to keep those I love safe."

"All true," said the elf. "But in time, it will burn your mind and drive you mad. You will endanger everyone near to you. Even the ones you love."

"Has this ever happened to an elf?" asked Gewey.

"Long ago. It is why elves are taught to use it sparingly. And there's something else. You are able to use many times more of the flow than any elf. It may accelerate any adverse effects."

"It doesn't change the fact that we need to know if more of those creatures are about," insisted Gewey.

"True," admitted Theopolou. "But I will not have a mad godling roaming the earth. Be mindful."

"I will," said Gewey, aware of Theopolou's implied threat.

Theopolou got to his feet. "We will rest for two hours. That should be enough time to eliminate any suspicions about you." With that, he walked away toward three of his guards who were talking near the fire.

Kaylia and Linis sat next to Gewey a few moments later. "What did he say?" asked Kaylia.

"Nothing important. He just wanted to know if I was tired."

"I see," said Kaylia, clearly not believing him. "I would rather you say nothing at all than tell me a lie. Even if it is to spare me worry or hurt."

"I'm sorry." Gewey sighed. "I sometimes forget I cannot fool you."

"I think I know what Theopolou wanted," said Linis. "He was concerned about you using your power for too long. Am I right?"

Gewey nodded. "He said it could drive me insane."

"Unlikely," said Linis. "I've heard the same tales of caution, but as wise as Theopolou is, he has no real experience with this matter. It would take many weeks of constant use to have any lasting effect."

"He said that, because I can use so much more of the flow than any elf, that it might take less time," said Gewey.

"He may have a point," admitted Linis. "How do you feel now?"

"Good," Gewey replied. "In fact, better than good. I've never felt so strong in my life. I think I could run for days without stopping."

Linis thought for a moment. "Tomorrow I want you to release the flow when we rest. I and the others should be able to keep watch well enough."

"Okay," said Gewey, smiling, though the thought of releasing the power of the earth made his heartache. Kaylia at once picked up on this feeling.

"I'll see to it," she said.

Linis threw his head back in laughter. "Then I have no need to worry. I am sure all will be well, so long as you are keeping watch over our young man." He moved to his bedroll. "Don't forget, you must at least pretend to rest, Gewey."

Gewey lay on his blanket and closed his eyes. He could hear the forest's sweet song as the wind caressed the trees and moved across the grass. Nocturnal predators stalked their prey, and high above, an eagle soared in the direction of the sea. It was now so much more natural than the first time he had done this. In fact, he couldn't imagine a time when his ears were deaf to such marvels.

Sleep was not a possibility.

# CHAPTER 9

When the elves broke camp, Gewey was bursting with energy. His mind raced with the thoughts of the coming days. The elves seemed satisfied that Gewey had had enough rest and took little notice of his energetic behavior.

In the hours before sunrise, they covered many miles. Gewey was astounded by the pace the elves maintained. His original journey from Sharpstone would have taken half the time had they been able to move at this speed. He was certain Lee could match it, but doubted he would have been able to at the time.

When the sun broke the horizon, Linis called for a halt, though no one put down their packs. Each helped another to retrieve bread and a flask from their gear and they continued, eating and drinking along the way.

By midday the sun was blazing, but the elves did not appear affected by this as the party increased its pace. Gewey, still using the power of the earth, was as strong as he'd been when they left. In fact, with each hour that passed, he felt stronger.

"Does the human need rest?" asked Akakios, a short, stocky elf with sandy blond hair.

"The human has a name," said Gewey irritably.

Akakios laughed and slapped Gewey on the back. "I meant no offense, young one. Come. Walk beside me and perhaps you can instruct me on human manners and customs."

Gewey allowed his irritation to subside and gave the elf a friendly smile. "I'd be happy to. If you can, call me Gewey."

Akakios bowed his head. "Agreed."

Akakios and Gewey walked together until the light of the day began to fade. Gewey told him stories of his home and his upbringing, and he found Akakios to be an elf of good humor. Just as Kaylia had first done when hearing of his old life and upbringing, Akakios also told Gewey that he and many other elves also longed to live in such a way.

"To live a simple existence is the desire of many of my people," said Akakios. "Perhaps when all of this nonsense that plagues the world is done, we can."

"Do you hate humans?" asked Gewey, then realized the rudeness of his question. "I only ask because..."

"I know why you ask," Akakios said. "The answer is no. Though I have no love for them either. Hatred is a useless emotion. Though I would not choose to live among your kind, I see no cause to dwell in the past. The world is big enough for all to live within it."

Gewey thought for a moment. "So are you against what Linis and others like him are doing?"

"I am," Akakios admitted. "They invite the destruction of our culture. The result of living side by side with humanity would be a mixing of the races. I would not see the blood of our people corrupted." He lowered his head. "I hope I have not offended you, but it is how I feel."

Gewey's thoughts turned to Dina. "I'm not offended. I don't agree, but you have the right to feel any way you wish. But then why spend the day in my company?"

"You have shown yourself to have great strength and courage. I would know the man behind it. I am not close-minded. I realize that virtue does not live within my people alone, and your company does not cause me discomfort."

"I'm glad," said Gewey. "Maybe in time, I can change your mind even more."

"One can never know the future," said Akakios. "You're welcome to try."

When they had made camp, Theopolou informed Gewey that they would be resting until the morning. Gewey insisted that he could continue, but Theopolou would not be dissuaded.

"Your stamina is already causing talk," said Theopolou. "Besides, as I understand, you will be releasing the flow tonight. You may find that your body needs to recover."

A chill shot through Gewey's body. He had all but forgotten that he would be spending time without the power of the earth inside him.

Gewey was sat on his bedroll, staring at the fire, when Linis approached.

"It's time," said Linis. "Release it."

Anger swelled in Gewey's chest. "I'd rather not."

Linis studied him for a few minutes. "I was not certain before, but I am now. You must release the flow ... now."

"I will not," he growled. "There is no reason to. I'm fine."

"You are not fine," shot Linis. "If you were, you would have no trouble doing as I request. I can see that you should not hold it for so long."

Gewey jumped to his feet, rage swelling inside him. His eyes focused on Linis, and his hand felt the urge to slide to his sword.

"Gewey," called Kaylia. Her voice came from just outside the light of the fire. "Come here—now!"

Gewey's mind snapped to attention. It was then he realized that the entire camp was staring at him. He lowered his head and started toward Kaylia.

She was stood with her eyes fixed on him. Once he was beside her, she took his hand and led him away from the camp.

"You must release the power," she said softly. "And you must do it quickly before you lose yourself."

Gewey pulled away, his anger returning. "Why? Why must I become weak again?"

"Do not call yourself weak," she said. "You insult me. My spirit would not bind itself to the weak. Your strength, your true strength, does not come from the flow. It comes from within." She placed her hand on his chest. "Do this for me."

His heart raced at her touch. He lowered his head, allowing the power to drain away. Gewey felt weakness and fatigue wash over his entire body, and he fell to his knees, weeping. The absence of the flow made him feel hollow and afraid. The sounds and smells he had found so enthralling were gone, and he was left in silence. It was like the world had been ripped away.

Kaylia kneeled down in front of him, pulling his head to her shoulder. "It will pass." She stroked his raven hair. "I am here."

After a few minutes, Gewey regained his composure. He wiped his face and his eyes. "It's dark," were the only words he could manage.

Kaylia smiled sweetly and kissed his cheek. "And it will get darker still. But not tonight."

"Thank you," said Gewey, weakly. "You were right. I must not hold the power for that long again. I nearly lost myself."

"But you have returned to us, I trust," came the voice of Linis from a few yards away. He walked into view, Theopolou at his side.

Gewey rose to his feet. "I'm back to normal. I'm sorry for what I did at the camp. It won't happen again."

"No apologies needed," said Linis. "The fault was mine. I should never have asked you to hold the flow for so long without knowing what it would do to you."

"Indeed, you should not have, seeker," said Theopolou. "I hope you will heed my advice from here on."

"In matters such as this, I will," said Linis.

"What about the others?" asked Gewey. "I'm sure they noticed what happened."

"They believe you pushed yourself too far and your human body affected your mind," replied Theopolou. "A fiction I am not inclined to correct at this time."

"If you are able, we should get back," said Linis. "You need to rest."

Gewey nodded and followed the others back to camp. The elves all watched him closely as he made his way to his bedroll. Embarrassment welled up inside. He rolled onto his stomach and hid his face.

"All is well?" It was Akakios.

Gewey turned over to see the elf smiling down at him. "I'm fine. Just tired."

"I must admit I was amazed that you kept pace with us with so little rest," said Akakios. "Don't feel bad. We may not show it, but we are tired as well. If it were not for the demons that attacked us at Valshara, we would not be moving at this speed."

"I appreciate your words," said Gewey, forcing a smile. "I'll be better once I've had some sleep."

"I will leave you to it, then." Akakios walked away to join a group of elves gathered on the other side of the fire.

It didn't take long for sleep to take him, and his fatigue held off any dreams. Kaylia woke Gewey just as the sun breached the horizon.

"Theopolou has said we will stop at the home of Kephalos." Kaylia handed Gewey a piece of bread and some dried meat. She huddled close.

"Why?" asked Gewey. "I thought we were in a hurry."

"Theopolou wants to show him the head of the Vrykol," she replied. "Kephalos is very knowledgeable in ancient lore and may be able to give us information we need."

The thought of seeing an elf dwelling excited Gewey. "When will we arrive?"

"We should be there by sundown tomorrow."

Gewey smiled with satisfaction. Having Kaylia next to him seemed more natural than before, though the others stared with disapproval. The next day he woke before dawn, ready for a new march. By midday, the trees began to thicken, and the ground was covered by dense, moist grass that made walking at speed difficult. The heat of the sun made the air like earthy steam, and sweat beaded on Gewey's forehead.

"How is it so hot this close to winter?" Gewey asked Linis.

"We are near the fire hills."

"I've heard of them," said Gewey. "My father said it's like summer all year there, and that great plumes of steam erupt from the ground. I had no idea we were so close."

"Your father was correct," said Linis. "But we will only be just outside the hills. Not within them. One day, if you wish, I will show them to you properly. They are truly a wonder."

"I'd like that," said Gewey.

By late afternoon, they had found a narrow trail that wound through the forest. Here, Theopolou called a halt and asked Gewey to speak to him privately. He led him into a small clearing about one hundred yards east of the trail. Kaylia tried to follow, but Theopolou stopped her.

"When we arrive at the home of Kephalos, it is important that you do not speak unless spoken to," Theopolou warned Gewey once they were alone. "He is a kind elf, and not prone to violence, but he fought in the Great War for many years and feels the same way as I do regarding human and elf living together."

Gewey had almost forgotten that Theopolou was not really on his side. If not for The Dark One and his bond to Kaylia, Theopolou would never suffer the company of a human, let alone a god.

"I'll keep quiet," said Gewey. "I don't want any trouble. At least, not until it's time for it."

"And that time will come soon enough," Theopolou added. "If I can, I will convince Kaphalos to come with us. If he agrees, you may be forced to travel in silence for the remainder of the journey. I tell you this because I would not have you feel it is an insult from my guard or me. Once we arrive at my home, you are under my protection and may speak as you wish."

Gewey almost laughed but managed not to. "I won't be insulted. I understand that this Kaphalos might hold hatred for me, and I don't want to make things more difficult than they have to be."

"One other thing," said Theopolou with a sigh. "You must refrain from speaking to Kaylia in his presence."

This irritated Gewey, but he nodded slowly. "If he comes, I won't speak to her—at least, not until we get there."

"You must convince her of this as well," said the old elf with a hint of embarrassment that amused Gewey. "She is strong-willed, and has never been one to take orders well."

"You're not kidding." Gewey chuckled. "I'll speak to her."

"Thank you." Theopolou held out his arm, motioning Gewey to return to camp. "I advise you speak to her before we arrive."

When they got back to the others, Gewey told Kaylia what Theopolou had said.

Kaylia was enraged. "If he thinks I'll pretend to be some close-minded, human-hating fool, he has lost his senses." Her voice rose with each word.

"I understand," said Gewey, trying to calm her. "But until we reach Theopolou's home, I think we should listen to him."

"You would have this?" she demanded.

Gewey could feel her fury through their bond. "As it is, we are deceiving the others. They don't know what has happened between us. What does it matter if we keep it up a bit longer?"

"It's one thing to hide a spirit bond," she countered. "It's quite another to pretend we do not know each other. That is what he is asking."

"I don't like it either. But if it keeps things calm until we get there, then I think it's best."

"Fine," she huffed. "But once we arrive, I plan to reveal the bond between us to every one of those closed-minded morons." With that, she stormed off, staring daggers at Theopolou.

Linis came up to Gewey and slapped him on the back. "That went better than we thought."

"She's right," said Gewey. "I entered into a bond with Kaylia by means I didn't understand, but I am not ashamed of it. I don't like hiding it any more than she does."

"You won't have to hide it for very long. In fact, I doubt you will be able to."

"It's time," called Theopolou.

They continued for another hour until they came upon a smooth stone path leading east. Either side of this was dotted with tiny white flowers and waist-high shrubbery that had been meticulously manicured. The scent of lavender and magnolia wafted through the air, bringing a smile to Gewey's face. The path wound on through the forest for about half a mile, ending with an elegantly carved wooden gate bearing ancient elfish symbols etched along the outer braces. Beyond this gate, the forest ended, and the land opened up, revealing lush grass similar to that which Gewey had seen when they'd drawn close to the fire hills. But this grass was much thicker and was covered with beads of dew.

As the house came into view, Gewey was both surprised and disappointed. It appeared rather like a human dwelling.

It was a single-story wooden structure with a white tiled roof. The windows were small and round, and a well-kept flower garden surrounded the entire building. In Gewey's eyes, it looked like a house he might expect to find in any human town.

"What's wrong?" asked Linis.

"Nothing," Gewey replied. "I just imagined something, well ... different."

"Really? Like what?"

Gewey shrugged. "I don't know. I always thought that elves lived in different kinds of houses to humans." He waved a hand. "You know. More tree-like."

"Tree-like?" Linis laughed. "Do you think us birds or squirrels? We live in houses, my friend. Though I must admit, I was expecting something a bit grander from an elf of Kaphalos's stature and reputation."

They were about fifty feet from the front door when it flew open. A tall elf stood in the doorway, dressed in a gray robe made from a fabric Gewey had never seen before. It looked heavy, but it flowed like silk. His hair was silver and tied in a ponytail that fell loosely down his back and shoulders. His face was wrinkled and looked ancient. This was another shock for Gewey. The elves he had seen so far did not show the ravages of time as a human did. Theopolou was old. Gewey guessed him to be well over five hundred, yet he could pass for a human in his forties.

The elf looked over the group and shook his head. "What do you bring to my door, Theopolou?" His voice was deep and menacing.

"I wish to speak to you, old friend," Theopolou replied.

"You bring a human to my door and expect my welcome?"

"I am an elder and your friend," said Theopolou. "So I do indeed expect your welcome."

"And who else is this I see?" said Kaphalos, looking at Kaylia. "Is it the elf who comes to judgment? Or does she still defy her kin?"

Kaylia stepped forward to speak, but Theopolou held out his hand to silence her. "She is under my protection," he announced. "As is the human."

"Times have surely changed when the great Theopolou harbors a filthy human and a fugitive elf," Kaphalos sneered. "I would know why. Enter." He disappeared inside.

# CHAPTER 10

Theopolou gave Gewey a quick glance before leading the group inside.

The interior of the house was a bit more like Gewey might have imagined. The main hall just beyond the doorway was roughly fifty feet wide and equal in length. The walls were built from a material, the like of which he had never encountered. Though rough in texture, it shone and sparkled with countless tiny, semi-precious stones, causing the entire room to change hue from moment to moment. The floor was covered with a thick carpet that resembled the grass outside. It even looked as if it bore the same beads of dew, though it was not slippery. Opaque glass orbs hung from each corner of the room, giving off a soft and pleasing light that mixed perfectly with the sparkle of the walls. No pictures or tapestries hung, but on the far wall, carved into the stone and inlaid with pure gold, was the perfect likeness of an ancient willow. The room itself was devoid of furniture, apart from a round oak table that stood only one foot off the ground.

The elves kneeled around the table. Theopolou motioned for Gewey to sit beside him. Kaphalos placed himself directly across from Theopolou and stared intensely.

"Tell me, Theopolou," said Kaphalos. "When did you begin befriending humans and traitors?"

"I am no traitor," Kaylia blurted.

"Silence, girl," Theopolou scolded.

Kaphalos sneered. "I was referring to the seeker."

Linis glared. "You dare name me traitor? I should take your life for that insult."

"I would expect as much," said Kaphalos. "You would kill your own kind while saving a human animal. But be warned, I am not unprotected. If you strike me down, you will not leave these woods alive. My kin are nearby and know that you are here."

"That is enough," commanded Theopolou, "from everybody. I did not come here to fight. Nor did Linis."

"Then why did you come?" asked Kaphalos.

"To ask you to accompany us to my home," Theopolou replied. "Surely you have received my invitation."

"I have," said Kaphalos dismissively. "I have no desire to listen to the elders bicker. I am content to remain here."

Theopolou nodded to Linis, who brought forth the cloak containing the Vrykol head. Kaphalos stared, stunned, as the cloak was opened. "What is this abomination?" he gasped.

"We hoped you would know," Theopolou replied. "It claimed to be a Vrykol."

"Vrykol?" Kaphalos whispered. "Certainly not. That is impossible." He reached across the table and pulled the cloak in front of him.

"I thought the Vrykol were merely a legend," said Theopolou.

"In a way, they are," said Kaphalos. "Their true nature has been lost to all but a few. Most stories you hear today are but myths with not an inkling of fact."

"What are they then?" asked Linis.

"The damned," replied Kaphalos. "They are spirits forced to serve the gods within the decaying remains of mortals."

"The gods created these beasts?" asked Linis. "Why?"

"To punish those who dared to defy them," said Kaphalos. "They were cursed assassins ... roaming the earth. How is it you came by this?"

Theopolou told of the encounter.

"You say this human killed two Vrykol?" Kaphalos laughed. "Are you certain? Or is this merely what he told you?"

"He saved the life of one of my guards in the process," said Theopolou. "You may doubt the word of a human, but surely not that of an elf."

Kaphalos glared at Kaylia. "Depends on the elf."

Kaylia glared back furiously.

"In any case," Theopolou continued, "it was not the gods who created these creatures."

Kaphalos threw his head back in harsh laughter. "The Lord of Angrääl has seen to that, hasn't he?" He rose to his feet, turning his back on the table. "You think I am ignorant to the goings on in the human world? I know what you would have our people do, and I will have no part in it."

"Then you would sit idle while the fate of our people hangs in the balance?" Theopolou challenged.

"The fate of our people was sealed the moment the human plague set foot on this world," said Kaphalos. "The Great War was only the end result."

"But it does not have to be the end," Linis cried. "Can't you see that?"

Kaphalos spun around. "I see more than you know, seeker." His eyes fixed on Gewey. "I see what you have brought among us. You think he will save us? Don't you?"

Gewey's heart raced. Did he know?

"You're wrong," said Theopolou. "Our people may still rise again. But we must not succumb to our own stubborn nature. We need the humans if we are to resist Angrääl."

"Resist?" Kaphalos scoffed. "What resistance can you offer? The humans will scatter before the might of the army that now gathers. Once they are gone, we will be annihilated."

"There is something you do not know," said Theopolou. "We have recovered the Book of Souls."

Kaphalos raised an eyebrow. "Have you? How nice. But even if you can open it, and even if it tells you how to defeat your enemies, what then? Do you not see what will happen?"

"I see that we will survive," said Theopolou.

"Survive, yes," Kaphalos retorted. "But to what purpose? The humans will not suffer those unlike themselves. Our people will be absorbed, and our race will cease to exist. I have already heard rumors that one half-breed walks the earth even now."

Gewey tensed. This did not go unnoticed by Kaphalos.

"Human," said Kaphalos to Gewey. "If that is even what I should call you. Somehow I think not." His face was one of disgust. "Theopolou wisely instructed you not to speak. But I would know your thoughts. Would you have human and elf live as one?"

Gewey took a deep breath, trying to steady his nerves. "Yes, I would." There was a long pause.

"That's all you have to say? Surely you have more than that."

"I don't know what you want of me," said Gewey. "I know you are wise, and I know that you believe you are of a right mind." He chose his next words carefully. "I would not presume to debate with you in matters that are beyond my understanding. So I don't see what I can offer you."

"You offer nothing," agreed Kaphalos. "At least nothing I would have from you. Still, I am interested in your reasons for trying to deceive me."

Gewey was aghast and suddenly afraid. Kaylia shot him a glance, feeling his dismay through their bond.

Kaphalos let out a malicious laugh. "You have not told them that you have bonded yourself to an elf woman?" This caused the elves to stir. "Theopolou has kept this a secret as well, I see." He shook his head slowly. "Did you really think I wouldn't know? I knew the moment I saw them."

"I don't see what that has to do with anything," Gewey growled with irritation.

"You wouldn't," said Kaphalos. "But it just confirms what I have already said. You are the first, but you will not be the last."

"Is this true?" Akakios asked Theopolou, appalled.

"It is," said Theopolou. "Gewey and Kaylia have bonded their spirits."

"Why keep this from us?" he demanded.

"It was not for me to reveal," Theopolou replied. "The bonding is a personal matter and not to be spoken of lightly. I made my choice. You do not have to agree with it."

The elves were clearly upset, but calmed themselves and continued to listen.

"I am bonded to Kaylia," announced Gewey in a clear, strong voice. "I know this may anger you, but it was not my intent to do so. But know that I'm in no way ashamed."

"Nor am I," added Kaylia.

"It matters not," Kaphalos said. "It is unlikely either of you will live long enough to regret it. Angrääl will march soon and slaughter us all."

"Is there nothing I can say to convince you to come?" asked Theopolou.

"You know there is not," Kaphalos replied. "But you needn't fear. I will not hinder you. There would be no point."

Theopolou bowed his head. "Then we will take our leave." Linis gathered the Vrykol head.

"Farewell," said Kaphalos. "Perhaps we will meet again before we rejoin the creator. If not, know that I hold you in high regard, even though we do not see eye to eye."

"As do I," said Theopolou.

They left the house and filed back down the walkway. Once they had reached the beginning of the trail leading to Kaphalos's house, Akakios halted.

"My Lord Theopolou," said Akakios. "We must speak ... all of us." The other elves nodded in agreement.

"And what would you speak about?" Theopolou asked.

"I think you know," replied Akakios. "I have never questioned you before. But to knowingly protect someone who has..."

He could hardly bring himself to speak the final words. "Bonded with a human," he finally said.

Theopolou crossed his arms. "So you would have me kill her here and now, I suppose? You would have me break my word? You ask if I would dishonor myself?"

"No!" Akakios was clearly uncomfortable. "But you help her to avoid judgment by offering your protection."

"I am doing nothing of the kind," said Theopolou. "Kaylia has agreed to face judgment according to our laws upon the completion of her task, and not before. She entered into this bargain in good faith. You should know that, despite our laws, her life is sought even now by the very elders with whom we are going to meet."

"Before judgment?" gasped Akakios. "Why?"

"They feel as Kaphalos," Theopolou explained. "They harbor hatred from the Great War, and they fear a mixing of the races will be the end of our kind. I share some of these fears. But I will not turn my back on our traditions because I lack the courage to do what is right."

Akakios bowed his head. "You are right, of course. Forgive me."

Theopolou smiled kindly. "There is nothing to forgive. But you should know that there are other things I hold as secret and have not told you. I will tell you now if you feel you must know." His eyes scanned his guard. They looked embarrassed to have questioned their master's motives.

Gewey snapped to attention. "You cannot," pleaded Kaylia.

"I can," corrected Theopolou. "And I will if I must."

"Lord," said Akakios. "If you feel we should not know, it is enough."

Theopolou thought for a long moment. "No," he said. "You deserve to know what is so important that I would hide things from my most trusted companions." He turned to Gewey. "Step forward."

Gewey obeyed, keenly aware that Kaylia was at his right side fingering her knife. Linis slid to his left.

"You may have wondered how Gewey was able to kill two Vrykol so easily," Theopolou began. "Some may have guessed that he is a half-man." A few of the elves nodded. "You are only half right. Before you, stands the only being ever born from the union of two gods. Before you, stands a god who walks the earth as a human."

There was dead silence as all eyes fell on Gewey. Akakios was the first to speak. "This is true?"

"It is," Gewey affirmed, "but I only found out a few weeks ago. I've lived my entire life as a human. Until Lee proved what I am to me, I didn't know anything."

"That is why he is here," said Theopolou. "We hope he will be able to open the Book of Souls."

"Why would he need it?" asked Akakios. "Could he not simply go and defeat the Lord of Angrääl? If he is a god, does he not possess such power?"

"I don't know much about my power, or what I can or can't do," admitted Gewey. "I am only now discovering my abilities."

"But you're a god?" countered Akakios. "A god!"

"True," interjected Linis. "But he is not all-powerful. He can be injured—maybe even killed. It would be foolish to send him to confront The Dark One until he is ready."

"Angrääl is not what concerns me," said Akakios. "It was the gods that split our people. It is our lives I worry about."

"I would never harm you or your people," said Gewey. "I swear it. If my kind have hurt you, I am sorry. But I am not them."

"Even so," said Akakios. "You are one of them."

"I would ask that you trust my judgment in this matter," said Theopolou. "Gewey is not to be harmed in any way. We need him."

"I beg that you give us a few moments to consider what you have revealed," said Akakios.

Theopolou nodded his consent. Gewey, Kaylia, Linis, and Theopolou watched as the others gathered in a tight circle, speaking in hushed tones. Minutes ticked by as Gewey's nerves began to unravel. Kaylia gave his hand a light squeeze and smiled. This calmed him.

After several more minutes, the elves finally broke their circle and slowly advanced toward Gewey. "You have done me no harm," said Akakios. "And I trust my Lord. We will do nothing against you as long as Theopolou commands it. That you have bonded with one of our kind is troubling, but I see nothing that can be done, short of killing you both. And as you are not subject to our laws, I see no call for that."

"I thank you," said Gewey, bowing low. "But understand that should Kaylia face judgment, I will stand with her."

"As her mate, that is your right," said Akakios.

"We have yet to complete the bonding," interjected Kaylia. "And should I be sentenced to death, I will not."

Gewey turned to Kaylia. "What do you mean?"

Kaylia locked eyes with him. "If the bond is sealed and I die, you die as well. I will not have that."

"You would doom his soul?" asked Theopolou.

"What do you mean?" asked Kaylia. "I would save his life."

"You know as well as I what happens when the bond is left unsealed for too long," said Theopolou. "It is the same if you die. His soul will be torn apart."

"Is there nothing to be done?" she asked.

"To my knowledge, no," he answered. "You should have considered this beforehand."

"It wasn't her fault," said Gewey. "It wasn't something either of us planned."

"I see," the old elf muttered. "Then there is only one thing to be done. You must seal the bond between you. If your souls reached out without prior knowledge, then there can be no other choice."

Kaylia stared in disbelief. "You would have me complete the bond? But I..."

"You should think more, and act less," said Theopolou. "I have no desire to see you, or any elf, bonded to anyone other than another elf. But that does not change the facts. Keep in mind that I advise you as your uncle, not as an elder. As an elder, I would see you judged."

"I understand, uncle," said Kaylia. "Thank you."

"We should depart," said Linis. "There is a clearing about two hours' march ahead where we can make camp."

"Agreed," said Theopolou. "We have tarried long enough."

# CHAPTER 11

Travel for the next two days was uneventful. At first, the elves kept their distance from Gewey, but by the morning of the second day, their curiosity had gotten the better of them. Gewey tried to answer their questions as best he could, but soon it became apparent that he didn't have the information they wanted. He knew nothing about heaven, the Creator, or immortality.

The day before they arrived at Theopolou's home, Theopolou asked to speak with Gewey and Kaylia alone. They walked a few yards from their evening camp and sat on a large fallen dogwood.

"When we arrive tomorrow," Theopolou began. "I will ask that you keep to your quarters until you are summoned." He looked at them disapprovingly. "And you will be housed separately."

"We do not share quarters," said Gewey, turning bright red.

"Good," said Theopolou. "Until you have completed your bond, you should not."

"I may not share your opinions on humans," said Kaylia. "But I am no scortus."

"What's a scortus?" asked Gewey.

"A woman of ill repute," Kaylia replied.

"I was not implying that you are," said Theopolou. "But I'm still your uncle and am protective of your honor."

"I would not dishonor Kaylia," said Gewey, with all the sincerity he could muster through his embarrassment.

Theopolou cracked a smile. "I believe you." Then his smile faded. "Now listen to me, both of you. You must keep out of sight until I call for you."

"How long will we have to wait?" asked Gewey.

Theopolou shrugged. "An hour. A day. There is no way to know. But you must stay put no matter what. Each of you will have a guard outside your door."

Kaylia's eyes narrowed. "Do you expect treachery?"

"No," Theopolou replied. "But I will be prepared, nonetheless. Timing will be crucial, and I will get us every advantage I can. Since I opposed your assassination, I have lost support. I still hold position and influence, but not as much as before. You must do exactly as I tell you."

Gewey and Kaylia both nodded in agreement.

"Good," said Theopolou, satisfied. "Now we must rest. Tomorrow we will arrive. I can only hope that we get there before the others."

They slept for only a few hours and were on their way once again long before daybreak. By midday, the forest grew thicker until it was nearly impenetrable. Gewey snagged his clothes countless times on thorns and brambles—insects swarmed around him, making a feast of his flesh. The elves seemed unaffected by the conditions, deftly hopping between the trees and thick brush, avoiding thorns and low-hanging branches as if they weren't there.

Linis noticed Gewey's difficulty. "Stay just behind me," he said. "Do as I do." Gewey tried his best to follow Linis's every move, and as a result, was able to lessen his hurts considerably. Even so, he still managed to inflict a few extra scrapes on himself before the forest thinned.

"How can he stand to live in such a place?" Gewey asked.

"A bit much to get through for anyone other than an elf," Linis said, chuckling. "It is why we choose such places. Most of our dwellings are not easily accessible, even our towns. Some you could never find unless you knew exactly where to look."

Gewey tried to imagine what an elf town would look like. Majesty and magic must be everywhere. Then he dismissed the notion. So far, he had been way off the mark. Kaphalos lived in a house, and though it was well-built and beautiful, it was nothing like he had pictured.

The forest thinned even more, and soon Gewey found himself walking along a colorful cobblestone street. It was wide enough that the party could comfortably walk four abreast.

Theopolou turned back to Gewey. "Once we reach the end of the road, Akakios will guide you and Kaylia to your quarters. You should be able to get there unseen. The servants will be preparing the house, and we are the first party to arrive."

"How can you tell?" asked Gewey.

"It's my house," replied Theopolou. "I know when someone is about. Not even Linis could enter my land without my notice."

The road ended at an immense gateway, twenty feet high and solid as steel. It shone like silver and bore long, carved ivory handles. A polished granite wall spanned east and west farther than Gewey's eyes could see. He stared in wonder. Even the walls of a human city weren't so well constructed, and the gate looked as if nothing could bring it down.

The rest of the party halted while Theopolou approached the gate. He placed his hand upon one of the handles. Suddenly, the handle hissed and glowed with a pale, white light. Then, as if by command, the gate swung outward without a sound.

"Magic," whispered Gewey as they moved closer.

Theopolou sniffed. "It is not magic." His eyes fell on Kaylia. "If he is to be yours, then you should teach him properly."

Gewey could feel Kaylia's embarrassment. "I'm sorry," he apologized to her. "I shouldn't have said anything."

"It is not your fault." Kaylia lowered her eyes. "I have not told you enough about us. I should have instructed you more about our ways the moment we were bonded."

Gewey was on the point of trying to console her, but Theopolou held out his palm. Akakios moved in front of Gewey and Kaylia.

"Wait for the rest to enter," said Akakios. "Then follow me to your quarters."

Once Theopolou and the others were about fifty feet ahead, Akakios led them through the gate. Gewey sucked in his breath.

A solid, polished white marble path lay before him. Each stone was etched with an intricate golden inlay of elf ruins. The grounds were dotted with ancient willows and strong oaks and wildflowers covered the area like a glorious carpet of color and splendor. Directly ahead stood a ten-foot-tall, solid crystal statue of an elf maiden. Her right arm held aloft an orb surrounded by tiny vines of ivy. As the sunlight struck the orb, it sparkled and split, causing rainbows of light to dance playfully. The craftsmanship was far beyond anything Gewey had ever imagined possible.

But what impressed Gewey most of all was the house—if such a structure could indeed be called a house. The entire building was constructed from pure white marble, and it stood three stories high, rising to an apex. Elaborate carvings of horses, wolves, bobcats, and many other animals Gewey did not recognize decorated the facing. Not a speck of dirt blemished its beauty, and it showed no sign whatsoever of weathering. A massive flight of stairs, as wide as the entire house, led to broad double doors made from the same gleaming metal as the gates. Lining the front and supporting the lip of the high ceiling stood six massive columns, ten feet apart and as big in circumference as a mature oak.

As Theopolou and the others passed by the crystal statue, each stopped in turn and bowed their heads.

"Come," Akakios commanded.

He led Gewey and Kaylia to the west side of the house where three small, round buildings stood in a line separate to the main dwelling. They were crafted from smooth white stones, and the roofs glittered with quartz tiles. The doors were blond maple with a silver doorknocker in the center.

"All of the rooms are identical," said Akakios. "Each is equipped with a shower. Food and fresh clothing will be brought to you right away."

They thanked Akakios. Kaylia took the room nearest to the main house, and Gewey the one next to her.

When opening the door, Gewey immediately felt the welcome relief of cool air. The room was large enough for four people and was well-lit by the same strange orbs he had seen at the home of Kaphalos. Four of these orbs hung from a silver chain near to the wall. To his right was a single bed with fine linen sheets and a plump, comfortable-looking round pillow. On his left stood a small circular oak table with four chairs. A plush couch with a brass table at each end had been placed at the far side of the room. But what really caught Gewey's eye was the area between the table and the couch—the shower.

Gewey nearly forgot to close the room door behind him before throwing down his pack and stripping off his clothes. Apart from slightly more elaborate fixtures and a small marble table provided for the soaps and bathing implements, this shower looked much like the one he had previously used in Lord Ganflin's manor.

Once inside, he pulled the curtain around. Remembering the shock of the water from his first experience, he twisted the knobs carefully on this occasion. Soon he lost himself in the glorious feeling of steaming hot water pouring over his body. When he finished, he grabbed a towel hanging on the wall and stepped out. To his amazement, a fresh set of clothes lay neatly on the bed and a bowl of hot stew and fresh bread had been placed on the table. He had not heard the slightest sound of anyone entering or moving about.

He dried off and donned the clothes that had been provided. They were simple tan pants with a thin leather belt and shirt of the same color. The fabric was comfortable, fitted nicely, and was highly durable. A pair of calfskin moccasins and cotton socks completed the ensemble. Gewey was sat at the table and had begun to eat when the door swung open. It was Linis.

"You look very much the elf in those clothes," remarked Linis, smiling.

"This is what elves wear? I've never seen an elf dressed this way."

"Of course not." Linis laughed. "This is what we wear at home while relaxing. Do you find it comfortable?"

"Very." In fact, the longer Gewey wore the clothes, the more he noticed they had certain properties. His skin felt cool and alive, and the moccasins hugged his feet to the point that he barely noticed he was wearing them. "I'd love to know how they're made. The tailors back home would go crazy for this. The cobblers, too."

"I am sure they would," said Linis. "But you may find it is easier to sway the minds of the elf elders than to pry the secrets from our craftsmen. They are very protective of their art." He sat across from Gewey. "It may be some time before you can leave this room. Do you need anything? I can have it brought."

Gewey thought for a moment. "Some books would be nice. About the elves, if possible."

"I'm sure that can be arranged."

"Have you seen Kaylia?"

Linis shook his head. "Not yet. I am going to see her after I leave here. Do you have a message?"

Gewey hated that he couldn't speak to her when she was just yards away. "No. I'll deliver it myself."

Linis frowned. "You must not leave this room. Give it to me and I'll convey it."

Gewey flashed a mischievous grin. "I don't need to leave this room to deliver my message. I agreed to stay here, and I will. But where my spirit travels is my business."

Linis burst out laughing. "I sometimes forget what you are, and what you're capable of. Mind that you keep this ability to yourself for now. Once the elders are told of your heritage, many are likely to fear you. Give them no more reasons than necessary to do so."

"I was wondering," said Gewey. "The gate. How did it open?"

"By the same means you gain strength when you use the power of the earth," Linis replied. "We can create tools and objects that can harness the flow just as you do. It is said that in ancient times, the elves created things of such power that they could upend the very earth, moving entire mountains."

Gewey's eyes widened at the thought. "Incredible. Have you ever seen such a device?"

Linis shook his head as sadness washed over him. "No, I have not. No one has in many generations. The wisdom and knowledge of our forefathers were said to rival that of the gods. But I fear we will never regain what we have lost."

"Maybe together we can rediscover the secret."

Linis forced a smile. "Perhaps. I fear I will not live to see such a thing."

"Don't say that," said Gewey. "We're all going to make it through this alive. I swear."

Linis furrowed his brow. "Never make a promise you cannot keep. Besides, I have no fear of death. It comes to us all—except perhaps to you."

"I may be a god, but I am not immortal. Whatever I am, I'm part of this world, just as you are." He stood and turned his back. "What bothers me is that, if I am bound to earth as a human, I may have a human lifespan. Kaylia could live for four or five hundred more years."

Realization washed over Linis. "You're afraid that if you complete your bond, she will only live a human lifetime."

Gewey nodded and lowered his head.

"Your fears are justified," said Linis. "But certainly that should compel you to value the time together you will have." He stood and placed his hand on Gewey's shoulder. "Do not dwell on it. You and she are the first to have such a bond. It could be that if you have a human life, it may be extended to that of an elf. There is also the possibility that you may not die at all and that the two of you will be able to live together forever. Whatever the case, there is nothing to be done."

"You're right." Gewey sighed. "But sometimes it's hard not to think about it."

Linis gave Gewey's shoulder a light squeeze. "I'll have the books sent. Perhaps they can occupy your thoughts."

Gewey turned and smiled. "I'd appreciate that."

After Linis left, Gewey lay on the bed and closed his eyes. He reached out with his mind, hoping to touch Kaylia's, but found this to be more difficult than expected. It felt as if something was blocking him. He looked inside his pack, retrieved a small flask of jawas tea, and took a long draught. He could feel its effects at once. His body and mind relaxed and his breathing deepened. He reached out again, but even now he was unable to make contact. It seemed as though a brick wall was barring his way. He tried a few more times, but always with the same result. Frustrated, he got up and began pacing the room.

The desire to leave the room and ask Kaylia if she was experiencing the same thing was nearly unbearable. But he knew to do so would cause serious trouble. Instead, he busied himself by first unpacking his things, and then by polishing and oiling his sword while sitting on the edge of the bed. The weapon never seemed to need such care, but he enjoyed the task, anyway. Simply by holding it, he could feel the throbbing pulse of the earth.

He closed his eyes, allowing the flow to move through him. More and more, he opened himself until every fiber of his being was saturated.

"Stop this!" cried a loud, deep voice. Theopolou was standing at the doorway, fury in his eyes.

Gewey released the power. Immediately, he longed to hold it once more.

"You must not do that again," Theopolou told him, slamming the door behind him.

"Why?" asked Gewey. "What can it hurt?"

"Fool," the elf grumbled. "You expose yourself when you draw that much power."

Gewey got to his feet. "I don't understand."

"Then understand this. Should an elder be nearby when you draw that much of the flow, you will not need to tell anyone what you are." Theopolou sat at the table and motioned for Gewey to do the same.

Gewey, irritated by his inability to contact Kaylia, resisted. "I'll stand."

"You tried to contact Kaylia through your bond," said Theopolou. "Did you not?"

Shocked, Gewey sat. "How did you...?"

"I know everything that happens within these walls," he said. "And though another elder may not be as sensitive as I am within my house, they will know that you are not as you seem if you do that again. You are fortunate that no one has arrived yet."

Gewey nodded but still felt angered. "Why can't I contact Kaylia? It's as if I'm being blocked. And why is it that you can feel when I use the power, but your guards do not?"

Theopolou's mouth tightened. "I am not inclined to be your instructor, but I suppose on this occasion I must be." He folded his hands on the table and leaned forward. "As far as your inability to spirit travel is concerned, I prevented it. I cannot risk you accidentally ruining my plans. And as for why I can feel you using the flow, it is a trait of my race. As we age, we become more sensitive. Seekers develop this ability, which is why Linis can feel it, but it would come naturally with time, anyway."

Theopolou stood. "That is all you need know. Any further instruction will be from Kaylia, or perhaps Linis." He walked to the door. "Do not be a fool and try that again, or we will be undone."

Left alone to feel like an ignorant child, Gewey sat in silence. When first departing from home with Lee, he'd been rebuked many times, but Theopolou's words had struck home keenly. He had thought his experiences had matured him, but now he was forced to question himself and his worth. There was still so much he didn't know.

The door opened and Akakios entered, carrying an armload of books. "Linis sent these." He placed them on the table. "Mostly children's stories, but Linis thought it best for you to learn our culture from the beginning."

"Thank you." Gewey picked up a leather-bound book with the title 'Songs of Lilith' embroidered on the cover.

"Something troubles you?" Akakios asked.

"It's only that sometimes I realize I have much to learn."

Akakios smiled warmly. "It is good to know that about yourself. Even the very wise are not all-knowing, though some may think so. I take it Theopolou had harsh words for you?"

Gewey shrugged. "He didn't say anything I didn't deserve. It's just that for a while I was starting to feel like I was my own man, and then I'm reminded of how young and inexperienced I really am."

"Then take comfort from the fact that you are the first being, other than an elf, to grace the home of Theopolou or his family in more than five hundred years. That is an honor that you, and you alone, can boast. If it is experience you desire, this is certainly a good start."

His words lifted Gewey's spirits. "Thank you. I guess I was just feeling a bit out of place and alone."

"Think nothing of it." Akakios turned and opened the door to leave. "I'll be guarding your door. I will see if Theopolou will grant me permission to keep you company. Linis may be tied up with the meeting of elders."

"I'd like that," said Gewey.

He spent the next few hours reading The Songs of Lilith. The book was a collection of stories about a young elf girl named Lilith who was kidnapped by a spirit and taken to the other side of the world. Each short tale recounted her quest to return home and ended with a moral lesson.

By the time Gewey had read the fifth story, his eyes were growing heavy, and he decided to go to bed. He examined the glowing orbs but could find no way of dimming them. Finally, still with all of his clothes on, he lay down and covered his eyes with a shirt from his pack. He thought it best not to undress, just in case he had to move quickly.

His dreams were filled with visions of Lilith and her struggle to return to her family.

# CHAPTER 12

Gewey awoke to find the lights dimmed and Linis sitting quietly on the couch flipping through one of the books he had sent over.

"Good morning," yawned Gewey. "Assuming it is morning."

Linis placed the book on the end table. "It is indeed. The elders began to show up late last night. Theopolou is hoping they will all be here today."

A breakfast of bacon, eggs, and juice sat on the table. Gewey stretched and walked over, his mouth watering.

"I noticed you were reading The Songs of Lilith," remarked Linis. He joined Gewey at the table. "It was a favorite of mine as a child. I hope you are enjoying it."

"Very much. Though the symbolism is hard to understand at times." He picked up his plate and breathed in the aroma.

"I thought you should start at the beginning. It will help you to know elf ways better if you understand us from childhood. These books are some of the first lessons we are taught."

Gewey swallowed a healthy portion of eggs. "They're certainly different from the stories I heard as a child. My father would have loved them. So would Lee, I bet."

"I'm sure he would." Linis's face grew concerned.

"What's wrong?" asked Gewey.

"The elders are taking a long time to gather. Theopolou was worried that we would arrive after the others were already here. But instead, it is we who wait."

"Maybe some of them were delayed," offered Gewey.

Linis shrugged. "Perhaps. But too many have yet to arrive. I fear they conspire against Theopolou."

"Conspire? To do what?"

"I do not know," Linis admitted. "Many who have yet to come are those who are openly against him. When and how they arrive will tell me much."

"Do you think they'd try something here?" asked Gewey.

Linis shook his head. "Within these walls—no. They would never break our customs to such a degree. To do violence in the home of another elf is one of our greatest crimes. We consider the home a sacred place. Besides, Theopolou controls the flow here. Even if they did the unthinkable, they'd be slaughtered." Linis stood and paced around in thought. "No. If they do intend to kill Theopolou, they'll first need to remove him from this place."

"Easy," said Gewey. "We just make sure he doesn't leave."

"I wish it were so simple," said Linis. "If there is a plot, it will be subtle. They will not simply threaten or force Theopolou to expose himself. They will dress it in a manner so that he will have no choice but to comply."

"How would they do that?" asked Gewey.

"I wish I knew. I am not as wise as Theopolou, nor as versed in the nuances of politics."

"What can we do?" asked Gewey, suddenly losing his appetite.

"Wait and see," said Linis. "I may be seeing intrigues where none exists. I hope so." He walked to the door. "I must leave you. I'm sorry that I cannot stay longer, but I have much to do before the meeting begins. Kaylia says to pay attention to the tenth story of Lilith." A smile crept over his face. "She is quite an elf."

Gewey laughed. "Yes, she is." He then remembered something. "Oh, one more thing before you go, Linis. How did you dim the lights?"

The elf laughed softly. "Rub your hand up the side of the glass to brighten, and down to dim."

"Thank you," said Gewey.

Linis nodded and left. Gewey immediately tried out the light. Just as Linis had said, it became brighter as he moved his hand up the side. He marveled at the skill it must have taken to make such a wondrous device.

Gewey spent the next few hours reading. He made it to the ninth story in The Songs of Lilith when there was a knock at the door. Gewey opened it to find Akakios standing there, a broad grin on his face.

"Theopolou granted me permission to keep you company," said Akakios.

"Then please come in," Gewey responded, happy to have someone to talk to.

Akakios sat down at the table and gestured to the book Gewey held. "What do you think?"

"I'm loving it," said Gewey as he sat across from the elf. "Do you know who wrote it?"

Akakios raised an eyebrow and chuckled. "You think you might know the author?" He picked up the book and thumbed through the pages. "Anyway, if I told you, you wouldn't believe me."

"Try me."

"Legend says it was written by Lilith, herself, thousands of years ago."

Gewey's eyes widened. "You mean these are true stories?"

"Perhaps. But I think not." He leaned back and crossed his legs. "More likely, Lilith was just the one who invented the stories."

"Of course." Gewey felt foolish. "Has the meeting begun?"

"Yes," Akakios replied. "About an hour ago. The last of the elders arrived just before they were going to start without him."

"How is it going so far?"

Akakios shrugged. "I would not know. The only non-elder allowed inside is Linis. I'm sure he'll fill you in later. In the meantime..."

He pulled a set of eight-sided dice from his pocket. "How would you like to learn an elf game?"

Gewey beamed. "I'd love to. But I must warn you, I'm not a very good gambler. And I really don't have much money."

Akakios leaned back in his chair and gave Gewey a devilish grin. "Don't worry. We can play for fun—for now."

Gewey fetched the few coins he had with him: three coppers and a silver, plus one gold coin that Lee had given to him. He tossed these onto the table. "That won't be necessary."

"Don't worry," joked Akakios when he saw Gewey's money. "I'll give you a loan if you need one."

The game was similar to others played at the tavern in Sharpstone, and though Gewey had not been one to visit the place at night very often, he caught on to this new game quickly. Soon, he had nearly doubled his money.

"Not a gambler, you tell me?" teased Akakios as he fiddled with his dwindling pile of coins.

"Is that what I said?" said Gewey, feigning innocence.

Linis entered, looking very unhappy. Akakios quickly gathered his remaining coins and excused himself.

"From the look on your face, things aren't going too well," said Gewey as they took a seat on the couch.

Linis lowered his head and rubbed his neck. "That is putting it mildly. Things are turning sour, and fast."

"What happened?"

"To begin with," started Linis. "They knew you were here."

"How?" asked Gewey.

Linis shook his head slowly. "I don't know. But somehow they discovered in advance that both you and Kaylia are here. Some of the elders are calling for Theopolou to face judgment for treason, and for harboring a fugitive."

Gewey shifted nervously. Without Theopolou's protection, he wasn't sure what could happen. "They can do that?"

"It's doubtful. It's just a prelude to another move." Linis looked disgusted. "Even if they can get enough support to call Theopolou to judgment, they would never be able to convict him."

"Then why do it?"

"To force him to expose himself," said Linis. "If he is called to judgment, he will have to go to the Chamber of the Maker."

"What's that?" asked Gewey.

"It's where all judgments are made, and where the council meets during times of war." Linis stood up and began pacing. "If he leaves these walls, he is vulnerable."

"You don't really think they'd try to kill him—do you?"

Linis sighed heavily. "If you had asked me that question a year ago, I would have said no. But now..."

Gewey thought for a moment. He needed to speak to the elders and convince them to join him against Angrääl. If Theopolou were brought to judgment, he didn't know if there would be another chance.

"There's more," said Linis. "They want to speak to you—and Kaylia."

This sent a chill throughout his entire body. "Together?"

"Yes," Linis replied. "They know about your bonding. Needless to say, they are not pleased."

Gewey shot to his feet. "What will they do?"

Linis grabbed Gewey's shoulders, trying to calm him. "They can do nothing so long as you are under Theopolou's protection. If they tried, the elves who are undecided in this matter would move against them. And don't forget, this is the house of an elf sage and council elder. Only a great fool would attack him here. He controls the flow within these walls."

"But if we are forced to leave?"

"Then you have the greatest living seeker to fight at your side," Linis assured him. "Even the elders will pause at that."

"But that will put you at war with your own people." Gewey shook his head. "I won't have that."

"I'm already at war." Linis held a deep sadness in his eyes. "I've been called to judgment."

Gewey's eyes shot wide. "What? What are you going to do?"

Linis forced a weak smile. "I've refused to recognize their authority. Once I leave these walls, I am to be considered a fugitive and a traitor."

"I'm so sorry," said Gewey

"Don't be. I knew this would happen. It was just a matter of time." He squared his shoulders. "I have made my choices, and I do not regret what I have done."

The door opened, and Theopolou entered, dressed in a long white robe. He looked weary.

"I imagine Linis has filled you in," said Theopolou. Gewey nodded.

"The council wishes to extend you an invitation to join them at the Chamber of the Maker," said Theopolou in a clear, even tone. "Do you accept?"

"Why?" asked Gewey. "Why do they want me to go there?"

"They feel that your presence has jeopardized the gathering," Theopolou replied without conviction. "They fear you may have led others here."

"That is a lie and you know it," Linis roared. "They are luring you into a trap. You must see that. Once you're outside of these walls, they will kill you—and Gewey."

"I pray that you are wrong, seeker," said Theopolou. "But if you are not, you must take the Book of Souls and keep it safe. I'll entrust it to you before I leave. Keep it hidden."

"No need," said Linis flatly. "I'll be going too."

Theopolou nodded. "Very well."

"What about Kaylia?" asked Gewey.

"She will be accompanying us," Theopolou answered.

"I won't let you march her to her death."

"She is not to be judged," said Theopolou. "At least, not yet. She has been called to bear witness and give testimony."

"Testimony?" said Gewey. "What kind of testimony?"

"Against me," Theopolou replied. "I have been called to judgment."

"You cannot do this," said Linis. "Your enemies know that you will not be found guilty. It can only mean they intend to move against you once you are away from the safety of your home."

"If so," said Theopolou. "I shall count on you to come to my aid."

"My seekers should come as well," Linis told him.

"No," said Theopolou. "If you insist on coming, they must not. It will be taken as a sign of aggression. You must help me to keep the Book—and Gewey—safe."

"So I won't be opening it here?" asked Gewey.

"I do not think that would be wise," Theopolou replied. "It would cause more trouble than I care to handle at this point. The council is aware that I have re-acquired the Book, and that has gained me some support. But introducing a god into the situation this soon would be most unwise. Linis is right. I will not be found guilty. Once that happens, we can move on from there. I will gather the council once more after I am found guiltless, and then you will open it."

"Is Gewey still to meet with the council before we depart?" asked Linis.

"Yes," Theopolou replied. "Though his petition to have the elves join his cause must wait."

Gewey's heart sank. "Isn't there any way for me to speak to them about this before we reach the Chamber of the Maker?"

"It would be a foolish risk," said Theopolou. "Beyond the grounds of my house, I cannot protect you. Certain revelations may cause my kin to react poorly."

"I have to risk it," said Gewey. "Every day wasted brings the Dark Knight closer to our doors. I need to do what I came here to do."

Theopolou sighed. "If you must, I cannot stop you. But I think you would do better to listen to my council." He turned to Linis. "The road ahead may hold danger. Prepare."

Linis nodded. "I may not be able to bring my seekers, but I can see to it that they are not far away." He shot a stare at Theopolou before he could argue. "I insist."

"They must say out of sight," said Theopolou reluctantly.

"They are seekers," said Linis. "The finest the tribe of Melanctha has ever produced. That bumbling group of fools could not spot my elves if they were standing on top of them."

"I know you are angered by them naming you traitor," scolded Theopolou. "But they are not fools. If your seekers are not careful, they will be discovered."

"They will not be discovered," said Linis. "But I must take my leave now to inform them."

Theopolou nodded curtly as Linis left the room. "What happens now?" asked Gewey.

"Now you will speak briefly with the elders." Theopolou looked Gewey up and down. "You may keep your present attire."

"And Kaylia?" asked Gewey.

"She awaits us."

Theopolou led Gewey out of the door and around to the front of the main house. The opportunity to see the interior of such a magnificent building excited him, and his sense of anticipation grew further when the great metal doors automatically swung open as they approached.

What Gewey saw as they stepped inside made even the exterior of the house seem trite and common. The immense receiving hall was brightly lit by the same type of orbs that were in his room, only these were much smaller and vast in number. The floors were of deep emerald green marble, polished to a bright shine and veined with ivory. The walls, made from the same gleaming silver metal as the door and gate, were etched with elf letters and symbols of such artistry that it brought tears to Gewey's eyes.

Above him, running along the entire length and breadth of the hall, was a green marble balcony. Darkly stained wooden doors lined the wall leading to various rooms and chambers.

In the center of the hall, a crystal statue, similar to the one outside, was holding a book. Gewey immediately thought of the Book of Souls. Theopolou's family had guarded this for generations. It must have pained the elf over the years to look upon the statue and know that it no longer held the same meaning that it once had.

At the rear of the room, a broad staircase led up to the next level. There was a set of double doors positioned on either side of the stair base, with another matching set of doors at the top. Gewey stared, mouth agape, as he passed the statue. He could hardly wait to see the rest of the house. While cresting the staircase, Gewey caught sight of Kaylia. She was dressed in the same type of white robe as Theopolou, and her hair hung loosely down her back. She smiled when she saw Gewey, and he could feel her relief through their bond.

Kaylia appraised his Elven garb. "You look good dressed this way."

Gewey blushed. "It's very comfortable, but I feel under-dressed to meet elf elders." He decided not to mention that he had also slept in them.

"Are you ready?" asked Theopolou. Gewey and Kaylia both nodded.

Theopolou clapped his hands loudly, and the doors swung silently open. As they followed the elf inside, Gewey took a deep breath, hoping that this trip had not been a huge mistake.

# CHAPTER 13

The High Lady of Valshara paced the halls of the temple, immersed in thought. She had hardly been able to sleep ever since Linis had reported the presence of possible agents from Angräal watching them. Then, two of her scouts had disappeared three nights ago. On top of that, the temple watch had reported seeing shadowy figures lurking just beyond the walls. Their location was compromised, and she felt sure that an attack would come soon.

The few knights she had available were not enough to hold off an attack should the walls be breached. They had attempted to convince her to escape, but she'd refused. The High Lady of Valshara would not scurry away in the night, and she would not leave her people behind. If evacuation became necessary, everyone would go. Of course, if their enemies had found the hidden exit, then they would all die.

Her mind wandered to thoughts of her son. She yearned to speak to him one more time. Their reunion had been all too brief, though she was thankful that she had at least been able to see him before the end.

"My Lady." It was Ertik.

Selena forced a smile. "Brother Ertik, how are the preparations coming?"

"They go well, My Lady," he replied, though not convincingly. "If the walls are breached, the knights will be able to slow any invaders long enough for everyone to get out."

"I want you to spread the word," commanded Selena. "Gather all packs and gear and place them in the receiving hall at once. If it comes to that, I want nothing to hinder our escape."

"Yes, High Lady." Ertik bowed and left.

Selena busied herself by inspecting the provisions and defenses. The knights tried once more to convince her to leave, but she would not be moved. When it was time for the evening meal, fatigue was setting in. Her feet had swelled and her legs ached. However, even after a hearty meal and a hot bath, she still could not bring herself to sleep.

After lying in bed for an hour, she decided to read. She sent for some hot tea and settled into her favorite chair, curling up with one of her favorite comedies. She needed a laugh. But she had barely gotten beyond the first paragraph when a loud knock sounded at the door. It then burst open before she could even respond. Jericho, the captain of the knights, stepped inside the chamber. He held his sword tightly.

"We are besieged, High Lady," said the captain. "We must evacuate."

"I heard no alarm raised." Selena reached for her coat. She was thankful that she had begun the habit of dressing in clothes suitable for travel rather than her cotton nightgown. "Have they breached the defenses already?" She slipped into a pair of short leather boots.

"I don't know how it was done," Jericho admitted. "But they killed three knights before we even knew they were there. Whatever they are, they're neither human nor elf."

A cold knot twisted in her stomach. "How many are there?"

"We can't be sure," said the captain. "But they fight as if possessed. We cannot hold. You must leave now."

Selena squared her shoulders, standing straight and tall. "Begin the evacuation. Then, and only then, will I leave."

Jericho lowered his eyes but made no move to obey. "My Lady, if you do not come with me willingly, I regret that I must take you by force."

"You wouldn't dare!" she hissed.

"It is my duty to protect this Order." He took a small step forward but did not lift his eyes or place his hands on her. "You are not only our leader, you also symbolize what we are. Should you die, we die with you. The knights are falling back as we speak to aid in your escape. Every second you delay, more of us meet our end."

Selena boiled with anger, but she had no other choice. She nodded sharply and allowed Jericho to lead her through the temple to the receiving hall. Screams echoed everywhere as the enemy found new victims, but Jericho wouldn't allow her to pause. Tears streamed down her face. Her people were being slaughtered, and she was helpless to do a thing about it.

She hoped desperately that the gathering in the receiving hall would be large. But as they entered, those hopes were dashed; just three knights, Ertik, and two novices were waiting there.

"So few," Selena whispered in horror. She felt her legs begin to give way, but Jericho caught her.

"Come High Lady," said the captain softly. He led her to the tunnel entrance. "Others may yet follow."

Selena tried to fight back her tears.

"I will stay behind and help others get out," said Ertik.

"No!" Selena shouted. "You will escape now."

Ertik bowed and helped Selena to the ladder once Jericho had descended. When they reached the door, Jericho motioned for them to wait before creeping outside into the cool night.

"All clear," whispered the captain. "My Lady, stay close behind me."

Jericho led the group down the trail, sword in hand. The others followed as closely as they could without tripping on each other.

They had walked for about half a mile when they suddenly heard footsteps approaching from out of the darkness. Jericho crouched, and the rest followed suit. As the footsteps grew louder, the lights from three torches came into view.

"Off the path," whispered Jericho.

They scampered into the nearby brush, trying to stay quiet. Soon, the torches were right next to them. Selena's heart raced, her breaths short and swift. Then the torches halted. From where they were behind a small bush, she couldn't see who it was.

"Come out," hissed a foul, unearthly voice. "I can smell you, hiding like scared rabbits."

Selena was the first to stand. "Who are you?" she shouted. "Why have you attacked the sacred Temple of Valshara?" She stepped onto the path. The others quickly jumped up and followed. The knights stood at her side, while the others stayed close behind. Ertik had drawn a small dagger.

What she saw shocked and revolted her senses. Two soldiers stood in full chain mail, each one bearing a vicious-looking curved scimitar in one hand, and a rope attached to a bound and blindfolded elf in the other. Selena recognized the elves as being part of Theopolou's guard. They had been badly beaten, but there was no mistaking who they were. Standing in the center was a creature she had never seen. Even in the dim torchlight, she knew it wasn't human. Hunched over and swaying from side to side, it was wrapped in a long, flowing, black cloak, and wore heavy boots of leather and iron. Though its face was hidden behind the drawn hood, she could feel its eyes on her. It took a step forward and drew a long, jagged sword. The creature's movement was unimaginably quick and fluid. Jericho and the knights leaped in front of the High Lady.

"Stay back, demon," commanded the captain.

"The Vrykol bid you greetings, High Lady," said the creature. "You will come with us—or all of your companions will die."

"You will not lay your foul hands on the High Lady of Valshara," growled Jericho.

The Vrykol hissed a laugh. "Brave words, human. I think I'll kill you slowly."

"You will harm no one," said Selena. In a flash, she reached inside her sleeve and threw a small glass vial straight at the Vrykol's head. The sound of breaking glass was followed by another foul laugh.

"Holy water has no effect on me, foolish woman," said the Vrykol. "Your gods have no power in this world."

Selena smiled fiendishly as smoke began to rise from the Vrykol's hood. A second later, it burst into intense, blue flames. The two soldiers standing beside the Vrykol stepped quickly back as the creature desperately tried to beat out the flames, eating away at it. It was no use. The fire grew larger and hotter until the light was blinding. The creature dropped to its knees and let out a short series of unearthly screams. The sound caused Selena to wince and cover her ears. Then, abruptly, the noise stopped. The smoldering remains of the Vrykol crumbled to the ground.

The two human soldiers immediately dropped the ropes they were holding and ran off into the night. Jericho started after them, but Selena ordered him back.

"We can't waste time chasing them," said Selena. "We must move quickly."

They untied the elves and examined their wounds.

"You are Theopolou's guard, are you not?" asked Selena.

The elves nodded. "I am Stintos, and this is Haldrontis. We owe you our lives, High Lady."

Selena smiled. "We are happy to aid you. How did this happen?"

Stintos explained how they had been attacked by the Vrykol, and how Gewey and Linis had slain them. "We were to return to the temple until I was able to travel, but we were ambushed and held captive." Anger raged in his voice. "They tried to get us to turn spy, but I would not dishonor myself, or my kin, with treachery. They are devils. And they have elf allies. Now that we are free, I must get this information to Theopolou."

"He will be told," assured Selena. "But your wounds must be tended. We go to Althetas, and the two of you are coming with us. I will send word the moment we get there." Stintos opened his mouth to protest, but Selena shot him a stern look that told him there would be no argument.

"Can you travel?" asked Jericho.

"Yes." Haldrontis spoke with fierce determination. "And we will fight if need be."

Jericho turned to one of the knights. "Give him a dagger." The knight obeyed, while Jericho gave Stintos a dagger from his own belt. "I wish I could arm you better..."

"This will be fine," said Stintos. "An elf with a dagger is a thing to be feared."

The elves struggled to their feet.

"What was that thing?" asked Selena. "It called itself a Vrykol."

"I'm not certain," Haldrontis replied. "But they fight like they are possessed. And the only way I know to kill one is to remove its head." He glanced at the smoking corpse. "And it would seem they do not like fire either."

The entire group erupted into uneasy laughter.

"Let us go," said Selena, still chuckling. "It's many miles to Althetas."

Despite their injuries, the elves easily kept pace. By the time dawn pierced the darkness, they had traveled many miles. To everyone's relief, there was no sign of pursuit.

# CHAPTER 14

Several days had passed since Millet and Jacob had parted with Malstisos, Maybell, and the caravan. Once they arrived in Manisalia, Maybell discovered that the Oracle had fled more than a year before, and no one knew where she had gone.

Malstisos arranged for Maybell to have her own tent, and they purchased enough provisions to last the rest of their journey.

Though it was bitter cold, the blizzard had not reached the far west, and the roads were clear enough to allow travel after only a few days. The nights brought cheer and laughter as Maybell and Malstisos made friends among the merchants. Maybell instructed the men in manners, and the women in how to keep a man in his place. Soon she became viewed as a sort of caravan elder, settling disputes and advising the merchant leaders.

Malstisos spent a great deal of his time with Grentos and Vadnaltis, exchanging stories and news from their tribes. Maybell checked in on them from time to time, but her new-found duties kept her busy.

On the eighth night, Maybell was preparing for bed when Malstisos came to her tent. He looked worried and anxious.

"What is it?" asked Maybell.

Malstisos's lips pressed tight and his brow furled. "I fear my kinsmen are not what they seem."

Maybell's back stiffened. "How do you mean?"

Malstisos kneeled down near to the entrance of the tent and peered outside before speaking. "First of all, they are seekers."

Maybell looked confused. "Why is that odd?"

"Because seekers do not hide who they are," he explained. "And they have attempted to mask what they are from me."

"Is that all?" asked Maybell. "There could be any number of reasons for that."

"Perhaps," he agreed. "And if it were only that, I wouldn't be so concerned. Seekers can be an odd bunch, and the ways of my kin in the steppes are different. But these two have been probing me for information—the kind that can only be for one purpose. And they have underestimated me. I am not a seeker, but I am a worthy diplomat. Much more so than either of them. I know when I am being manipulated."

Maybell tensed. She knew how vulnerable they were. "What do they want to know?" she whispered, suddenly afraid that they were being spied on.

"The identity of allies who are hiding their sympathies, the location of Valshara and its strength—things of that nature." He fingered the knife on his belt. "The thing is, if they had asked me directly, I wouldn't have become suspicious. But they hide their questions behind other, seemingly innocent questions. Their poor attempt at subterfuge has made it clear to me that they are not what they seem."

"Should we run?"

Malstisos shook his head. "No. We are better off remaining with the caravan for now. I do not think the humans are aware of their deception, and I doubt my kinsmen will want to draw attention to themselves so far from home. If we run, we are vulnerable. They are seekers. They will hunt us down and kill us both."

Maybell's eyes brightened. "I know what to do." She stood and began to pace the tent. "We will be near Farmington in two days' time. I have friends there who will give us shelter. We should say that we need to pick up extra supplies, then take refuge."

"Good plan," said Malstisos, nodding in agreement. "It is unlikely they will openly attack us in a human village. Until then, behave normally. I will quietly gather what we can carry without being noticed."

"Good," said Maybell, satisfied. "Then if you'll excuse me. An old woman needs to sleep. Especially if we're going to be running for our lives in two days' time."

Malstisos bowed and left the tent. He took a deep breath and returned to the fire, where the humans were laughing and singing. He knew that he should join Grentos and Vadnaltis so as not to raise their suspicions, but he needed time before he could face them. The thought of being deceived by his kin caused his blood to boil, and if they were to escape, he needed them to believe he knew nothing. He just hoped that the place of refuge Maybell had in mind would be secure enough to stop two seekers.

After a couple of hours of socializing and singing with the merchants, Malstisos finally steeled his emotions sufficiently to join Grentos and Vadnaltis in their tent. The talk was light and cheerful, and for once they didn't try to gather any information from him. Around midnight, they all went to sleep, though Malstisos found it nearly unbearable to stay in the same tent as the treacherous seekers. He slept lightly and woke several times.

He decided he would find a reason to stay with Maybell in her tent the following night.

# CHAPTER 15

Salmitaya cursed as she slapped a horsefly stinging the back of her neck. Her plain wool dress was stained with mud and grime, and her brow was beaded with sweat. She was not accustomed to humid climates or the way she was now being forced to live.

For two weeks, she and Yanti had been in Baltria, and for two weeks she had worked for him as a slave. The home they stayed in was a modest, single-story dwelling, though well-decorated and comfortable. Located on the northern outskirts of the city, populated mostly by merchants and store owners, it had a decent yard and a small flower garden in the back—a garden well tended by her own backbreaking efforts.

There had been two servants at the house when they'd arrived, but Yanti promptly dismissed them both.

"You are all I need, my love," he'd told her in his melodic tone. "I wouldn't want you to feel useless."

He'd then made a list of her daily duties, though they changed from moment to moment on his whim. The first day had nearly killed her. She'd been forced to rearrange all of the furniture, tend the garden, prepare the meals, and then go to the market to pick up a week's worth of food and supplies. After she completed each task, Yanti would inspect her work.

"You must do better, my love," he would say. "Otherwise you will never leave my service."

Angrääl had forced her to give up her position and wealth and had indentured her to Yanti until he felt she had earned the right to regain her status. She had gone from a powerful High Priestess to a lowly servant overnight. At first, she had hoped it wouldn't be so bad, but it didn't take long to realize that despite Yanti's smooth and cultured demeanor, he was, in truth, a vicious and cruel monster.

She had attempted to escape during the very first week, only to be caught less than an hour into her flight. She still cringed at the thought of the beating he had given her, and at his promise that should she try to do the same thing again, then he would most certainly kill her—very slowly.

Today, her duties consisted mostly of scrubbing the house clean from a black mold that seemed to cover everything in Baltria. Yanti had commanded that she be finished by midday because he had other errands for her to run later on. She looked up. The sun was high in the sky, and she was still only halfway done. Her back ached and her hands were blistered from constant scrubbing.

"Taya, my love," called Yanti from behind her.

She jumped. Yanti moved silently and was constantly sneaking up on her. "Yes?" She tried to hide her hatred by averting her eyes.

"I need you to check the inns again. See if your friends have arrived yet." He turned and strode away. Just as he reached the corner of the house, he paused. "Later this evening, we'll discuss the fact that you weren't able to finish your work on time again. Perhaps we can find new ways to motivate you."

Salmitaya shuddered as she watched him disappear around the corner. She dusted herself off, put away the bucket and brush, and headed to the tavern district. The streets of Baltria were filthy by Kaltinor standards. Though well-paved and maintained, you could actually hear the mud and grime crunch beneath your feet. The city was situated in the very center of the largest delta in the world. The soil was rich and black, and the humid climate meant that the ground was wet for most of the time. It was nearly impossible not to track mud wherever you walked. Frequent rain helped to wash away the buildup before it could get out of hand, but it left a strong musty odor to which Salmitaya swore she could never grow accustomed.

The houses were mostly single-story, brick-and-mortar structures, even those owned by the nobles. However, as she drew closer to the docks, she began to notice the many houses and shops built on tall pylons in order to avoid the occasional extreme high tides.

One of the largest cities in the world, Baltria was known mostly for its massive ports and marketplaces that were as big as some towns. A colossal variety of goods were shipped both into and away from the Goodbranch River, and from there spreading to all points near and far.

Salmitaya despised the tavern district. Yanti had her coming here every two or three days to check the local gossip and pay his informants. At first, she feared she might be spotted by someone from the temples. Word of her betrayal had certainly traveled this far by now, and if she were caught, then she would be doomed to spend the rest of her life in a dark temple prison cell. However, it soon became clear that, in her present state of filth and dishevelment, no one was likely to recognize her. Twice before, she had seen sisters and brothers whom she had known quite well, but they simply walked right past without so much as a second glance. After that, she removed the mirrors from her room.

Snow would be falling at this time of year in Kaltinor, but here it was unbearably hot. Her heavy clothing made the heat feel like torture, and the humidity made the countless patches of filth on her skin cling like leeches.

"Taya," called the raspy, uncouth voice of Saul Milspend.

Salmitaya clenched her jaw and stepped up her pace. Saul was a fish merchant and one of Yanti's local informants. His bald head, short round frame, and smile that was missing several teeth caused her to recoil every time she saw the man. Worse, he was constantly trying to touch her on the hand or shoulder in a clumsy attempt at flirting.

"Taya!" he called out louder.

Salmitaya dropped her head and stopped. She could hear Saul's lumbering footsteps running up behind her.

Saul seized her by the shoulder. "I am glad I caught you."

Salmitaya recoiled. "What is it, Saul?" The stench of rotten fish caught in her nostrils.

"The innkeeper at the Malt and Mane said you should come by. He said to make sure you come through the back." He held out his hand and gave her a toothless smile.

Salmitaya reached into the small pouch that hung from her belt and gave him a copper. Saul tried to thank her, but she walked quickly away in the direction of the inn.

The streets were crowded with city dwellers and merchants, both local and foreign. Fashions from the farthest reach of the world could be seen everywhere. Salmitaya was particularly fond of the silk wraps and colorful dresses of the eastern desert, though every time she saw one, it reminded her painfully of her own poor appearance.

It took her the better part of an hour to wind her way through the city to the tavern district.

The Malt and Mane was typical of the many inns in Baltria. Not particularly nice, but not a flophouse either. Still, as a lady of culture and dignity, it was not a place she wanted to be. That she was instructed to enter from the rear was as much of an insult as she could bear, but she dare not ignore it. Yanti had intrigues everywhere and was constantly gathering information. Salmitaya reckoned he had dirt on every influential person in the city, and he made sure they knew it.

She was still thinking about this as she rounded the corner leading directly to the inn. Suddenly, she froze. Not twenty feet away stood Celandine. She was talking to a fruit merchant. Salmitaya immediately spun around and returned quickly the way she had come, pressing her back flat against the building on the corner.

Slowly, she peered around the edge of the building, taking care not to be seen. Celandine was wearing a tan linen dress rather than her novice robes, and her hair flowed loosely about her shoulders. Even so, there was no mistaking who it was. Salmitaya watched her until she entered the Malt and Mane, then sped off back to the house, unsure what she was going to tell Yanti.

By the time she reached the house, she was drenched in sweat and her legs were burning. She paused, composed herself, and entered. It took a moment for her eyes to adjust to the gloom. A small lamp in the living room to her right was the only source of light. Yanti sat cross-legged in a plush chair, dressed in a white cotton shirt and trousers, reading a small, leather-bound book. How he could see to read, Salmitaya couldn't imagine.

Yanti looked up and smiled, closing the book. "Well, my love." His voice was honey. "I see that you're back quickly. A bit too quickly."

Salmitaya tried to meet his eyes but couldn't. "I saw Celandine in front of the Malt and Mane."

"Celandine?" he remarked, raising an eyebrow.

"She was a novice..."

Yanti raised his hand, silencing her. "I know who she is." He rose from his chair. "Interesting choice."

"I don't understand," said Salmitaya. "You..."

Yanti shot her a glance and drew close. "My love, there is much I know that you don't. The sooner you accept that ... the easier your life will be." He reached out and held her chin, lifting her head to meet his gaze. "You should stay out of sight for the time being. I wouldn't want you to come to harm. At least, not yet."

She began to tremble. Whatever his plans were, she knew she was disposable to him. She needed to prove her value in order to stay alive. "Let me help you," she begged. "I can watch her without being seen."

"I am pleased with your enthusiasm," he replied, sounding almost sincere. "And I'm certain you could do a wonderful job. But I have enough eyes. No. I will restrict your movements to inside this house for the moment." He released her. "You should be happy. It will be a respite from your normal duties."

"Thank you," she said in her most submissive voice. Yanti laughed softly. "Get yourself cleaned and rested." Salmitaya bowed her head and turned to leave.

"I don't want you to worry," Yanti called after her. "I will have much for you to do, soon enough."

A chill ran down Salmitaya's spine. Tears welled in her eyes. Whatever he had in mind, she knew it wouldn't be good.

# CHAPTER 16

Dina entered the Malt and Mane carrying a basket of fresh strawberries. She let the scent fill her nostrils. As a child, her father would often take her into the forest to go strawberry picking. Most of the time, they would eat half of them before they even got home. Dina hadn't thought of this in many years, and a small smile crept across her face.

"You look far away," remarked Lee, sitting at the table next to the kitchen door.

The inn was typical of the area. There were two large common rooms, one on either side of the entrance. The room on the left was furnished with a dozen tables, each large enough to accommodate six people. The room on the right offered customers a bar on the far side, with tables scattered along all the walls; it also featured a raised platform in the middle for entertainment purposes. Just next to the bar were two doors, one leading to the kitchen, and the other to the guest rooms. Brass lamps hung from the ceiling, and two small fireplaces were in opposite corners.

Dina joined Lee at the table and handed him a strawberry, which he took gratefully. "I was just thinking about when I was a child," said Dina, still with a faraway look on her face.

"Is your father still alive?" asked Lee.

"No," she replied. "As you know, I'm older than I look. And I was very young when I found the Order."

"I'm sorry."

"It's fine," she said, shaking off her melancholy. "It's just that I haven't been home in a very long time. I'm still rather tired as well."

Lee and Dina had only just arrived the previous night. Their trip was uneventful, but their rapid pace had pushed her limits. Lee figured that Millet and his son would make their way to the Goodbranch River and sail down. That would certainly cut down on their travel time, and he had wanted to be sure of arriving ahead of them.

"Perhaps you should rest," Lee suggested.

"I think I will." Dina picked out a large strawberry. "But not before I enjoy a few of these." She popped the fruit into her mouth and sighed with pleasure as she bit down.

"Good," said Lee. "In the meantime, I'll check with my contacts here. I should like to get the feel of things."

Dina nodded in agreement. "I can check the temples this evening," she said, still chewing.

"I don't want you going off by yourself. I'm certain there are agents of the north about. Probably informants among the locals as well."

"How would they know who we are, or what we're doing?" she asked, swallowing the remains of the berry.

Lee lowered his voice to a whisper. "They knew about us from the moment we left Sharpstone. And we were followed, at least for a time, out of Valshara. Clearly, they have a more efficient system for gathering intelligence than we do." He scowled. "I intend to change that situation."

"How do you plan to do that?" She picked up another strawberry.

"I am very wealthy, my dear," he stated. "And so are many of the people we have met, such as Lord Broin and Lord Ganflin. Information is nothing more than a commodity. If you have the coin, it's yours."

"But won't the informants have already been bought?"

"Almost certainly," he affirmed, smiling. "But the one dependable thing about scum is that they will always serve as many masters as can pay. But I won't be contacting the street dregs directly. I have friends among the nobility. I'll make my inquiries through them."

Dina furrowed her brow. "And what happens if your friends have been bought as well—or worse, joined our enemies?"

He shrugged. "Then that will tell me what I need to know. But I doubt they'd betray me openly. Most know me from my days studying under local sword masters. I had a reputation as a very skilled swordsman." He chuckled and shook his head. "The nobles aren't what you would call courageous, at least, not in the way a soldier is courageous. They wouldn't risk my wrath unless they were certain they could get away with it."

Dina recalled watching Lee battle the elf seeker, Berathis. "I don't imagine any of them would want to upset you."

Lee grinned fiendishly. "Not unless they want me to pay them more than a social call. But I know one lord I can trust. I saved his life."

"Really, how?"

"He made the mistake of drinking and gambling at the wrong tavern," Lee replied. "And he tends to flash his money when he's had too much wine. Not something you want to do in Baltria after dark. I stopped three thieves from killing him for his foolishness."

"Well, I certainly hope that would buy you a bit of loyalty," said Dina. She yawned and blinked her eyes. "And on that note, I need to rest for a bit. Wake me before sunset."

Lee nodded. "Just don't leave here until I return."

"And you remember that you are not invulnerable," she said as she got up from her seat, making sure not to forget her remaining strawberries.

Lee laughed, sprung up, and snatched a berry for himself. "I'll be fine." He made his way to the door and ventured out into the city streets.

The sun was still high in the sky, and the heat reminded Lee of how far removed from Sharpstone he was. He had sent a messenger to his friend early that morning, asking that they meet near the docks. He couldn't risk being noticed. Dina was right to think that the nobility could have been bought off. Their entire world revolved around the acquisition of wealth; in some ways, they were no better than bandits. Then there was the real possibility that they had sided with Angrääl, which would be worse still. Bought loyalty could be changed, but a true believer...

It wasn't long before the houses transitioned from typical Baltria dwellings into the structures that had been built on tall pylons. Lee had been in the city during a particularly bad flood year when the water had risen sufficiently to cover even the high porches. He'd wondered why the entire city hadn't been drowned but then discovered that Baltria was equipped with a system of drains and manual pumps that could be used to keep the majority of the city reasonably dry.

The mold stench of the docks filled the air as Lee neared. Sailors in brightly colored shirts and hats stumbled drunkenly through the streets, while merchants enthusiastically shouted their wares to passers-by. It wasn't long before he could see the tall masts of the ships peeking over the rooftops, and hear the sounds of orders being barked and bells ringing. A minute or so later, the massive dock came into view. It stretched out from east to west as far as the eye could see. When he had first come here, many years ago, there had been hundreds of ships coming and going, loading and unloading. But now there were less than fifty ships in all.

He frowned. *The dark times have struck everywhere.*

The Plank Walker's Café, where he was to meet his friend, was located only a few yards from the docks. Mostly patronized by officers and merchants, Lee knew the place well. It boasted the best seafood stew in the known world, a claim well supported by popular opinion. Lee had once tried to get the owner to give him the recipe but to no avail.

Lee climbed the stairs to the deck where a short, plump, young woman greeted him. She smiled warmly and showed Lee to a table.

"And what'll you be havin' today, sir?" she asked cheerfully, with a thick Baltrian accent.

"Seafood stew, of course," Lee replied.

"Right away." She spun around, heading for the kitchen.

A few moments later, a young, dark-haired boy brought him some bread and a bottle of wine.

"Careful, Starfinder," said a voice from the steps. "That isn't weak northern wine you're drinking."

"Lanson Brimm." Lee laughed. "I don't think it's my drinking that needs to be monitored."

Lanson was a tall, slender, middle-aged man. His fine, sandy blond hair blew carelessly in the sea breeze. He wore a blue cotton shirt and trousers with white silk embroidery. A silver-handled short sword hung from his black leather belt.

Lee stood and embraced the man tightly. "It's good to see you." He offered him a chair. "Are you eating?"

"I'm sorry, my friend," said Lanson. "I must leave you soon. Frankly, I was surprised to receive your invitation."

"Why is that?" asked Lee.

Lanson shook his head and wagged his finger. "You've made some powerful enemies. Every noble in the city has been paid for information on you, and the gods only know how many street vermin are on the lookout."

Lee straightened. "Paid by whom?"

"Don't be naïve, Starfinder." He reached over and took a piece of bread. "The ambassador from Angrääl started making inquiries months ago."

"Ambassador?" Lee exclaimed. "In Baltria?"

"I'm afraid so," said Lanson. "He and his attendants have set up residence inside the governor's mansion."

Lee suddenly felt exposed. "The King allowed that?"

"Allowed?" laughed Lanson. "He gave it to him."

"And the governor?" Lee asked.

"He moved into his own private home, claiming it was his decision." He bit off a piece of bread. "I personally think the man is no longer running the city in any capacity."

"Why would you think that?" asked Lee.

Lanson shrugged. "Because crime is down, and in spite of the empty docks, profits have never been better. Governor Greenly is a moron. He couldn't even manage the city in good times. If he wasn't the King's nephew, he would never have been appointed in the first place. No, Angrääl is in charge around here. They're pumping gold on top of gold into the economy."

Lee was appalled. "So you want them here?"

Lanson nodded indifferently. "Sure. They're good for the city. So long as they don't send an army our way, I don't mind." He could see Lee's apprehension. "Don't worry. I'm not one of the faithful. Those people are lunatics."

"The faithful?" said Lee. "What in the name of Dantenos are the faithful?"

Lanson cocked his head. "You have been gone a long time, old friend. The faithful follow The Reborn King of Angrääl. They claim he's the reincarnation of King Rätsterfel, and spend most of their time causing trouble for the temples. Lately, it's become fashionable to become one of them if you're nobility. But if you ask me, it's a bunch of hogwash.

None of them really believe it. They just like the idea of their purses getting ever fatter."

"What are the temples doing to stop them?" asked Lee.

"What can they do?" Lanson replied. "King Talminian doesn't seem to care what the faithful do, just so long as the gold keeps flowing into his coffers. As for me—I have found it wise to stay out of it."

"Talminian has always been a fool," Lee grumbled. "And weak."

"Dangerous words," said Lanson. "But as you're already in danger, I suppose it doesn't matter. Speaking of which…"

He reached in his pocket, pulled out a small key, and pushed it across the table. "I assume you'll not heed my words and leave the city at once. So, in that case, you remember my rental house?"

Lee nodded.

"It's vacant," continued Lanson. "I want you to hole up there until your business here is finished. Which brings me to the next question. What is it you need me to do?"

"I need you to tell me when Millet arrives in Baltria," he answered. "And if I'm found out, give me warning."

"You didn't drag poor Millet into your adventures again, did you?" he scolded. "But I already know the answer to that, don't I? Even if you tried to leave him behind, he wouldn't let you."

Both men burst into laughter. Just then, the server arrived with Lee's meal. Lanson stood from the table. "I must leave you to eat alone, I'm afraid. I'll make inquiries regarding Millet. But please, stay out of sight. The gods only know what will happen if you're discovered."

Lee smiled warmly. "I'll be careful, my friend."

Lanson twisted his mouth and shook his head. "I doubt that very much. But at least I can say that I warned you."

Lee watched as Lanson turned and walked away. Alone, he felt even more exposed. He ate quickly and headed back to the inn. His paranoia grew with each step. He knew he couldn't leave the city until Millet and Jacob arrived, but should the servants of the Dark One realize his presence, that could get them all killed. He briefly considered sending Dina away but dismissed the idea. If they were aware of him, they would most likely be aware of her as well. She would need his protection.

When he arrived at the inn, Dina was still in her room, sleeping. Lee regretted waking her, but considering what Lanson had told him, he felt he had no choice. She came to the door, yawning and wrapped in a blanket.

"Get your things together and meet me in the common room," Lee ordered.

Before Dina could ask questions, Lee moved off down the hall to his own room and began packing his gear. Twenty minutes later, they were both in the common room. Lee had the horses brought from the stables and walked with Dina to the door.

"What's going on, Lee?" she asked.

He recounted his conversation with Lanson as they secured their gear onto their mounts. "At least your friend didn't betray you," said Dina.

Lee nodded. "He's a good man. But I still hate that he goes along with what's happening here."

Dina mounted her horse. "What would you have him do? Besides, from what you said, Angräal isn't acting aggressively. He has no reason to suspect their true intentions."

"That's just it," Lee countered. "They're not a bunch of uneducated fools. They know what's going on. Some even welcome it. So long as they stay rich, they'll go along with anything."

"But you thought that might be the case," said Dina. "Why are you so angry?"

"I'm angry because we have been lazy," said Lee. "We've allowed The Dark One to spread his lies unchallenged. Now, who knows if he can be dislodged? He'll conquer the world one city at a time before even one battle is fought."

"What can we do?"

"We can play his game better. The moment I've secured Millet and my son, Valshara must be told what is happening here. In fact, when you visit the temples tonight, I'll have you send a message to Althetas."

They wound their way through the streets to Lanson's rental house. Lee remembered Lanson using it to rendezvous with his mistresses in years past. The man had had a bit of a wild side and a reputation with the ladies. But it seemed his friend must have settled down these days if he was now renting the house out. It was a modest, single-story dwelling, typical of the merchant class. Its solid brick walls and tan tile roof were well-built and suited for the climate. The yard was small but well-kept, and a wrought iron fence surrounded the property.

Lee led them to the rear of the house and put the horses in a small stable at the back. They entered through the back door and he set about lighting lamps. The interior was well-decorated and deceptively spacious. The main living room was equipped with a small fireplace, a plush suede couch, and two matching chairs. With the local hot climate usually preventing any need for a fire, the fireplace was more for decoration than anything else. Elsewhere in the house, the three bedrooms were each big enough to accommodate a married couple comfortably, and the beds had thick, goose down mattresses.

There was a bathing room that had running water and a tub heated by coals placed in a compartment beneath its base. Lee and Dina each picked a bedroom and washed and changed in turn. Once dressed, they relaxed in the living room.

"I'll go out later for food and drink," said Lee. "There's an eatery a few blocks from here that serves wonderful mince pies."

Dina smiled, trying to hide her apprehension. "I should go with you," she said. "I don't think I like the idea of either of us venturing out alone."

Lee nodded. "I'll walk you to the temple and we'll pick something up on the way back."

There was a knock at the door. Lee drew his dagger and peered out of the window. Lanson stood uneasily outside. Lee opened and let him in.

"I see you're prepared," said Lanson, glancing at the dagger. "Good."

"Has something happened?" asked Lee.

Lanson eyed Dina. "Such matters can wait until after we've made proper introductions." Dina smiled and got to her feet.

"Lanson," said Lee. "This is my dear friend Celandine..."

He paused and looked at Dina, embarrassed. "I'm afraid I don't know your last name."

"Such things have not come up," Dina replied. "Lord Lanson Brimm I presume." She curtsied, elegantly. "I am Celandine Selborne."

Lanson took her hand and kissed it lightly. "My dear, it is an honor." He tilted his head. "Do I detect a Baltrian accent?"

"I lived here in my youth," she said. "That is to say, when I was a little girl."

"Indeed," said Lanson. "Well, our city has certainly missed your beauty."

Lee slapped him on the shoulder. "And here I was thinking that you've settled down."

"Me?" Lanson smiled mischievously. "Never." He made his way to the couch and sat down while Lee and Dina took the chairs. "I thought you might want to know that I was told to be on the lookout for you just after we parted company."

"By whom?" asked Lee, leaning forward.

"One of those blasted faithful," he replied. "I think they must know you're in the city. And it's no secret that we are friends."

"Isn't it dangerous for you to come here?" asked Dina.

Lanson smiled. "It will be after today. I had only walked a few blocks from the cafe before they stopped me. I'm afraid I can't risk returning here until you've left Baltria."

"Did anyone see us together?" asked Lee.

"I don't think so," said Lanson. "I followed them after they spoke to me, and they gave me no indication that they knew anything. They spoke to three other nobles, then went to the governor's mansion." He held up his hand. "And before you ask, I wasn't followed."

"We should leave," said Dina. "I wouldn't want to put you in danger."

"My dear," Lanson replied. "I may not be the hero that Lee is. But I do not abandon a friend—especially one who has saved my life. Besides, no one will think to look here, even if they suspect me of helping you. As far as anyone knows, this house is still occupied. The last tenants only moved away a week ago." His face was grim with resolve. "I'm having food and supplies brought for you within the hour."

"We had planned to visit the temples," said Dina.

"Don't," Lanson objected. "All the temples are being watched by the faithful. They like to know who comes and goes. There's no way for you to enter unnoticed."

Dina crossed her arms in disappointment.

"How will you communicate with us?" asked Lee.

"Do you remember my servant Jansi?"

Lee nodded.

"He'll bring you any word of Millet." Lanson stood up. "I wish I could say I'll see you soon but..."

Lee and Dina got to their feet. Lee embraced Lanson tightly. "Thank you," he said, smiling. "I think we're even now."

Lanson laughed and turned to Dina. "My dear, I only wish I could behold your loveliness once more—but alas."

Dina kissed Lanson's cheek. "Thank you for your kindness."

Lanson put his hand over his heart and walked to the door. He turned just before he crossed the threshold. "I know you were upset by my attitude regarding Angrääl. But I think that attitude is changing." He bowed and left.

Soon after his departure, a young boy showed up with a wagonload of food, wine, and other essentials. Dina and Lee busied themselves by putting things away, then prepared the evening meal. Dina tried to convince Lee they should attempt to get into the temples, despite Lanson's warning, but Lee wouldn't allow it.

That night Lee slept in one of the chairs in the living room, his sword across his lap.

# CHAPTER 17

Millet and Jacob disembarked from the river craft. The heat in Baltria was causing no small amount of discomfort, and both were sweating profusely.

"I'll never understand how people live in this wretched heat," said Jacob.

Millet had never been around anyone so contrary and bad tempered in his life. Even though he'd tried to be understanding over the boy's situation—that his mother was in captivity, and that his entire life had been stripped away from him—Millet still couldn't help but be irritated by his behavior. On more than one occasion, he marveled at how this ill-mannered youth could possibly be the son of Lee Nal'Thain.

"You had better be grateful that they do," remarked Millet. "Most trade goods in Hazrah arrive through here. Without Baltria and its port, most of the world would starve."

"Hazrah is starving," snapped Jacob.

Just for once, Millet felt as Jacob did. The thought of Hazrah's people suffering caused anger to swell inside him. He quickly changed the subject. "You said you have friends here?"

"Yes," Jacob replied. "But I'll need to visit them alone. They do not enjoy meeting new people."

"I assure you that I can fit in," said Millet. He didn't like the idea of Jacob venturing into Baltria alone. "I know this city very well. I think you'd be better off..."

"I said I'm going alone," he growled. "Besides, don't you need to find my father?" The word 'father' dripped with hatred.

"Your father will find us," said Millet. "You can count on that."

"If you say so." Jacob shrugged, trying to appear indifferent. "I don't care. You wait for him, and I'll do what I have to do."

Millet led them through the city into the tavern district, and then directly to the Green Barnacle Inn. He knew that Lee had stayed at the Green Barnacle for a month when they'd first come to Baltria many years ago, and he would often return there to see the jugglers or musicians and relax. Lee had always enjoyed less sophisticated company. Millet also considered the Malt and Mane, another of Lee's old haunts, but Millet had never cared much for the place. If Lee were staying there instead, he would know to look out for them at the Green Barnacle too.

Millet was carrying a considerable amount of money on him. He had plenty left over from the trip, and more still from the sale of their horses. His clothes were dirty and worn from travel, so he decided to spend out on some new attire after they had checked in. He smiled, thinking of the many trips and hardships he had endured in his travels with Lee, and, despite the boy's ill temper, he was pleased to have had this experience with his son.

Millet and Jacob stowed their belongings in their rooms and then took time to eat a modest meal of roast pork and wine. As they ate, Millet remembered the seafood stew at the Plank Walker's Cafe and began to regret filling his stomach. If Lee were already in Baltria, he would have made that place one of his first stops.

Once he was finished, Jacob stood from the table and moved toward the door. "When should I expect you to return?" asked Millet.

"When my business is done," he shot back, without turning around. With that, he left.

Millet spent the next few hours wandering the city, buying the new set of clothes he had promised himself, plus a few other odds and ends. Once finished, he had a messenger deliver his goods to the inn and headed off to the Malt and Mane.

As he sat listening to a bard spin a tale to the music of a lute, he scanned the common room for signs of Lee. Disappointingly, there were none. He knew there was the possibility that he had arrived ahead of his master; the river was swift, and the vessel had only made two stops before arriving in Baltria, and those had only been for a brief time to offload a small portion of their cargo and take on fresh water.

Just as he was about to give up and head back, the barmaid handed him a folded slip of parchment. He glanced around, but couldn't see anything out of the ordinary. Slowly, he opened the paper. Meet me for the best seafood stew you've ever tasted. There was no signature.

Millet left the inn and made his way to The Plank Walker's Café. Once there, he scanned the dining area for a familiar face but could see none. He took a table near the edge of the deck so that he could see people as they approached and ordered a bowl of seafood stew.

After a few minutes had passed by, a tall, slender man with dark, shoulder-length curls that fell about his shoulders approached Millet's table. His sharp, angular features and soft, white cotton outfit spoke of wealth and breeding. A small dagger sheathed in a jeweled scabbard hung from his belt, and he was carrying a bottle of wine and two glasses.

"Millet, I presume," said the man. His voice was deep and masculine, yet smooth and pleasing. "May I join you?"

Millet tensed but held out his hand, motioning for him to sit. "And you are?"

"You may call me Yanti," he replied, bowing his head. "It was I who sent you the note at the Malt and Mane."

"How do you know me?" Millet shifted in his seat.

Yanti smiled. "My good man. I'm the enemy, so to speak."

Millet started to rise.

"Don't fret," said Yanti. "You are in no danger just yet. But that could change should you leave before I've had a conversation with you."

Millet slowly sat back down. "What do you want?"

"From you, nothing," said Yanti. "From Lord Starfinder, however—from him I want a great deal."

"You waste your breath, Yanti," said Millet. "I have no idea where he is. And even if I did, I would not tell you."

Yanti covered his mouth, laughing quietly. "My good man. I would not presume to think you would betray your master. No. I only want to convey my deepest respect and admiration in the hope that we can come to an agreement."

Millet's face hardened. "If you think Lee Starfinder will come to terms with you, or any servant of the Dark One, you're mistaken."

"That may be," said Yanti. "But I would have you deliver my message, nonetheless. And to show you my goodwill, I will make no move against you, or his son—Jacob, I believe his name is."

His final words sent a chill down Millet's spine. "If I were you, I would leave Lord Starfinder and his family alone."

"I know how formidable Starfinder is," Yanti responded with a tinge of amusement. "But rest assured, I mean his family no harm. In fact, I wish to reunite them if only he can be reasonable."

"Then deliver your message and be gone," said Millet, his fear turning into anger.

Yanti laughed softly, unimpressed with Millet's display. "Simply tell him that, should he decide that his wife and son are more important to him than a race of gods that has long since abandoned this world, he can leave this conflict behind. We promise to allow him and his family to live in peace. They can even return to his home in Hazrah, if that's what he would like. In fact, we can ensure that his remaining years are quite rewarding."

"Is that all?" asked Millet.

"One more thing," Yanti continued. "Should he consider an unwise course, remind him that his wife resides in the court of the Reborn King."

"I will see to it that he receives your message," said Millet. He tossed a couple of coppers on the table and rose to his feet. "You'll pardon me. I've lost my appetite."

Yanti smiled and nodded. "It was a pleasure."

Millet's face was stone as he turned and headed back toward the inn.

Yanti watched him disappear into the distance. He waved for the serving girl to bring more wine. As he waited for this to come, Salmitaya walked up and took a seat.

"Did it go as you hoped?" she asked.

"It went as I expected," Yanti replied. "And I expect you to do your part as instructed, my love."

"You can depend on me, My Lord," she replied.

"Considering the dangers involved, you seem remarkably at ease. You aren't thinking about betrayal, are you?" His eyes darkened.

"I will do exactly as you have told me," she said. "You have no need to worry about my loyalty to you or my commitment to our cause."

"That's good to hear. I would hate to think of you sharing the fate of Lord Starfinder."

"What fate is that?" she asked.

Yanti flashed an angry look. "You know perfectly well not to ask such questions."

Salmitaya lowered her eyes.

# CHAPTER 18

**M**illet struggled not to break into a dead run. His conversation with Yanti unnerved him to the core. All of their attempts to go unnoticed had failed. It seemed that no matter where they went, The Dark One wasn't far behind. In fact, most of the time, it was as if he were ahead of them—waiting.

He was hoping to find Jacob already back at the inn but was disappointed to find that the boy had not yet returned. Millet decided there was nothing he could do but hope Lee would contact him soon. He sat in the common room, staring at the door, waiting for Jacob's return. If this Yanti fellow was as smart as he suspected, he was unlikely to make a move on Jacob until he'd first of all found Lee. And so far, it seemed as if he hadn't managed to do this. Or, if Yanti had, he obviously didn't want Millet to know about it. But Millet couldn't think of any reason at all why Yanti would bother pretending such a thing in view of the message he was asking him to deliver.

The door opened, and Millet straightened, hoping to see Jacob. Instead, he saw another familiar face. It was Jansi, long-time servant of Lord Lanson Brimm. Jansi scanned the room until he spotted Millet, then strode over to the table.

Jansi was of medium build and average height, with pale skin and short-cropped gray hair. He wore a light green cotton shirt and trousers. Millet noticed how much he had aged since he had last seen him. He stood up, smiling, and embraced the man warmly.

"It is certainly good to see you, Jansi."

"And you, Millet," Jansi replied. "Though I wish it were in more pleasant circumstances."

"Then you know what I'm doing in Baltria?" asked Millet, trying to hide his anxiety.

"My Lord filled me in," he said. "At least to the extent I need to know. He wants you informed that Lord Starfinder is in Baltria. He and a young woman named Celandine are staying at his property near the merchant district."

Millet nodded. He was familiar with the house. "I require your help. My presence is known to our enemies. I was approached by an agent of Angräal earlier, and they know where and who I am."

Jansi's eyes widened. "Do they know where Lord Starfinder is?" he asked.

"No," replied Millet. "At least he didn't seem to. He asked me to give him a message when I find him."

"Good." Jansi sighed. "It would not do for Lord Lanson to get mixed up with those people."

Millet looked confused. "What people?"

Jansi lowered his voice. "The ones from Angräal. They're everywhere these days—you didn't know?"

Millet shook his head. "I have only just arrived in the city."

"I see." He took a deep breath and proceeded to inform Millet about the faithful and the Angräal ambassador, along with recent events regarding the assaults on the temples.

Millet was dumbfounded. "You must take me to Lord Starfinder. But I must get there without being seen."

"I have a carriage waiting just outside," said Jansi. "If you leave through the kitchen, you can get to it through the alley. I'll meet you there."

Millet nodded and got to his feet. "I'll be there in a moment."

As soon as Jansi had departed, he made his way to the kitchen. He slipped the innkeeper a gold coin and instructed him to tell anyone who might ask that he was feeling unwell and had retired to his room. Also, to tell Jacob on his return to stay there and wait for him.

He was relieved to find no one at the rear entrance as he made his way around the back of the inn and then along the alleyway. He could see the carriage. Jansi was in the driver's seat and the door was open. Millet raced inside and slammed the door shut.

Jansi expertly navigated the streets until they reached their destination. The sun was sinking over the horizon when Millet looked out of the windows for signs of pursuit. To his great relief, only a few people were about, and none seemed to be taking any notice of them. He jumped from the carriage and moved rapidly to the front entrance.

Lee opened the door just as Millet was about to knock. He pulled him inside. Jansi quickly followed.

Lee embraced Millet so tightly he could hardly breathe. "It's so good to see you, my old friend."

"It's good to see you too, My Lord," Millet grunted through the embrace.

Lee released him and together they walked to the living room. Dina awaited them on the couch, a cup of wine in her hand. She was wearing her wool traveling clothes. When she saw Millet, she sprang from her seat and flung her arms around him.

"I knew you'd make it," she said.

"Indeed," said Millet, smiling. "And I'm pleased your trip was uneventful."

"We moved too quickly to have any adventures." Dina laughed. "People scarcely knew we had passed."

Millet's face turned grave. "They know now, I'm afraid."

"Sit," said Lee. "We can tell our tales later. First, I must know where my son is."

Millet and Dina took their seats, Millet just beside Lee. Jansi excused himself and went outside to the carriage.

"Your son is safe," said Millet. "By now he's probably back at the inn. But now that I've found you, we should leave the city immediately." He recounted the conversation with Yanti.

Lee lowered his head, deep in thought. "I want you to take Jacob to Dantary in the eastern desert," he said finally. "He'll be safe there."

"That might be a problem, My Lord," replied Millet.

"Why is that?" asked Lee.

Millet took a deep breath before he spoke. "Your son is a bit ... stubborn. I don't think you will be able to talk him into leaving. He's quite determined to rescue his mother."

Lee nodded with understanding. His suppositions about his wife's temporary safety and the boy's intentions had both been proved correct. And he knew full well what Millet meant by Jacob being stubborn.

"Then I'll have to convince him," he said. "I'm sure he holds no love for me, but I'll not have him die needlessly."

Lee got to his feet. "If this Yanti person knows you're here, he may very well know where I am, too. If so, it's likely he's waiting until we're all in the same place at the same time before striking." He walked to the window and peered out.

"If that's the case," said Dina. "We should split up and leave the city in different directions."

Lee shook his head. "I'll not let any of you out of my sight." There was no hint of compromise in his tone. His hand slid to the hilt of his sword, his knuckles white. "If the Dark One thinks I'll bend to his will, then he's a bigger fool than I thought. And as for this Yanti—if he's stupid enough to hinder us, I'll make him regret the day he was born."

"What about these people who call themselves the faithful?" asked Millet. "Even you cannot fight a hundred men at once."

"We'll move with speed," said Lee. "We won't give them a chance to do anything about it. It takes time to organize enough men to stop the likes of me, and if Yanti has the same intelligence as Harlando, then he'll know what I am."

"But what if he's like you," said Dina. "You know, a half-man."

Lee flashed an evil grin. "Then I'll kill him first and slaughter his followers last. It's more than my blood that makes me formidable. I have trained under the greatest warriors the world has ever known. Unless he has done likewise, it is he that should fear me."

"Still, it may not be so easy to convince Jacob to leave Baltria," said Millet. "His dislike for you is quite strong. I think we should overcome that obstacle first, don't you?"

"No doubt," Lee agreed. "Go back to the inn and bring him here. If you're not back within an hour, I'll know something is wrong."

"You don't mean to send Millet out alone, do you?" Dina protested.

"If they wanted to harm Millet, they would have already done so," said Lee. "No. It's me they want." He turned to Millet. "Still, be careful all the same."

Millet nodded and left. The streets were busy, and it took Jansi nearly twenty minutes to get back to the inn. Millet didn't bother trying to hide his presence. *If they see me, they see me*, he thought. As soon as he was inside, he spotted Jacob sitting at a long table. The boy was playing dice with two other patrons and draining a large jug of wine. Millet walked straight up to him and pulled him by the arm.

"What do you think you're doing?" Jacob protested.

"We need to leave," said Millet as quietly as he could manage. "Now."

Jacob pulled himself free from Millet's grasp. "Let me go, old man," he bellowed. "I've only just arrived. And I've yet to have my fill."

Millet leaned down and whispered into the boy's ear. "You will have your fill when agents from Angrääl get here. Now get up and gather your things."

Jacob glared at Millet but eventually relented. "I'm sorry, fellows," he announced. "I must be off." Jeers and boos sounded as he rose to his feet and followed Millet to their rooms.

"There's a carriage out front," said Millet when they stood at Jacob's door. "Meet me there."

"Wait," said Jacob, catching Millet's wrist. "Where are we going?"

Millet twisted himself loose and simply said, "Where it is safe." He turned and entered his own room.

Minutes later, he waited at the carriage. Jacob followed shortly after carrying his gear and looking none too happy. Millet opened the door, and the boy entered, tossing his pack carelessly aside.

"Now tell me what's going on," Jacob demanded once they were underway.

Millet explained his encounter with Yanti but said nothing of the message the man wanted passed on to Lee.

Jacob's face twisted. "I take it you plan for us to run like cowards?"

Millet remained silent. He didn't want to mention Lee until they arrived at Lanson's house.

"Well?" pressed Jacob. "Is that it, or not?" He sniffed with disgust. "I'm not running. I'm not finished with my business, so you should let me out right here."

Millet sighed. "If you're worried that your mother will be left in the hands of the Dark One, let me assure you, she will not be."

"What? Are you going to rescue her? You joke, of course."

Realization then washed over Jacob's face. "Oh, I see now. My father—that's where we're going. You've found him and thought to bring me to him without my knowledge. And I suppose he intends to save her."

Millet's mouth tightened. "He has not told me what he is planning. But I would wager that is part of his plan."

"Don't worry, old man." Jacob laughed. "I'll speak to the dog. But don't think that this will change anything."

"I wouldn't presume," Millet muttered.

Lee was waiting at the door when the carriage arrived. Millet could see the nervousness in Lee's posture as he shifted uncharacteristically from side to side.

Jacob leaped from the carriage first, striding straight past his father and into the house without so much as a word. Millet shrugged at Lee and helped Jansi with the gear. Lee went inside and found that Jacob had already taken a seat in the living room. Dina was on the couch, her eyes moving from Lee to Jacob. Lee dragged the other chair directly in front of the boy and sat down. Millet put the packs and other gear near the door and asked Jansi to wait outside.

"So you're Lee Nal'Thain," said Jacob. "I hope you're not expecting a warm reunion."

Lee rubbed his hands together. "I know you must not think much of me," he began.

"I don't think about you at all, father," said Jacob, anger seeping into his voice. "As far as I'm concerned I have no reason to think anything—or feel anything either."

Lee lowered his eyes. "I truly am sorry for what I had to do. But please understand, it had to be this way. I was trying to protect you and your mother."

"Good job," he spat. "I've been forced to leave my home, and my mother is imprisoned in Angrääl. We're so lucky you were watching out for us."

"You may not believe this, son," said Lee. "But if I had stayed, things would have been much worse. The Dark Knight would already have what he wants, and he'd have no further need to keep you or your mother alive."

"And just what does he want?" Jacob leaned back in his chair. "What is it that is more important than your family? I would really like to know."

"I can't tell you," Lee replied. "At least, not yet. But know that it was the only thing that could force me to make such a choice. And know that you and your mother never left my thoughts—not for a minute."

Jacob's mouth tightened. "I see. You abandon your family, start a new life, and when I ask you why, you can't tell me? I listened to my mother cry herself to sleep for years, and you can't tell me why? I watched as my home was invaded and my people murdered, and you can't tell me why?"

"I'm sorry," said Lee. "I will tell you soon. I promise."

"Keep your promises," he growled. "I don't need them— or you." He moved to get up, but Lee caught his shoulder.

"You do need me," said Lee sternly. "That is ... if you expect to free your mother."

Jacob tried to free himself from Lee's grasp, but Lee held him firmly. "I know you think you can find a way to do this alone," Lee continued. "But you can't."

Jacob ceased resisting and reluctantly sat back down. "And you can? Just because you have the blood of Saraf coursing through your veins, you think you can take on the armies of Angrääl by yourself? At least I did not inherit your stupidity."

"You have a plan then?" Lee asked.

Jacob hesitated. "No. But I'm forming one. I have friends in the city, and I've already contacted some of them."

"Then you've almost certainly let the agents of Angräal know that you plan to save your mother," said Lee. "They have eyes and ears everywhere in Baltria. Even among the nobility."

"Then what do you think you can do?" asked Jacob.

"First, I can keep you safe. I want to you go with Millet to the oasis of Dantary."

This time, Lee was unable to stop Jacob from rising. "You don't tell me what to do," his son shouted. "I'll not be shipped off to the desert."

Lee heaved a sigh. "I need to know that you're safe if I'm to save your mother. As long as you're in danger, I can't focus on what needs to be done. I must protect you first."

"It's too late to start trying to protect me now," said Jacob. "And forgive me if I don't trust that you'll follow through with anything you promise. No. I think I'll do things my own way."

"Listen to me," said Lee. His tone was dark and intimidating. "If you ever want to see your mother alive again, you'll forget your hatred for me and do as I tell you."

Jacob opened his mouth to speak, but no words came.

"If I may, My Lord," interjected Millet. Lee nodded his approval. "Jacob, let me take you to Dantary. I promise that I will reveal everything once we get there. I have been with your father through it all. There is nothing he could tell you that I don't already know."

"And if I fail," Lee added. "Then you are free to do as you will."

Jacob glared at Lee, then at Millet. "I'll do as you ask. But know that if you fail, I will kill you."

"If I fail," Lee replied. "I will be dead already." He held out his hand, but Jacob turned his back.

"I need to check my gear," Jacob said and walked toward the front door.

Millet placed his hand on Lee's shoulder. "I'll watch over him. I swear it."

Lee bowed his head. "I don't blame him for hating me. I hate myself for leaving him."

"You did what you had to do," said Millet. "You did not choose this."

Lee pretended not to hear. "Do you have mounts?" he asked.

"No, my lord," Millet replied. "We sold them."

Lee reached into his pouch, retrieved several gold coins, and handed them to Millet. "Have Jansi purchase horses and saddles for you and Jacob."

He began to walk toward his room. "We leave as soon as he returns."

# CHAPTER 19

Maybell had inconspicuously made ready their gear for a quick getaway—they would be in Farmington in less than an hour. Meanwhile, she was doing her best to remain calm. She had spoken to Malstisos several times about their exact route and timetable, but she knew how dangerous the two other elves could be. One mistake might cost both of them their lives. Right now, Malstisos was out scouting the surrounding area with Grentos and Vadnaltis. Maybell feared that the seeker elves would suspect that they were on to them, but so far, they had shown no indication of knowing this.

She was riding in a wagon with the family of a silver merchant from Althetas. Both her and Malstisos's horses had been tied to the rear. She passed the time by playing a card game with the merchant's wife, Lilly, and their two children—Anna, who was six years old, and Beth, who had just turned eight.

They were among her favorite people in the caravan. Lilly was kind and cheerful, and in spite of a life spent traveling and raising two children, she was always well-groomed. Maybell enjoyed spending time in their tent when they camped. Lilly kept it much like a home. She even took the time to display personal keepsakes.

"It helps me not to miss Althetas so much," Lilly had explained. "And the children are reminded that there is a home waiting for them."

Her husband, Gaylan, though not as cheerful as Lilly, was a good and decent man. Tall and thin, with narrow eyes and wind-burned skin, he was not particularly handsome, yet Maybell could see why Lilly, who was very fetching, loved him dearly. He was a man who would always do his best to make his family comfortable. Though reasonably well off, he was not exactly rich, but still, he provided the best that money could buy when it came to comforts. They had goose down mattresses and cotton sheets to sleep on, though he admitted these were a burden to carry along, and their clothes were of the finest quality. When it was time for meals, Gaylan wouldn't touch a bite until Lilly had sat down to join him. Clearly, he loved her very much.

Before long, Malstisos returned and joined Maybell in the wagon. The children cheered with glee when they saw him. They loved the elf and couldn't get enough of touching his ears. One of the favorite activities for all the children in the caravan had become listening to Malstisos telling stories at bedtime. In fact, on the nights when there were no stories, you could hear the wail of crying children throughout the camp.

"Will you join us, master elf?" asked Lilly. "I am afraid Anna keeps getting all the best cards."

Malstisos smiled. "No. I'm afraid I cannot. We will be stopping in a matter of minutes, and Maybell and I must venture into town to resupply."

"Nonsense," said Lilly. "My husband is going into town. He can pick up whatever you need."

"I'm afraid I must go myself," said Malstisos. "I often don't know what I need until I see it."

"Yes," said Maybell. "And there is a matter I must attend to personally."

Lilly frowned. "Very well. But you must join us tonight for supper."

Maybell reached over and hugged the woman, then the children, in turn. "If we are back in time, we will." She hated misleading them.

Soon, the caravan halted and began to make camp. After setting up their tents, Maybell and Malstisos detached their horses from the wagon and headed in the direction of Farmington. They hadn't traveled even half a mile when they heard a voice calling out to them from behind.

"Wait" It was Grentos. Vadnaltis was just behind him. Both carried their long knives at their side and had bows slung across their backs.

"I was afraid we'd miss you," said Grentos.

"I wasn't aware you intended to go to town," said Malstisos, trying not to sound alarmed.

"We noticed you were leaving and thought we'd keep you company," said Grentos.

"I thank you," said Maybell. "But our day will be tedious and long. I would not want you to waste your time on such trivialities."

"You are kind," said Grentos. "But we don't mind." He turned to Vadnaltis. "Do we?" Vadnaltis did not reply. His face was expressionless, his eyes fixed on the road ahead.

"You carry a bow, I see," Malstisos remarked.

"Yes," Grentos replied. "We thought we'd do a bit of hunting later. I'd ask you to join us, but as you have no bow…"

"That's quite all right," said Malstisos. "The game here is small and sparse, and I have no need for food or clothing. Besides, such a hunt requires great skill."

Maybell noticed a sudden change in the elves' walk and movements.

"I see," muttered Grentos. "Then we were correct."

"About what?" asked Maybell.

"We suspected you had found us out, Malstisos," Grentos continued. "But we couldn't be certain. Seekers are not as adept at reading people as an elf such as you. Luckily, those dull humans believe whatever they are told."

"What is your intent?" asked Malstisos. If he was afraid, it did not show.

"That has been a thing much debated between Vadnaltis and me," Grentos replied. "I would not have you escape to the temples." He glanced over at Maybell. "I can only assume that is what you were planning. Nor can I simply kill you. That would not sit well with Vadnaltis."

"What's your solution?" asked Malstisos.

"You will face my challenge," Grentos answered, sounding pleased with himself.

Malstisos reigned in his horse. "You cannot be serious."

Grentos backed away a few steps. "I am. Do you accept?"

Malstisos slid from the saddle but made no move to draw his weapon. "You have no right to do this."

"Don't I?" scoffed Grentos. "I think I have every right to call out a traitor."

"What's going on here?" Maybell demanded. "What is this challenge?"

"If I were a seeker and had broken their code, or if I had refused judgment of the elders," Malstisos explained, "Grentos would have the right to challenge me to single combat. But as neither is the case, he has decided to take matters into his own hands."

Vadnaltis placed his hand on Grentos's shoulder. "He is right, brother. You cannot do this. Call him to face judgment instead. You have that right."

"He will not honor it," Grentos countered. "He's just like the rest of our kin who have taken up with the humans."

"Perhaps," said Vadnaltis. "But then he shows his dishonor and can be put to death. As it is, you have no authority. The elders have not given any such edict, and our laws forbid it."

"We have already been through this," Grentos let out, his frustration clearly showing. "The elders have already ordered the death of a traitor without judgment. What is the difference?"

"They were wrong to do so," said Vadnaltis. "And the difference is, we are from the steppes, and we hold to the laws that have guided our people for thousands of years. Would you behave as the rebels and throw away the laws because they are inconvenient?"

Grentos shook off Vadnaltis's hand and turned his back. "We've been over this. I will not be swayed."

"And if Malstisos refuses the challenge?" he asked. "What then?"

"Then not only will he die," Grentos replied darkly. "But his human pet will die with him. As it stands, I'm willing to let her go in peace."

Sadness washed over Vadnaltis's face. "I will ask you, one more time, to reconsider."

"I will not," Grentos replied. He spun around to face Malstisos. "Do you accept or not?"

Malstisos opened his mouth to answer, but Vadnaltis stepped in front of him.

"I challenge you, brother," said Vadnaltis. His eyes were full of tears. "Do you accept?"

"What is this?" Grentos cried. "You cannot do this."

"I ask again," he pressed. "Do you accept?"

"I..." Grentos stammered. "I ... I do."

The two elves stepped away from the horses and took opposite positions on the road. Maybell moved close to Malstisos and grabbed his arm. "What is going on?" she whispered.

Malstisos bowed his head. "A tragedy," he said. "And an act of pure honor."

The two elves put down their bows and quivers, and each drew their long knives. "Why?" asked Grentos. "Why do you do this?"

"Because I love you too much to see you live in dishonor," Vadnaltis replied. "Should you strike me down, it is unlikely you will be strong enough to defeat Malstisos after, even if he is not a seeker. And as you well know, the challenge made cannot be withdrawn."

"Then I hope I die by your hand, brother."

Grentos charged.

Vadnaltis stepped aside, narrowly avoiding Grentos's initial onslaught. For several minutes, the battle then raged. Time and again they traded blows, each unable to gain an advantage over the other.

Eventually, it was Grentos who struck first as his blade cut deep into Vadnaltis's left thigh. Blood poured from the wound, soaking the elf's leather trousers. Any human would have collapsed in agony, but Vadnaltis showed no signs of weakening. He spun around and brought his blade across the right shoulder of Grentos. Grentos staggered forward but quickly regained his balance. Both elves stepped back for a moment, blood dripping from their blades.

Grentos felt the wound on his shoulder and smiled sorrowfully. Tears streamed down the face of Vadnaltis.

"Deep enough," said Grentos, looking at the blood on his hand. "You have killed me. I beg you—finish it." He dropped his weapon and fell to his knees.

Vadnaltis slowly approached his comrade and stood over him. "I will join you soon enough, brother," he said, placing his hand on top of Grentos's head and muttering a prayer. "I send you to the Creator." With that, he plunged his knife through Grentos's heart. The elf gasped, then crumpled over onto his side.

Maybell was weeping uncontrollably. Her thoughts went to the death of Berathis.

Vadnaltis pulled his knife free and cleaned it on his shirt. "Malstisos of the Finsoulos Clan." he said without looking up, "I call you to judgment for crimes against our people."

Malstisos took a step forward but did not approach Vadnaltis. "I am bound to see this woman to safety," he replied. "But upon the fulfillment of that duty, I will face judgment."

"Then go in peace," he said. "I would perform the rites alone."

Malstisos bowed low and motioned for Maybell to mount her horse. They urged their steeds on in the direction of town in silence. Once they were a few hundred yards away, Malstisos began to weep. Maybell rode in silence, tears stinging her eyes also. They halted just before they got to town.

"I know you don't understand what just happened," said Malstisos softly.

"I think I do," Maybell replied. "At least part of it. What I don't understand is why Grentos allowed himself to be killed."

"He was dead either way," answered Malstisos. "The fight would have continued for some time, and Grentos was losing too much blood. Even if he were victorious, he would have been so weak that he could not have challenged me successfully. He chose to die by his brother's hand, instead."

"Seekers and their ways are beyond my understanding," said Maybell. "I could never kill a sister—not even that devil Salmitaya."

"Yes," said Malstisos. "But they were more than just seekers. They were brothers."

"You don't mean..." she gasped.

Malstisos nodded slowly. "I do. They were brothers by birth."

"How do you know?" She reeled at the thought.

"He is performing the burial rites alone," he replied. "That is only done under two circumstances. If there are no others there to help—or if it is blood kin, killed by your own hand."

"Monstrous," Maybell cried. "And you intend to let such people judge you?"

"They are my people!" he yelled, causing Maybell to recoil. He then took a breath and calmed himself. "I'm sorry. I shouldn't expect you to understand. Forgive me."

"There is nothing to forgive," she assured. "It's just... I can't..."

"I don't expect you to understand all of our ways," Malstisos said. "But know that I am not afraid to face judgment. In fact, after today, I welcome it. I am tired of the division within my people. Perhaps this is the only way that we can heal." He urged his horse forward.

They spent the rest of the day in utter silence. Maybell picked up a few supplies but was in no mood to linger. The only thing she wanted to do was get back to her tent and sleep. On the trip home, she could smell the funeral pyre burning somewhere in the forest and began to weep once again.

Vadnaltis did not return to the camp, not that Maybell or Malstisos expected him to. When asked, they said that the two elves had gone off hunting. When they didn't turn up the next day, a search party was sent out to look for them. However, after a time, it became clear that they were gone. The camp divided their belongings, giving Malstisos a purse with coin matching the value of the gear and possessions. Malstisos promised to pass this on to them should he see them again.

But something had changed in him. Maybell could sense it but did not know what it was. As the days passed, Malstisos became more and more withdrawn, sometimes disappearing for hours. When she tried to speak to him, he would just say that he was fine and only needed to think. But somehow, this didn't ring true. It was as if his spirit was broken. She prayed to the gods that she could help him to heal.

# CHAPTER 20

Lee hurriedly packed their gear and helped Dina prepare a quick meal of dried meat and fruit. Jacob refused to eat at the same table and took his meal into the living room. By the time Jansi returned, the party was ready to depart. The sun had been down for more than an hour, and only the faint lights from the windows of the nearby houses lit the streets. They said farewell to Jansi, mounted up, and made their way out of the city. The gloom of the streets pleased Lee. The darker the better. He had even planned their exit from Baltria to avoid sections that were lit by lamps.

They wound their way through the streets, Lee leading the way and keeping watch for signs that they were being followed. At first, there was nothing out of the ordinary. Then, just as they entered the main avenue leading to the city gates, they noticed a small group of five people wearing dark cloaks. They were carrying torches and standing to their right on the walkway. As they passed, the group fell in behind them.

"The faithful, I presume," whispered Millet. "What should we do?" "Nothing," Lee replied. "Do nothing until they make a move."

As they continued, more began to emerge and follow. By the time the gates were in sight, there were nearly thirty behind them.

"Be ready," said Lee. "When I give the signal, we'll make a dash for the gate."

A lone figure stepped in front of them, barring their path.

"Move aside," Lee commanded.

"Peace, Lord Starfinder," said the figure in a distinctly feminine voice. She pushed back her hood, revealing a familiar face.

"Salmitaya," Dina hissed. "I should have known you were behind this rabble."

"You're wrong," she replied. "I am just a servant—and a messenger."

"Then deliver your message." Lee gripped the hilt of his sword. "I have no patience for the likes of you."

Salmitaya smiled, amused. "Very well. Reconsider your present course. Yanti knows you intend to refuse his offer. He also assumes you intend to attempt to free your wife. This will fail, and you and your family will die." She took a step forward. "Yanti begs you to reconsider. You could live in peace and wealth. You need not sacrifice any more than you already have. He promises this, and more. You could even return to Hazrah as governor if you wish. You can go home and have the power to protect your people."

"I already intend to protect my people, witch," snarled Lee. "Perhaps I should begin by taking your head." His sword sang as he pulled it from its sheath.

"That would be unwise," said Salmitaya, pointing to the faithful grouped behind them.

Lee let out a hearty laugh. "You think that rabble frightens me?" He sprung from the saddle and turned to the mob. "Many of you know who I am. You know my reputation. So open your wretched ears and know this. I swear that should you attack me, or any of my friends, that I, Lee

Starfinder, son of Saraf, God of the Sea, will kill every last one of you." He took a long step toward the faithful. The mob stirred uneasily.

"I await your response," called Salmitaya.

Lee spun around. "My response is this. Tell this Yanti creature that before this business is over, I will bathe my sword in his blood. If he wants to save his own life, he should run as fast as he can to Angrääl and return my wife to me at once. Then, he should pray to whatever he worships that I decide it is enough for me to spare him."

Salmitaya bowed her head. "I will convey your message. He will be disappointed, I'm sure." She snapped her fingers and the mob slowly dispersed. "Farewell Lee Starfinder. I'm afraid we will not meet again." With that, she vanished into a nearby alley.

Lee tensed, awaiting an attack, but none came. Finally, he remounted his horse. "I guess they are choosing to strike later, rather than sooner." He clicked his tongue to urge his horse forward.

They passed through the gates unhindered. Lee noticed the lack of city guards. So did Millet.

"The guards seem to have abandoned their posts," Millet remarked.

"We just met the keepers of Baltria," said Lee. "They've taken the city with a force more powerful than any army—fear."

"Perhaps it's time we gave them a taste of their own medicine," said Dina.

Lee turned and smiled maliciously. "I intend to."

They headed north through the delta roads for several hours. Dozens of small bridges made good spots for an ambush, but they passed them all unmolested. From time to time, they would see lights from torches several hundred yards ahead, but these always disappeared before they reached them.

"They seek to unnerve us," said Millet.

"They only succeed in angering me." Lee slowed his horse, allowing Jacob to catch up with him. "Are you all right?"

Jacob glanced over, unaffected by their situation. "I'm fine. Worry about yourself."

Lee tightened his lips and spurred his horse forward to retake the lead position. Millet joined him.

"It will take time, My Lord," said Millet. "He's had many years to form his opinions, but I know you can make him understand."

"Thank you, my friend," he responded. "I hope I live long enough to do so."

"You've never failed before," said Millet. "You will not fail now. You will put your family together again."

"I have to tell you," said Lee. "This Yanti person made a tempting offer. If I wasn't so certain that it was a lie, I might have taken him up on it."

Millet nodded with understanding and dropped back to join the others. They rode until it was near dawn and Lee had found a decent place to rest and eat.

"We rest for three hours," he said. He turned to Millet. "Tomorrow night, you'll take Jacob east. I'll take Dina with me as far as Sharpstone."

"I really wish you would consult me about these things," said Dina, scowling.

"I can't take you with me," said Lee. "There is a good chance I'm marching to my death, and I won't be responsible for yours."

"I know I can't go with you," she said. "But I have no intention of being left in the middle of nowhere. I'm a cleric in the Order of Amon Dähl, and I have my own duties. I will go with you as far as Sharpstone, but from there I will return to the temple."

Lee nodded. "You're right, of course. I apologize."

Dina smiled, reached in her belt, and pulled out a small flask. "Here." She tossed it to Lee.

Lee opened the flask, and the air filled with the scent of plum brandy. "Ahhh!" He smiled, took a sip, and closed his eyes, savoring the sweet taste. He offered it to Millet, who refused and then called out to Jacob. As Jacob turned, Lee threw the flask to him. Without a word, Jacob took a sip and then threw it back.

"Manners, young man," said Dina.

Jacob glared at her for a moment. "Thank you for sharing your flask—Dina."

Lee kept watch as the others tried to catch a bit of sleep. Later, while they were preparing to leave, he walked up to Jacob and handed him a sealed letter.

"What's this?" the boy asked.

Lee pressed the letter into his hand. "Should anything happen to me, or should Millet somehow be unable to fulfill his promise to tell you everything, I have written it all down here. Please, just don't open it until after you've reached Dantary."

Jacob paused, then stuffed the letter into his pocket. "I'll wait."

They kept to the road north until reaching a fork. Here, they veered to the right, heading northeast. By mid-afternoon, they neared the spot where they planned to split up. Up ahead, Lee spotted a figure standing in the road. He scanned the area for signs of an ambush but could sense no one else nearby. When they were less than one hundred yards away, Millet sat up straight in his saddle.

"That's Yanti."

Lee nodded. "I'll deal with him."

Yanti was dressed in a black shirt and trousers; even his leather boots were black. His hair was tied back in a tight ponytail, and a long sword hung loosely at his side.

Lee halted his horse and slid from the saddle. "Yanti, I presume." His tone was dark and vicious. "Unless you are here to tell me that you're on your way to retrieve my wife, you've signed your own death warrant."

Yanti smiled, unconcerned. "Lord Starfinder. At last we meet. I've looked forward to this for quite some time." He tapped the hilt of his sword with his index finger. "I am saddened that you have chosen to refuse my offer. Unwise."

Lee slowly drew his weapon.

Yanti cocked his head. "I see you are in no mood for idle talk. Still, I would be remiss if I didn't give you one more chance to abandon this course of action."

Lee turned to the others. "Should this go badly, ride hard. Follow Millet. He knows where to go."

"What say you, Jacob?" called Yanti. "Will you follow Millet?"

"Leave my son alone," Lee roared. "You..."

He stopped short as Jacob walked past, holding out the letter he had given to him.

"He gave me this," his son said, handing Yanti the letter. "Probably no more than sentimental drivel, but there might be something useful in it."

"What is this?" Lee demanded.

"I'm sorry," said Yanti. "Jacob and I are old friends. He's been quite helpful to our cause. Without him, Hazrah would have been much more difficult to subdue."

"Jacob! You can't do this?" Lee appealed. "Your mother..."

"Is weak," said Jacob, cutting him off. "If she had her way, Hazrah would still be under the yoke of the temples." Hatred poured from his eyes. "You know, she never stopped believing that you would return one day. She probably still thinks you're going to save her. But she is as big a fool as you are."

"As you can see," said Yanti. "The things you fight for are in fact fighting against you. By now, your dear wife has joined us, and as you see, your son has been with us all along."

"She would never betray her people." Lee's face burned with fury. "And whatever it is you've done to my son to make him this way—for that, I swear you'll pay with your life."

Yanti drew his weapon and took a step back. "Come then. Let us see if your reputation is deserved."

Lee sprang forward, slashing through the air in a wide arc, attempting to end the fight in a single blow. But Yanti spun to his left with a speed Lee had never before encountered. If not for his training and physical power, his momentum would have sent him sprawling.

"Hasty, Starfinder," taunted Yanti. "Mind the things you have learned." But he made no move to counter.

Lee cursed himself for such an arrogant and foolhardy attack. Yanti was no ordinary opponent. He should have suspected as much.

This time, Lee attacked with more caution and finesse. Short, powerful strokes rained down on Yanti as he attempted to throw him off balance, but to Lee's dismay, Yanti parried each blow easily. Lee became concerned by Yanti's lack of aggression. The man had not yet made a single move to attack, seeming to be content to fight off Lee's onslaught.

"You're trained well," admitted Lee, taking a step back. "But if you think to tire me out, you'll find that will not happen."

"No, no," replied Yanti, still smiling. "I only wish to admire your skill. You have indeed been well educated in the art of the sword. It is a pity you won't allow my master to make you even more powerful—as he has done for me."

With these final words, Yanti charged, bringing his sword hard down at Lee's head. A deafening clang of metal on metal shot through the air, causing a flash of sparks to fly. Lee had only just been able to raise his own sword in time. A second blow from Yanti whizzed by his ear and he was forced back, nearly losing his footing.

Now Yanti began to toy with him, slashing and feigning. Lee tried to regain advantage, but Yanti kept forcing him further and further back. Finally, Lee dropped to one knee from the sheer force of yet another attack. He pushed with all of his strength and somehow managed to get back on his feet, but he knew now that Yanti could finish him at any time. He glanced over long enough to see Dina and Millet still on their horses, staring in horror.

"Ride, you fools," he shouted. "Ride before it's too late."

"It is already too late, Lord Starfinder," said Yanti, pointing to Jacob, who had a bow drawn and pointed at Dina's head. "At that range, he won't miss."

"If you let them go, I will do what you ask," said Lee, bowing his head.

Yanti laughed softly. "Being that you are in no position to bargain, I cannot help but be amused. Still, you have shown courage. A quality my master values greatly—as do I. Still, I am not foolish enough to simply kill you and allow your companions to roam free."

Lee tensed, ready for another assault. "Then we end this."

"Indeed, we do," Yanti agreed.

In a flash, Yanti raced forward. Lee attempted to sidestep and counter, but Yanti was too fast. His own blade had barely moved when he felt Yanti's blow striking home on the back of his skull. He fell to his knees with a grunt, and his sword flew from his hand. His head was swimming as he looked up to see Dina weeping and Millet in silent prayer. He marveled that he still lived. His head should have been split in two. Then he realized that Yanti had hit him with the hilt of his sword, and not the blade.

"You fought well." Yanti's voice sounded far away. Then he felt his entire body jar as Yanti delivered one final blow.

His last thoughts before darkness took him were of his wife. He had failed her.

# CHAPTER 21

Consciousness came slowly—and very painfully. The world around Lee was spinning violently. Then realization washed over him. Feeling anything at all meant that he was still alive. Yanti must have spared him. But why?

He opened his eyes and let the light filter in. The wound on the back of his head throbbed, but he knew he had to sit up. He had to find out if Millet and Dina still lived. Taking a deep breath, he struggled to his knees. As his vision cleared, he could see that their horses had been tied to a fallen log and their gear neatly placed beside them. Millet and Dina were lying tied and blindfolded just off to the side of the road. Near them, Jacob was bound and blindfolded in the same way, only judging from the bruises on his face, he had also been beaten and was unconscious.

"Millet—Dina," called Lee. "Are you hurt?" He struggled to his feet and stumbled toward them.

"We are both fine, My Lord," said Millet. "Yanti decided to leave us unharmed." Lee was about to search for a knife in the gear but then saw that his weapons had been placed beside Millet. He cut their bonds and helped them to their feet. Dina immediately noticed Jacob and ran over, seething with fury. She stood over him momentarily, then spat on the ground.

"If he wasn't your son," said Dina. "I'd slit his throat here and now."

"I wouldn't blame you," admitted Lee, gingerly touching the back of his head. "But his fate is in my hands, and I alone must decide what to do with him."

"Well, that can wait," said Millet. "First I must treat your injuries." Lee didn't protest and allowed Millet to examine his wounds.

"Your skull must be made of stone to have taken such a blow," Millet muttered. He retrieved some medicine and bandages from their gear and finished the dressings.

"What happened after I was knocked out?" asked Lee.

Millet's face twisted in anger, then relaxed as he regained his composure. "He told Jacob to bind and blindfold us. After that, I heard Jacob arguing with him that he should kill us all and be done with it. But Yanti just laughed at him. Next thing I heard was a thump and what sounded like a body hitting the ground. I can only assume that was Jacob. After that, Yanti must have tied off our horses and searched through our gear. Before he left, he told us that you were still alive and that once you woke up, there would be a gift waiting for us. I suppose he was referring to Jacob."

"How could your own son betray you like that?" asked Dina, still furious. "And his own mother..."

"I know," snapped Lee.

He took a deep breath. "I know," he repeated, this time more calmly. Millet placed his hand gently on Lee's shoulder. "What will you do?"

"I'll keep my word," Lee replied. "I will save my wife." His eyes fell on Jacob. "And he will go with me."

"You can't be serious," Millet protested.

Lee's eyes remained fixed on his son. "I've never been more serious. Yanti knew what he was doing, leaving me alive."

"What do you mean?" asked Dina.

Lee glanced sideways at her. "He wants me to go north, and he wants me out of the fight. If I am captured attempting to rescue my wife, then they will try to turn me. If the Dark One was able to empower Yanti so much as to make short work of me, his own power must be unfathomable. If I went with him willingly, he would worry about treachery along the way. This way, I deliver myself into their hands. And he knew exactly what he was doing by leaving Jacob behind as well."

"I still don't follow," said Dina.

"By doing so," Lee explained, "he leaves me with an impossible choice. If I decide to return to Gewey and continue aiding him, I will be forced to kill my own son. I cannot trust Jacob, therefore I cannot take him with me. Nor can I simply let him go."

"Why not?" argued Dina. "He clearly wants you dead. Why not just leave him to return to his masters?"

Lee looked at Dina angrily. "He's my son. He is what he is because I abandoned him. I'll not simply leave him to his fate. No. If I can save him, I will. And if we are killed, we'll die together."

"And I will go with you," said Millet.

Lee smiled at the man with intense affection. "No, my friend. You must continue to do what I cannot. You must return to aid Gewey as best you can."

Millet opened his mouth to protest, but Lee held up his hand, silencing him.

"You must do this," pleaded Lee, his eyes welling with tears. "I have never given you a command, dear friend—not until now. I must break the oath I made to Gewey, so you must have more honor than I. You must keep the word of the house Nal'Thain, as you are bound to do. But you will not do so as my servant."

He walked over to his pack and retrieved a sealed parchment. "From this moment on, you shall be known as Millet Nal'Thain. I empower you with the rank and privileges of Lord and Patriarch of my family. I officially step down from all titles and pass them to you." He held out the parchment.

Millet took a step back. "My Lord," he cried. "You cannot do this. I am your servant, and shall remain so. I refuse this."

Lee smiled and pressed the letter into Millet's hand. "You cannot refuse. As the Lord Nal'Thain, it is my right to choose my successor. You are the only man I can trust with the challenges that lie ahead. And I am sorry. I leave to you a broken house of a broken land, and it will be up to you to heal them and restore our honor. I likely ride to my death, and even should I survive, I cannot return to my former life. I beg you to do this service."

By this time, Millet was weeping openly. "I cannot restore your honor. I could only ever maintain it. The honor of Nal'Thain is embodied in you. I will not fail you, My Lor..."

He took a step back and bowed. "Lee."

Lee smiled, then bowed low in return. "I know you won't, My Lord."

Jacob began to stir. "You must leave before he wakes," Lee said. "I don't want him to see what direction you are heading in."

"What about Yanti?" asked Dina. "Do you think he will follow us?"

"I doubt it," Lee replied. "He doesn't consider you a threat. The only reason he left you alive was to confuse and hinder me, making my choices even more difficult. If he had plans for you, he would have taken you with him. No doubt he had the means to transport you north, or have you imprisoned here. Still, I suggest you ride hard until you can take rest within a temple."

Jacob groaned.

"Now go," Lee commanded. He embraced them both and helped to repack their mounts. Millet glanced back one last time before they spurred their horses to a run. "Good luck, old friend," Lee whispered.

"Wh..what's happening?" Jacob moaned, struggling with his bonds.

Lee took a deep breath and kneeled down beside his son. "What's happening is that you've been abandoned and left in the hands of your foe. Luckily for you, that foe is also your father."

Jacob stiffened. "Yanti—that dog. I will kill him for this."

"Shut your mouth, boy!" barked Lee. "You have much to answer for—both of us do. If you choose, I will give you a chance for redemption."

"Just kill me and get it over with," Jacob grumbled.

"Why do you think you deserve such a kindness? You have betrayed your mother, you have betrayed your father, and you have dishonored your family name." He cut Jacob's bonds.

Jacob pulled down his blindfold and rubbed his wrists. "And what have you done, father? What crimes have you committed? How are you any better than me?"

"I have committed crimes I can scarcely describe. And for those crimes, I suffer ... and will continue to suffer." Lee stood and offered his hand.

Jacob stared at Lee for a moment, sneering. "You should kill me now. If you don't, I will kill you."

"And in whose name will you kill me?" Lee asked. "Will you kill me for the Dark Knight, the Reborn King of Angrääl? The one who has just left you behind now that your usefulness to him is over? Or perhaps you will kill me in the name of your mother? Or do you mean for her to die? Do you? Has the Dark One blackened your heart so much that you turn your back on the one who loves you the most?"

"Loves me?" he roared. "She loves you—not me. She never loved me!"

"Of course she does," said Lee, withdrawing his hand. "I have never known her to love anything more than you, and if you don't see that, then you are as blind as you are foolish. You think she wept for me?" He paused. "She wept because she knew you had to grow up without a father. She wept because of my absence in your life. She wept because I had stolen something precious from the true love of her life. Did she love me? Yes. And I love her still. But you do not know the depths of your mother as I do. From the moment you came into this world, you became her very reason for living. It was I who was second in her heart, not you."

He re-extended his hand. "Come with me to Angrääl and I'll prove it."

Jacob hesitated for a moment, then allowed Lee to pull him to his feet. "I'll go with you," said Jacob. "If only to take my revenge."

"That's good enough for now," said Lee. "If you can refrain from killing me, at least for the time being, I may even be able to show you a thing or two about the power that flows in your veins."

"As I said," he replied. "I'll go with you. I promise nothing else."

"I suppose that will do," said Lee. "Perhaps together we will both find retribution and redemption."

They loaded the horses and began making their way north. Lee whistled a traditional Hazrian travel song. Jacob did not join in at first, but after a time, he started to hum along.

# CHAPTER 22

Gewey's heart pounded as he passed through the massive double doors. Kaylia followed close behind, and though she didn't show it, he knew she was nervous too.

Once inside, Gewey was amazed to see a room that looked much like a theater. On either side, rows of marble benches curved along the walls, forming a semi-circle that met at the back of a raised, stone platform. The ceiling was vaulted and covered with the familiar orbs that had been used to illuminate the other rooms in the house so brightly it took Gewey's vision several moments to adjust to their brightness here. Already standing across the stage, tall and proud, a group of six elves faced him, arms crossed and hoods drawn. Theopolou quickly took his place on the platform beside the other elders. Gewey and Kaylia walked down the narrow center aisle until they were only a few feet away.

"That's far enough, human," said the elf just beside Theopolou. Her strong, feminine voice echoed throughout the room. She pulled back her hood, revealing long, elegant features. Her skin was the same dark bronze as Kaylia's, but her hair was jet black and wrapped tightly with silver ribbons.

She glared down at the duo, not attempting to mask her disgust. "I am Lady Bellisia, Chief Elder of the clan Hastriatis. You know Lord Theopolou. To my left are Lord Chiron, Lord Endymion, Lord Syranis, Lady Leora, and Lord Aneili. We are here to determine whether you are to give testimony on behalf of Lord Theopolou, who has been called to judgment according to our laws."

"That has already been decided," corrected Theopolou. "Do not taint my house with deceit."

Lady Bellisia glared angrily at Theopolou. "It was not my intention to deceive," she said. "I merely misspoke." She turned her attention back to Gewey. "I do admit that some of us were curious to see you." She glanced at Kaylia. "The human who could ensnare one of our people in the bond."

"I was not ensnared," barked Kaylia.

"Silence, girl," Bellisia commanded. "You have no right to speak."

"That's odd," said Lord Chiron. "I thought this was an open forum. Or have the rights of an elf changed?"

"Just because you support Theopolou and this madness," shot Bellisia, "do not think I will tolerate your insults, even within these walls."

"I give no insult," Chiron retorted. "But as you well know, Kaylia has been invited to these proceedings. She has the same right as an elder here—as does the human."

"I mean no disrespect," said Gewey, "but I am called Gewey Stedding. You may use my proper name."

"Indeed," said Bellisia. "So Gewey Stedding, Lord Theopolou has told us that you are quite remarkable—for a human. And he says you saved the life of one of his escorts."

Gewey nodded. "We were attacked by Vrykol."

Bellisia laughed. "Yes, I've heard. The ancient evil of the gods returned to plague the world. What is next? Shall the Elder Race return to reclaim the world?"

"Once again, you name me a liar," said Theopolou. "You have all seen the head."

"I do not call you a liar," Bellisia replied. "I merely say that you have been deceived. The creature you showed may or may not be what you claim. Perhaps it is an abomination created by human hands in order to cause fear among us."

"And how would they have done such a thing?" Theopolou asked. "Could they create a creature that is as fast as an elf, and will only die when you take its head?"

Bellisia paused. "We are not here to discuss the Vrykol." Her gaze returned to Gewey. "And now that you are in our presence, I have a question. What are you?"

A chill crept into Gewey's stomach. "I don't understand what you mean."

"Do you not?" Bellisia pressed. "It's a simple question. We can all feel the flow that saturates your being. Humans cannot do this. So I ask again—what are you?"

"You do not have to answer," said Theopolou, just as Gewey was opening his mouth to speak.

"Do you seek to deceive us, Lord Theopolou?" Bellisia asked. "Do you seek to bring danger among us?"

"The boy is no danger and you know it," said Theopolou.

Bellisia crossed her arms. "Is that so? I think you are hiding something, and if he is not a danger, then there is nothing to prevent him from revealing his origins." She looked at the other elders. "We all know that this Gewey Stedding is no ordinary human. How could he be? Perhaps he is a half-man, or perhaps something else. Whatever the case, do we not have the right to know?"

"You do not," announced Gewey. "As I understand it, you are asking me to testify for Theopolou, and that is all. I see no reason to explain myself to you or anyone else. If you no longer want me to testify, I will respectfully take my leave. I have urgent matters to attend to, and time is short."

Bellisia raised an eyebrow. "And you think you can just leave? You think we can allow you to wander the world, bonded to one of our own?"

"Do not threaten my guests," boomed Theopolou. "I have given them both sanctuary."

Bellisia smiled innocently. "I make no threat. And your offer only extends as far as your domain. Unless you intend to have them reside here forever." She waved her hand dismissively. "In any case, the boy can keep his secrets—for now. But he must be guarded if he is to accompany us to the Chamber of the Maker." She looked down at Gewey. "Do you agree to this?"

Gewey nodded.

Bellisia looked up and down at the group of elders. "Are there any objections?" She smiled with satisfaction when there were none. "Good. Then we depart at once." Theopolou turned and walked off the stage, pushing past Gewey and Kaylia, who followed close after him. The other elders lingered until they had left the chamber, their eyes following them out.

"She is up to no good," Theopolou muttered.

"What do you mean?" asked Gewey.

"There was no reason for this meeting in the first place," he explained. "The questions she asked were meaningless. You had already agreed to come, and a guard would have been put on you, regardless. I thought she simply wanted to see you out of sheer curiosity, but now I suspect she may be hiding something."

"Do you think she knows about Gewey?" whispered Kaylia.

"Perhaps," Theopolou replied, his brow creased in thought. "If she does, there is only one way she could have come upon this knowledge, and that worries me."

Thoughts of the Dark Knight exploded in Gewey's mind, and he remembered the dream he'd had the night he left Sharpstone. "What should we do?" he asked.

"There is nothing to do," the old elf answered. "We must allow this to play out. If Bellisia and her allies plan to join with Angrääl, we must call them out in front of the others. I will send word ahead to the elders who chose not to attend here today. They will not ignore a summons to the Chamber of the Maker."

"I thought all the elders were already here," remarked Gewey.

"No," said Theopolou. "The seven elders here, including myself, are chiefs among our people, and can speak for our tribes in the absence of the others."

"Will they have time to get there?" asked Kaylia.

"I hope so," said Theopolou. "I should be able to get word to them quickly enough for most to arrive ahead of us, though those from the northern tribes will never be able to get there in time." Theopolou walked them to the front door and left them just outside.

"I'm worried," said Kaylia, as they made their way around to their rooms. "I have never seen my kind behave with such malice and deceit toward one another. Linis was right all along. The second split is inevitable."

"Does that mean you will change your mind about facing judgment?" asked Gewey.

Kaylia smiled and touched his hand. "I don't know. At least, not yet."

"Whatever happens, I'll be there beside you," said Gewey, with grim determination.

"That reminds me," said Kaylia. "I have decided we shall complete the ritual of bonding once we arrive at the Chamber of the Maker." She glanced sideways at Gewey. "That is ... if you are agreeable."

"I..." he stuttered. "That is..." He stopped short and cleared his throat. "Of course I am."

"Good," said Kaylia. "Linis will instruct you on the ceremony along the way. Also, you need instruction in our customs if you are to be mine. I will see to that personally."

Gewey's heart raced with a mixture of excitement and apprehension. If the Sharpstone Village Mothers could see him now. They had tried to play matchmaker for him more times than he cared to remember.

Once in his room, Gewey packed his gear and changed into his own tan leather pants and thin wool shirt. As he strapped on his sword, he heard a knock at the door. "Come in."

The door opened and Akakios walked in with three other grim-looking elves. All were wearing hard leather armor, a long knife, and a bow and quiver across their backs.

Gewey bowed. "I take it you are my guards?"

"We are," Akakios affirmed. "These three are from the personal escort of Lady Bellisia. They wish me to tell you that they have no desire to speak with you, and any questions should be directed to me."

Gewey couldn't help but be amused and laughed softly. This brought angry stares from the three elves and a smile from Akakios.

"You are not permitted to carry your weapon," said Akakios. "I will carry it for you ... if you wish."

"That's fine," said Gewey, unbuckling his sword. "But take care not to touch anything but the scabbard or you will be burned."

Akakios looked in wonder at the sword as Gewey handed it over. He couldn't help but test what Gewey had told him and touched the blade, anyway. Immediately, he withdrew his hand, wincing in pain.

"I have never heard of such a weapon," marveled Akakios. "How did you come by it?"

"Perhaps I'll tell you along the way." He couldn't help but get in a quip, designed to get under the other elves' skin.

"That is ... if I have time. Linis is to instruct me in the bonding ceremony, and Kaylia is to teach me more about elf ways and customs."

The three elves stirred uneasily but said nothing. Gewey smiled with satisfaction. Akakios closed his eyes and shook his head with a groan.

Gewey grabbed his gear and allowed himself to be led from the room to the front of the house. At least thirty elves awaited him. Theopolou and the six other elders, along with their armed escorts, stood near the base of the statue. Kaylia and Linis stood a few feet away from them, talking quietly. Gewey began to approach Linis and Kaylia, but Akakios stopped him.

"You must remain with us until we make camp," said Akakios, almost apologetically. "You are free to speak to whoever you wish, then. But you are to stay silent as we travel."

This irritated Gewey, but he could see no alternative other than to concede. It was then that Linis walked straight up to him and slapped him on the back. At first, it seemed as if the guards would try to prevent him, but one glance from Linis made it very clear that he would not be hindered.

"They have no jurisdiction over me, Gewey," said Linis. "I'll walk with you." He noticed Gewey looking at Kaylia. "She'll walk with her uncle and his escort—for now."

This satisfied Gewey. He could see that Linis had unnerved the elders, but they did nothing to stop him.

They set off through the front gate, the elders and escorts leading the way, followed by Gewey, Linis, and Gewey's guards. As they traveled, Gewey spent the rest of the day listening to Linis tell stories about his exploits and adventures.

For such a large group, they covered ground swiftly, not stopping to rest until it was time to make evening camp. By then, they had covered nearly forty miles. Akakios and the other three elves set up their bedrolls a few feet away from Gewey and Linis. Kaylia stayed near Theopolou until they had settled in, but joined Gewey and Linis soon after, as they were retrieving some bread and dried fruit from their packs. Linis had already warned Gewey that they would not be building a fire for cooking along the way, explaining that the elders intended to travel swiftly and unnoticed. At first, the lack of a fire worried Gewey. He only had the provisions he'd arrived with, and some of these required cooking. But Linis assured him there would be enough dried meat and fruit to go around.

"Have you gone over the ceremony with Gewey?" Kaylia asked Linis.

"I will tomorrow," he replied. "I do not think the others are comfortable with the idea, so I thought it best to wait a day or two."

"You don't have to worry about that," said Gewey with a mischievous grin. He told them about the remark he had made at Theopolou's house in front of his guards.

"You should not provoke them," Linis warned. "Bellisia is one of Theopolou's main opponents, and they serve her."

"It's not like it's a secret that Kaylia and I are bonded," Gewey argued. "Besides, they deserved it. I mean, really. Akakios isn't in favor of human-elf relations, but he still manages to act decently toward me. The others have refused to even address me properly."

Linis couldn't help but smile. "It would have been amusing to see them squirm. But still, they could be dangerous, and now you are unarmed."

"I may be unarmed," said Gewey, "But I am far from defenseless."

"A fact we don't want them to know," added Kaylia. "Some of them probably suspect you of being a half-man, and that's bad enough. But at least it explains your ability to channel the powers of the earth. If you were forced to defend yourself and unleashed those powers upon them, we would be faced with a whole new set of problems." She reached over and touched Gewey's arm, causing him to blush. "After we complete the bonding, then there will be nothing they can say or do."

"Which brings a question," said Linis. "Who shall preside over the ceremony?"

"Theopolou would do it if I asked," replied Kaylia, "but I fear it would jeopardize his position among the others. I was hoping you might do us the honor. As a seeker, it is within your right."

Linis bowed his head. "I would be honored to do so. But I still think you should speak to your uncle about this. He has done nothing to oppose your union with Gewey, though I am certain he is not happy about it. In fact, if I am not mistaken, he has pressed you to follow through with it."

"You are right, of course," said Kaylia. "I will speak to him tomorrow."

"Do you think Theopolou is really in danger?" asked Gewey.

"I do," answered Linis. "But from whom,, I cannot say."

"Bellisia seems to be the most likely candidate," said Gewey. "She all but threatened to have me killed."

Linis furrowed his brow and shook his head. "I would not be so quick to pass judgment on Lady Bellisia. Her hatred is limited to humans and, well—the gods. She opposes Theopolou, but it is hard for me to imagine her conspiring with humans for any reason. Even if it meant regaining our kingdoms and lands."

"Who then?" asked Kaylia. "Certainly not Lord Chiron. He has been as a brother to Theopolou since they were children. Lord Aneili is the only other elder who wanted Theopolou called to judgment, but it's hard to imagine him doing anything so dishonest. And the rest are Theopolou's allies."

"Are they?" asked Linis. "I'm not so sure. You cannot be betrayed by your enemies, only your friends."

"Are you sure there is a plot?" asked Gewey.

Linis shook his head. "You hit upon it, my friend. I suspect there is. I feel there is. But I do not know it. Everything I have predicted would happen, and needed to happen, has happened. Theopolou is exposed, and you are unprotected—at least, they believe that you are." Linis leaned in and whispered. "My seekers are near should we be attacked, or should someone attempt to follow us."

This comforted Gewey, and he could feel Kaylia's mood lift as well. "How long until we arrive?" he asked.

"Normally, it would take more than a week," Linis replied with amusement. "But they seek to exhaust you by maintaining a pace no human could endure for very long. At this rate, we will be there in five days, maybe less."

Gewey smiled. "I'll try to look tired."

"I will rejoin Theopolou," said Kaylia. "I suggest you use this time to prepare for our ceremony." She rose to her feet and walked off in the direction of the others.

"She's right," said Linis. "You would not wish to anger your unorem on your first day of bonding."

"Unorem?" asked Gewey.

Linis laughed. "Wife is how you would say it. But partner might be more accurate."

Gewey blushed and whispered, "Unorem." He looked up at Linis. "I hope I'm ready for this."

"You're ready," assured Linis. "And if you are not, then you soon will be. In fact, I envy you. It takes courage to enter into the bonding. To share that much of oneself is not a matter to be taken lightly, yet I cannot help but wonder what it would be like."

"Do you have an ... unorem?" asked Gewey.

"No," Linis replied. "I loved once. But my life as a seeker kept me ever from her. In time, she chose another."

"And now," he asked. "Is there anyone?"

Linis paused for a long moment. "There is someone I desire. And I believe she desires me. But I fear I will never have the chance to find out for certain."

"Who is it?" Gewey pressed. "Tell me."

Linis smiled dolefully. "It is not in our custom to ask such questions."

"I'm sorry," said Gewey. "But it's not like I would know her. The only elves I know are mostly here with us."

"And what makes you think she is an elf?" asked Linis.

"You mean she's human?" exclaimed Gewey. Akakios and the other guards looked up for a second but then returned to their meal.

"You must learn discretion," Linis scolded. "I did not say she was human. I did not say anything." He sighed. "I will tell you. But you must keep this knowledge to yourself."

"I swear." Gewey leaned forward.

"Celandine," said Linis.

"Dina?" Gewey laughed as quietly as he could manage.

"Is it in your custom to make sport of a friend's emotions?" he said.

Gewey calmed himself. "I'm sorry. Really. It's just unexpected. When did this happen?"

"I knew I felt something for her from the moment we met," said Linis. "Though at the time I thought she was fully human, so those feelings were easy enough to dismiss. I would live for hundreds of years, and she would grow old and die. I would not court her only to watch her slip away. But when I touched her hand for the first time and felt the elf blood coursing through her veins, it quickly became clear to me that I could no longer simply ignore what was in my heart."

"And you say she feels the same way?" asked Gewey.

Linis shrugged. "I can tell she feels something. But what exactly that is, I don't know. If we both live through this adventure, I intend to find out."

Gewey slapped him on the shoulder. "We'll live through this. And when we do, I just know it will work out for you."

"Perhaps," he said. "But that is a question only the future can answer. For now, we must concern ourselves with more immediate issues."

Linis spent the next few hours going over the ceremony with Gewey, having him repeat it back to him over and over. Once Linis was satisfied they had covered as much as they could, the two of them lay down to sleep for what little rest time remained.

Gewey could feel Kaylia through their bond and was tempted to reach out to her, but in the end, decided not to risk causing trouble with the elders. He still wasn't sure about the extent of their abilities, and it would be wise not to stir things up until he really needed to.

# CHAPTER 23

An hour before sunrise, they were underway again. Linis spent the first few hours picking up where they had left off the night before. The bonding ceremony wasn't particularly complex, but he made it clear to Gewey that each part held great significance, and it was very important to get it exactly right.

"I have never seen the bonding performed," he said. "And I don't really understand the bonding in the same way that Theopolou would. But as you are connected with Kaylia's spirit already, I don't think it will be difficult for you."

"I hope not," said Gewey.

Linis threw his arm around Gewey's neck. "Don't worry. Things will go as planned. Besides, you are about to become the envy of many an elf."

They went over the ceremony a few more times, then let their conversation drift to lighter subjects. Gewey's guards kept their distance, but by midday, Akakios joined in. He had heard of Linis and held him in high regard, despite the fact that he had been named a traitor.

They covered another forty miles before they stopped. Gewey noticed the elves occasionally glancing over at him to see if he was tiring yet. He knew it would be wise to feign fatigue, but his pride simply wouldn't allow this. Every time he caught one of their eyes, he just smiled happily and whistled a bright tune. This brought fierce stares and chatter among the elders—all except Theopolou, of course.

Once camped, Kaylia joined them again. She looked burdened with worry. "What's wrong?" asked Gewey.

"Theopolou," she replied. "He doesn't seem well."

"You mean he's ill?" asked Gewey.

Kaylia shook her head. "Not ill exactly. It's more like he is slowly being drained of all energy."

Linis smiled sympathetically. "Theopolou is very old, Kaylia. Perhaps this trip, and our quick pace, is too much for him."

Kaylia shook her head. "I know, but it's more than that. It's as if his very spirit is being gradually taken away from him."

"I might be able to help," offered Gewey.

"How do you mean?" asked Linis.

"I could give him part of what I have," Gewey said. Then he shook his head. "No. That's not what I mean. I can't really describe it, but I think I can put power from the earth inside him."

Linis looked at Gewey in wonder for a moment. "How did you learn to do such a thing? Only the greatest of elf sages have ever been able to do this."

"I don't know," he admitted. "I don't even know that I can do it for sure. I just feel that I can. Ever since I journeyed to the spirit world for the first time, I keep getting these ... impressions. It's like I know I can do a thing, but I don't know what it is." He rubbed his chin. "I don't understand it, but I still think I can help Theopolou—if he'll let me."

"I'll ask him," said Kaylia, rising to her feet. She paused and looked down at Gewey, smiling. "Thank you," she said. With that, she walked off to speak to Theopolou.

A short time later, she returned, accompanied by her uncle. The old elf sat next to Gewey, though he did not look directly at him. "Kaylia says you have the ability to transfer the flow from yourself to another," he remarked.

"I think so," said Gewey.

Theopolou turned to Kaylia, then to Gewey. "But you are not certain?"

"Not entirely," Gewey admitted. "As I told Linis and Kaylia, after I woke up from being in the spirit world, I felt as if I knew things—but without really knowing them. I know I can do this. And if you're ill, you really should let me try."

Theopolou scrutinized Gewey for a long moment. "I'm neither ill nor tired as Kaylia might think, but something is wrong." He stood up slowly. "I feel as if the energy of the earth is somehow being drained from me."

"Drained how?" asked Linis.

"I don't know. I have never encountered this before. I have attempted to track down the source, but so far, unsuccessfully."

"Could it be one of the elders?" asked Gewey.

"I don't think so," said Theopolou. "Of all the elders and other elves here, only Chiron, and perhaps Linis, have a stronger connection than I. Neither of them could do this."

He looked straight at Gewey. "Actually, you are the only one here with such ability."

"I swear..." Gewey began to protest, but Theopolou held up his hand.

"I did not mean to suggest that you had anything to do with this," he said. "Just that you are the only one here I am aware of who has such power. Of course, it is possible that another has also somehow gained this ability. And then again, it may not be anyone. It just may be an anomaly."

Theopolou's eyes grew sad. "Our people have lost so much knowledge. Even the wisest of us are mere children compared to our ancestors. They had such vast knowledge in matters of the flow, it is said they could trace it to its source."

Linis joined Theopolou in his melancholy. "Yes. The seekers of old were said to have been able to outrun a deer, and hear the heartbeat of a rabbit from one hundred yards away."

"I do not think it is wise for you to give me your flow," said Theopolou. "But I would ask that Linis help me track down the culprit ... if there is one." Then, as if a wave had hit him, he staggered.

Gewey jumped up and placed his hand on Theopolou's shoulder. He could feel the elf tense at the unfamiliar contact, so he withdrew and took a step back. "Are you..."

Theopolou waved him off. "I'm fine."

"No, you're not," argued Kaylia. "You should let Gewey try to help you."

Linis nodded in agreement. "I..."

Suddenly, he looked up to see Akakios standing a few feet away, eyes ablaze, his bow drawn and pointing at Gewey. Linis reached for his dagger, but it was too late. The arrow loosed.

Time stood still as it flew through the air and Kaylia tried desperately to throw herself into its path. But instead of piercing Gewey's flesh, the shaft flew past him, missing his throat by a hair's breadth and burying itself into the chest of an elf wielding a vicious-looking dagger just a few feet further back. The attacker gasped and clutched at the arrow before falling to his knees. Kaylia and Linis were already running toward him, while Gewey threw his arms around Theopolou and pressed him toward the guards.

"Unhand me, boy," boomed Theopolou.

Gewey ignored his protests. When he was in range of the guards, he shoved Theopolou in their direction. "Protect him," Gewey commanded. The elves obeyed without question, surrounding the elder.

Gewey ran to Akakios's pack and retrieved his sword. It sang as he pulled it free from its scabbard, and he could feel the warm throb of the earth rush through him. By this time, Kaylia and Linis had reached the assassin and were trying to remove the arrow.

"To arms," yelled Gewey, alerting the others, who by this time knew something was wrong and had begun forming a protective circle around the elders.

Gewey ran to Kaylia and Linis. The wounded elf was struggling against them, trying to reach into his belt. Gewey dropped to the ground, and with all his strength, grabbed the elf's wrists and pinned them to the ground. The assassin's eyes shot wide as he felt the power in Gewey's grasp. Realizing that he was far outmatched, the elf ceased resisting. Even so, Linis, Kaylia, and Gewey did not release their holds.

"Who are you?" roared Linis.

The wounded elf said nothing, instead simply turning his head away.

Gewey could hear the camp organizing a search of the nearby forest. He looked at the wounded elf carefully. Then he closed his eyes, allowing the power of the earth to flow like a relentless tide and reach every fiber of this being.

"Gewey," whispered Kayla. "What are you doing?"

Gewey took a deep breath. "I am going to get some answers." Releasing the elf's wrists, he instead placed his hands on the captive's chest.

The ground hummed for a moment as Gewey let the power flow from him into and around the elf's body. "You can let him go," he said to Linis and Kaylia. "He cannot move."

Slowly, the other two relaxed. They marveled at the sight they beheld. Gewey smiled as he also removed his hands. Still, the wounded elf could not move.

"What have you done to him?" gasped Linis.

"Nothing," Gewey replied. "I am just using the same power that you do. Only I'm using it to hold the elf down."

"Amazing," said Linis, half smiling.

Gewey nodded, then turned his attention back to his prisoner. "You will tell me what I need to know." His voice was grim and intimidating. "Who sent you?"

The elf glared with hatred and fear. "Curse you, and all of your kind," he hissed. He shifted his gaze to Kaylia. "And you…"

"Careful," Gewey warned, then let the power squeeze in tightly.

The elf gasped. "Traitor," he managed to say.

Gewey could hear some of the other elves making their way quickly toward them. In a flash, Theopolou appeared with a knife in hand and slit the wounded assassin's throat. Blood soaked the elf's shirt and spilled onto the ground. Gewey immediately released his hold on him, but it was too late. His eyes met Gewey's for one final moment before death overcame him. Pure hatred was the only thing Gewey could see. Then came the blank stare of oblivion. He heard a thud as the knife hit the ground beside the slain captive's head.

Theopolou turned to the others, who were still a few feet away. "He is dead. I have killed him."

Chiron walked up to the body and examined it carefully. "He has no markings, and his clothes could be from any-where. The dagger is common as well. The stains and scrapes on his boots suggest that he has traveled through the moun-tains." He turned to the others. "Does anyone recognize him?"

Each elf in turn examined the body, but none could place his face or guess at his origin. Even Linis could not find a clue. After it was clear that no one could solve the puzzle, the elders gathered in a small circle to decide their next move. They invited Linis to join them but made it clear that Gewey and Kaylia were to remain with Akakios and the other three guards. Akakios looked as if he wanted to ask for Gewey's sword, but he did not.

The elders talked for about an hour before splitting up to tell their plan to the others. Linis approached Gewey, his eyes aflame.

"Fools," spat Linis. "Bloody fools!"

"What is it?" asked Gewey.

"They want to press on even faster," Linus replied in disgust. "And still, they will not allow my seekers to join us."

"You told them they are near?" asked Kaylia.

"I had no choice. Whoever that assassin was, he possessed the skills to slip past my people. If there are more like him out there, we won't be able to notice them if we travel too fast. But if the elders were to allow my seekers to come amongst us, we could move at speed and avoid a trap." He checked his weapon. "I need to speak to my comrades. I'll return soon." He dashed off into the woods and disappeared.

"Your weapon," came Bellisia's voice from behind them.

Gewey turned to her as she approached, accompanied by two escorts with long knives drawn.

"If there is someone seeking to kill him," said Theopolou. "He should be allowed to keep it."

"You misunderstand," she corrected. "I only wish to know where he acquired that sword."

"It was a gift," said Gewey.

"And such a gift it is," she said. Her eyes locked with Gewey's. "I will not ask you to give it up, and I suspect that forcing it from you may prove to be more difficult than we would have originally suspected. Because of that, I think that you shall be dealt with first. Theopolou's judgment must wait." She turned to Theopolou. "Once we arrive, be prepared to present your arguments in favor of this boy and inform him of his rights."

"You cannot do this," said Theopolou.

"I can and will," Bellisia shot back. "Do you think me blind? Did you think he could use that much of the flow and it would escape my notice?" She stepped toward Gewey, looking him up and down. "Whatever you are, I will get to the truth of it. And if you are a danger to my people, we need to know. That gives me the right." She spun on her heels and strode off.

"I am sorry, Gewey," said Theopolou in a half whisper. "I fear this trip may go ill for you."

"I don't understand," said Gewey. "What just happened?"

"Bellisia is calling you to appear before the council to determine if you are a danger to our race. If they decide that you are, then they will kill you—and me for bringing you among us."

Gewey tightened his jaw and re-sheathed his sword. "They may find that more difficult than they think."

"Then you will be forced to slaughter your allies," said Theopolou. "We will fall and the Dark One will triumph."

"If he allows himself to be killed, all is lost anyway," said Kaylia.

Theopolou nodded. "The only hope is for you to convince them to spare you. You must show them that you are not a threat."

"I need to do more than that," said Gewey. "I need to convince them to join me. That's why I came to begin with."

"True," said Theopolou. "But I fear you will have little success. The only way is to gain the support of the majority of the elders. The others will fall in line to avoid a second split."

"How should we proceed?" asked Kaylia.

"My way is usually one of caution," replied Theopolou. "But now is a time for bold action." He turned and took a few steps. "Face each other. Do it quickly." He turned back around. Gewey and Kaylia stood motionless for a moment, then obeyed.

"Are you still sure you wish to be bonded?" the old elf asked. His voice was soft and melodic.

Kaylia didn't hesitate. "I am."

Gewey was speechless but still managed a short nod.

"But won't this anger the others?" asked Kaylia. "How can Gewey convince them if they're too incensed to listen?"

"Anger will fade," he explained. "You have chosen this ... man. And he, you. If you expect to touch the reason of the elders, you must make them face their fears and see what is possible. Talk is not enough. Though you may be right; this may be a mistake."

"It is no mistake," said Kaylia, smiling. "If Gewey faces death, I will face it with him. I would have the bond completed before our fate finds us, and it is too late." She turned to Theopolou. "Now is the time."

"Then prepare yourselves," said Theopolou. "I will gather the witnesses."

They watched as Theopolou walked away into the fading light toward the elders. Gewey was shocked. "They will be our witnesses?" he laughed.

"They cannot refuse," Kaylia explained. "The bonding ceremony is one of our most sacred rituals. It strikes at our core beliefs. They would not dare say no, regardless of who is being bonded."

"What do I need to do?"

Kaylia suppressed a laugh. "If you still have the clothes Theopolou gave you, you should put them on. They are a bit more appropriate." She reached out and squeezed his hand. "As for me, I should change as well." With that, she danced off, leaving Gewey reeling with emotions that flowed between their connections.

*If this is what it's like now*, Gewey thought. What must it be like when it's completed? He shook his head vigorously in an effort to steady his nerves and went to his pack to retrieve his elf clothing.

"Gewey," called Akakios. He came trotting over, holding a tiny flask in his hand. "There is a stream nearby where you can wash. I've sent the other three ahead to make sure it's safe." He slapped Gewey on the back. "Come. Let's get you ready."

Gewey paused and extended his hand. "I didn't thank you for saving my life."

Akakios looked thoughtful. "I'm not sure I did. Anyway, you might not have been the target."

"What have they done with the body?" Gewey asked, noticing that it had been removed.

"Two of my kin have taken it to the forest to perform the funeral rites," he replied. "Assassin or no, he was an elf, and should pass from this life as one."

"Of course," said Gewey.

"But enough of that," said Akakios. "You need to get ready, and I will not face Theopolou for failing to have you back on time." He threw his arm around Gewey, pulling him along.

Gewey allowed himself to be led into the surrounding dense forest. About half a mile in, he heard the light trickle of a stream. The three guards were waiting there; they did not smile.

Akakios halted. "You'll find the stream just a few feet through that brush." He handed him the flask. "Essence of the star lily. It is a tradition among us to perfume ourselves during high rituals, and it does not get more lofty than this."

Gewey opened the flask, and the air filled with a sweetness he had never experienced. "Thank you," he said gratefully before heading to the stream.

"Just see that you give it back," Akakios called after him. "I need some for myself as well."

Gewey washed and dressed. He wished he had a mirror. The stream moved too swiftly to see his reflection.

"Gewey," called a voice a few yards away, just beyond the brush.

Gewey glanced over to see Linis striding toward him. A smile beamed across his face.

"How do I look?" asked Gewey.

Linis examined him carefully, then said: "Presentable—all things considered. How do you feel?"

Gewey took a deep breath. "A bit nervous, but excited, too." He took another breath. "Mostly nervous."

"Just remember what I told you and you'll do fine," Linis reassured. "However, if you'd like, we can go over the ceremony once again."

"Yes, I would like that," admitted Gewey. "But tell me. Did you speak to your brethren?"

"I did," he replied with a brief flash of anger. "I am not pleased that they let someone through. It will not happen again."

His smile then returned. "I can't wait to see the look on the elders' faces." He began to laugh. "Their own arrogance has forced them to witness their worst fear."

"I'm sorry," said Gewey. "But I don't think it's very funny."

Linis forced back his laughter. "Forgive me, my friend. I forget myself. This is a joyous occasion, not to be tainted by the petty squabbles between me and the elders."

As they returned to the camp, Gewey and Linis went over the ceremony one last time. Upon arrival, Gewey could see that the elders had gathered. All of their eyes were fixed upon him.

"This should be interesting," muttered Gewey as he approached the group. The grim expressions on their faces told him that they were none too pleased.

"Gewey Stedding," said Lord Chiron. "As you probably know, we are not in favor of this union."

"I understa..." Gewey began, but Chiron held up a hand to silence him.

"Allow me to finish," he continued. "We are not in favor, but there is nothing we can do to stop it. As you know, this is among our most sacred rites, and you and Kaylia are the first in more than one hundred years to be bonded in this way. Because of this, we would not have it done here in the middle of nowhere. We feel that to be a sacrilege." All but Theopolou nodded in agreement. "We ask only that you delay the ceremony until we reach the Chamber of the Maker. It is a far more fitting site for such an event." He took a small step forward. "Kaylia has already agreed, but only if you do as well. What say you?"

Gewey's eyes drifted to Theopolou, but his face was stone.

"It may be a wise choice," Linis whispered in Gewey's ear.

Finally, Gewey squared his shoulders and said, "I do understand that this ritual is sacred to you. And if Kaylia is in agreement, then so am I. We can wait until we arrive."

Chiron bowed. "I thank you." The others bowed and dispersed.

"One more thing," called Gewey. The elders turned. "We will complete the bonding before I face your judgment."

"Agreed." Chiron walked away.

Only Theopolou lingered.

"A wise decision," said Theopolou, almost smiling. "This could go a long way to furthering your cause. The rite of bonding, performed in the Chamber of the Maker, is symbolic beyond your understanding."

"Who suggested this?" asked Linis.

"Lord Chiron," Theopolou replied. "He could be an important ally to you. He has been a friend to me for many of your lifetimes."

"And the others?" asked Gewey. "How do they feel about it?"

"Their opinions are mixed," Theopolou admitted. "Though they all agree that the rite should be performed in a more appropriate location, they still have a difficult time with the fact that a human is to be bonded to an elf. They may try to convince you not to do this, though they cannot stop you—or Kaylia."

"They can try all they want," said Gewey. "The choice has been made."

"Do not underestimate their guile," Theopolou warned. "They have far more experience in bending the will of others than you. Their arguments will be persuasive."

Gewey nodded with understanding.

Bellisia approached. "Gewey Stedding. I would speak with you alone." Theopolou and Linis bowed to her and walked away out of earshot.

"If you are here to talk me out of completing the bond with Kaylia..." Gewey began.

"I am here to warn you," said Bellisia.

"Warn me?"

"I know that you intend to try and sway the elves to join you in your fight against Angräal," she said. "And you may accomplish your goal. But should you bond with Kaylia..."

"Stop right there," said Gewey angrily. "My relationship with Kaylia has nothing to do with Angräal, or my reasons for being here."

"You think not?" she shot back. "Do you think the powers in the north are fools? What will they do once they discover that you are bonded to an elf woman?"

She paused. "They will kill her."

Gewey opened his mouth to speak, but no words came.

"That's right," Bellisia continued. "They will hunt Kaylia down and kill her. And they will do it to kill you."

A cold chill filled Gewey's chest. "Why would you think they care about me?"

Bellisia sniffed. "You imagine we do not know that the King of Angräal is searching for you? Every elf tribe knows your name. We have all been made aware that he seeks you and have been made offers of friendship for your deliverance—or death."

"Theopolou hasn't said anything about this," said Gewey. "He would have told me."

"Theopolou," she scoffed. "You think Theopolou is your friend? He is no more a friend to you than I am. But at least I am not trying to make you think otherwise. Theopolou has no love for humans. He is motivated by his love for his niece. Make no mistake, if he had his way, he would break your bond to Kaylia and see you dead."

"I don't believe you," said Gewey. "It was his idea that we complete the bonding. Why would he do that if what you say is true?"

"His idea?" she laughed. "And who suggested that you wait until we get to the Chamber of the Maker? Theopolou's closest friend—Lord Chiron."

"That doesn't prove a thing," said Gewey. "You're just trying to confuse me."

"No," said Bellisia. "I am trying to clear your mind."

She glanced over to Theopolou. Kaylia was at his side, talking quietly. "He will not allow you to complete the bond. He thinks there is a way to break it. He is wrong, of course. But his love for his niece blinds him." She turned back to Gewey. "That your spirit was able to combine with Kaylia's has caused much doubt among the elders. Enough that you might be able to convince them to side with you against Angräal. But you will not get the chance."

"What do you mean?" asked Gewey. "I'm supposed to prove that I'm not a threat to your people."

"Yes. And you intend to use that as an opportunity to plead your case. But I assure you, it will not happen. You will be dead before you utter your first word inside the Chamber."

"Are you saying Theopolou plans to have me killed?" he cried.

Bellisia shrugged. "I am saying that Theopolou will do everything he can to stop you completing the bond. But have you forgotten the assassin? Someone sent him. Perhaps someone among us. Whether it was Theopolou, I cannot say, but he certainly has the motivation to do so."

"And what are your motivations?" asked Gewey.

"I only want my people to be safe and free," she replied. "You are a being of great power. That much is clear, even though I don't know what you truly are. If killing you protects my people, then I would not hesitate. But I do not think that would do any good. And I do not believe that Angrääl will leave us in peace. You may be the only way we can escape destruction."

"Then why not join me?" asked Gewey.

Her eyes locked with Gewey's. "Because I am not willing to sacrifice our souls in order to survive. Whatever you are, your heart is human. To join you is to join them. That I cannot do."

"What would you have me do?" asked Gewey. "You said it yourself. Angrääl will not leave you in peace. The Dark One will march over the land like a plague, and both our peoples will suffer. Our only hope is to cooperate, even if it's only for a short time."

"That may be," she admitted. "And you may be able to convince the others. But my mind is set. I have seen what the humans do. I will not be a part of it." She took a small step back. "I have said what I came to say. Think on my words. Speak to Kaylia if you wish. But know that I have not lied to you."

"What would you do if you were me?" he asked, just as she began to walk away.

Bellisia paused and glanced back. "I would run. I would take Kaylia and run." With that, she left.

Gewey stared at Theopolou and Kaylia for a time before heading over to them. His mind was confused. Only one thing was for sure. He had to speak to Kaylia. He had to know what they were walking into.

# CHAPTER 24

Gewey approached Theopolou and Kaylia. Excusing himself from the old elf, he took Kaylia by the hand and led her far enough away so they would not be overheard. After Gewey told her what Bellisia had said, Kaylia sat thoughtfully for several minutes.

"Do you think she's telling the truth?" he asked.

"I think she believes so," Kaylia replied. "But do I think Theopolou means to break our bond and assassinate you? I honestly don't know. I wish I could dismiss it, but it does fit. He was the one who killed the assassin, and it was his friend who suggested we wait until we reach the Chamber of the Maker. All the same, I have never known my uncle to be dishonest."

"He deceived his own elves about what I am," Gewey reminded her. "And he only told them after Kaphalos had revealed our bond to them."

"True. And it was to his advantage to do so. But I don't think the assassin would have told us anything, regardless of what we did to him. Theopolou would have known this as well. Anyway, we still are not certain that you were the real target. Remember, it was Akakios who shot the assassin, and Akakios serves my uncle. No—even if what Bellisia said is true, I don't think he had anything to do with that."

"We could just ask him, I suppose," Gewey suggested. "I don't like feeling as if I'm being manipulated, and whether it's Bellisia, Theopolou, or anyone else, I want it to stop."

"Yes," she agreed. "I feel that confrontation is best. I want to know his motives before we get there. And if Bellisia is trying to drive a wedge between us, then we should know that, too."

Kaylia and Gewey found Theopolou talking with three of his escorts.

"Can we speak?" asked Gewey.

Theopolou nodded and dismissed the elves. Kaylia recounted Gewey's words and waited for a response. At first, Theopolou was expressionless, but then he began to laugh.

"Crafty," said Theopolou. "Very crafty. And correct."

"What?" cried Kaylia. "She was telling the truth?"

"Of course she was," said Theopolou. "At least from her perspective. I do not wish you to bond with Gewey. And yes, if there were a way, I would seek to break it. But Bellisia is wrong to suggest that I believe I can. The bond is unbreakable—even by the two of you. I certainly couldn't force it to break, and even if I could, it would likely kill you. As she said, I act out of love for you. That is my motivation." He turned to Gewey. "She told you I was no friend to you, and she is correct. But I am an ally."

"What do you think she was trying to do?" asked Gewey.

Theopolou smiled. "I think she was being honest. And I am glad for it. I had suspected her of many things until now."

"In what way does this rest your mind, uncle?" asked Kaylia.

"Bellisia has been an opponent to me for quite some time," he explained. "Even in better times, she and I have rarely seen eye to eye. But her actions have usually been to protect our people—even when in opposition to me. That she would open her mind to a human, knowing that I would likely hear of it, tells me much. And her words have merit, though not in the way you might think."

He placed his hands on Kaylia's shoulders. "I swear to you that I mean your suitor no harm. Though this is not a bond I would have chosen for you, I know I must accept it. Should you wish, I will perform the rites here and now if that will prove my intentions to you."

Kaylia smiled warmly and hugged Theopolou. "I believe you."

Theopolou turned to Gewey. "I am your ally. But you must be mine in return." His eyes fell lovingly on Kaylia. "You must protect her."

"I swear I will," said Gewey. "But something Bellisia said still bothers me. She said that the Dark One will try to kill Kaylia to get to me."

"She is right," said Theopolou. "But they could do that already. Were either of you to die, it would rip the other apart, even without completing the bond. You would be useless shells, unable to fight. In fact, death would be kinder. But I think it is more likely that the Dark One would wish to capture Kaylia and use her to control you. Were that to happen, you could be made into a powerful weapon."

Gewey nodded. "What will you do now?"

"I shall speak with Bellisia," he replied. "Now that I feel I can trust her, I should like her council."

Theopolou embraced Kaylia once more and walked away to find Bellisia. "Do you believe him?" asked Gewey.

"Yes," she replied. "He is not plotting against us."

The elders announced that they were to remain where they were for a few hours, then start out again before daybreak. Kaylia, Gewey, and Linis went off a few yards from the others while Theopolou spoke privately with Bellisia.

Chiron approached. Gewey and the others stood and bowed. Chiron bowed in return. He looked different than

Theopolou. Though he was the same age, he seemed younger and less careworn of spirit. His hair still held its deep brown color, and he walked with a light spring in his step.

"You have courage, Gewey Stedding," said Chiron, once he reached them. "To face the council of elders within the Chamber of the Maker, and do so after bonding with one of our own kind..." He laughed softly. "Truly remarkable."

"Are you here to convince me not to go through with it?" asked Gewey.

"Not at all," Chiron replied. "Besides, what can be done now? Your spirits are already joined. You have very little choice in the matter. That is unless you intend to allow your souls to rend asunder."

"You are a friend to my uncle," said Kaylia.

"I am," he replied. "For many years, we have been as brothers."

"Then I am a friend to you," she said.

Chiron smiled. His eyes then fell on Gewey. "And what of you? Shall you be a friend to me as well?"

"If you would like," Gewey replied. "I am eager to befriend the people of my future unorem."

Chiron cocked his head. "I see you have been learning our customs. In that case, allow me to educate you further." He took a seat on the grass. Gewey and the others did likewise. "Has anyone told you of the rite of pudnaris?"

Gewey shook his head.

Chiron glanced briefly at both Kaylia and Linis. "Then your friends have been neglectful of your education."

"I..." began Linis. But one look from Chiron silenced him.

"Let me explain," said Chiron. "Pudnaris is when a suitor is challenged for his right to join with his intended mate. This challenge can be made by anyone as long as they can give valid cause."

"Who could have cause?" asked Kaylia. "I have accepted no other suitor."

"True," said Chiron. "But there are other arguments to be made to support the pudnaris besides a potential rival."

"Like what?" asked Gewey.

"In this case, anything," he replied.

"Why are you telling me this?" asked Gewey.

"I tell you because you have the right to know. Many will oppose this union. Perhaps enough to risk their lives to stop you." He scrutinized Gewey for a moment. "We know that you control great power, and open battle with you is a risk. We also know of your fight with the Vrykol. If Theopolou is correct, and that is what they truly were, the fact that you defeated them tells us everything we need to know about your skill." He pointed to Gewey's sword hanging at his side. "And to face that weapon in the hands of someone who can use the flow to gain strength is to face death."

"You know something about my sword?" asked Gewey.

"I know a little," Chiron replied. "It was made during a time when elves first walked the earth and our knowledge was vast. The art of its construction has been lost in time, but the legends remain. Only small objects can be made now and with limited uses. Whoever gave you that sword had no idea what they possessed, or they would have never given it away. It was said that such weapons could make someone powerful beyond measure."

Gewey looked down at his sword, remembering the first time he had used it when fighting Salmitaya's soldiers. "Do you think someone will challenge me?"

"Who can say?" the elf replied. "I tell you this only to warn you." He rose to his feet. "I will inform you if I hear of anything." He spun about and strode off before Gewey could utter another word.

Gewey watched Chiron as he walked away. "I don't trust him," he said quietly.

"He is Theopolou's friend," said Kaylia. "And my uncle trusts him."

"Gewey's right," Linis interjected. "I get the same feeling. He seems all too willing to accept you. It may be nothing, but I feel something is amiss." He rubbed his chin in thought. "Still, if Theopolou trusts him, I suppose we should as well."

"Did you know about this pudnaris?" Gewey asked, looking to both Kaylia and Linis.

Kaylia nodded. "Yes, but I did not think it important. As an elf facing judgment, and with my well-known relationships with humans, I could not imagine why anyone would call for it. Not to mention that we are already bonded. That should be enough to deter any potential rivals."

"True," said Linis. "But if someone thought to use it to prevent your union with Gewey, things could get complicated."

He looked at Gewey with a grave expression. "If it happens, you will be exposed. The amount of flow you will need to channel in order to defeat a determined elf will be immense. I remember when I saw you holding the power within you for the first time."

"But you didn't guess what I was," said Gewey.

"No," said Linis. "But I knew beyond doubt that you were something different. And remember, I am not as versed in such matters as the elders. There will be many more of them at the Chamber when we arrive. You can bet that they will figure it out. The only reason they have not as of yet, is that the idea of a god in human form is beyond most of our understanding or imagination."

Gewey thought for a minute. "I don't see anything I can do about it," he said finally. "They'll know about me one way or another in time, anyway."

"You have a point," Linis agreed. "But it would be better if they found out by watching you open the Book of Souls. If Theopolou has not deceived us, you may get the chance to do so." He reached out and placed his hand on Gewey's shoulder. "Whatever happens, Kaylia and I will stand by you. Until then, we should keep our wits about us and look for signs of trouble."

"You still suspect Theopolou?" asked Gewey.

"I suspect there are plans set in motion against us. That much is clear. I have not heard anything thus far that eases my suspicions." Linis glanced over at Theopolou, then Bellisia. "Of course, our true enemy may yet to be revealed. Mistrust can be a powerful weapon."

Gewey thumbed the hilt of his sword. "I want to trust Theopolou. My heart tells me to. I suppose we'll know soon enough, won't we?"

Linis nodded. "That we will."

Kaylia was oddly silent, but her eyes never left her uncle.

The rest of the evening was uneventful. Gewey and Kaylia sat a few yards away from the others, talking, while Linis rejoined the elders to discuss their route. The two elves that had been sent into the forest to bury the assassin returned about an hour before it was time to depart. Their faces were somber when they rejoined their companions, and they clearly had no wish to speak.

Gewey gathered his gear and checked his sword. Akakios and the other three guards had already rejoined the others, leaving Linis as Gewey's sole companion.

"I guess there's no point in guarding me any longer," Gewey remarked.

"I think they realize it is a useless gesture," said Linis. "They are of more use protecting their masters than watching you."

# CHAPTER 25

The spirits of the party did not rise with the sun. The events of the previous day weighed heavily on their minds, and aside from their footfalls and the rustling of gear, not a sound could be heard to disturb the gloomy silence. Kaylia continued to stay by Theopolou's side, while Linis and Gewey remained at the rear. Gewey felt more at ease where eyes could not easily watch him. Though the pace had slowed a bit, they were still able to cover many miles before they made camp for the night. The evening mood was as dreary and quiet as it had been during the day, though it was decided that a few small fires could be lit.

Linis and Kaylia, along with Theopolou and Chiron, joined Gewey beside the fire he had built a few yards away from the main camp. Six guards surrounded them, although far enough away not to intrude. Even so, Gewey still felt uneasy as he noticed the contemptuous stares they threw at him whenever he met their eyes.

"I thought it would be best to display our unity to the others," explained Chiron as he took a seat by the fire.

"I appreciate it," said Gewey. "I need all the help I can get."

"Indeed," said Theopolou. "The coming days will be difficult. Lord Chiron and I both agree that we must find a way for our people to survive the coming storm. Even if it means allying ourselves with the humans for a time."

"Others will argue that it is the humans who march," added Chiron. "The King of Angrääl was himself a member of Amon Dähl, and his armies are human, even if it is their own kind, they march on."

"The humans who follow him have been deceived," said Linis. "They have no idea what is about to be unleashed upon the world. And the elves that think him the reincarnation of King Rätsterfel are just as blind and twice as stupid."

"I cannot argue," Chiron admitted. "But you must take into account that many of our people are wary of what has become of us. They no longer want to live in the shadows, yet they cannot bear to live side by side with humans."

"What do you think?" Gewey asked Chiron.

"In my opinion, the elves should leave," he replied. "There are legends of lands beyond the great Western Abyss. It is said that my people once dwelt there. Perhaps it is time we returned."

"Those are just legends, as you say," said Theopolou. "And we have sent ships across the Abyss before. None have ever returned."

Chiron smiled and laughed softly. "I suppose this will be a discussion to be had once our people are no longer facing extinction. In the meantime, we have matters to resolve."

He turned to Gewey. "You will face intense opposition when you are before the entire council of elders. Some, perhaps many, will wish to aid you, but few will be prepared to say so openly. It is important that you convince more than just Theopolou and me to speak in your favor. To do this, you must open the Book of Souls." He eyed Gewey intensely. "Theopolou is confident that you can do this. Can you?"

Gewey thought for a long moment before admitting: "I don't know."

"That's not the answer I was hoping for," said Chiron. "But it will have to do. If you are challenged for the right to bond with Kaylia, you must wait until after the bonding before speaking to the council. You have until sunrise of the next day to answer the challenge, so you must not act before then. If the Book is opened and you are proven to be the fulfillment of prophecy, then not only will you likely avoid further challenges, but almost certainly you will also gain the support you need."

"What if we waited until after I've opened the Book to complete the bond?" suggested Gewey.

"Risky," remarked Linis. "If you are not successful…"

"Then Gewey and I will still complete the rite," Kaylia interjected.

"The fact is," said Theopolou, "there is no way to tell what will happen until we arrive. I suspect that all of our plans will be useless. We will be entering an atmosphere alien to us all. Not since the Great War have so many elders been summoned."

Chiron nodded in agreement.

A commotion sounded at the edge of the camp. Gewey and the others sprang to their feet and drew their weapons. One of the elves who had been guarding Gewey ran up to them.

"We have an intruder," he told them.

"An intruder," Linis exclaimed. "How did anyone get past the watch?"

The elf shook his head. "I don't know. He just appeared out of nowhere."

"Is it an elf?" Theopolou asked.

"No," the guard replied. "He looks human but…"

"But what?" Chiron pressed.

"I'm not sure what to make of him," the elf stammered. "He doesn't smell like a human."

"Take us to him," ordered Theopolou.

The guard bowed sharply and led Theopolou and the others to the camp's opposite edge. A group of elves was gathered in a circle with weapons drawn. They were surrounding a small cloaked figure leaning on a long, ash walking staff. Theopolou pushed his way between two elves and stood directly in front of the newcomer.

"Who are you?" Theopolou demanded. "What do you want?"

The figure did not look up. "I seek a child of heaven, I do. Oh, yes. Among the young ones, I find him."

Gewey knew at once who it was. "Felsafell!" he cried out.

An audible gasp could be heard throughout the elves. Clearly, they knew the name well.

Felsafell pushed back his hood, revealing his haggard features and crooked grin. "I see you remember old Felsafell—but of course, of course. You are not daft. Your mind is sharp. Oh yes, it is." He took a few steps toward Gewey. The elves gave way.

"What are you doing here?" asked Gewey.

"I have come again to see the world," he replied. "The spirits are gone, and the wind has risen. Blown away my friends, it has. The darkness comes, and the firstborn shall have one final adventure."

Bellisia stepped forward. "You claim to be Felsafell. How do we know this is who you really are?"

"Ah yes," Felsafell laughed. "The child of discontent, who sought me out. Did not find me. Could not find me. Cannot find herself. Lost you became and lost you are still. Indeed, indeed. With troubled past and uncertain future. She still seeks the thing she once lost."

Bellisia glared at Felsafell but fell silent.

This time, Theopolou stepped forward. "If you are Felsafell, we welcome you. Your wisdom has helped our people for many ages past. But please, explain to us why you are here."

Felsafell's smile vanished. "The wisest of the fallen speaks. Fallen from grace you are, yet in you, the spark remains. But I fear it fades. Like me and my brothers and sisters, fading from memory. Sad, sad, sad. The end nears for us both. But perhaps you may be saved. Oh, yes, I have seen the many paths. The trails of joy and sorrow join together."

"You speak in riddles," said Theopolou. "If you know something, tell us."

"Know?" Felsafell sighed. "I know many things. Yes, I do. But none to help you. Alone is the journey of the second-born. To what end shall be your task to discover? I come to aid the heaven child. Nothing less and nothing more."

Gewey walked up to Felsafell and bowed low. "I never had the chance to thank you for what you did for me. If it were not for you, I'd still be trapped."

"How did he help you?" asked Bellisia.

"The why's and what's will have their time," Felsafell said. "I know much and will share what I can. I will indeed. Oh, yes." He looked across the gathering. "I know you have questions. Always questions for old Felsafell. But be mindful of what you ask. You may learn what you should not know."

"So you intend to accompany us?" asked Chiron.

"I do, I do," he replied. "If you will have me. To learn to speak in the world again. An adventure that I did not see. Thought I would fade. Fade away and join my kin. But they have been stolen. The first are all gone."

"You may join us," said Gewey.

"You speak without authority," snapped Bellisia. "We must..."

"He joins me, or I don't go," said Gewey.

Bellisia paused, then turned and walked away, muttering.

"An old man is tired," said Felsafell. "Rest is what I need. At least for a while. Questions after. Questions waiting."

"Come with me," said Gewey, offering his hand.

Felsafell smiled cheerfully and allowed Gewey to lead him through the camp to where he had set up his bedroll.

"You can take my blanket," said Gewey. "I'm not tired."

"A kind child of heaven you are," said Felsafell. He plopped down on the ground and wrapped himself in the blanket. In seconds, he was breathing deeply.

"I can't believe he is here," remarked Kaylia. "I wonder what he wants."

"Whatever it is, he sure has stirred up the elders," said Gewey, amused.

Theopolou approached. "We would like to speak with you," he said. It was clear he did not share Gewey's amusement.

Gewey, Kaylia, and Linis followed Theopolou to the far side of the camp where the elders, along with their escorts, had gathered. They eyed Gewey as they shuffled uneasily and whispered to each other.

"How is it you know of Felsafell?" Bellisia demanded.

Gewey considered for a moment whether or not to mention his experience in the spirit world and decided not to. "I met him in the Spirit Hills, after escaping from an agent of the Dark One."

"And how did you come upon him?" asked Lord Aneili.

Gewey recounted the story of his encounter, leaving out the details that would suggest his origin.

"You stayed in his home?" said Chiron. "Remarkable. Many of my people have sought out Felsafell. Some never to return. But even those who found him have never been afforded such a privilege."

"We're still not certain that is the real Felsafell," countered Bellisia.

"You seemed certain enough when he spoke to you a moment ago," said Theopolou. "Gewey appears to believe him, and of all of us, he seems to have the most personal knowledge."

"Suppose this is Felsafell," said Lady Leora. "Is it wise to have him among us?"

Lord Endymion laughed. "Just what would you have us do, Leora? Kill him? He walked straight into our camp without being noticed. Do you think he gives us a choice?"

"I think we should hear what Gewey has to say." Theopolou turned to Gewey. "You clearly want him with you, but is there anything you can tell us that might explain his being here?"

Bellisia leveled her gaze on Gewey. "Indeed, child of heaven. That is what he called you, is it not? What do you think are his motives?"

"I don't know why he's here," said Gewey. "But I don't think he is here to harm us. That's not his way."

"Tell that to my brother," cried one of Chiron's escorts. "He vanished in the Spirit Hills seeking Felsafell's so-called wisdom, never to be seen again."

"I don't think Felsafell did anything to your brother," said Gewey. "He warned me when I was with him that the spirits would try and play with my mind. That they could make people lost and confused. If your bother disappeared, I would think the spirits are the villains, not Felsafell."

"So you say," scoffed Bellisia. "Apparently, he has much interest in you. But why now? Why has he appeared just as we are preparing to gather? Are you sure you cannot answer this riddle—child of heaven? Can you be certain that he means us no harm? Perhaps he just means you no harm."

"I'm certain he is who he says he is," replied Gewey, trying to ignore Bellisia's repeated reference. "As for anything else, I was not alone when I met him, and Felsafell made no move to harm my companion. In fact, he did what he could to make sure the spirits left both us in peace."

Bellisia scowled. "That proves nothing. There is something you are not telling us. No one shows as much trust as you show Felsafell without good reason."

"Perhaps Gewey is not as jaded as some," said Chiron, in an obvious dig at Bellisia.

"We are talking in circles," said Theopolou. "We either allow Felsafell to continue with us, or we ask him to depart." He looked at Gewey. "You say that you will not go without him?"

Gewey nodded. "As long as he wants to come with me, I will have him."

Theopolou turned to the others. "There you have it. As Gewey is called before you to give testimony, you must make your decision. Do you withdraw your invitation?"

The elders looked at each other, but none said a word.

"Very well," Theopolou continued with satisfaction. "Felsafell will be welcome among us." He turned to Gewey. "Watch over our new guest. I will be with you in a moment."

Gewey bowed and walked back to where Felsafell was still fast asleep, Linis and Kaylia close behind.

"Sometimes I can't tell the difference between an elf and a human," muttered Gewey.

"What do you mean?" asked Linis.

Gewey had not meant his words to be heard. "I'm sorry. I meant no offense. It's just that since I've met the elders, I've seen nothing but petty squabbling and disagreements. The council back home in Sharpstone gets along better than they do."

"You are not wrong to say so," Linis agreed. "Once we were a noble people, with honor and understanding. Our forefathers would be disgusted with us now. It is as if a veil of mistrust has been brought down upon us, and we do not know how to lift it."

"My father thought that the generation who fought in the war would have to leave this world before we are healed," added Kaylia. "He believed that the bitterness it caused prevents us from regaining what we have lost."

Linis nodded. "I think he may have been right. It is a new way of thinking we need. Our race must find how to exist in a new world."

"Where does he fit in?" asked Gewey, motioning to the sleeping Felsafell. "What is he? He's certainly not an elf. He looks human, but he isn't."

"What am I?" said Felsafell, popping to his feet. "I am the oldest. I am. The most withered."

"I'm sorry," said Gewey. "We didn't mean to wake you."

Felsafell smiled cheerfully, stretching his arms. "I wake myself. Sleep I did. Sleep well. Sleep soundly. Sleep plenty."

"But you've only just laid down," said Linis. "Even an elf needs more rest than that."

"An elf I am not," said Felsafell. "And the child of heaven is right. I am not human."

"Then what are you?" asked Kaylia.

"I am the first," he replied. "But not the last. No. I shall soon fade. But before I do, I must rescue my kin. Rescue my past."

"I don't understand," said Gewey.

"All will be clear," Felsafell assured. "Clear as glass. But not now. Now, with enemies about, we must be swift and silent."

"Enemies?" said Gewey

"Don't fret," said Felsafell. "No swords or arrows will hinder us. A clear path we have. But enemies don't always carry swords. Be silent and still and all will be well."

The party gathered and continued toward the Chamber of the Maker. Felsafell walked just behind Gewey and Kaylia, while Linis ventured a few yards ahead of everyone, scouting for signs of an ambush.

As the day progressed, elves gradually began to approach Felsafell, each requesting a private talk. Felsafell's wisdom was legendary among the elves, and they did not want to miss a chance to benefit from it. True to his word, Felsafell was more than willing to speak to all comers. Some walked away smiling, others angry, and others in tears. Gewey wondered what he had told them, remembering the words the strange little man had for him while on his porch in the Spirit Hills, and how those words had upset him.

They stopped once for the midday meal. Gewey listened for signs of pursuit, but to his relief, all he could hear was the sound of the wind and various small animals. Even though he informed Linis of this, the elf still insisted on searching the area. And while Linis could remain invisible to all the others, Gewey enjoyed the fact that he alone was able to hear exactly where the seeker was.

"Your power grows," said Felsafell, munching on a bit of bread. "No longer weak. No longer frail."

"How do you know what I am?" asked Gewey.

"I am old, not blind."

Gewey stared into Felsafell's watery, gray eyes. Something was there, deep inside. Something different. Something unfamiliar. "You're really not human, are you?" he said.

"Human?" he laughed. "No, no, no. I am too old for that. I am the first, yet I will not be the last."

"You said that before," said Gewey. "But what does it mean?"

"Me and kin wandered the hills and valleys, we did," said Felsafell. "Happy and free. Before the elves and their ways. Before humans and their wars."

Gewey raised an eyebrow. "So you're saying your people were here first? Where are they now, and why haven't I heard of them?"

"We are all gone." A tinge of sorrow filled Felsafell's voice. "All but me. Poor Felsafell. Gone before the humans gathered were we. We saw the coming of elves. But too small the world became. Too prideful were we to remain. Deep in silence, we escaped until only our voices were left."

"So your people were here before the elves," said Gewey. "But what about the gods?"

"Oh, how wonderful they were," said Felsafell. "We loved them so. We love them still. But in time, we lost our way and our will. Spirits we became—companions to your mother and father."

"Do you know who my real mother is?" asked Gewey. "I've guessed that my father is Gerath. But who is my mother?"

"I tell what I know," he replied. "But I speak of only what I know. And this I do not. Perhaps the Book of Souls has what you seek."

"You know about that?" said Gewey in a hushed tone.

"Oh, yes," said Felsafell. "I was there. I saw the Book. I hear its cry. It longs to be opened. But beware. A bell that is sounded cannot be un-rung."

"What's in it?" asked Gewey.

"Many things," he replied. "Some I know, and others I do not. But now is not the time for telling these secrets. Soon enough. Yes—soon enough."

Kaylia walked up and took a seat beside Gewey. "You have caused quite a stir," she told Felsafell. "The entire party can't stop talking about you."

The old man smiled. "I have not left home in the lives of many an elf. It is good to see the world. Better to know I'm remembered."

"I've noticed your speech has changed a bit," said Gewey.

Felsafell cocked his head. "Has it? I guess living in the world does that. Oh yes. Practicing with the living makes it easy. Spirits have no need for speech, and elves rarely visit."

"What about humans?" asked Kaylia. "Do they ever seek you out?"

"No, no," he answered. "They know nothing of me. They think me a ghost. A rumor. But time for more talk will come later. Now we must march."

The elves had already begun to gather their packs and gear, and soon they were on the move once again. The day was warm, with the sun shining brightly in the sky. Traveling with Felsafell was enjoyable for Gewey. He never tired of the old hermit's stories, though he understood very little at times, and had never heard of most people and places that were mentioned. Before he realized it, they had walked thirty miles, and it was time to stop for the night.

The following days were much the same, though Gewey was becoming increasingly apprehensive as they neared their destination. The night before they were due to arrive, Theopolou asked Gewey to accompany him away from the others.

"Are you prepared?" asked Theopolou.

"I'm not sure," Gewey admitted. "I really have no idea what I'm going to say to convince them."

Theopolou looked at Gewey thoughtfully. "The appearance of Felsafell should help with that. Word will spread fast that he is with us. That you have such an ancient wisdom as your ally will go far to sway the doubters. The main thing you must remember is not to allow yourself to get angry. Your opponents will try to twist your words. If you show anger, they will see it as a sign of weakness and you will lose support quickly."

"I'll do my best." Gewey sighed, trying to anticipate just what might be said to anger him. No firm ideas formed.

When he returned to camp, Gewey sought to temporarily forget concerns about the day ahead by listening to Felsafell sing songs in an ancient forgotten tongue. Though he couldn't understand the words, he imagined an epic battle between good and evil being waged across time. He wondered what the song was really about, but did not bother to ask. Once the song was done, Gewey shut his eyes and listened to the music of the forest until he felt the dawn approaching.

Linus kneeled beside him. "Today is the day."

Gewey opened his eyes and smiled. "I'm ready."

# CHAPTER 26

I t was mid-morning when Gewey noticed the terrain around him beginning to change. The woods became thicker—so dense, in fact, that even when he used his powers to listen, the sound bounced straight back, startling him.

The party funneled into a narrow trail, causing their progress to slow. No sound could be heard at all, not even their footfalls. Gewey nestled himself between Felsafell and Linis as Felsafell began to whistle. The sound pierced the dead silence of the woods, making some of the elves uneasy.

"We're nearly there," whispered Linis.

"Nearly there indeed," said Felsafell. "There and back we go. Once more and again."

Gewey couldn't help but smile at Felsafell's words, though most times they made no sense to him.

After about an hour, they came to a narrow stream spanned by an elegant, wooden bridge. Theopolou motioned for everyone to halt.

"We come in brotherhood and friendship," he called out.

There was a long pause before a voice called back from the other side. "Then enter and be welcome."

Theopolou and the other elders slowly led the party over the bridge. Here, the landscape soon opened up into a soft grassy meadow dotted with multicolored wildflowers. Tents lined the far end, and Gewey could see elves walking among them. Far beyond the tents, a white, vaulted roof peeked out. A group of three elf women dressed in tan leather shirts and trousers, each with a long knife at her side, approached from among the tents. Theopolou raised his hand in greeting, but the women made no reply. When they were a few feet away, Theopolou stopped and bowed.

"Matrons of the Creator," said Theopolou, without looking up. "I offer you my friendship. As the eldest among my party, I claim the right to beg entry for all."

The matrons examined the group, only pausing for a second when their eyes passed Gewey and Felsafell. They looked at each other and nodded.

"Be welcome," said the woman in the middle. "But be warned. You bring two humans with you, and will be responsible for their well-being, and answerable for their actions."

"I understand," he replied, lifting his head. "We need to be shown to our quarters at once. There is much to do."

"You, along with the other elders, have already been seen to," said the matron on the left. "Your tents and provisions had been made ready and await you."

Her gaze fell on Gewey and Felsafell. "However, we did not expect to accommodate humans."

"They need no special consideration," said Theopolou. "They will lodge with me and mine."

"Very well," said the matron on the right. "I assume you know your way." With that, they turned and walked back in the direction of the tents.

Theopolou waved Gewey over. "Stay with me." He turned to the others. "Farewell for now."

The other elders and their escorts bowed in turn and headed off in different directions to their own tents.

Theopolou led Gewey, Linis, Kaylia, Felsafell, and his own escort to the left, toward the western edge of the encampment. Gewey glanced several times at the domed roof, hoping to get a better look, but to his disappointment, the dome disappeared as they drew close to the campsite. From the far end of the meadow, Gewey hadn't been able to tell how many tents had been erected. But now they were passing amongst them, he was surprised to see that they numbered literally in the hundreds. Elves were everywhere. Most were dressed in plain leather or linen, but some were attired in fine silks and adorned with exquisite jewelry.

"I never thought to see this many of your people at the same time," whispered Gewey to Linis.

"I'm shocked as well," said Linis. "I thought to see less than half this many. It seems Theopolou's call has caused quite a stir."

"All the more reason to be cautious," Kaylia interjected over her shoulder.

They wound their way through the camp until they reached a large silver tent. It was twelve feet tall and at least forty feet across. Gewey figured it could easily house three times the number they had with them.

Theopolou pulled back the tent flap and disappeared inside. Kaylia, Felsafell, and Theopolou's escort followed close behind. Gewey and Linis entered last.

Gewey looked around, impressed. The interior resembled a house more than a tent. Just past the entrance was a large open area with a dozen plush chairs lining the walls. In the center was a round table, low set but big enough to accommodate twenty people; an assortment of cushions rested on the ground beneath this. The scent of mint filled the air, emanating from the roasted lamb that had been placed on the table. Along the ceiling hung light orbs set just dimly enough to give the room a warm feel. The floor was uncovered, but the soft grass was as lush and beautiful as any carpet. At the far left corner, another tent flap led to the back areas.

"There are enough rooms for everyone," said Theopolou, pointing to the rear flap. "They are all the same, so choose as you will. Hot water should be waiting for you ... unless you prefer to eat before you wash."

"No, thank you," said Gewey. "I prefer to be clean when I eat if I can."

Theopolou nodded and led the group through to the back. A hall lined with several cloth-covered doorways stretched before him. Gewey chose the third room, and Linis the one just beyond. Kaylia and the others continued to follow Theopolou and disappeared around a corner. Felsafell whistled merrily and turned to wink at Gewey before heading after them.

Gewey's room was rather sparse compared to the main dining and lounging area. A small bedroll had been placed in one corner, and opposite this, a washbasin with a cotton towel folded neatly beside it. One light globe hung from the ceiling, and a soft, thin, brown rug covered the floor.

Gewey washed and changed into a cotton shirt and pants, then strapped on his sword. He could still smell the mint lamb, and his stomach growled loudly.

"Are you ready?" came Linis's voice from just outside his room.

Gewey threw back the door flap and smiled at the elf. "I'm starving."

Linis noticed Gewey was wearing his sword. "You will want to take that off at the table," he said. "It is considered rude to be armed at the table of your host, and for all intents and purposes this is still the home of Theopolou."

Gewey removed his sword. "Should I leave it behind?"

"No," Linis replied. "Keep it with you, but place it on the floor beside you."

Gewey nodded before following Linis into the dining hall. Theopolou and a few of his escorts were already seated. Gewey took a seat opposite them, while Linis sat on his left. Kaylia was not yet there.

Theopolou nodded at the lamb. "We serve ourselves here. Felsafell will not be joining us. He said he needs to rest."

One of Theopolou's escorts passed them a bottle of wine. Gewey gratefully accepted it, then gave it to Linis.

"I'll wait until we're all here," said Gewey, noticing that the other plates were still empty.

"We only await Kaylia," said Theopolou. "The rest are running errands."

"No need to wait any longer," said Kaylia, entering the room.

She was dressed in a loose-fitting, white cotton shirt, together with trousers and a pair of soft leather shoes. Her hair was tied into a long braid, and she carried a long knife in her left hand. After surveying the group, she took the seat on Gewey's right.

Theopolou cut off a portion of lamb, then passed it around to the others. One of the elves rose from the table to retrieve a basket filled with flatbread, and this was also handed around. To Gewey's relief, they dined in silence. It was all he could do to maintain his table manners. Not only was he famished, but the lamb was also exceedingly tender and juicy.

Once they were finished, two elves cleared the table and brought out a decanter of plum brandy. Gewey's mouth twisted as the sweet fragrance filled the room.

"I see you don't care for plum brandy," Theopolou observed. "I have more wine, if you would rather."

"Brandy will be fine," said Gewey. "I've never had elf brandy. I would try it before I decide."

Theopolou smiled slightly while passing the bottle over. To Gewey's relief, though the smell was similar, it was not as sweet as the brandy he had tasted in the past. In fact, it was quite pleasant. A smile crept over his face as he sipped it.

"Word of you and Felsafell will have begun to spread by now," said Theopolou. "I have called for a gathering in the Chamber of the Maker this evening for the joining between you and Kaylia." His eyes darkened. "Do not expect a warm reception."

Gewey nodded. "Do you expect me to be challenged?"

"I hope not," Theopolou replied. "It would complicate matters. On one hand, you could show your strength and resolve it. On the other hand, you may be prematurely exposed. That Felsafell is your friend and companion may give any would-be challengers pause—at least, that is my hope." His eyes fell on Linis. "I have debated as to the virtue of your presence. You are cast out and have refused to face judgment. Those who do not know this soon will. Yet your name still carries weight and respect, even among your ene-mies. You shall also stay by Gewey's side."

"I never intended to do anything else," Linis stated. "And I will offer again to perform the bonding. That is, if you think it will go ill for you, should you do it."

Theopolou's jaw tightened and his eyes narrowed. "I will not be denied my right, nor ignore my obligation as Kaylia's guardian and uncle. Though some may abandon me for what I am to do, I will not let politics cause me to act with dishonor."

"I meant no offense," said Linis. "I think only of your safety."

"Then I will have Lord Theopolou bond us," said Kaylia. "And no other."

Theopolou couldn't help smiling. The old elf got to his feet, accompanied by his escort. "Then you should both prepare. I must make the arrangements." He turned and left the tent.

"What do we do?" asked Gewey.

"If you are to be bonded in the Chamber of the Maker," said Linis, "I think I will try to find you some appropriate attire."

"Won't you be in danger if you go wandering around outside alone?" asked Gewey.

Linis flashed a smile. "I think not. There are few who can hope to attack me and live. Besides, with you and Felsafell around, I doubt I'm of much interest. At least, not yet." Linis stood and fastened his long knife to his belt. "If I were you, I would take advantage of your time together alone."

Gewey blushed as Linis departed. Kaylia forced back a laugh.

"Are you nervous?" asked Gewey.

Kaylia took Gewey's hand and kissed him lightly on the cheek. "No—not really. At least, not in the way a human might be." She could see that Gewey did not understand. "I feel as if I am beginning a new chapter in a life that I know nothing about. This does not make me nervous. It makes me excited." She scrutinized Gewey for a moment. "And you? How do you feel?"

Gewey thought for a moment. "I don't know. Not for sure. I do know this is what I want. I can feel that in my heart. It's just..."

He shook his head in frustration. "I wish I had the words. But I don't. In truth, I'm still just a simple farmer. I guess I feel small among the company I have been keeping. It's confusing."

"Even with me?" she asked.

"Especially with you," he admitted. "You are so far beyond anything my wildest dreams could have imagined. And I'm to be bonded with you. How am I worthy of this? How? Me, a hay farmer from Sharpstone, married to an elf princess."

Kaylia pulled Gewey to her and kissed him again, this time deep and hard. Gewey felt dizzy when she finally released him.

"For a farmer with no words, you seem to speak them well," she whispered. "You are worthy because I deem you worthy. Never forget that. And never forget that it is the company you keep that stands in awe of you." She stroked his cheek and smiled sweetly. "One more thing—I'm not a princess."

Gewey gazed deeply into her eyes. For the first time in days, he felt confident and at peace. He took Kaylia's hand and pulled it to his chest. "Thank you."

Kaylia cocked her head. "For what?"

"For showing me what I must do."

"And what is that?"

He squeezed her hand, then kissed it. "Bond with you. Bond with you, then see to it that we are never in fear again."

He jumped to his feet and pulled Kaylia up with him. "I guess you should get ready." He embraced her for a long moment. "As for me—I'll count the minutes."

Kaylia laughed softly. "It is tradition that I be attended by two elf maids." She looked around the tent. "Sadly, I seem to lack them."

As if on cue, two young elf girls dressed in blue satin dresses entered the tent. One carried a thick bundle bound with a thin twine. The other had a large leather bag thrown over her left shoulder. They stopped just inside the tent and bowed.

"We have been sent by Lord Chiron to attend Lady Kaylia," said the elf holding the bundle.

Kaylia beamed. "A kind gesture. And well received." She leaned over and kissed Gewey lightly on the cheek, then allowed the two maids to lead her away into the back of the tent.

Gewey took a seat back at the table and nibbled on a piece of bread while waiting for Linis to return. After half an hour, the tent flap opened. But instead of Linis, Akakios entered. He wore a grave expression.

"What's wrong?" asked Gewey.

"Word of your bonding has spread," he replied. "Lord Theopolou was nearly assaulted." Gewey jumped up. "How did it happen?"

Akakios peered outside for a moment. "An argument broke out regarding his presiding over the bonding ceremony. Linis stopped it just as knives were being drawn." He looked around the tent. "Where is Kaylia?"

"She's getting ready," Gewey answered. "Lord Chiron sent two maids to attend her."

"That's good," said Akakios. "The sooner this is over, the better. I have a feeling tensions will keep rising. Perhaps once the two of you are bonded, there will be no further need for this nonsense."

"I wish I could say I am sorry," remarked Gewey. "But Theopolou knew this could happen. I think he knew it must. Change is always hard. I will not apologize for my bond with Kaylia. It's important. Not only for us but for everyone."

Akakios sighed heavily. "When I first met you, those words would have angered me. Now—I think I understand why this must be."

He walked to the side of the tent and sat in one of the chairs. "I've heard the words of Felsafell. He speaks of us as a broken people. I think he is right to say so. When I hear of the grace and wisdom of my ancestors, I cannot help but long for us to regain what we once were. Not power. Not to be as we were before the Great War. But to be as we were in the times of our legends. I used to think that they were just stories. But now I feel they are more than that."

He reached behind him and touched a glowing globe that hung from the wall. Sadness washed over his face. "Once we created such things as to rival the craft of the gods. Now..."

"Compared to the darkness and fear that exists in the human world, your people are still great and wise," Gewey said.

Akakios raised a hand and shook his head. "No. We are not as humans think we are. Not as good, nor as cruel. We have hidden ourselves away for so long that we have become ... something else."

"I'm hoping to change that," said Gewey. "Perhaps when all is done, the elves can learn how to become what they once were. Perhaps something even greater." He took a seat next to Akakios. "I've only begun to learn about your legends, but what I've read tells about a people who led open and adventurous lives. I believe it is time for your people to live that way again."

Akakios turned his head to Gewey and smiled. "Yes, I believe you're right. For too long, we have stewed in our own hatred. It is indeed time for us to live in the world again."

"Indeed," said Lord Chiron. He was standing just inside the tent, wearing a crimson robe tied at the waist by a black silk rope. His long knife peeked out as he moved toward them.

Both Gewey and Akakios stood and bowed.

"Forgive me, my Lord," said Akakios. "The threat to my Lord Theopolou so close to the Chamber of the Maker caused me to despair."

"You are right to be upset by such events," said Chiron. "But we should look to happier matters." He turned to Gewey. "I trust Kaylia is well attended?"

Gewey bowed again. "She is. I thank you for your kindness."

Chiron waved his hand. "Not at all. I am honored to have taken part in such a momentous event." His eyes strayed to the flap leading to the sleeping quarters. "And I shall further my participation by inviting you to join me in my tent until it is time for the ceremony. It would not do to have you here while your future unorem is getting dressed mere feet away."

"I thank you again," said Gewey. "But I am still waiting for Linis to return."

"Akakios can remain here and tell him where you have gone," said Chiron. "As I understand it, he is combing the encampment for more appropriate attire for you. I doubt he will be successful, and this I can provide."

"Then lead the way," said Gewey. He turned to Akakios. "You do not mind waiting?"

"Not at all. The tent should not be unattended in any case, especially with Kaylia and Felsafell both here."

"Good point," said Gewey.

Chiron led Gewey out of the tent and through the camp. Along the way, Gewey couldn't help but notice the constant stares. Some were of amazement, others of contempt. The sun was now low in the sky and the smell of hundreds of cooking fires filled the air, lending a soft glow to the vast number of tents.

"I can't imagine what this must look like at night," muttered Gewey.

"It is quite a sight," remarked Chiron. "So many have not been gathered here in quite some time."

Gewey looked north to the domed roof of the Chamber of the Maker. Even before the fullness of night, the lights from a thousand illuminated globes caused it to shine like a shimmering jewel.

"How old is it?" asked Gewey.

"I don't know," Chiron replied. "Older than history itself, it is said. It was ancient, even in the time of my ancestors."

Gewey marveled at the idea. "It looks as if it were newly built. At least, it does from here."

Chiron nodded. "The stone never ages. Not that we can tell, at least. It looks just as it did when I was a boy, and never once has it needed repair. A monument to the ancient craft of our people. One long forgotten, I'm afraid." He looked back over his shoulder. "Perhaps you can change that."

Chiron's tent was nearly identical to Theopolou's in size, but instead of being silver, it was emerald green. Two guards stood just outside the entrance. They bowed as Chiron and Gewey passed. The interior was also similarly set up to Theopolou's tent, apart from the table being oval-shaped and colored green to match that of the tent. At least a dozen elves buzzed about. Some Gewey recognized from their journey, other faces were new.

"I presume you have eaten?" said Chiron.

"I have."

Chiron smiled. "Then allow me to show you to where you'll prepare."

He led Gewey to the back of the main hall and into the sleeping quarters area. Chiron showed Gewey into the first room along. Unlike his quarters in Theopolou's tent, this room was equipped with a soft bed, a dresser, and a wardrobe.

"You will find fitting attire here. I will send someone to attend to your grooming shortly."

Gewey thanked Chiron and explored the contents of the wardrobe. He found a white silk shirt embroidered with the likeness of two eagles facing each other, together with a pair of matching trousers. The fabric was finer than any he had ever felt. A tan vest completed the ensemble.

An elf girl entered with a tray of grooming items. Gewey was thankful he had not yet begun to undress. His hair had grown long since the last time it had been cut in the home of Lord Ganflin—a fact that he hadn't noticed until that very moment. The girl motioned for him to sit and immediately went to work. Unlike the woman who had groomed him the last time, she spoke not a word, nor did she bother to allow him to gaze at his reflection, even though she carried a mirror on her tray.

Once she left, Gewey donned his attire and rummaged around in the wardrobe until he found a pair of black leather boots. They were a bit tight on his feet, but not so much as to prevent him from wearing them. The only thing missing was a belt, so he used the shirt he had just taken off to polish the belt he was already using.

"Are you dressed?" called Chiron from outside Gewey's room.

"Please, come in," called Gewey.

Chiron entered, dressed in the same white robes he had worn at the home of Theopolou. Chiron scrutinized Gewey for a moment. "You look ... acceptable. Though that belt of yours could use some attention."

"I couldn't find another," said Gewey. "But this one will do once I've cleaned it a bit more."

"I could provide you with another if you wish."

"Thank you, but no," said Gewey. "This was given to me by the same man who gave me my sword. It may be dingy now, but it's a fine belt when polished. Besides, it fits my scabbard perfectly."

Gewey had placed his sword on the bed. Chiron eyed the weapon and nodded in its direction. "Might I see it?" he asked.

Gewey picked it up and handed it over. "Certainly. But be careful not to touch the blade. It will burn you."

"I see," muttered Chiron as he slid the sword free, careful to touch only the leather that wrapped the hilt. A high-pitched ring filled the air, then faded away.

"A true wonder," said Chiron. "That you possess this is a miracle. Such things were thought lost. There isn't an elf alive who wouldn't give up everything he or she owned to possess such a sword."

"They couldn't wield it unless it was truly theirs," said Gewey. "Once it is first drawn, the blade can only be touched by the one who drew it."

Chiron re-sheathed and handed the sword back to Gewey, though his eyes never left it. "I see. You should take care never to lose it."

Gewey suddenly felt uneasy. "I will."

Chiron blinked and regained his focus. "If you are ready, I would have you join me in the main hall. It may be several hours until Theopolou has everything in order. We can relax there and wait. That is ... unless you are tired and would rather sleep. I can certainly provide a bed."

"I'm anything but tired," Gewey replied with a grin. "In fact, I wish I could explore the camp."

"That would not be a good idea, unfortunately." Chiron chuckled. "You will have to make do with the simple conversation of an old elf."

Gewey's cheeks flushed. "I didn't mean..."

Chiron threw his head back in laughter. "I jest. I am not offended. I, too, would like to wander the camp. There are many friends I have not seen in some time. But I fear that my association with Theopolou has lost me many of them."

"And your support of me, I wager," Gewey added.

"True."

Chiron rose to his feet. "Come. Let us relax and tell tales. It may be the last of simple pleasures we have for quite some time."

Gewey nodded and followed Chiron into the main hall. The table was empty and only a couple of Chiron's guards were visible.

"Where did everybody go?" asked Gewey.

"Most are in the back preparing for the ceremony," Chiron replied. "The rest are running errands for me."

Gewey and Chiron took seats on opposite sides of the table. One of the guards brought them a bottle of wine.

"Careful with that," warned Chiron. "We wouldn't want you too lightheaded." Gewey stared at the bottle, then pushed it away.

Chiron smiled and ordered a pitcher of water.

They talked of Gewey's home and upbringing until Linis arrived. It wasn't until he saw Linis enter that he realized Chiron had not spoken a single word about himself.

"Forgive my absence," said Linis. "But I've been busy assisting Theopolou. Akakios told me you were here, so I knew you were in good hands."

"No worries," said Gewey. "Lord Chiron has kept me quite occupied. Though I regret I must have rambled on. But it's been wonderful to take my mind off things for a bit."

Chiron bowed his head slightly. "It was a pleasure. So seldom do I have such a chance to hear of the human world." He turned to Linis. "All is ready?"

"It is," said Linis. "Theopolou and the others are awaiting us in the Chamber of the Maker. Even Felsafell is there."

"And Kaylia?" asked Gewey.

Linis laughed heartily. "Don't worry. She will be there as well."

"Then let us go," said Chiron.

Gewey's stomach began to quiver. Suddenly, he felt faint. Linis rushed up and put his arm around him.

"He can face the Vrykol," Linis teased. "But an elf woman makes him weak in the knees."

Gewey blushed and tried to regain his composure. "I'm fine."

He took a deep breath. "Let's go."

# CHAPTER 27

As Gewey left the tent, he was awestruck. In the fullness of night, the camp was an ocean of multicolored lights. The tents glowed brightly, their fabrics silhouetted by their inhabitants moving about inside. Although not as bright as the light of day, he could see just as clearly. It was as if a shadow had been removed from his eyes, allowing him to see the cool, natural beauty of the night. He could feel eyes upon him as they walked toward the Chamber.

"Before we enter, you must receive permission from the keepers to enter," said Chiron.

"The keepers?" said Gewey.

"Guards with a title," mocked Linis. "Most are elves who didn't have the talent to become seekers."

Chiron frowned at Linis. "They are more than that, and you know it. They stand watch over all that enters the Chamber of the Maker, and keep the peace within its borders."

"They are arrogant fools," grumbled Linis. "It took Theopolou twenty minutes just to convince them to allow him entry. Then it took more than an hour of debate to have them open the Chamber for the bonding."

"It is well within their right to question petitioners," said Chiron. "In fact, it is their duty. You should know this."

"I know that they tried to deny us," Linis replied. "And that is not within their right."

"You dwell on things that do not matter, seeker. You should keep your focus on the matter at hand."

Linis's jaw tightened. "You are right, of course." But his tone still held a tinge of irritation.

"Do you think they'll try to stop me from getting in?" asked Gewey.

Chiron smiled. "No. That has been dealt with. You will only be following tradition by requesting entry."

As the entire chamber slowly came into view, Gewey very nearly gasped out loud. The dome was supported, not by columns, but by a series of immense crystal statues of elf women, their arms held aloft and their eyes turned skyward. The craft and skill needed to carve these were beyond his imagination. Light emanated from the base of each statue, spraying out a myriad of colors that washed over the surrounding area. The statue bases themselves were much like the glowing spheres used to light the houses and tents, but many times more intense. He could feel the power of the earth radiating from the entire structure. There were no walls beyond the statues, and Gewey could see that the interior was in fact a gigantic amphitheater.

The path that led to the main entrance was made from a smooth red stone that radiated the same energy as the building itself. Elves could be seen pouring in, and by the time they were fifty yards away, he could hear a cacophony of voices from inside. When he reached the base of the Chamber, he stopped.

"What's wrong?" asked Linis, placing his hand on Gewey's shoulder.

Gewey took a deep breath. "Nothing. Nothing at all."

"Intimidating sight, is it not?" remarked Chiron.

"Yes, it is," said Gewey. "It's beautiful as well, though. The craft is beyond anything I have ever imagined."

"If only we could build like this today." There was a tinge of sadness in Chiron's voice.

"I think it was more than mere skill with crystal and stone," said Gewey. "I sense the flow within everything here. I'm sure it was put here. It's almost like the flow itself was made a part of the structure."

"Our ancestors were said to have a powerful connection to the earth's energy," said Linis. "No doubt they used it in their craft."

Gewey squared his shoulders and took a deep breath. "How do I look?"

"Ready," said Linis. "You look ready, my friend."

Two elves strode up; each one adorned in brightly polished leather armor and helmet and armed with a curved sword attached to his belt.

"What business do you have at the Chamber of the Maker?" asked the elf on the left. Linis stepped forward. "You know well what we are doing here."

The keeper ignored Linis and fixed his eyes on Gewey.

"I am here to complete my bond with Kaylia," he said, his voice clear and strong.

There was a long pause, then both keepers nodded and moved aside. Gewey nodded sharply and marched forward. As he passed into the Chamber of the Maker, he could feel the flow growing stronger and stronger until it threatened to penetrate him. He was barely able to keep it at bay.

The Chamber's interior, though without decoration, was still impressive. The seats were carved from white, silver-veined marble that surrounded the entire hall. In the middle was a smooth floor made from the same crystal as the statues. It glowed with power from the flow, illuminating the entire building. Hundreds of elves filled the seats, talking and whispering, but they all fell silent as Gewey came into their view. Theopolou and Kaylia were already down below on the theater floor. Felsafell, still dressed in his ragged skins, and holding his gnarled walking stick, stood quietly, several feet behind them, a quirky smile on his wrinkled face.

Gewey was taken aback at the sight of his future unorem. She was clothed in a silver gown that shimmered in the light of the Chamber. The cloth hung to her curves flawlessly, and though her back was to him, he knew she was smiling. Her hair fell loosely about her shoulders and was decorated with tiny, delicate white flowers. He could feel the bond between them growing stronger with each step he took. He no longer noticed the elves in the gallery.

"Your sword," whispered Linis.

Gewey removed the blade and carefully handed it over. Linis stayed just behind him as he continued down.

Theopolou's eyes were closed, his hands folded in front of him. As Gewey finally reached the stage, Theopolou opened his eyes. The old elf held a grave expression, denoting the seriousness of the ceremony.

As he stepped beside Kaylia, Gewey saw the slightest of smiles on her lips. Theopolou bowed slightly and held out his hand, palm down. Gewey and Kaylia slowly dropped to their knees. All voices were silent. All eyes were focused on them.

"We are here on this night to bear witness," said Theopolou. His voice echoed throughout the Chamber. "The Creator has deemed that the two here before me be bonded in spirit. Their souls forever as one. Their lives, a single life. It has been many years since such a thing has taken place, so it is fitting that these most sacred vows be made here in the Chamber of the Maker for all the elders of our race to see." He stepped forward and placed a hand on Gewey and Kaylia's heads. "Is there anyone here that can find just cause to stand against their bond?"

This caused a stir among the crowd. Gewey's heart raced, but no one spoke. "This is good," Theopolou continued. "Then..."

"I claim the right of pudnaris," called a voice from the crowd.

Both Kaylia and Gewey turned. From amongst those gathered, a lone elf pushed his way through. He was dressed in plain tan leathers and wore a long knife on his belt. He was tall, nearly as tall as Gewey, though not as broad in the shoulders. His long, silver blond hair was tied back in a tight braid. His eyes were aflame with determination.

"Eftichis," whispered Kaylia.

"By what right do you challenge?" Theopolou demanded.

Eftichis reached the floor and stood tall, just a few feet away from Gewey. Linis moved in between them.

"Still yourself, seeker," said Eftichis. "I will do no violence yet."

"Answer the question," said Theopolou. "By what right do you challenge?"

"Kaylia was promised to me," Eftichis replied in a loud, clear voice.

Kaylia sprang to her feet. "I was never promised to you, or to anyone else."

"You dare to tell untruths in this sacred place?" Eftichis challenged. "Your father made this arrangement during the Great War as a symbol of unity between our families. You were yet to be born, but the promise still holds. Certainly, you know this."

"I know nothing of the sort," Kaylia countered. "Were you to ever make this claim, I would have refused, and you know it. I am already bonded to Gewey, and I will not be forced to accept a promise made by my father before I was born—if indeed he ever made such a promise."

"You doubt my honor?" Eftichis asked. "You doubt the word of my father?"

"You think to trick me into naming you a liar," said Kaylia. "I will not. But if you wish to see the Maker, so be it."

Eftichis laughed. "You think much of your human mate."

Gewey rose to his feet and met Eftichis's gaze. "You speak from ignorance, so I will ask you not to do this. I have no desire to spill your blood. But if you stand between us, I will."

Gewey allowed the flow to wash over him. Audible gasps came from the gallery.

"I see," said Eftichis. "It would seem there is more to you than meets the eye. Still, I will not be deterred. Do you accept?"

"He has until sunset tomorrow to answer," Theopolou interjected.

"I don't need to wait," snapped Gewey. "I accept. I am sorry. I had hoped I would never have to spill elf blood. But if you force me to, so be it."

"We will see whose blood will spill, human." Eftichis sneered. He turned to Theopolou. "And unless you dare to dispute my word, then you have no choice. The right is mine, and I claim it."

He looked out over the gallery. "Does anyone here question the truth of my claim?"

A full minute passed, and the Chamber remained silent. Eftichis smirked with satisfaction.

Theopolou bowed his head and sighed. "Then it is done. When the dawn breaks, you will return here. You may bring with you your weapon, your clothes, and nothing more. One elf of your choosing may stand with you, but he is not to interfere. Do you understand?" Both Gewey and Eftichis nodded.

"A shame, it is," rang the voice of Felsafell. "To see blood of the young wasted. But blood there will be and nothing more."

"I have heard you were here," said Eftichis. "What wisdom do you bring us? Do you think to stop me?"

"No, oh no," Felsafell replied. "I am no mover of elves or molder of fate."

"Then why are you here?" called a voice from the crowd.

Felsafell surveyed the gallery, then his eyes fell on Gewey. "I am here to live in the world one last time. Oh, yes, once more before the end. To see a child of heaven walk the earth. To hear the wails of the elves and cries of men. To free my brothers from winter's cold grasp." He reached out and took Gewey and Kaylia by the hand. "Come with me. The dawn comes early, and there is much to say."

The three made their way back out of the Chamber, followed closely by Theopolou and Linis. Once they had reached Theopolou's tent, Felsafell released them and took a seat at the table. Gewey, Kaylia, and Linis did likewise, while Theopolou gave orders to his escort. This done, he joined the rest of the group.

"Did you know this would happen?" Gewey asked Felsafell.

"A fortune teller I am not," he replied. "Things I know, I do indeed. But the future. A mystery difficult to grasp."

"I suspected someone may try to stop you," said Theopolou. "But I never thought Eftichis would lie openly on the Chamber floor."

"He was lying." Gewey turned to Kaylia. "Wasn't he?"

Kaylia stared down at the table. "Perhaps. His father was close to mine. They fought together during the Great War. If he promised me to another, I was never told. But I suppose it is possible. Eftichis would have been a good match for me had my life taken another path."

A pang of jealousy shot through Gewey, but Kaylia smiled and placed her hand on his.

"You will have to kill him," said Linis. "There is no way to avoid it."

"Perhaps," said Felsafell. "Always choices. Always new roads to travel. Listen to me, child of heaven." His eyes fixed on Gewey. "My time in this place is at an end. A new road I must travel. But this you must know. The cold of the north comes swifter than you can imagine. Not ready to face it, are you? But you must. Hard choices you will make, and many deaths will you see. Your true mother will soon be revealed, and with this knowledge will come madness. Your bonded mate will save you if you allow it. But the cost may be more than you can bear."

He rose to his feet. "One last thing. Do not falter. Do not retreat, and all will be overcome." With that, he walked toward the back of the tent. "Until the morning I remain, I will. Then off to free my kin." He pushed back the flap and disappeared down the hall.

"I really don't understand him," said Gewey.

"You're telling me that he walked all this way, just to tell you that?" said Linis. "Now he's leaving?"

"Felsafell has his own reasons," said Theopolou. "He comes and goes as he pleases and speaks in his own time. Besides, I think you have more urgent matters to attend to."

Gewey nodded. "Is there anything I should know about Eftichis?"

"He's strong," said Kaylia. "Had his father not been the leader of his people, he would have likely been a seeker. It is known that he has great skill with a weapon. You should be cautious."

"Indeed," said Theopolou. "Do not underestimate him, as he will underestimate you. Though your display in the Chamber will have given him pause, not to mention the others watching. The best thing you can do is get some rest and gather your strength. In the morning you will face him, and we shall see."

"I wish there was another way," Gewey grumbled. "Why must everything be life or death? I really don't want to kill him."

"But kill him you must," said Theopolou. "Otherwise Kaylia will be taken from you, and there will be nothing I can do to stop it."

Gewey's fist clenched until his knuckles turned white. "Then death it is."

Kaylia put her arm gently around Gewey's shoulders. "This will only be the first of many, I fear. But I'll be with you until the end."

"I'm afraid you are not allowed to attend the pudnaris," said Theopolou. "You must remain here until it is over."

Kaylia turned to Theopolou, her eyes burning with fury. "I will not wait here while Gewey faces death."

"Yes, you will," said Theopolou. "You have no choice."

"Don't worry," said Linis. "I'll be with him. I know he will prevail."

Kaylia scowled. "The moment it is over, I expect you to send word." She turned to Gewey. "And you—show no mercy. I will not have you killed. Forget everything else. Just win."

Gewey smiled and said, "I will, I swear." He kissed her lightly on the forehead. "I haven't come this far to die now."

"Then you should rest while you can," said Theopolou. He rose to his feet. "As should I."

"How are you feeling now? Are you still being ... drained?" asked Gewey.

"No. It ended once we neared the Chamber. Whatever the cause, it has no effect in this place. Do not be concerned. We have more pressing matters at hand."

"Agreed," said Linis. He looked at Gewey. "Come. I know it will be difficult, but you need to at least try to rest."

Gewey gave a deep sigh and nodded. "I'll try."

Linis led Gewey to his room, Kaylia immediately behind them.

"Don't worry," Gewey said to her just before he entered. "I'll be fine."

Kaylia smiled sweetly and put her hand on his cheek. "I know."

Through their bond, she allowed him to share her emotions. Gewey's heart pounded as he felt the love come pouring through. He watched as Kaylia walked away, then went inside.

Linis smiled broadly.

"What?" said Gewey, suddenly embarrassed.

"Nothing," Linis replied, still smiling. "You have come a long way since I first met you in that tavern. Even then, I knew there was strength in you. But I think Kaylia has made you invincible. I pity Eftichis."

"I'm trying not to think about it," said Gewey. "I know what I have to do. But I still wish there was another way. I've killed before, but this time it's different."

"Why?" asked Linis. "Because it's an elf?"

He shook his head. "Listen to me, Gewey. This will not be the last time you will face one of my kind. There is a split among my people. The idea of a second split once weighed heavily enough on our hearts to prevent it. But now it is inevitable. The world is changing, and the new ways are struggling with the old. I regret to say that means more blood will be spilled. We have already been attacked once by our own kin."

Gewey remembered the assassin and the hatred in his eyes.

"War is upon us," Linis continued. "And this time, the victor will shape the future for both races. Even the most reluctant elf knows this. When you face Eftichis in the morning, you are fighting for much more than just you and Kaylia. Your victory will see that your voice is heard by all elves. Many think humans weak and without honor. Tomorrow you will show them differently."

"But I'm not human," argued Gewey. "Not really."

"That may be," Linis countered. "But you were raised as one. You have their values, and you are what is best in men. The strength I speak of has nothing to do with a sword, though admittedly it helps. That you have the courage to face the elders and speak your mind shows the rest of my people true power. That you fight for the bond between you and Kaylia shows that you will not be deterred, and should be treated with respect."

He placed his hand on Gewey's shoulder. "Tomorrow is about more than the pudnaris. By striking down those who would challenge your rights, you send a message that will echo throughout all the elf nations."

Gewey's face twisted into a sour frown. "Thanks. Nothing like a bit of pressure just before a life and death struggle."

Linis chuckled. "I think you can handle it. But sleep now. I will keep watch."

"For what?" Gewey began to remove his clothes.

"Who knows?" Linis replied and dimmed the light.

Gewey lay down on his bed and closed his eyes. At first, he tried to calm his mind and sleep, but soon realized that this was not going to happen. He decided to reach out to Kaylia, hoping that Theopolou wasn't able to block him, though he couldn't imagine any reason why he would. To his relief, he found her. As their spirits became one, his body relaxed, and he became lost in the sheer emotion.

Is this what it will be like after we're completely joined? he asked.

It will be better, replied Kaylia. Much better.

# CHAPTER 28

Yanti lounged inside his cabin aboard the Moon Shadow. It was sturdy, as river vessels go, though not as lavish as he would have liked. But the wine was good and the food, passable. It had taken them quite some time to navigate the delta and enter the Goodbranch River; pushing against the wind and current with oars made for slow progress.

Fortunately, he was in no hurry. Plans were already in motion, and his direct intervention was no longer necessary, at least for now. There was a soft rap at the door. He took a sip of brandy and got to his feet.

"Enter."

The door opened and Braydon, the first mate, stepped timidly inside. "Beg your pardon, My Lord."

"What is it?" Yanti asked irritably. He did not care much for midday interruptions.

"A small craft has pulled alongside." A bead of perspiration appeared on Braydon's brow. "Says he has a message for you."

Yanti furrowed his brow. "Did he give his name?"

"No, my lord," Braydon replied. "But I don't like the looks of 'im—all covered in black, and all. He smells foul, too. Like death. And his voice. He hisses more than speaks, he does."

"Let him on board and bring him to me. And be quick."

Braydon bowed awkwardly and hurried off.

A few minutes later, the door swung open and there stood the figure of a man covered in a long black cloak. His face was hidden, but Yanti could hear a slow growl coming from beneath the hood. Braydon stood just behind, his face pale and fearful.

"You may go," said Yanti to the first mate, who eagerly did as instructed. The door slammed shut and Yanti took a seat, crossing his legs in his usual aristocratic fashion. "To what do I owe the pleasure of a visit from the Vrykol? I assume our Lord knows you are here."

"He knows," the Vrykol hissed. "He knows much. He knows of your plans and is unhappy. They will not succeed."

Yanti cracked a smile. "Unhappy you say—I see. Well, my pungent friend, we shall see how unhappy he is when I deliver the godling to him, as well as his elf mate." He picked up his brandy and held it under his nose for a moment. "All is in order, I assure you. Oh, and he can look forward to having Lee Starfinder among the converted as well."

"The Great Lord is not so optimistic," said the Vrykol. "He foresees problems."

"What kind of problems?" Yanti tried to conceal his concerns.

The Vrykol reached inside his robes and withdrew a sealed letter. Yanti took it, doing his best not to touch the Vrykol.

"By the by," Yanti remarked. "A bit bold of you to be out in the open, don't you think?"

The Vrykol gurgled with grotesque laughter. "The Master has perfected us. Only a few mindless beasts still roam. Humans fear us and choose what they see or don't see."

"Then I can look forward to more visits, I take it," said Yanti.

"No," replied the Vrykol. "I will stay with you—until the end."

Yanti scowled. "Then I hope your kind can bathe." He opened the letter, reading it carefully. "Wait here," he said, getting to his feet.

Stuffing the letter inside his jacket, Yanti threw open the door and made his way on deck, where he found the captain busy navigating the river. The sun was high in the sky and there was a winter chill in the air, despite the fact that they were still far south. His Master's doing.

"Pull along the bank and retrieve my horse from the hold," Yanti ordered as he strode up. "I'll be getting off here."

Captain Tarn, a stout, broad-shouldered man, did not shift his eyes away from the river. Unlike the first mate, he was clearly not intimidated by Yanti. "Not here," he said gruffly. "Too dangerous."

"Here," Yanti demanded. "Now." Tarn ignored him.

Yanti turned and sought out the first mate. He found him in the galley, eating a bowl of fish stew.

"Can you pilot this vessel?" asked Yanti.

"Aye," Braydon replied. "As well as the skipper, I'd say."

"Good," said Yanti. "Come with me."

Confused, the first mate pushed his bowl aside and chased after Yanti, who was already making his way back on deck. The moment the captain came into view, Yanti drew a small dagger. Before Braydon could utter any kind of protest, Yanti hurled the weapon. The captain's eye shot wide as the blade buried itself deep into his throat. He grabbed at the knife, falling to his knees and letting out a gurgling groan. Blood poured from his throat and mouth. Yanti walked slowly over, and with one strong kick, sent the man crashing through the railing and into the river. Three sailors stepped forward but backed away when Yanti drew his sword.

"You are promoted." Yanti smiled as if nothing had happened. "Now land on the bank and retrieve my horse from the hold."

Braydon gaped in stunned silence. Yanti snapped his fingers, bringing the first mate out of his stupor.

"Get to it," Yanti ordered.

Braydon grabbed the wheel and carefully guided the boat to the western bank, while one of the deckhands retrieved Yanti's horse from below.

Yanti returned to his cabin and gathered his belongings. The Vrykol stood patiently in the corner.

"I hope you don't mind walking," Yanti said, feigning concern. "We have far to go."

The Vrykol made no response and followed Yanti topside. The gangplank had been lowered, though it did not quite reach the shore.

"This is as close as we could get without running aground, My Lord," Braydon explained, his voice filled with trepidation.

Yanti looked at the first mate for a long moment, then turned to stow his belongings onto his saddle. At the same time, the Vrykol leaped to the shore with unworldly strength, drawing gasps and murmurs of amazement from the crew.

"If I were you, I would forget you ever saw me—or my companion." Yanti mounted his horse. He reached into the pouch on his belt and held up a silver coin. "Do we understand each other?"

"I ... I understand," replied Braydon, trembling.

Yanti tossed the first mate the coin and urged his horse down the gangplank. He cursed as water drenched his boots. For a moment, he considered returning to kill the first mate but dismissed the idea. Braydon had already ordered his men to pull up the plank and shove off.

"I know your kind are fast," Yanti said to the waiting Vrykol. "You will need to be." He spurred his horse west into a dead run, not bothering to see if the Vrykol was following. He knew the creature was not far behind.

He reached into his jacket and touched the letter. He would not allow his plans to fail—even if it meant that the godling had to die.

# CHAPTER 29

"It is time," said Linis.

Gewey opened his eyes slowly, allowing the connection with Kaylia to slip away. He felt rested and strong. The echo of Kaylia's final thought rang through his mind. I'm with you always. He sat up, swung his legs over the side of the bed, and stretched.

"I've laid out your clothes," Linis told him, nodding to the corner. "I've chosen soft leather for you. It will allow you to move freely while giving you some protection."

Gewey smiled. "Thank you." He rose to his feet and dressed. As he attached his sword to his belt, Theopolou entered. Akakios followed just behind.

"I will be awaiting you in the Chamber," said Theopolou. His eyes were somber, and, for the first time, Gewey noticed age on his face creeping in. "You should wait here for only a few minutes after I leave. I am told Eftichis is already there."

Gewey's lips tightened. His connection with Kaylia had released the stress of the coming fight, but the mention of his opponent's name brought it flooding back. "I'll be there. Is Felsafell with you?"

"No," Theopolou replied. "He was already gone when I went to his room." Before Gewey could reply, Theopolou and Akakios bowed and left.

Gewey took a deep breath and squared his shoulders.

"Remember why you fight," said Linis. "And remember what you are. To face you is to face death."

This stabbed at Gewey. He knew it was true. Since leaving his small village, death had become a part of his existence. He had killed many times. Now he was to once more be the bringer of death. He steeled his wits. So be it.

Linis studied Gewey for a moment. "Good. You have the same look in your eyes that Lee had just before he fought Berathis."

Gewey checked his sword and moved to the room's exit. "I know what I must do." With that, he pushed back the flap and made his way into the main hall.

Following Theopolou's instructions, he waited there for only a few minutes before leaving. Once outside of the tent, the chill of the morning air washed over him. He filled his lungs and surveyed his surroundings. The camp was quiet. Only a few scattered elves roamed about. Gewey guessed that most were already waiting in the Chamber of the Maker to witness the pudnaris. The stillness made him shiver.

As he made his way to the Chamber, the few elves he encountered stared at him, not with hatred as he would have thought, but in wonder.

"Why are they looking at me like that?" Gewey asked.

"They marvel at your courage," Linis replied. "I imagine most thought you would flee."

"Perhaps I should," Gewey joked. "Maybe I should just grab Kaylia and head east."

"I wish that were possible, my friend. If it were, I might even come with you."

"I doubt that very much," said Gewey, with a short laugh.

The Chamber of the Maker was no less impressive by day. In fact, the light of the morning sun caused it to glow even brighter than last time he had seen it. As they approached, the rumble of the crowd grew more intense. Gewey dreaded the silence his arrival would cause. His heart pounded in anticipation. Just as he reached the entrance, he spotted Felsafell leaning lazily against the statue base. He was dressed in his customary skins and carried his gnarled walking stick.

"I see you come," said Felsafell. "I see you go."

"Aren't you coming inside?" asked Gewey.

"I care not for fighting," he replied. "No, indeed. When the young fights the younger, sadness only—sadness and pain. I wish not to see such things. Oh, no."

"Then you are leaving?" asked Linis.

"For now," answered Felsafell. He took a few steps forward. "We'll meet soon enough. Again and again, I think."

"You know more than you're saying," said Gewey.

Felsafell grinned impishly. "I know much. I tell much. But do not tell all, as I do not know all. Find your road child of heaven. I'll meet you alongside." As he walked past Gewey and Linis, he stopped and pressed a small key into Gewey's hand. It was gold and bore no markings.

"What's this for?" Gewey asked.

"What is a key for, you ask?" Felsafell laughed. "You know this already. Oh, yes, you do. And now I say farewell." He continued until he was out of sight. Gewey shoved the key into his pocket and looked at Linis, who only shrugged.

"I suppose it's just another one of his mysteries," said Gewey. "If I live through this, maybe I'll solve it."

The moment he and Linis entered, the Chamber fell silent. He peered down to the Chamber floor. There stood Theopolou, Eftichis, and another elf who Gewey assumed was Eftichis's second. Eftichis was dressed as he had been the night before, with a long knife hanging loosely from his belt.

As Gewey approached, his eyes met with his opponent's. Their gazes locked for what seemed like an eternity. Gewey knew that soon those eyes would be dull and lifeless by his hand. He pushed the thought from his mind and turned his attention to Theopolou.

Theopolou addressed Eftichis. "I ask you one last time to withdraw from this challenge."

Eftichis drew his weapon slowly and leveled his gaze. "I will not." His voice was even more determined and commanding than the previous night. "This human shall either flee, never to return, or die."

Gewey drew his weapon, allowing it to take in the flow. The power within him rapidly grew until the very foundation of the Chamber trembled. The world around him seemed to grow smaller and insignificant. The elves before him, as well as those in the gallery, were as children to his eyes. The Chamber of the Maker itself was at his command. He had never before felt so much of the flow passing through him.

Then it occurred to him. The building itself had been created by channeling such power. Inside this structure, it was as if a river with the power of the earth had become a raging hurricane. He took another look at Eftichis. The elf was now clearly frightened, though he was trying hard to mask it.

"I ask you one last time," Gewey's voice boomed, causing the others to wince. "Do not do this."

"What are you?" screamed a voice from the crowd.

"Demon," cried another.

"I am no demon," Gewey said to the crowd. "You will find out soon enough what I am." He turned back to Eftichis. "Do you still wish to fight me?" He tried to lessen his hold on the flow, but it was replaced with an aching sadness, along with a yearning for its return. Still, after a few moments, he managed to release it.

"Now more than ever." The elf, though shaken, was grimly determined. "I would not have one of my kin bonded to such a creature, nor would I have my people follow you to their doom." Gewey was taken aback.

"Oh, yes," Eftichis continued. "I know why you are here. We all do. And I would spit my last breath in your face before standing by your side." This brought cheers from several throughout the gallery.

"Give me your knife," Gewey said to Linis as he sheathed his sword.

Linis did as he was asked. "What are you doing?"

"Only what I have to," Gewey whispered, then turned back to Eftichis. "Linis shall hold my blade and I shall fight with his." He removed his sword and gave it to Linis. Linis opened his mouth to protest, but a quick glance from Gewey stopped him short.

"What is this?" Eftichis demanded. "You think to mock me?"

Gewey examined the knife, then looked up. "I am not mocking you. If I use that sword, you will die without a fight. I would not see you come to such an end. If I have to kill you, you will die with honor."

Eftichis could only stare in amazement. "Are you certain?" asked Theopolou.

Gewey nodded and stepped forward. "Linis has trained me well, as has Kaylia, my future unorem. I will not have our union tainted by dishonor."

Eftichis removed his long knife and took a dagger from his second to replace it. "Then we shall face each other as equals."

Gewey smiled as he felt the flow entering his opponent. Though it was far less than he, himself, could channel, it was nearly as much as Linis, or even Theopolou, would be able to manage.

Theopolou, Linis, and Eftichis's second backed away to the edge of the platform.

"Are you ready?" Eftichis's voice dripped with menace.

Gewey crouched low and allowed the power to rush through him. "I'm ready." This time, the flow was much less than before. And though he could feel the power held within the Chamber, he could no longer use it. He waited for Eftichis to lunge.

He didn't have to wait long. The elf rushed at Gewey with blinding speed, fast enough to rival even Lee, but instead of striking directly, the elf rolled left and slashed at Gewey's right thigh. Gewey was only just able to avoid the cut as he spun away.

Eftichis smiled with satisfaction. "You have been well trained, I see." The dagger shifted in his grasp. "That is good."

Again, the elf charged, but this time he did not strike. Instead, he whirled around and pushed Gewey's shoulder hard with his empty hand. Gewey nearly lost his balance and staggered back a couple of steps. Eftichis pressed his attack, attempting to drive his knife into Gewey's stomach and only just missing.

Gewey knew what he needed to do. He drew back, allowing his blade to hang loosely in his hand. Bring him close.

Once again, Eftichis charged, but this time Gewey was ready. Eftichis feigned left, then thrust underneath Gewey's guard. Gewey caught the arm of his attacker and heaved upward, sending the elf sprawling.

Gewey did not hesitate. He sprang after his opponent and slashed the hand that wielded the knife. To Gewey's surprise, the elf somehow managed to regain his footing and flip the dagger into his other hand. Blood gushed from the open wound onto the pristine floor.

"Well struck." Eftichis grimaced in pain. "But this fight is far from over yet."

In a flash, Eftichis was on Gewey again, twisting and thrusting—driving him back. Gewey tried to counter, but the elf's skill was astounding. Even with the power flowing through him, he was only just able to avoid being slashed to ribbons. Finally, Gewey saw an opening. The elf dodged left, attempting to get behind him, but he stepped just a hair too far. Instead of bringing his blade down, Gewey's left hand came across, his fist smashing hard into the temple of Eftichis. The elf staggered and fell to one knee. Gewey raced in, grabbing his opponent's wrist and twisting hard. As Eftichis's knife slid across the floor, Gewey pinned him firmly down.

"You must yield to me," he demanded.

Eftichis's eyes were aflame with fury. "We do not yield, human! Finish it and be done."

"You would have me end your life?" asked Gewey. He released the elf and got to his feet. "As you would end mine?" He turned his back.

Eftichis glanced at his dagger several feet away but made no move to retrieve it. "I would. It is our way."

Gewey spun around and tossed his dagger onto the floor directly in front of Eftichis. "Then kill me."

Eftichis reached down and picked up Gewey's weapon. He stared at it for a long moment before rising slowly to his feet.

Gewey walked up to Eftichis and placed his hand on the elf's shoulder. Eftichis tried to back away, but Gewey held him fast.

"What are you doing?" the elf cried. "This is not..."

"Not what?" said Gewey. "You want me dead. You think my bond with Kaylia is wrong. So kill me."

Their eyes met.

"Do it," Gewey whispered. "Or yield."

Eftichis pressed the knife to Gewey's chest. The gallery was silent. Then came the sound of metal against stone as the dagger fell to the floor. Eftichis dropped to his knees and bowed his head. "I yield." He raised his head and looked to Theopolou. "I release my claim and yield to the mercy of my adversary."

Theopolou stood silent for a moment, then stepped forward. "Gewey Stedding. The life and honor of this elf is yours. What shall you do with it?"

"Eftichis is master of his own life," replied Gewey. His voice echoed throughout the Chamber. "As for his honor—in my eyes, it is without question."

Theopolou bowed his head slowly. "Then the pudnaris is at an end."

The twang of a bow sounded. Gewey, still awash in the flow, saw the arrow coming and twisted his body just as it reached him. He felt a sharp pain as it tore through his shirt and cut across his chest.

A voice cried out from the entrance. "We are attacked!"

Suddenly, the entrance was flooded with sword-wielding elves clad in black leather armor. The gallery erupted. Elves from the gallery drew their swords, trying to make their way into the fray, while the attackers cut down all who stood in their way.

"Gewey!" Linis tossed him his sword and drew his own long knife. Gewey turned to Theopolou. "Get behind me."

Another arrow whizzed through the air, striking Eftichis's second in the chest. The elf fell, desperately grasping the shaft.

Gewey drew his sword, holding the scabbard in his left hand. The flow raged inside him. The sound of clashing steel rang throughout the Chamber as he lowered his eyes, drawing in more and more power. The building shook violently, throwing many of the combatants off their feet. Gewey's eyes snapped open and the world in front of him became chaos as the very air appeared to contract and then explode. Attackers and members of the gallery alike were thrown aside like paper dolls by the blast, leaving a clear path to the entrance.

"With me," shouted Gewey as he started up.

Linis, Theopolou, and Eftichis filed in behind him. By the time they reached the top, several of the attackers had recovered and were moving in to cut them off. Gewey cleaved the first nearly in two. Linis took down the second. This gave the others pause, allowing their escape.

Bursting out of the Chamber, Gewey's eyes scanned the campsite. Fires had erupted everywhere, and the screams of the dying sent a chill to the pit of his stomach. There was only one thought in his head. "Kaylia!" he screamed, taking off in the direction of Theopolou's tent.

The sights of battle were a blur as Gewey ran straight through the camp. One of the attackers tried to stand in his way, but Gewey cut him down without even pausing. Finally, he reached the tent. It was untouched.

"Kaylia!" he shouted again as he burst inside, ripping the flap to shreds. There was no answer. He rushed to her room, only to find she was not there. From room to room, he rapidly searched, but there was no sign of her anywhere.

Linis and the others finally arrived. "Where's Kaylia?" the seeker exclaimed.

"She's gone!" cried Gewey, and started to leave the tent again. Theopolou stood in his way.

"Think, Gewey," said the old elf. "The camp is too big and the battle still rages. You will not find her like that."

"Out of my way," Gewey commanded, his eyes dark with rage.

"Use your bond," Theopolou continued. "Use it to find her."

The sense of what Theopolou was saying suddenly got through to Gewey. Lowering his head, his chest trembling with each breath, he tried to calm his mind and reach out to her. At first, there was nothing. Then, like a faint light, he found her. "She's alive," he exclaimed, unable to contain his joy. "But I can't find where she is. It's like there's a shroud around her."

"It would take someone powerful to accomplish this," said Theopolou. "I was only able to do such a thing in my own home."

"How do we find her?" asked Linis.

Gewey's jaw tightened. "I know how." He walked to the entrance. "Wait here."

Linis stepped forward, but Gewey's eyes stopped him short. "Be careful," was all he could say before Gewey disappeared from view.

"What is he doing?" asked Eftichis.

"Getting a prisoner," Linis replied. "And woe be unto him if he does not tell Gewey what he wants to know."

"Should we not help the others?" said Eftichis. "The elders..."

"One of whom stands before you," shot Linis. "The others are well protected. I doubt that whoever attacked us could pass their guards. Until we know what has happened, we protect Lord Theopolou."

Minutes seemed like hours as the party waited for Gewey's return. As the sounds of battle filtered in, Eftichis grew more unsettled.

"I can wait no longer," he roared. "Our kin are dying."

Barely were the words out of his mouth when the body of a black-clad elf flew through the door and slid onto the table. Gewey entered just behind, his face and clothes covered in blood. The elf groaned and rolled onto his back.

Linis rushed over and held his blade to the elf's neck. He then glanced back to Eftichis. "Watch the door," he ordered. Eftichis quickly obeyed.

"The attackers are moving away," said Gewey. "I caught this one about to set fire to the tent."

He kneeled down over his captive. "Now you will tell me everything I want to know." The elf glared defiantly.

A malicious smile crept over Gewey's face. He reached down and ripped open the elf's shirt. "I'll ask you one time..."

He placed the flat of his blade on the elf's chest. The sizzle of burning flesh immediately rose up.

The elf winced with pain, but his jaw tightened. "A curse on you," he hissed.

Gewey turned the blade, allowing the edge to dig into the elf's flesh. "Not the words I wanted to hear. And you didn't wait for my question."

He pressed the blade in harder. "Where is Kaylia?"

The elf moaned but said nothing.

"Gewey," warned Linis.

Gewey ignored him. He began to drag the blade across the elf's chest. "If you don't start to answer me, I'm going to cut you apart—piece by piece."

"Gewey," said Linis again, this time more forcefully. Gewey glared at him, but Linis was undeterred.

"Stop this," said Linis. "This is not what you want on your heart."

"I think I do," snarled Gewey. "And I think that if he doesn't tell me what I want to know, I'll make good on my promise." He pressed the blade even deeper.

The elf wailed, and the smell of burning flesh filled the tent.

"Allow Linis and I to do this," said Theopolou. "If we fail, then you may do as you wish with him."

"Please," said Linis.

Gewey paused, glaring at his captive with hatred. Then, in one smooth motion, he released his hold and walked to the entrance.

"Make it fast," he said, staring outside at the smoldering tents. The sound of fighting had faded, replaced by the cries of the wounded and the sobs of the survivors.

Linis dragged the captive to the back of the tent and bound his hands and feet. He and Theopolou leaned in close, speaking in soft whispers. After several minutes, Theopolou rose to his feet and walked over to Gewey.

"They have taken her north, toward the steppes," said Theopolou. "Along with the Book of Souls."

"So the northern tribes are responsible for this," growled Eftichis in disgust.

"It would seem," Theopolou affirmed.

"I leave now," said Gewey. "They can't have gone far."

"True," Theopolou agreed. "But I don't think the northern tribes could have acted alone. They knew exactly when to strike."

"Then we were betrayed," said Linis.

"Yes," said Theopolou. "That seems certain. But betrayed by whom?"

"Bellisia?" Linis offered.

"Possibly," Theopolou replied. "Though not likely. I can think of no one who would do this."

"I don't care who did it," said Gewey. "The only thing I care about is getting Kaylia back." He pushed his way past Theopolou and Linis and stalked to his room. A few minutes later, he returned wearing a set of brown travel leathers, his sword, and a small pack thrown across his back. He took a moment to stare at his captive, then walked to the entrance.

"Gewey," said Theopolou. "I understand your urgency. You are bonded to her, but she is also my niece. Allow me one hour to gather more information. I fear you will fail if you simply march off without knowing what you face. If we were betrayed, you could be walking into a trap." He placed his hand on Gewey's shoulder. "Just one hour."

Linis walked over and placed his hand on Gewey's other shoulder. "Give him one hour. Besides, I'll need to scout their trail to find out where they have taken her. That will take time." He met Gewey's eyes. "I promise we will find her."

Gewey's muscles tensed, and his body shuddered. He let out a terrifying scream. "One hour," he roared. "That's all."

Theopolou nodded. "Stay with him, Linis." He turned to Eftichis. "Come with me."

The two left the tent. Gewey watched as they vanished into the smoke and carnage. "One hour," he muttered through his teeth.

# CHAPTER 30

Gewey paced the tent, occasionally stopping to look outside for Theopolou's return.

"Try to be calm," advised Linis. "You must have your wits about you if you want to save her."

Gewey took a deep breath. He knew Linis was right. He must be able to think clearly. He reached out once again, attempting to touch Kaylia's mind, but the result was the same. No matter how hard he tried, he could only sense that she lived. Whatever was blocking him was indeed powerful. He prayed they would not harm her.

"Why would they take her, anyway?" asked Gewey. "Why single her out?"

"I can only imagine the purpose is to get to you," Linis replied. "Strong leverage."

"If they harm her…" The words stuck in Gewey's throat.

"You cannot let such thoughts enter your mind," said Linis. "They will cloud your judgment and cause you to make a mistake that could cost both of you your lives." He handed Gewey a rag. "Clean your sword and recheck your gear. Make certain you have everything you need."

Gewey nodded and obeyed. He soon realized that he had not packed any clothing for Kaylia. She might well need some. He searched her room, rummaging through her wardrobe until he found a set of travel clothes. He could smell her scent everywhere, and tears welled in his eyes. Swallowing hard, he focused his mind.

By the time he'd finished, Theopolou had returned. Chiron, Bellisia, Syranis, and Eftichis stood beside him.

"Where are the others?" asked Linis.

"Lord Aneili was slain," said Theopolou. "Lord Endymion and Lady Leora were injured in the fray and are being tended to. The rest are gathering nearby."

"Have you figured out who is responsible?" asked Gewey.

"Not yet," answered Chiron. "But we will."

"We should join the others," said Eftichis.

"Indeed," said Theopolou. "But first—what to do with our captive?"

"I would like the chance to question him," said Chiron.

"As would I," agreed Bellisia.

"As you wish," said Theopolou. "But I doubt you will learn anything I have not. I do not think he has any answers that can help us. Those who planned this attack would not have allowed anyone to know too much."

"All the same, I will try," said Chiron.

As Bellisia, Syranis, and Chiron approached the captive elf, Bellisia noticed the wounds on his chest. Her eyes met Gewey's with disapproval, but he met her gaze, unmoved.

Chiron kneeled beside him. "What is your name?"

The elf looked broken and weary. "I have told you all that I am willing to say." He turned his head and looked away. "Kill me and be done with it. Or better yet, give me to the human. I'm sure he would love to make sport of me."

"You attacked your own kin," said Bellisia. "And you took a captive, one bonded to this human. You are fortunate he is human and not an elf. An elf would have made more of you than sport."

She moved closer. "An elf would have you screaming so loudly it would wake your ancestors." She drew even closer, forcing him to meet her eyes. Her voice dropped to a whisper. "And if Kaylia dies, I will give you to him."

Fear struck the elf, but he forced it down. "All I know is that you have a traitor among you." He closed his eyes. "I will say nothing more."

Bellisia stood up and turned to Theopolou. "Kill him," she said, lowering her head. "But do it without pain."

"No," shouted Gewey. "His life is mine."

"And just what will you do with it?" asked Bellisia. "Will you kill him? Do you wish to torture him further?"

Gewey was speechless.

"Then allow this elf to die," said Bellisia. "Without pain."

"Release him," said Gewey.

The elders stared at Gewey, stunned.

"Release him?" exclaimed Syranis. "Don't be a fool."

"Linis and Theopolou were right to stop me when I was torturing this elf," said Gewey. "Though I did not see it." He closed his eyes and steadied his nerves. "I will not kill him—I will not murder a helpless person. That will not be on my soul."

Linis placed his hand on Gewey's shoulder. "Is this the best way? If we let him go, our enemies will gain knowledge."

"Then keep him captive," offered Gewey.

"How shall we do this?" asked Theopolou. "We have no prison. Our people are reeling from the attack. Where should we keep him?" He drew his knife. "Unless you intend to take him with you, there is nowhere for him."

"It just feels wrong," said Gewey.

"Did it feel wrong when you were cutting into his flesh?" Bellisia challenged. "If Linis and Theopolou had not stopped you, would you be so kind now? This elf attacked his own kin and abducted your bonded mate. His death is warranted."

"You're right," said Gewey. "If I had continued to hurt him, my heart would have changed. I see that now. And I'm grateful I didn't." He met Bellisia's eyes. "How could I face Kaylia with a stain on my heart?"

"If you wish him to live," said Bellisia, "you can only release him." She looked down at their captive. "Would you like that? Would you simply wander off and not warn your kin that Gewey is coming for them?"

The elf squirmed and shifted until he could meet Gewey's eyes. "If you wish to let me go, then you have nothing to fear from me. I will not interfere. I will go east. This I swear." He lowered his eyes. "But they are right. You can only kill me. It is what I would do in your place."

Gewey's eyes narrowed, and he straightened his back. "You will wait until I am gone three days, then release him. If his word is good, then he will not follow. If he does—he had better pray that we do not meet again."

"I do not agree with this," said Theopolou. "But I will do as you ask. I will have what remains of my guard to watch him." He called outside and two elves entered. He instructed them to guard the prisoner.

"We should meet with the others," said Chiron.

They made their way through the smoldering ruins of the camp to the field near the bridge. Gewey could see more than a hundred elves gathered there in a loose circle.

Several yards away, a pavilion was being erected to house the wounded. From the crowd, Akakios came limping toward them, carrying a bundle under his arm. His leg was bandaged and his left cheek bore a deep gash.

"My lord," said Akakios. "It is good to see you unharmed."

"Thank you," said Theopolou. "I feared you were slain."

"I nearly was," he replied. "I have only just bandaged my leg. I was caught in the tempest Gewey unleashed when you made your escape."

"I'm sorry," said Gewey. "I didn't mean..."

Akakios held up his hand. "You saved the life of my lord and an elder of our people. A small price. Besides—I live."

He smiled before continuing. "I do have some good news, My Lord. I was stopped by Felsafell just before I entered the Chamber of the Maker. You had already descended to the floor." He handed Theopolou the bundle. "He gave me this and told me to place it back with you."

As Theopolou unwrapped it, his eyes widened. "The Book of Souls," he whispered. "This is good news."

"But that means Felsafell must have known of the attack," said Chiron. "And that he refused to warn us."

"Perhaps," Theopolou replied. "Perhaps not. I do not pretend to understand the motives of Felsafell. But the fact that he safeguarded the Book of Souls means we have not lost hope." He turned to Gewey. "I must ask one more thing of you before you leave." He handed Gewey the box containing the Book. "You must open it and read from its pages."

Gewey ran his fingers over the smooth, polished wood. "Then we must do it now. I will not wait much longer."

"Agreed," said Theopolou. "Come."

"I need to see what has become of my seekers," said Linis. "I must know if they live. And I also need to find the trail of our attackers. I shall return soon, Gewey. Then we will depart."

Gewey nodded, and Linis dashed off over the bridge.

Theopolou led the group to where the elves were gathered. All eyes turned to them as they drew near.

"He has brought this on us," called a voice. "He must leave." This was met by loud shouts of agreement.

"He will leave," said Bellisia, her voice rising over the crowd. "He will pursue our attackers and free Kaylia. While you bicker and argue, he will take action." The crowd became silent.

Theopolou nodded to Gewey. "I think it is time for you to speak."

Gewey squared his shoulders and stepped forward. He was unsure what he was going to say. All he could think about was departing on his quest to save Kaylia, and how precious seconds were slipping away. He took a deep breath and began to speak.

"I am Gewey Stedding, and I am here to ask for your help. A dark force is rising in the land of Angrääl. A force that threatens to destroy both humans and elves alike. A force that turns brother against brother. A force that will not stop until it has conquered the whole world. I know that you have been promised your lands, and the freedom to rule them. Some of you may believe this promise, others may not. Some of you think you should join Angrääl, and some think you should stay out of it entirely. But I think today's attack should now prove to you that there is no way you can safely follow either choice."

"We do not know that the King of Angrääl had anything to do with this," said a tall, silk-clad elf.

"So you think it's a coincidence that your own kin attacked you while the north gathers for war?"

"I am saying that we do not know," retorted the elf. "I am saying we have as much reason to suspect you of being involved as we do to accuse Angrääl." This brought murmurs of agreement. "I am Marinos, lord and elder of the western isles. We too have been offered lands that we already hold, just as the human says. But what he does not say is that, for us, it is the human threat that spreads like a plague. They move ever closer to our lands and keeps. They disregard our borders and poison the spirits of even the most wise."

His eyes fell on Theopolou. "Now you say that Angrääl is gathering for war. You tell us what we already know. You pretend to offer us a way out of danger, but in truth, you only offer us destruction. If we join you, the Lord of Angrääl will sweep down upon us like a storm. There will be nothing of our people left to save."

"I had nothing to do with this attack," said Gewey. "Have you forgotten that they took Kaylia from me?"

"Exactly," Marinos countered. "Why was she not killed? The field is littered with the dead. Why did they spare her? Perhaps that was what you intended. Perhaps she awaits you now."

Gewey's anger swelled, but he managed to keep it at bay. "If that is so, then why didn't I kill Theopolou or any of the other elders? Why did I help them to escape? Why am I still here?"

"Who can know the motives of a human," said Marinos. "If that is what you are. We all saw you in the Chamber of the Maker. What human can control so much of the flow without destroying himself?" More murmurs of agreement sounded.

"I told you all that I would reveal who and what I am," said Gewey. "I have told you who I am. I am Gewey Stedding and nothing more. As for what I am..."

He held up the box containing the Book of Souls. "I assume you know what this is."

Marinos glared at Theopolou. "You recover what your family was sworn to protect, only to put it back into the hands of a human?"

Theopolou stood expressionless.

"You have heard that only one who possesses the power of heaven can open the Book of Souls," said Gewey.

Marinos let out a mocking laugh. "So you propose to open the Book of Souls? You claim to possess the power that resides in heaven? Do you even understand the claim you are making?"

He turned to the crowd. "A god indeed! The one that the prophecies speak of. Here, amongst us." His gaze returned to Gewey. "A half-man, most likely. You cannot open the Book with the diluted blood of a god in your veins."

Gewey decided that things had gone far enough. It was time for actions, not words. Grabbing the lip of the box, he pulled.

At first, nothing happened. But then the lid moved a little. Gasps could be heard throughout the crowd as the box slowly opened. A strong wind blew across the field, and the only sound to be heard was the flapping of the nearby pavilion.

"You..." Marinos stammered. "How is this possible? What trickery is this?"

Gewey reached inside and pulled out the Book of Souls. The cover shimmered like gold and radiated a soft light. Intricate writing in a language that not even Theopolou could recognize was clearly visible on the spine and cover.

"Can you read it?" asked Theopolou.

Gewey studied the writing. At first, the symbols made no sense at all, but slowly he began to understand them.

"I can," he declared.

"What does it say?" asked Chiron.

Gewey ran his hand over the cover. "It says: Within these pages is written the true history of Heaven, of Earth, of Man, of Life, and of Gods and Elves." He looked out on the crowd and said. "Now you know what I am."

"How is this possible?" asked Bellisia, in wonder.

"I don't know," admitted Gewey. "In fact, I know almost nothing. All I do know is what I am, and what I must do."

"Do you expect us to follow you?" asked Marinos. "If this is true, then it was your kind that caused our people to fall in the first place. By all rights, we should kill you, here and now."

"The gods had nothing to do with the split," Theopolou said. "All of us who are old enough to have fought in the

Great War know this. It is time this lie was exposed. It is time for us to become the people we once were."

"So, you would have us follow this—this creature?" asked Marinos. "You would have our people mix their blood with that of humans?"

"I would have us become a better people," Theopolou replied. "The idea of mixing with humans is as disturbing to me as is to you. But how much different are we, really? We plot and scheme against one another. We kill our own kind. We lie to ourselves and deceive our children. In fact, is there even one of you who sees the virtue and grace of our ancestors in the people we are today?"

No one spoke.

"Gewey Stedding has shown me much," Theopolou continued. "Though he is not a human, he was raised as one. He has defended our people, upheld our values, and kept his word. He has shown courage and determination. He has placed the lives of others ahead of his own. And he has bonded to my kin. I am not fool enough to believe that all humans are as he. But he does represent what is best in man. Perfect? No. But most certainly he is honorable, strong, and true. Something I have not seen in elves of late."

He looked Gewey directly in the eyes. "I admit that when I started this journey, I had hoped for you to reveal yourself as false. The idea of one such as you leading my people into a new future repulsed me. My mind has been changed. I pledge my house and my family to your cause."

"As do I," said Chiron.

"And I," said Eftichis.

"There is still the matter of the traitor," said Bellisia. "Before I make any decision, I will know how we came to this pass."

"The traitor is among us," said Theopolou. "And I know who he is."

"Who?" shouted several voices.

Theopolou let his eyes scan the gathering. They finally came to rest on Akakios. "The Book of Souls was never in the possession of Felsafell. It went missing just after we arrived."

Akakios opened his mouth to protest, then lowered his eyes. "I did it to protect you, My Lord. Forgive me."

The crowd erupted. Two elves seized Akakios and disarmed him.

"Traitor," Eftichis roared, drawing his sword.

"Stay your blade, Eftichis," Theopolou commanded. He turned back to Akakios.

"You pretended to befriend Gewey. You were instrumental in the slaying of dozens of your kin. You betrayed your lord and dishonored your name."

"I did what I did to help you keep your honor," Akakios replied angrily. "You would have us bow to this abomination. You would lead our people to their doom. Don't you see? I was protecting you from yourself." Tears streamed down his face. "But I swear I never meant for so many to die."

"For just one elf to die by your actions is unforgivable," said Chiron furiously. "You have sealed your fate."

"No," said Theopolou. "Gewey has taught me a lesson this day. Akakios is in my service, and I will decide what is to be done with him." He walked close to Akakios and leveled his eyes. "He is to be questioned. After that, release him with the other prisoner in three days' time. He is exiled to the east. If he has any honor left, he will abide by this decision. If not, so be it."

"Is that wise?" asked Chiron.

"Probably not," Theopolou admitted. "But we must be better than those who oppose us. We must not succumb to vengeance or hatred. I will see elves return to grace, even if that means showing mercy to our enemies." He stepped back and the two guards took Akakios away.

"What now?" asked Chiron.

Gewey handed the Book of Souls to Theopolou. The old elf gazed at it for a full minute before looking up again.

"I need to leave," said Gewey. "I have to rescue Kaylia."

"I understand," said Theopolou. He put the Book back inside the box and closed it. "I will guard this for you until you return. In the meantime, we have much to discuss amongst ourselves."

"I will come with you, Gewey Stedding," said Eftichis.

"No," said Theopolou. "You are needed here. Many are still not convinced that this is the way. I will need your help."

"He's right," said Gewey. "You must help Theopolou. Linis and I can track down the elves who have taken Kaylia."

"But you will be outnumbered," Eftichis argued. "At least let me send some of my guard with you."

"Thank you," said Gewey. "But I think Linis is all the help I'll need. If it comes down to a fight, I'd rather not risk more lives than I have to."

As if on cue, Linis returned, his face grave. "There are no signs of my seekers."

"Perhaps they were driven away," said Eftichis.

"Perhaps," said Linis. "Whatever the case, I have no time to look for them. I have found the attackers' trail. They flee north at great speed. Some on horseback. We must leave now, or we will struggle to catch up." He turned to Gewey. "Are you ready?"

Gewey checked his pack and sword. "I'm ready."

"Good," said Linis. "You can tell me later what has happened while I was gone. I'm sure it is worth hearing."

"Indeed, it is," remarked Chiron.

Gewey placed his hands on Theopolou's shoulders. "I am in your debt, and I promise that Kaylia will be safe."

"I have no doubt of that," replied the old elf. "We will await your return."

Without another word, Linis and Gewey raced off in pursuit of Kaylia.

# CHAPTER 31

Linis took the lead as they raced across the bridge and back down the forest path. When they reached the end, Linis came to a halt.

"They went north through the woods from here," he said. "Some on foot, some on horseback. We must hurry. If they are smart, they will split up soon."

From the corner of his eye, Gewey noticed something resting on the ground. It was a tiny white flower—exactly the same type of flower that Kaylia had worn in her hair for the bonding ceremony.

"This was hers," Gewey said.

"Then perhaps we are in luck," said Linis, hopefully. "If this was indeed left by Kaylia, then it should make finding her easy. Of course, it's possible that her captors may be using it to throw us off their trail. Can you tell if she is conscious?"

Gewey reached out to Kaylia but with no better result than before. "No. I only know she lives. Still nothing more than that." He brought the flower close and smelled the sweet fragrance. "But I feel that she dropped this for me to find."

"Good," said Linis. "Then our chances are greatly improved. Still, we must be careful."

They continued for several hours, running as fast as they could without risking missing a sign. Gewey allowed the flow to rush through him, and soon it was Linis who lagged behind. Several times Gewey tried to hear their quarry, but to no avail. He had no idea of how far behind they were, and each step caused him greater anxiety. By mid-afternoon, he was becoming frantic.

They paused to check the trail. "Why haven't we caught them yet?" demanded Gewey.

"I do not know." Linis shook his head. "I have never seen such a large group move so swiftly."

Gewey sensed something approach. Something foul. Linis sensed it a moment later.

"Vrykol," Linis whispered.

They both drew their weapons and fixed their eyes on the forest ahead. As it approached, the air chilled, and the woods became silent. From behind a thick pine, the Vrykol then appeared, cloaked in a long black robe. It was taller and straighter than the ones they had faced outside the Temple of Valshara, though it moved with the same terrifying speed. It stopped short, fifty feet away, and drew a long sword. Its face was hidden in the shadow of its hood, and Gewey could hear the hiss of its breath.

"This one is mine," thundered Gewey.

But he had barely taken another step forward when the Vrykol suddenly burst into flames. This was followed by a blinding flash of light that blasted him violently over onto his back. Then there was nothing but darkness.

When Gewey regained his senses, he opened his eyes, but there was still only blackness.

*Blind,* he thought. He struggled to stand, but something was wrong. He couldn't feel his limbs. He shouted for Linis and was relieved to hear the sound of his own voice. But there was no answer from the elf.

"Linis cannot hear you, boy," came a voice from the darkness.

Gewey recognized it at once, although he had heard it only once before—the night his adventures had first began. "That's right," said the voice. "I am here. You know me, don't you?"

"What do you want?" demanded Gewey. "Why have you brought me here? Wherever here is."

The Dark Knight laughed softly. "Where you are is not important. As for why—I think you already know that."

"Why can't I see you?" asked Gewey, his eyes straining to pierce the blackness.

"Do you want to see me?" he asked, amused.

"No," replied Gewey. "I don't. We will see each other soon enough."

"Indeed, we will, little god. But until then, I would make you an offer."

"I am not interested in anything you have to say," said Gewey.

The Dark Knight's voice grew deep and menacing. "I have gone to a great deal of trouble in bringing you here," he said. "I will not release you until I have said what I have to say. You will hear me."

"You cannot hold me forever," argued Gewey. "I am not the naïve boy you tried to trick the last time you spoke to me."

"No?" he mocked. "If that fool of a half-man hadn't filled your head with lies and convinced you to flee, you might see things differently. You continue to challenge me, yet you still do not understand that I am not your enemy."

This time it was Gewey's turn to laugh. "Is that so? How many people have you sent to kill me? How many more will come? You're a liar. You're nothing more than a deceiver with a sword. Release me now."

"I have sent none to kill you," he replied. "I have only wished for you to join me. Those I have sent could do you no lasting harm. If you used your mind, you would see that. You cannot stop me, regardless of what you have been told by anyone. And once my labors are completed, you will be the last of your kind. Though I do despise the gods, I do not see you as one of them. Don't you see what we could accomplish if you joined me?"

"Accomplish? You mean destroy, don't you? You think I don't see what you mean to do to the elves?"

"I mean the elves no harm. Why should I? They can go about hiding from the world until the stars fade for all I care. They do not concern me."

"Again a lie," said Gewey. "If they don't concern you, then why attack them?"

"I have not attacked the elves," he said. "Though I hear they attack each other."

Gewey thought on this for a moment. What if Angrääl really wasn't responsible for the attack? He would have drawn them into a war based on a lie. "You expect me to believe that?"

"I expect you to do what you know you must," he replied. "And that will lead you to me."

"That it will," said Gewey. "But it will be on my terms, not yours."

The Dark Knight let out a deep, thundering laugh. "That is where you are wrong. You will come to me now—before you are able to do more harm. The half-man and his son are on their way here as we speak. They think to rescue his wife. They will fail. And my Vrykol have taken your elf mate from her captors." The air stirred. "As you can see, I have all that you hold dear in my hands. And though it would pain me, I will flay them alive if you continue to oppose me. You may be willing to sacrifice Starfinder, but I doubt you would be so willing to allow your dearest Kaylia to suffer."

Fear struck Gewey's heart. "If you harm her…"

"You will do what?" he boomed. "Kill me? I think not. You will do as you are told, or the ones you love will suffer for your lack of wisdom."

The darkness pressed in. Gewey thought back to that first night in Sharpstone. This time, Lee would not be coming.

"Gewey?" It was the voice of Linis.

The darkness faded as light from the waning day crept in. "Gewey?" Linis repeated.

Gewey groaned as he tried to sit up. "Stay still," said Linis.

Gewey ignored him and forced himself upright. "There is no time. We must catch up with Kaylia." He tried to reach out to her, but couldn't focus his mind. "What happened?"

"The Vrykol just burst into flames," Linis answered, shaking his head. "Then you fell. Other than that, I don't know."

Gewey struggled to his feet. "How long was I out?"

"Less than a minute," replied Linis. "There's nothing left of the Vrykol." He pointed to a smoldering pile of ashes several yards away. "Tell me what you saw."

Gewey gathered his wits and recounted what happened.

"If the elves are in league with the Vrykol, that would explain why they move with such speed," said Linis.

"Unless the Dark One is telling the truth," Gewey offered. "What if Angrääl had nothing to do with this?"

"I doubt that," said Linis. "But even so, it changes nothing. Even if what you were told is true, his armies will still march across the land very soon, and I do not believe he will just leave us in peace."

Gewey reached out again. This time he was able to touch Kaylia's mind—though only for a moment. "She still lives," he said.

He checked his pack and sheathed his sword. "I'm ready. And I will get her back." His eyes narrowed as he steadily drew in more and more of the flow until the ground directly beneath them began to shake.

Linis nodded in approval. "Then let our quarry despair."


## End Book Two

# BOOK CLUB QUESTIONS

1. Who is your favorite character? Why? And what about them make them enjoyable to read about? Has your favorite character changed since the last book?

2. How well does the author follow the formula of the hero's journey while making the story unique in its own right? Has the journey held true from book to book?

3. How well developed do you feel the character arcs are? And how do you think they develop throughout the book and series?

4. Do you feel Gewey will be the savior he is prophesied to be or will he succumb to the temptations of power? Have your feelings on this changed since the last book?

# SPECIAL THANKS

George Panagos- Kitty Bullard (GMTA Publishing)- Gerald and Donna Anderson- Vincentine Williams- Hunter and Sarah Anderson- Hector and Athena Ramos (I didn't forget Deserae, Raquel, and Nataly aka. Stormageddon)- Alex, Cassy, Ariel (of course Mia and Malaki), and Kyle DiBastista- Richie and Katie Gnyp- Jacob, Elizabeth, and Jennie Bunton- Tara Ramerez-Tom Riddell (one of the first people to give me a shot)- Lilly Jean- Laura Will- Lisanne Cooper-(for the amazing editing job). Jen Frith Couch- Miklos Bartha- Christopher Martyn Smith- The folks from my home town (too many to name but I love you all)- Helenic Classical Charter School- All my new fans in India, the U.K. and Germany (thanks for reading)- And all the fans and supporters who have made this possible...

You're the best!!!
Authors Brian D. Anderson and Jonathan Anderson

# ABOUT THE AUTHORS

Brian D. Anderson was born in 1971 and grew up in the small town of Spanish Fort, AL. He attended Fairhope High, then later Springhill College, where his love for fantasy grew into a lifelong obsession. His hobbies include chess, history, and spending time with his son.

Jonathan Anderson was born in March 2003. His creative spirit became evident by the age of three when he told his first original story. In 2010, he came up with the concept for The Godling Chronicles. It grew into an exciting collaboration between father and son. Jonathan enjoys sports, chess, music, games, and, of course, telling stories.

**Discover more at
4HorsemenPublications.com**

**10% off using HORSEMEN10**